Fortress of Evil

A Terra Alta Investigation

Other books by Javier Cercas

Soldiers of Salamis
The Tenant and *The Motive*
The Speed of Light
Anatomy of a Moment
Outlaws
The Impostor
Lord of All the Dead

Terra Alta Investigations

Even the Darkest Night
Prey for the Shadow

———

The Blind Spot: An Essay on the Novel

JAVIER CERCAS

Fortress of Evil

A Terra Alta Investigation

Translated from the Spanish by
Anne McLean

MACLEHOSE PRESS
A Bill Swainson Book
QUERCUS · LONDON

First published in the Spanish language as *El castillo de Barbazul*
by Editorial Planeta, S.A., in 2022

First published in Great Britain in 2025 as A Bill Swainson Book by

MacLehose Press
An imprint of Quercus Editions Ltd
Carmelite House
50 Victoria Embankment
London EC4Y 0DZ

An Hachette UK company

The authorised representative in the EEA is Hachette Ireland,
8 Castlecourt Centre, Dublin 15, D15 XTP3, Ireland (email: info@hbgi.ie)

A CIP catalogue record for this book is available from the British Library.

ISBN (HB) 978 1 52943 620 4
ISBN (TPB) 978 1 52943 621 1
ISBN (Ebook) 978 1 52943 623 5

1

Designed and typeset in Sabon by Patty Rennie
Printed and bound in Great Britain by Elcograf S.p.A.

Papers used by MacLehose Press are from well-managed
forests and other responsible sources.

For Raül Cercas and Mercè Mas,
my Terra Alta

Fortress of Evil

Part One

Terra Alta

The first memory Cosette had of her father was very vivid: she was snug in the deep well of a child's safety seat in the back of a car, and, in front of her, at the wheel, he announced that her mother had died. They were leaving Terra Alta and her father wasn't even looking at her in the rear-view mirror, only inside himself or ahead, at the ribbon of road that was taking them away towards Barcelona. Then her father tried to explain the significance of what he'd said, until she understood that she was not going to see her mother again, and from that moment on, they were on their own and would have to get along by themselves. There were two other memories associated with this first one, both just as vivid, both glazed with a sense of menace. In the first her father appeared beside Vivales, the lawyer who had been the closest thing to a father her father had ever known. This memory took place immediately after the first one, in a deserted cafeteria with huge windows, a place she would recognise years later as El Mèdol service station, on the Mediterranean motorway. Her father and Vivales talked while she climbed up and slid down a slide in a children's play area (she sensed that the two men were talking about her, about her and her dead mother); then her father drove back to Terra Alta and she went to Barcelona with Vivales. Her third memory was of Barcelona, and Vivales also appeared in it but her father disappeared or only appeared at the end, after she spent several days at the lawyer's house, with him and with Manel Puig and Chicho Campà, his two best friends, who didn't leave her side day or night, as if some abstract danger loomed over her and that outlandish trio of former military service comrades had assumed the mission of defending her, until one morning at dawn her father reappeared and, like a knight in shining armour, dispelled the danger and took her back to Terra Alta.

The memories Cosette had of her mother, however, were blurry or borrowed. More blurry than borrowed: because, no matter how much she interrogated her father as a child, he had barely told her anything about her mother, as if he had nothing to tell or as if he had so much to tell that he didn't know where to start. Her father's reticence contributed to Cosette's idealisation of her mother. Although for different reasons, she also idealised her father, which was not easy: after all, he was a flesh and blood person, while her mother was just a phantom or a mirage that she could embellish as much as she liked. When she was a little girl, especially when he was working as a police officer, Cosette considered her father a sort of hero, the knight in shining armour who came to her rescue at Vivales' house; more than once she'd heard him say that the worst bad guys are the ones who seem good, and she was sure that he possessed a natural talent for detecting and combatting them, that he was moulded from the same material as the heroes of the adventure novels that, as far back as she could remember, he'd been reading to her at bedtime, and the same as the sheriffs or gunfighters in the old westerns that Vivales liked.

Her relationship with her father was very close, especially in her childhood. He treated her with coldness or with what an impartial observer might have considered coldness, in a distracted way, self-absorbed and slightly absent. This didn't annoy Cosette, partly because she didn't know anything else and partly because she thought that, in real life, that's what heroes were like: cold, distracted, silent, self-absorbed and a little absent; also, Cosette counted on, at least for an hour or an hour and a half a day, her father emerging from his abstraction and devoting himself unreservedly to her. This was the moment when, before she let herself drift off to sleep, he read stories to her: then a warmth welled up from inside him, a deeper intimacy and enthusiasm than any display of affection; then a feeling of communion she would never feel with anyone else ended up binding her to him, as if the two of them shared an essential secret that was theirs alone. As Cosette approached adolescence, however, she gradually became convinced that her father's sombre reserve was not an inherent personality trait, but the poisoned fruit of her mother's absence; she was also invaded by the complementary suspicion that sometimes her father was searching for her dead mother when he looked at her and found only an everyday and diminished version of her. That was how the phantom (or mirage) began to take shape and that was how she began to fight against it unknowingly, or simply to try to live up to it. It was a combat destined to fail, of which she herself was not even completely aware and which could have destroyed her, or at least turned her into a diminished, subdued and insecure being.

It did not. During her childhood, Cosette and her father led a calm, orderly life. He took her to school every morning and, if he had an early shift at the station, he went to pick her up in the afternoon; if not, her best friend Elisa Climent's mother would pick up both of them and take them to play football or to do their homework at her place, until he came to get her once he'd finished work. Later, when her father left his job at the police station, the two friends would often go together to the library where he'd started to work, which was very nearby, and do their homework or read or study for exams, and then her father would take them to training or home.

Some weekends Cosette slept over at Elisa's place, and other times Elisa slept at Cosette's.

Cosette was not a bad student, but she wasn't a great one either. Although she loved reading, she wasn't interested in literature classes, or history, or the arts in general; she did have an innate talent for mathematics, though. Her teachers described her as a level-headed, measured, modest, stubborn student lacking a competitive spirit. This last trait did not prevent her from being very fond of sports and a member of one of the school's football teams; nor from showing a talent for chess, which led her to participate in several tournaments – she won three: two local and one regional – and forcing her father to learn the rules of the game to try to challenge his daughter in matches he initially lost with humiliating speed. Her teachers at school also described her as an imaginative girl, endowed with a great facility for escaping into her fantasies.

None of these descriptions surprised her parent; Cosette was only partly mistaken: he was a distracted and self-absorbed father, but he spent many hours with her and knew her well. Even though they both liked living in Terra Alta, every once in a while they ran off to Barcelona, and every summer they spent some time in El Llano de Molina in Murcia, with Pepe and Carmen Lucas, two friends her father had inherited from his mother. The older couple was in permanent contact with them, writing emails, phoning them, and encouraging them to visit during the rest of the year, which they did a few times. Cosette adored them and they adored Cosette, who over the years had built up a group of friends in the town, some of whom lived in El Llano all year-round. Cosette knew her father also enjoyed those bucolic interludes, in spite of the fact that all he ever did there was read, take long siestas, go running in the orchards and have long conversations with Pepe and Carmen, especially Carmen: her father was never able to develop an interest in horticulture, but in the afternoons he would accompany the former prostitute and last friend of his mother to her vegetable plot and spend hours sitting on the ground reading, leaning back against the wall of the shed where she kept her tools. As for Barcelona, after the death of Vivales, Cosette and her father started spending occasional weekends in the flat the lawyer had left them in his will. Her father had chosen to keep it exactly as Vivales had left it, not because of a sentimental superstition about conserving the phantasmal presence of the lawyer in the place he'd lived as long as he'd known him, but simply because he didn't know what to do with it. During those excursions to the capital, they went to the zoo, the Science Museum or the cinema, and more than once they had dinner with Puig and Campà, almost always at the home of the latter, who invited them to banquets in honour of Vivales where they dined like decadent emperors. They often spent Saturday mornings or afternoons at Internet Begum, the cybercafé the Frenchman ran in El Raval, chatting or reading or playing chess, or even helping her father's old friend with his business, who would later reward them for visiting by inviting them to a restaurant on the Rambla or in the Raval. One afternoon, after the three of them had eaten at Amaya, Cosette, fascinated by the expressive ebullience and enormous humanity of the former librarian of the Quatre Camins prison, asked her father where he had met him.

"Around," he answered.

"Around isn't anywhere," Cosette replied.

They were in a shop in Ensanche, buying breakfast for the next morning, and her father turned towards her with a box of Kellogg's cereal in his hand and an unmistakable look on his face thinking that, even though Cosette was only ten, she didn't deserve to be lied to.

"I'll tell you later," he said.

At that moment Cosette didn't know whether her father had made that promise to get her off his back or to fulfil it, but a couple of hours later, when she reminded him, she understood that he was not going to tell her the truth. He had never recalled his past previous to Terra Alta in front of her: he hadn't told her that, like Carmen Lucas, his mother had been a prostitute, or that she'd been brutally murdered, he'd never spoken of his wild childhood in Sant Roc, or his unknown father, or his furious orphaned adolescence, or his time in reformatories and job as a drug dealer and gunman for a Colombian cartel, or his arrest during a firefight in the Barcelona Free-Trade Zone, or his high court trial in Madrid, or even his time locked up in Quatre Camins and his lasting friendship with the Frenchman. Her father had never told Cosette those things, and nor did he now: he dispatched her curiosity by explaining vaguely that they had met when the Frenchman was working in a library, that thanks to the Frenchman he had discovered *Les Misérables* and that, thanks to *Les Misérables*, he had discovered his vocation and become a police officer. Cosette sensed that her father was lying, but also that he was lying with the truth.

"I don't believe you," she laughed. "The Frenchman has never worked in a library in his life."

Cosette felt that her intuition was confirmed when she saw the look of relief on her father's face when he answered:

"I give you my word of honour that he did."

From that night she drew three conclusions. The first was that the best lies are not pure lies, but lies mixed with truth, because they enjoy the flavour of truth. The second was that her father was hiding his past from her on purpose, which did not contribute to weakening the aura of a knight in shining armour or hero of adventure novels or sheriff or gunslinger her imagination had wrapped him in. The third was that she should read *Les Misérables*.

That very week she asked her father to read her *Les Misérables*, but he seemed unsettled by the request; in any case, he resisted. He argued that he hadn't reread Victor Hugo's novel since shortly after

8

Vivales died, he argued that he didn't know if it was a good idea to read it to her now, he argued that, even though it was a novel that had changed his life, she might not like it, or not yet (she might like it later, he argued, for example, when she reached the age he was when he first read it), he argued that it was vast, he argued using a sentence the Frenchman had said to him back when he first discovered it: "The writer supplies half of a book, the other half comes from you." To Cosette, who knew she was named after the daughter of the protagonist of *Les Misérables*, all these arguments seemed inadequate or absurd, and in the end they did nothing but increase her desire for her father to read her the novel.

Finally, she convinced him. They devoted three and a half months to reading *Les Misérables*. Cosette did everything she could to try to like it, but her disappointment was huge: from the first moment the book seemed to her like a tedious, sentimental, demagogic and ultimately boring melodrama, and Javert – the righteous and inflexible policeman who inflexibly pursues the former convict Jean Valjean throughout the whole story, and who for years had been a role model for her father – strikes her as a nasty, relentless, mechanical character lacking any trace of the moral courage or tragic greatness her father had admired in him. Cosette wouldn't have used those words to describe her impressions of the character and the novel, but that's how she felt. She also felt something worse, and it was that, even though her father had tried to read the novel with more warmth, intimacy and enthusiasm than ever, it did not awaken in her the usual feeling of communion between the two of them, as if that novel did not contain the essential secret they had shared up until then; or, on the contrary, as if precisely that secret were revealed in the novel, showing however its dramatic emptiness or its deceit. Despite that, Cosette did not ask her father to stop reading it to her every night and, while the experiment lasted, she made a superhuman effort to disguise her disappointment: perhaps expecting that at some moment the novel would take flight and acquire a belated but incomparable fulfilment; perhaps she thought that the responsibility for her disappointment did not reside in *Les Misérables* but in her, in her incapacity to add to the book the other necessary half, that which would allow her to access its complete meaning and which her father was able to add. Whatever the case, after he read the final page of the novel, Cosette only managed one lapidary response to the predictable question her father asked:

"A bit long, isn't it?"

It was the last book they read together.

1

Melchor is waiting for Cosette at the Gandesa bus station café, drinking a Coca-Cola and reading a novel by Ivan Turgenev called *Smoke*. Apart from him, there is only one elderly couple sitting at a table, holding hands, their travel bag on a nearby chair, and a man talking to the owner at the bar. Melchor doesn't know the old couple but he does know the others: the woman who runs the place is a single mother in her thirties from Arnes; the man, a youngster with tattoos and porcupine hair, is the owner's cousin, lives in Gandesa, is unemployed and comes in every evening to have a cup of coffee with her, chat for a while and, if it gets busy, give her a hand. It's half past seven. The amber-coloured light shining from some wall lamps makes the café feel vaguely like an aquarium. On the other side of the large windows, night has already fallen on the avenida de Catalunya, over the Hotel Piqué and, in the distance, over the Carvalls mountains, over all of Terra Alta.

Cosette has been on holiday for five days with Elisa Climent, and Melchor is looking forward to seeing her; he is also a little apprehensive. He wants to surprise his daughter, so he hasn't told her that he's waiting for her at the station. Now that she's seventeen, this isn't the first time Cosette has been away for that length of time, or even the first time without any adults. But this is not like the other times. Cosette and Elisa had been saving up for months to go on this trip; a trip that, in the imagination of the two friends, had or aspired to have, in principle, a symbolic or milestone aspect: that year they were finishing secondary school at the Instituto Terra Alta, and next year, also in principle, they were both planning to leave the region to start university, and might end up going their separate ways. In recent weeks, however, uncertainty had begun to undermine Cosette's plans: she's no longer sure she wants to go to Barcelona to study mathematics, as she's been planning for years, or if she even wants to take the selection exam, the preliminary step to admission to university. One concrete reason explains these sudden insecurities: weeks before setting off on that trip, Cosette discovered by chance that her father had been lying to her for fourteen years about her mother's death. She did not die in an accident, as her father told her at the time: she was killed; the hit-and-run that ended her life was not random, as she had always believed, but deliberate: the culprit was Rosa Adell's first husband and the main defendant accused of Rosa's parents' murder, who had run her over to intimidate Melchor and prevent him from continuing to investigate the Adell case. The exhumation of that buried crime by chance angered Cosette, who is furious not just because she's understood that her mother died as a result of her father's righteous obstinacy; she is also furious that her father hid the truth from her. Since then Cosette has been harbouring the feeling that her entire existence has been built on a fiction, the irrational certainty that she does not know her father and that all she believed she knew about him was a lie, that all the values he incarnated for her were mistaken, toxic, and all that she had lived until then was an utter fraud. This is the reason the father–daughter relationship has been poisoned and, a few days before she left, Cosette confronted Melchor and accused him of deceiving her. Melchor did not deny it, did not protest; the accusation was true: if he hadn't deceived her, he had at least hidden the truth from her (which represented a refined form of deceit). That's why he has spent these five days hoping that Cosette might reconsider and understand his motives for behaving as he did; he has also tried to arm himself with reasons that will enable him to convince her that, even though he might have made a mistake, he did it with the best intentions, thinking he was doing the right thing. And that's why he is now there, in the station café, anxious to see her again, ready to explain, to tell her he is sorry and persuade her to forgive him.

At eight the bus from Tortosa pulls in, parks in a loading bay, drops off some passengers and picks up the elderly couple who had been in the café now bustling with a group of hikers. There's still twenty minutes before the last bus from Barcelona gets in and Melchor feels like another Coke, but he changes his mind because the recent arrivals are laying siege to the bar, eager for sandwiches and drinks, which obliges the owner's tattooed cousin to help her.

Melchor goes back to Turgenev. He is still an indefatigable reader of novels, especially nineteenth-century novels. When his relationship with Rosa Adell began, he wanted to diversify his reading diet a little and tried to get into crime novels, which were Rosa's favourite reading then. He read quite a few and enjoyed some. After a while, however, he tired of them, or maybe he underwent a regression in taste, because he returned to his nineteenth-century novels, which Rosa, a reader of eclectic and changeable taste, also ended up enjoying. Melchor calls his relationship with Rosa a relationship because he doesn't know what else to call it. He can't call it a marriage because they're not married, although Rosa would like them to be; in fact, she has proposed to Melchor several times, but has always met with his refusal. His argument is invariably the same: the richest and most powerful woman in Terra Alta deserves something better than an ex-cop turned librarian; she would end up regretting it, he concludes. Rosa doesn't know if Melchor is serious or joking (in fact, she doesn't know if he knows himself), but she has tried to contend with that argument, always in vain; on occasion she has wondered whether the real reason Melchor doesn't want to marry her is because he doesn't want to marry a woman fifteen years older than him, not to mention a childhood friend of his first wife. In any case, Rosa has accepted the life they lead and is happy with it; much happier, she assures anyone who wants to listen, than she's ever been before.

Melchor and Rosa do not live under the same roof, but they see each other or speak on the phone every day, they sleep together with the frequency of newlyweds and Rosa's relations with Cosette are as cordial as Melchor's with Rosa's four daughters; the latter's is not as close, however, among other reasons because none of Rosa's daughters still lives in Terra Alta. Melchor, for his part, loves Rosa, admires her goodness, her cheerfulness, her intelligence, her discipline and her fabulous capacity to take on work; but, maybe because what he feels for her is nothing like what he felt for Olga, he doesn't know if he is in love with her, and he's not interested in finding out. He has not really understood that she is in love with him; in fact, deep down he thinks Rosa's love is based on a misunderstanding, and that this misunderstanding will sooner or later dissolve and their relationship will end. Apart from that, everyone around them, as well as half of Terra Alta, knows that the president and proprietor of Gráficas Adell is the romantic partner of one of the police officers who, fourteen years earlier, was involved in solving the Adell case, the murder of her parents; this slightly macabre coincidence was the region's top gossip at first, where a fleeting future was unanimously foreseen for the couple, but eventually it was accepted by everyone as one of the eccentricities of that uneccentric couple.

Melchor looks up from *Smoke* at the moment the last bus from Barcelona turns into Gandesa and drives up avenida de Catalunya towards the station. So he stands up, pays for his Coca-Cola and goes outside to meet his daughter. A group of passengers gets off the vehicle and swarms around the luggage compartment to collect their belongings, and for a moment blends in with the group waiting by the door to board. Melchor looks for Cosette in the crowd, but doesn't see her; he does, however, see Elisa, who is walking towards him with a backpack full to bursting, a spring tan and two octagonal boxes of *ensaimadas* hanging from a coloured ribbon. The girl stops in front of Melchor, who, still searching in vain for his daughter among the hustle and bustle of the station, asks:

"Where's Cosette?"

Elisa replies, with a serious look on her face, that Cosette has stayed in Mallorca; then she blinks as if she didn't know what else to say, or as if she knew, but didn't know how to say it. Melchor stares at her. The girl is the same age as his daughter, has a freckled face, blue eyes, straight, blond hair, which is a bit messy; she's wearing a pair of esparto sandals, a summery dress and denim jacket. Knowing something has happened, Melchor asks:

"Has something happened?"

"No." Elisa puts her backpack down on the ground, but not the boxes of *ensaimadas*, and looks at him again trying to appear more confident. "Cosette is fine. She told me she was staying because she needed to think. And that, when she arrives, she'll call you to tell you."

"Think?"

"Yeah. She says it'll just be a couple of days and that . . ."

Before she can finish her sentence, Melchor takes out his mobile phone and dials his daughter's number while urging her to go on:

"And what?"

"She's not going to answer," Elisa warns him.

She's right: Cosette's mobile rings, but no-one picks up. When it goes to her voicemail, Melchor turns his back on Elisa and takes a few steps towards avenida de Catalunya. "Cosette," he says. "It's Papá. I'm at the bus station with Elisa, she's just arrived. Call me, please." He hangs up and walks back over to the teenager, who has hoisted her backpack onto her shoulders again.

"Don't worry," Elisa insists. "Cosette is fine. She just wanted to take a couple more days' holiday."

"What about you?" Melchor asks. "Why haven't you taken them as well?"

"Because I've got things to do here."

Melchor nods without conviction. He's never had a real conversation with Elisa, but has known her almost since she was a baby, thinks he knows what she's like and he's sure that, although she will try not to lie to him, she'll also try to cover for Cosette. A bit dazed, he asks:

"Has Cosette met someone?"

She shakes her head energetically.

"No," she says. "Well, nobody like the way you're thinking."

A WhatsApp chimes from Melchor's mobile while the girl says something Melchor doesn't understand. The WhatsApp is not from Cosette, but from Rosa. "Is she back yet?" it reads.

"Dinner at my place?" Melchor looks up at Elisa, but, before she can finish her sentence or say anything, another WhatsApp arrives, this time it is from Cosette. "Papá, please don't call me. I don't want to talk to you. I'm fine. Don't worry, just give me a bit of space." Melchor raises his eyes to Elisa again, and for a couple of seconds looks at her without seeing.

"Is it her?" Cosette's friend asks.

Melchor shows her his daughter's WhatsApp.

"I told you she wouldn't pick up," Elisa reminds him, after reading it. "She wants to be alone. She told me that too."

Now it's Melchor who doesn't know what to say. After the first moment of surprise, he feels that what has just happened doesn't really surprise him so much, that perhaps he had gone to wait for Cosette because he had a feeling that, if not that, something similar to that might happen. "Do you have money?" Melchor types on his phone. "Yes," Cosette writes straight back. "I'll come back when I run out." Melchor is about to write another message, asking his daughter to be careful; however, he thinks it is too obvious, too paternalistic and, biting the bullet, he decides to show his confidence in her by sending a thumbs-up emoji.

"Well," Elisa says when Melchor looks up from his phone, abstracted again, looking at her again without seeing her. "I have to get going. My mother's waiting for me."

Melchor reacts, takes Elisa's backpack and, carrying it, offers to drive her home while telling Rosa by WhatsApp that he'll be coming for dinner on his own.

Elisa lives with her mother on the outskirts of town, on the road to Bot, not far from the first apartment Melchor had rented, eighteen years ago, when he took refuge in Terra Alta after shooting four armed Islamists on the promenade in Cambrils. During the drive, he interrogates Elisa. Elisa tells him

17

that the two friends spent the first two days of their holiday in Palma, in a hotel near S'Arenal, sunbathing on the beach in the mornings, walking around the old quarter of the city in the afternoons and going to bars and clubs at night. She also tells him that on the third day, instead of moving to Magaluf as planned, they'd taken a bus to Pollença or to be precise to Port de Pollença, got a room in a cheap hotel and spent the next two days lying on the beach, swimming in the sea and dancing in a nearby nightclub, and they only left the port one afternoon to visit the town of Pollença, and once to visit a place called Cala Sant Vincenç. He listens to his daughter's friend, paying close attention to her words. Just before his clash with Cosette, when she had been behaving in an unusual way, distant and surly, for several weeks, Melchor talked to Elisa, who had told him his daughter was going through something but she didn't know what it was, and now he can't bring himself to ask her if she's figured out what was going on with her and whether Cosette has told her about the argument they'd had the night before the trip, perhaps because he's sure the answer to both questions can only be affirmative. He does bring himself to ask, however, if she'd noticed if his daughter seemed worried during those days; Elisa says no, but then clarifies and says a little, although no more than she has been since, weeks ago, she began to have doubts about what she should study, or if she should even sit the selection exam or not.

"Has she told you she doesn't want to go to university?" Melchor asks.

"She's told me that she doesn't know what to do," Elisa says. "Maybe that's why she decided to stay away a couple more days. To figure it out. To have time to think."

It's the second time he hears Elisa say that, but this time he thinks he detects in her words a false note, as if the girl is rehearsing what she just said, as if rather than saying it she has recited it.

They have arrived at Elisa's house, and he doesn't want to pester her anymore. He gets out of the car with her and carries her bag to the front door, kisses her on the cheek while telling her to give his best to her mother and finally he cannot help but ask if she thinks she'll speak on the phone with Cosette that night.

"I don't know." Elisa shrugs. "I don't think so. But don't worry: if she tells me anything, I'll text you."

Melchor thanks her and attempts a smile, but can't manage one.

2

Melchor drives the five kilometres from Gandesa to Corbera d'Ebre on automatic pilot. Just outside the village he turns off the main road, takes a dirt track and, a short time later, pulls up in front of the entrance to Rosa's farmhouse and presses the remote control. While he waits for the gate to open he checks his WhatsApp, and, just in case, his email; neither of them contains any new messages: either from Cosette or from Elisa. Then he drives in, along a gravel drive and parks in front of the door, beside Rosa's BMW.

Melchor goes into the house, up to the first floor and into the kitchen, where he finds Ana Elena, Rosa's Bolivian housekeeper, who greets him with a smile and, stepping back from the stove and drying her hands with a cloth, tells him Rosa is in the shower.

"She said you should wait for her in the living room," she adds.

"I'll wait for her here," Melchor says. "Can I give you a hand?"

"No, señor, no way," Ana Elena answers, slightly scandalised. And, without waiting for instructions, she opens the fridge and takes out a can of Coca-Cola, she opens it and fills a glass with ice; offering both things to Melchor, she asks: "Where shall I serve it?"

Melchor takes the can and the glass from her hands and sits down at the kitchen table. Ana Elena is a short, round woman with plump, red cheeks, and of indeterminate age, who has lived with Rosa for years and takes care of the housework. When he began to frequent the farmhouse, he tried to get her to stop calling him "señor", but in the end he had to give up. Ana Elena has two children, a boy and a girl, who live in a village near Cochabamba with their grandparents; Melchor knows she sends them almost her entire salary every month. The two adults talk about the children often, and now, his phone in one hand and the glass of Coke in the other, Melchor asks Ana Elena how they are. To keep from thinking about Cosette, he tries to concentrate on her answer but only partially succeeds. After a while Rosa appears, kisses Melchor on the lips, opens her arms wide and asks:

"Where's Cosette?"

Rosa's hair is wet and she is dressed with youthful careless- ness in contrast to the formality her work obliges: flip-flops, baggy jeans and a thin white T-shirt that reveals her large breasts, and their prominent nipples. She is fifty-five years old (the same age Olga would be, if she were still alive) and is now a grandmother three times over but she still has a glowing com- plexion, a fresh face, clear eyes, a wide, bright smile and a slim body. Melchor shrugs.

"I don't know," he admits. "She stayed in Mallorca."

"With Elisa?"

"No. Elisa has come back. I just dropped her off. She told me Cosette is fine, that she hasn't come back because she needs to think. She told me that as well."

"Cosette?"

Melchor nods. Rosa crouches down next to him; with her hands on his knees, she asks:

"Did you speak to her on the phone?"

"We wrote to each other," Melchor answers, waving his mobile. "She told me not to worry. That I should give her some space."

In Rosa's expression, uncertainty has gradually given way to bewilderment, which is now displaced by acquiescence.

"If she told you not to worry, don't worry." Standing up again, she adds: "Let's talk about it."

Ana Elena has set the table in a little room with a big window that opens onto the first-floor balcony, and, while Melchor and Rosa eat the creamed vegetable soup and almond sole she has made for them, they go back to talking about Cosette, Melchor without taking his eye off his phone. When they started seeing each other, they barely mentioned their children, as if they didn't want their family lives to interfere with their personal relationship. The implicit pact didn't take long to crack, and it had already been blown apart long ago when, just a few weeks earlier and from one day to the next, Cosette became bad-tempered, souring the relationship between father and daughter. Since then, Melchor has kept Rosa informed; at one point he even asked her to sound out his daughter and try to discover what was going on with her. Rosa agreed, but it wasn't much use: Cosette refused to tell her anything, or maybe she was unable to. Only later did they both find out the reason for Cosette's fury and distress, when she revealed it to her father the night before leaving for her trip to Mallorca.

"You have nothing to reproach yourself for," Rosa assures him once they've finished dinner. "You only did what you had to do, which is to protect your daughter from the truth."

Ana Elena has cleared the plates from the table, but not the glasses, and Rosa runs her finger along the stem of her half-finished glass of white wine. Melchor asks:

"Can you protect a person from the truth, even if she's your daughter?"

"Of course you can," Rosa answers. "Señor Grau always used to quote an aphorism, I think it was by Santiago Rusiñol: those who search for truth deserve the punishment of finding it."

Melchor represses a self-destructive urge to ask Rosa if what she means to say is that he should not have been so set on finding out who killed her parents, because, in that case, his wife would not have died.

"What I mean is that, sometimes, truth is bad for life," Rosa continues, perhaps reading on Melchor's face that Rusiñol's maxim required some clarification. "And, if one can spare one's children that, one should. I tried to spare my daughters when my parents were killed, but I couldn't, because the truth I wanted to spare them was devastating. Too apparent and too horrible. And, since I couldn't protect my daughters, they suffered. On the other hand, you have been able to protect Cosette. Thanks to that she's had a happy childhood and, now that she's almost an adult, she is better armed to confront the truth. This is not an opinion: it's a fact. And, if you are able to explain it to her, Cosette will understand. I'm sure of it. It may take some time, but she'll understand."

Rosa argues with a conviction that seems suspicious to Melchor: he doesn't know if she's saying what she's saying because she believes it, or because she believes it can help him. Melchor admires Rosa's strength. Until the murder of her parents, she had lived an easy and slightly unreal life, made lethargic by the security provided by her family's economic power and her free decision to remain in her husband's shadow, raising their four daughters after having been an outstanding economics student and then having decided, of her own accord, not to pursue a professional career. Her parents' murder, on the orders of her husband, threw her savagely into reality, and since then she has devoted all her energies to a double purpose: on the one hand, enabling her daughters to overcome that familial calamity; on the other, maintaining and if possible expanding the business empire built by her father over half a century. As far as Melchor can judge, Rosa has achieved undeniable success on both fronts. These days, Gráficas Adell is making almost twice as much as fourteen years ago, when Rosa's father was still at the helm, employs twice as many workers and has three more subsidiaries, all in Latin America (one in Trujillo, Peru, and two in Colombia: one in Medellín and another in Pereira). This triumph is not solely due to Rosa, but also, as she herself emphasises every chance she gets, to Señor Grau, eternal manager of Gráficas Adell and eternal friend of the family, who acted as Rosa's mentor when she took charge of the business and died of old age three years earlier, when he was ninety-five, perched like a little bird in his big command chair in his office at Gráficas Adell. As for Rosa's daughters, they've all overcome the trauma of the Adell case, or that's what Melchor thinks; whether or not it's true, they all live ordinary lives, three of them are married or in stable relationships, two are mothers and, even though none of them live in Terra Alta, they all visit their mother regularly; all of them, as well, have disowned their father, who got out of prison not long ago after having been locked up there for thirteen years and since then seems to be living in Salou, not far from Terra Alta.

Rosa finishes her wine and, still referring to Cosette, repeats:

"She'll understand." Then she pours herself a bit more wine and concludes: "Don't worry. Everything will be fine. You'll see."

To try to distract Melchor, Rosa spends the rest of the evening telling him about her last visit to Medellín, from which she's only returned a couple of days ago, and about her friend the writer Héctor Abad Faciolince, who she's known for a few years now; she also tells him about a trip to La Inés, a farm belonging to the Abad family situated three and a half hours from Medellín, in the mountains in the jurisdiction of Támesis, where she spent the last weekend with Héctor, his wife and a group of friends.

"You'll never guess who Héctor is friends with," Rosa says; after a second, she tells him, without waiting for him to guess: "Javier Cercas."

The name sounds vaguely familiar to Melchor, but he doesn't know why.

"Don't you remember?" Rosa goes on. "The guy who wrote those novels about you. Have you still not read them?"

"No."

"Well, you should. That Cercas guy makes everything up, but they're entertaining. Héctor couldn't believe that I know you. He thought you didn't exist, that his friend had made you up as well . . . These novelists are a bunch of charlatans. Do you think they were like that in the nineteenth century as well?"

When they finish their after-dinner conversation they make love in Rosa's bedroom. She does so as she always does with him: possessed by an adolescent's desperation, euphoria and tenderness, as if she wanted to hide in Melchor's body. When they finish, she laughs, satisfied and sweaty.

"I'm a lascivious old lady," she pants.

"Lascivious," Melchor agrees. "But not old."

She laughs again.

"You better learn how to lie," she advises.

Melchor is about to say that Olga told him the same thing, but stops himself in time. Rosa gets out of bed and, as he watches her walk away towards the bathroom, her naked body glistening with perspiration, Melchor thinks he has not lied. He thinks so again when he sees her come back from the bathroom, slip between the sheets again and nestle up against him. A mahogany-coloured semi-darkness reigns in the room, created by a standard lamp at the back, beside an armchair. As if she knew Melchor has not stopped thinking about Cosette, Rosa comments after a few seconds of silence:

"Señor Grau always said that a tragedy is a fight in which both contenders are right."

"That's the second time tonight you've quoted Señor Grau."

"Is it?"

"It is."

Another silence.

"Well . . ." says Rosa. "The thing is that the relationship between parents and children is a tragedy."

Melchor thinks that, after raising four daughters, Rosa knows what she's talking about; also, that she misses Señor Grau much more than she does her father, which probably has something to do with the fact that it has taken her two and a half years of private deliberations and failed trials to find his replacement in Gráficas Adell, supposing she has actually found one and hasn't resigned herself to accepting that Señor Grau is irreplaceable. (Finally, Señor Grau's replacement or aspiring replacement is Daniel Silva, former finance manager of the business, who fourteen years earlier had been unwittingly decisive in Melchor's solving the Adell case.) Rosa goes on:

26

"We are right to try to protect our children. And our children are right to do everything they can not to be protected, trying to get away from us, getting us out of the way and freeing themselves of us to be able to get on with their own lives. That's the fight. And that's what's happening to you and Cosette, Melchor: a tragedy. But an essential tragedy. If you hadn't wanted to protect Cosette you'd be a son of a bitch, and if Cosette didn't want you to stop protecting her she could never free herself, and would never become an adult." Rosa stirs a little against Melchor, who is holding her tight, his arm around her shoulder. "I told you before, you did the right thing hiding the truth from her. What were you going to say to Cosette? That my ex-husband killed her mother by accident so you wouldn't keep investigating my parents' murder? How can you explain that to a child? What father would not try to spare himself? But it's also logical that she's angry with you, after all you hid something very important from her. Both things are true, and both are contradictory. Could you have done better? Of course, everything can be improved. Would it have been less bad if she had not found all this out the way she did? Absolutely. Has this confused her? Naturally. But she'll figure it out." Rosa pauses for a moment. "This is all normal, don't worry. Actually, there's only one problem."

"What's that?"

"That you don't trust her enough."

"Could be. Cosette is a little naive."

"Weren't you naive when you were her age?"

"At her age, I was in prison. Or about to be."

"Which means you were even more naive than Cosette. Besides, what if she is naive? She's also smart and strong. And maybe all this will help her lose her naivety. And kill her father. I don't want to get Freudian, but . . ."

27

"I didn't kill my father."

"You didn't have to, Melchor: you didn't have a father. Well, apart from Vivales."

"Vivales was not my father."

"Are you sure?"

"No."

Rosa laughs again. Even though she barely knew Vivales, he always pops up in their conversations sooner or later: maybe Melchor misses the old lawyer as much as Rosa misses Señor Grau. Without freeing herself of Melchor's embrace, she sits up a little, to look him in the eye and tell him something she's been wanting to say for some time.

"It'll do Cosette good to detach herself a bit from you." Since Melchor doesn't react, she adds: "She's always been too much of a daddy's girl. Not that I'm criticising her taste, but . . ."

"She's not anymore," Melchor interrupts her. "Now she hates me. Do you want me to tell you again about the scene the other day?"

Rosa nestles back against him.

"Cosette doesn't hate you," she murmurs. "She's just angry and disconcerted. It's normal, like I told you. She'll get over it. And a couple of days on her own in Mallorca might not be bad for her. On the contrary, they will most likely do her a world of good, Cosette needs to fly solo. Later, when she gets back, the two of you will have a good heart to heart and be done with it."

Rosa finishes off her statement by kissing Melchor on the lips and, while she strokes the curly hair on his chest, he picks up his mobile and sees that he still hasn't received any new messages from Cosette or from Elisa, at the same time as he tries to convince himself that Rosa's predictions will come true. Then, she runs her tongue over his nipples, slides down towards his

28

belly, takes him in her mouth and immediately makes him erect. They make love again. When they finish, he's the one who gets up and goes into the bathroom. He urinates. Then, as he washes his hands and looks in the mirror, he wonders what Cosette will be doing at that hour, alone in Pollença. When he gets back to the bedroom, Rosa has fallen asleep.

3

"For fuck's sake," Blai complains. "This girl's come to stir up a hornets' nest. That's all I needed."

It's eight-thirty in the morning and Melchor is sitting by the door of the bar on the plaza, drinking coffee. Beside him, wearing his uniform, the chief inspector of the Terra Alta police is ranting about the chief of the Investigations Unit, which he himself had been in charge of fourteen years ago, when Melchor began to work under his command after landing like a UFO in the region. The chief of the Investigations Unit is a sergeant who recently arrived at the station. Her name is Paca Poch.

"Besides, she does her own fucking thing," Blai goes on. "Do you remember Vàzquez on his good days? Well, more or less like that."

Although it's still cold, the sun is shining in a cloudless sky promising a bright spring morning, and the waiter has brought tables and chairs out onto the terrace, where Melchor and Blai are talking while around them the town begins its workday. The waiter is a Japanese man, called Hiroyuki, who strayed into Terra Alta a couple of years ago; according to him, he'd come to Spain to learn flamenco, but the local legend, which he denies with vociferous laughter and fuss, claims that he is

30

in hiding from one of the cruellest clans of the Yakuza, which wants to dismember him. Hiroyuki calls Melchor and Blai, in his broken Spanish, "the two amigos of Terra Alta", and always greets them and says goodbye with a small bow. Melchor and Blai have coffee every morning in Hiroyuki's bar, at least every weekday morning ever since, two and a half years after Blai left his job as head of the Central Jurisdiction of Personal Investigation at headquarters in Egara and took command of the station, Melchor left his job there.

"She's been to the library a couple of times." Melchor is also referring to the sergeant. "We've been chatting, she's asked me to recommend some novels. Truth is, I like her."

"Only a couple of times?" Blai asks, in a tone of voice between ironic and pedantic. "Must be four by now."

Melchor looks at his friend uncomprehending. The inspector is about to turn sixty, but looks ten or fifteen years younger; even though, as long as Melchor has known him, he's had his head impeccably shaved: he's never smoked tobacco, very rarely drinks alcohol, takes strict care of his diet and every morning, before meeting Melchor for coffee and heading into the station, he has already put his body through an hour-and-a-half-long workout at a new gym near his house, in Horta de Sant Joan. Furthermore, Melchor is aware that Blai uses those morning conclaves to blow off steam, but it doesn't bother him at all. First, and above all, because he is his best friend and he likes to listen to him. Second, because he knows that Blai can't unburden to anyone else, not even his wife, who doesn't understand what goes on at the station (and besides she's not interested). And, third, because he considers that his friend has more than enough reasons to want to let off steam: in recent years the crime rate in Terra Alta has increased tenfold, while the material and human resources available to combat it have been cut in

31

half. These two sombre statistics are not exclusive to the region – in some parts of Catalonia the situation is even more distressing – but Blai never stops reminding Melchor. "This is the jungle!" he ends up complaining every time. "And you, meanwhile, playing pocket billiards." "We've got problems at the library too," Melchor reminds him. "Go to hell, *españolazo*," Blai says.

"Look, Melchor," the police inspector explains, Paca is one of those aspiring cops who the first thing they do when they arrive at the Academy is ask about the hero of Cambrils . . . I'm not shitting you! Do you know she graduated fifth in her year? And why do you think someone who graduated fifth in her year asks to be sent to Terra Alta?"

"She told me she has a boyfriend in Tortosa."

"Yeah, pull the other one!" Blai explodes. "Bullshit. There's no boyfriend, she's been here for five weeks and has fucked half the station. Didn't I tell you she's stirred up a hornets' nest? And, don't think I don't understand, eh? You think I was born yesterday? You've seen what she looks like . . . ? But, shit, we have to be a little bit serious, don't we? Are we police officers or what the hell are we?"

To keep his friend from getting more worked up, Melchor does not remind him that he hasn't been a police officer for five years. The two men maintain one of those outmoded masculine friendships that almost completely exclude intimacies. Which explains that, in spite of meeting Melchor for coffee daily, Blai only discovered his friend was dating Rosa Adell because his wife told him, when the relationship was already public knowledge throughout Terra Alta. It also explains that, even though the previous week Melchor told Blai that Cosette was going to spend part of her Semana Santa holiday in Mallorca, this morning he hasn't even mentioned that his daughter has prolonged her trip without warning and stayed on the island by herself, even though her absence has been eating away at him for twelve hours. A couple of months before, when he discerned the first signs that something was going on with Cosette, Melchor didn't want to talk about it with Blai, but later he reasoned that his accumulated experience as father of a large family could possibly prove useful; his friend's reaction when he told him of his anxiety showed him he'd been wrong. "Don't worry," Blai attempted to calm him, with expert aplomb. "It's just hormones. It happens to all adolescents. When my daughters were Cosette's age, I had a hell of a time. I couldn't bear the idea that some idiot with testosterone coming out of his ears was going to have sex with my daughters. It was stronger than I was. In fact, if it was up to me I would have gelded anyone who came within three metres of them. So, forbearance, Melchor, lots of forbearance."

"More coffee for the two amigos?" Hiroyuki leans out the door. "Coffee good for everything. Ancient eastern wisdom says so."

"Get outta here," Blai laughs. "You wouldn't know wisdom if it bit you in the arse. East or west."

They order their second coffee, and once Hiroyuki leaves after bringing them, Blai goes back to talking about Sergeant Poch.

"I saw through her as soon as she started asking where the library was," he continues. "Look out, I said to myself. Here we have another novel reader. I bet she's read those books by that Cercas guy and swallowed all the bullshit he says about you, she must think you being at the library is a cover or something like that . . . Your legend pursues you, *españolazo*."

Blai is a one-track conversationalist: when he gets stuck into a subject, he does not let it go, he brings it up whether it has

33

any relevance or not, sometimes for weeks or months. For the last few days he's been talking non-stop about Paca Poch, but, years ago, Ernest Salom became an obsession for him. By that time the former corporal had been released from prison and returned to Terra Alta after almost six years of not setting foot there except on special leave. Salom's conviction in the Adell case had caused his expulsion from the Mossos d'Esquadra, but one of the circumstances that facilitated his early release was the fact that he had a job waiting for him when he got out of prison.

"He's living in Prat de Comte," Blai told Melchor, the same morning he told him that Salom was back. "Apparently he's looking after his daughters' country holiday homes."

That was the job. After the imprisonment of Melchor's friend and immediate superior in the Terra Alta Investigations Unit, his two daughters had dropped out of their university courses and returned to the region: Clàudia, the eldest, taught physics at the high school; her younger sister Mireia was married, had a daughter and was the manager of a wine-making cooperative in Arnes. Neither of the two earned a comfortable living, but, thanks to years of sacrifices, they had managed to restore an old, half-ruined family farmhouse as rural tourist accommodation, and after a while they rented and refurbished a second one. At first, it was Clàudia who took care of running them, which she could only make compatible with her classes at the high school in the beginning; later, when their father got out of prison, she got a good job as a maintenance technician at the nuclear power plant in Ascó and it was Salom who, after a short time learning the ropes, took over managing both houses.

"He likes the work," said Blai, who had visited Salom in prison on a couple of occasions in Lledoners, while the former corporal was serving out his sentence there. "That's what he says. Who could have imagined it, eh? Salom, working in the hospitality trade . . . Well, he'll have no shortage of customers."

It was true. Tourism had been a growing source of wealth for decades in Terra Alta. Couples on their own or with kids, groups of friends or relatives spent weekends or longer spells in the area, during the summer holidays, Easter or Christmas, sometimes taking in the larger fiestas of the region's towns: they hiked along the Vía Verde – a mountain trail that followed the old railway line – climbed the mountains, rented bicycles, rode horses or motorbikes, practised extreme sports or visited trenches, museums and interpretive centres on the Battle of the Ebro. The two establishments Salom ran were reserved on the internet, through a portal called Booking.com, and the ex-cop and ex-con took care of keeping the houses clean and ready to be occupied, opening them when tourists arrived and closing them when they left, giving them the keys and collecting them again at the end of their stay; he was also in charge of showing the houses to possible clients. With time, as well, he had begun to bake cakes to welcome them and offer supplementary services, such as preparing and serving breakfast every morning consisting of coffee, fresh fruit, toast with butter and marmalade, sausages, omelettes, tomato bread and orange juice.

"The truth is he seems happy," Blai concluded after telling his friend all about that. "It doesn't surprise me, after spending all those years in prison . . ."

Melchor had listened to the news of his two former colleagues meeting with suspicion and now listened to Blai's account with attention. When he seemed to be finished, Melchor asked him how many times he had seen Salom.

"Two or three," he answered. "He called me a month or so ago at the station and we met for a coffee. I was glad to see him out. After all, we worked together for years."

"You didn't tell me."

"That we worked together for years?"

"That you'd seen him."

"I'm telling you now."

Melchor nodded, but didn't ask any more questions or make any comment, and the conversation ended at that point. Days later, Blai told Melchor again that he had seen the former corporal.

"Do you know what he told me?"

"What?" Melchor asked.

"I've thought a lot about what happened," said Salom.

"What do you mean?" asked Blai.

"You know what I mean, said Salom; then he talked vaguely about the Adell case without mentioning it, and finally added, "You guys did what you had to do. I'm the one who was wrong."

"He said that?" Melchor asked.

Blai said yes. Then he added:

"He also asked after you."

"I heard he doesn't work at the station anymore," Salom said.

"No," Blai said. "He's at the library. Where Olga worked."

"That's what I heard," Salom said. "Maybe I'll go and see him one of these days."

"You should," Blai said. "He'd be happy to see you."

"Are you sure?" Salom asked.

"Of course," Blai answered. "At first he was furious, that's why he didn't want anything to do with you. To be expected, no? After what happened to his wife . . ."

"I had nothing to do with what happened to Olga," Salom said. "That was Albert."

"I know," Blai said. "And Melchor knows it too. But . . ."

"Tell him not to come to the library," Melchor said. "Tell him I don't want to see him."

"You're wrong," Blai said.

"Could be," Melchor said. "But I don't care."

"A comrade is always a comrade," Blai said. "Even if he makes a mistake. Even if you've sent him to prison."

"You said it," Melchor said. "But I don't want to see him."

"He's sorry," Blai insisted. "I've told you. He's not going to throw anything in your face. In fact, he just wants to ask your forgiveness.'

"If I'd been in Melchor's place," Salom said, "I would have done the same thing he did."

"To be reconciled with you," Blai said. "That's what Salom wants. Nothing more."

"Tell him there's no need," Melchor said. "Tell him that I never had any fight with him, so we don't need to reconcile."

"I understand that he's furious with me," Salom said. "He's right to be."

"It's true," Blai said. "More than me."

"More than you," Salom agreed. "We were inseparable. And I deceived him. I tried to cover up a murder and on top of that I deceived him."

"He said that?" Melchor asked.

"No more, no less," Blai said. "I told you he was sorry. And you're wrong. Know why you're wrong?" Melchor kept silent; Blai went on: "You once told me that hating someone is like drinking a glass of poison believing you're going to kill the person you hate."

"I didn't say that," Melchor said. "Olga did."

"It doesn't matter who said it," Blai replied. "What matters is that it's true. If you keep hating Salom you're going to end up poisoning yourself."

"I don't hate Salom," Melchor corrected him. "I just don't want to see him. I have nothing to say to him. And I'm not interested in what he has to say to me."

"You're wrong about that too," Blai said.

Melchor again asked his friend, when he next spoke to Salom, to tell him that he didn't want to see him. Although Blai delivered the message, that dialogue was repeated on a number of occasions with different variations, but always with the identical result. Until one Tuesday lunchtime, as he crossed the plaza on his way home after closing the library, Melchor thought he recognised Salom. It was market day, and most of the plaza was packed with stalls where merchants offered their weekly assortment of fruit, vegetables, salted fish, sweets, shoes, clothes, flowers, plants, accessories and household objects. At first, Melchor wasn't sure it was him, but his doubts soon vanished and he stood watching him from a discreet distance. Salom was there, leaning over a fruit stall, carefully selecting the items that, once chosen, he was putting in a bag. He'd put on a bit of weight, but he still had his dense beard and his big, outmoded plastic-framed glasses; his skin was the characteristic mousy grey of ex-cons, and, perhaps due to his hunched back and visible monk's tonsure, he had aged so much that Melchor had to remind himself that he was only two years older than Blai. For an instant he felt a stab of compassion, but the next moment he remembered some words he had forgotten, the last or almost last, as far as he could recall, he'd heard Salom say. "You are a murderer," he'd said to him the night Melchor discovered Salom was implicated in the Adell case and went to arrest him at his home, just before taking him to the station to hand him over to Blai. "That's what you are. I can see it in your face, in your eyes. I noticed the first time I saw you." And he'd also said: "Tell me something: You enjoyed killing those

kids, didn't you? Those four terrorists in Cambrils, I mean."
And also: "You liked it, didn't you? Tell me the truth, go on.
You can tell me. Don't worry. Did you enjoy it or not?" And
finally: "That's what you are: a murderer. Don't kid yourself. You were born like that and that's how you'll die. People
don't change. And neither will you." As he relived those words
and the tone of voice in which Salom had spoken them – a
sinuous and warm, confidential voice – his compassion disappeared; then he took a deep breath and started walking home
again. A few days after that chance encounter, Blai brought
up the subject again while they were having their morning coffee and again reproached Melchor for not wanting to meet
with Salom, but Melchor cut the conversation short so sharply
that they didn't discuss the matter again. That was seven years
ago.

"I have to say, she's great at her job," Blai admits, still talking about Paca Poch while he and Melchor pay for their coffees
at the bar. "Also, she knows how to lead. She straightened out
that lot in Investigations, who were a bit wild, as soon as she
arrived. And without shouting. If things were different, we
could invite her for lunch some Sunday."

"Why don't you?" Melchor suggests. "Rosa would like to
meet her."

"Well Gloria wouldn't," Blai says. "She's sure to think I'm
screwing her."

"You're monogamous, Blai."

"Yeah, but Gloria doesn't know that." Blai winks at his
friend. "And it's best if she doesn't find out." Collecting the
change that Hiroyuki hands him, he adds: "Besides, I already
see enough of Paca at the station."

"Goodbye, amigos of Terra Alta," the waiter bids them farewell. "Good day to you both."

"Adiós," Blai answers, pointing to the plaza through the glass door of the bar. "By the way, my people have seen a couple of sinister-looking compatriots of yours prowling around town. What do you think they're looking for?"

Hiroyuki laughs nervously.

"I'm not yakuza," he says, shaking his head and joining and separating his index fingers in front of his eyes. "I'm not yakuza."

Melchor and Blai cross the plaza in the shade of the mulberry trees and, while the inspector talks about a working lunch he has today in Móra d'Ebre, with the other regional station chiefs and the commissioner in charge of territorial coordination coming in from Egara, they turn right towards the plaza de la Farola, where they part ways each day: from there, Melchor walks towards the library along avenida de Catalunya, while Blai, who usually parks his car in that plaza, gets in it and drives to the station.

"By the way, Cosette came back from Mallorca yesterday, didn't she?" Blai asks. A leafy palm tree like a big vegetal fountain stands behind him, in the centre of the roundabout. "How did it go?"

"Fine," Melchor hastens to lie, surprised that Blai remembers that his daughter's holiday was ending the night before; he immediately corrects himself: "Well, actually she didn't come back."

Blai furrows his brow. Behind him, in the crystal-clear morning light, a delivery truck circles the roundabout in slow motion and takes the turn-off for Xerta and Tortosa.

"She didn't come back?" the police inspector repeats.

"No," Melchor says. "She's going to stay a few more days, seems like she's having a good time." He does not add that Elisa Climent has come back, and the explanation sounds false,

40

implausible, so he tries to counteract it with a vague hand gesture and a cliché: "You know what they're like at that age."

Blai's forehead smooths out again.

"Smart girl." The inspector nods emphatically while patting his friend's cheek. "Life must be enjoyed, *españolazo*."

4

Melchor spends the morning attending to library users, writing email messages, cataloguing a batch of new acquisitions and, most of all, trying not to worry about Cosette. He does not succeed. Mid-morning he sends a WhatsApp message to Elisa asking if Cosette had been in touch at all; the response comes back immediately: no. "Have you written to her?", Melchor insists. "Yes," Elisa writes back. "But she didn't answer me." Melchor waits until noon to phone Cosette, but, when he's about to, it occurs to him that it would be better if Elisa called her. So he writes to her again asking her to try to get in contact with Cosette, to tell her that her father is worried and to do her a favour and call him: he needs to talk to her.

Elisa agrees. After a while, when he's about to close the library and still has no news from Cosette or her friend, Melchor phones the latter again.

"I was just about to call you," Elisa says. "Cosette is not picking up. She's not answering my WhatsApps either.

"She hasn't answered any since yesterday?"

"No."

"How many have you sent?"

"Three. Four. I don't know. It's weird."

Melchor asks Elisa to stay by her mobile, hangs up and calls Cosette telling himself he shouldn't call her from his phone, but rather from a number she doesn't have registered in her phone and can't recognise. He hasn't finished telling himself this when he establishes that Cosette's mobile is not ringing: it's switched off. For a second, his legs go weak. Something's happened to her, he thinks. Immediately he reconsiders, he looks up at the library's glass facade and tries not to get alarmed. As he watches the Terra Alta high school students file by on the pavement in front of the library (baccalaureate students don't have classes the week before Semana Santa, but the rest do), he repeats the mantra he's been repeating to himself since yesterday: "Nothing's wrong. It's just that she doesn't want to talk to anybody. She's lost her bearings. She needs to think. She needs to be alone." He also thinks: "That's why she's switched off her phone: so we'll leave her alone."

He closes the library and starts walking home. As soon as he gets to avenida de Catalunya, however, he gets an idea, grabs his phone again and, still walking, asks Elisa by WhatsApp to give him the name of the hotel where Cosette is staying. "Hostal Borràs," Elisa answers, straight away. "It's in Port de Pollença." Melchor looks up the Hostal Borràs on the internet and finds it immediately: a two-star hotel, which, according to its website, is located a hundred metres from the beach and the marina.

Melchor calls the hotel phone number and a male voice answers on the first ring: no, Cosette Marín is not in her room. She had stayed there for two days, with a friend, but last night neither of the two girls had slept in the hotel.

"Are you sure?" Melchor asks.

"Completely," the man answers. "The beds are untouched.

One of the two girls' things and clothes are there, but . . . By the way, who am I speaking to?"

Melchor identifies himself, and at that moment he is overwhelmed by the certainty that something has indeed happened to Cosette.

"Do you know if your daughter is coming back today?" the man asks. "We need the room and—"

Melchor hangs up without letting him finish and writes a WhatsApp to Elisa. "Are you at home?" he asks. "Yes," she answers. "Don't move," Melchor writes back. "I'm on my way over." While he quickens his pace through the alley that leads off the plaza to the church of L'Assumpció, dotted with bakeries, florists, greengrocers and clothing boutiques, Melchor calls Blai and, as soon as he picks up the phone, blurts out:

"Cosette has disappeared."

"What?"

"Something's happened to Cosette. I've been calling her all morning and she doesn't answer. She hasn't answered Elisa Climent either. Her phone's switched off and she hasn't slept in her hotel room. Something's happened."

Blai does not respond immediately.

"Wait a moment," he finally says.

After a couple of seconds that feel like minutes to Melchor, the inspector speaks again: he asks his friend to repeat what he just told him. Melchor repeats it.

"Something's happened to her," Melchor insists.

"Cosette stayed in Mallorca on her own?" Blai asks. "You didn't tell me that."

"I didn't want to worry you," Melchor assures him. "What for? Lately we've had a few problems. I did tell you that. She's lost her bearings a bit."

"Do you think that has something to do with her disappearance?"

"Maybe. I don't know. Yesterday I went to wait for her at the station and, when I saw that she hadn't come back from Mallorca, I talked to her on WhatsApp. I wrote to her and she answered. She told me she was fine, that I should leave her alone, that she'd be back soon." While he's talking, Melchor is walking as fast as he can through the old centre of Gandesa towards the plaza del Ayuntamiento, between stately mansions and facades adorned with noble coats of arms, big wooden doors and balconies with iron railings. "I thought it was true. That she needed to think. To be on her own."

Trying not to omit a single detail, Melchor tells Blai what he knows, including what Elisa told him last night.

"You were right to call me," the inspector assures him when he finishes. "I could tell you we should wait a while, see if Cosette gets in touch, but it's better not to risk it. The sooner we report her missing and activate the search, the better. Do you know where Elisa is?"

"I'm on my way to her house."

"Perfect. Bring her to the station. We have to take her statement. Is she a minor?"

"Yes. I'll ask her mother to come with us."

"Great . . . Look, here's what we'll do. I'm in Móra d'Ebre right now, about to start lunch with the commissioner and the whole gang. I can't duck out, but, as soon as the meal ends, I'll be back at the station. Meanwhile, I'll tell Paca Poch to get ready to write up the report and get things moving."

"OK."

"Keep me informed. If there's any news, let me know. And do me a favour, eh? Don't worry: Cosette will show up any minute. I'm sure nothing's happened to her. It's what you said, she needs to think, to be alone . . . Whatever. She's probably partying over there. Or she's met someone she knows. Or she's got herself a boyfriend. Who knows. At that age, anything's possible. At Egara I was always slogging away with that kind of nonsense, kids who didn't come home because they were out on the piss or because they'd got up to some hooliganism and were scared of what their parents would say, but four days later they ended up coming back . . . Anyway, like I said: see you in a bit."

They hang up just as Melchor catches sight of his car parked in the plaza del Ayuntamiento. He gets in and drives the kilometre and a half as fast as he can through the emptied, silent, lunchtime streets, under a springtime sunshine that almost feels summery, and parks at the door of the three-storey building where Elisa Climent lives, just opposite the former headquarters of the Terra Alta Regional Council. Melchor presses the intercom and Elisa's mother buzzes him in and meets him on the second-floor landing with a question:

"Do you know anything?"

Melchor shakes his head.

"How about you two?"

Elisa's mother imitates Melchor's gesture and invites him in.

"We're just finishing lunch," she says.

Elisa's mother is called Lourdes and is Rosa's secretary at Gráficas Adell; Elisa's father also works for the company, but the couple separated years ago and he moved to Batea, where he remarried. Mother and daughter are eating at a table beside the kitchen window. Wearing a blue tracksuit, Elisa says hello to Melchor with a freshly bitten apple in her hand.

"Have you eaten yet?" Lourdes asks. "If you want, I could make you something."

"Thanks," Melchor says. "I'm not hungry. Besides, we should get going."

46

Elisa's mother looks at him with a combination of surprise and concern. Melchor has known her since their daughters became friends at nursery school. According to Rosa, this petite and cheerful woman is extremely efficient, and, although she had a bad run after divorcing Elisa's father, she's recovered her enthusiasm since she started dating the Hotel Piqué's Peruvian maître d', ten years her junior. She has a youthful hairstyle with reddish highlights, is wearing a bright print blouse, a tight grey skirt and high-heeled shoes; a discreet layer of make-up enhances her angular features.

"We should go down to the station," Melchor explains. "We need to file a report."

Elisa stands up without letting go of the apple.

"Are you sure Cosette has disappeared?" her mother asks.

"No," Melchor says. "But she's not answering messages or calls, her phone's switched off and she hasn't slept at the hotel. Something's happened. Or not. But, if we want to find her, we have to start looking for her now." He points at Elisa and explains: "She's the last person to speak to her, the last one to see her. They need to take her statement." He turns towards the teenager and adds: "Don't worry, you just have to answer a few questions. But the sooner we do it, the better."

Elisa looks questioningly at her mother, who nods and asks her to go and get dressed. The girl leaves the apple on her plate and heads to her room; meanwhile, her mother asks Melchor:

"Can I go with you?"

"You have to," he answers. "Elisa is underage and can only make a statement in front of a parent. Or legal guardian."

Elisa's mother nods.

"I'm going to call the office and tell them I can't come in this afternoon."

Before she can pick up her phone, Melchor pulls out his.

"Don't worry," he says. "I'll call Rosa."

While Elisa's mother tidies up the kitchen a little, Melchor phones Rosa and, looking out the window (through which he sees a field with the rusted skeleton of a tractor marooned in the middle of a sea of grass), tells her what is going on and that her secretary will not be coming in to work this afternoon, or that she'll arrive late, because she has to be present while her daughter gives a statement at the station. Rosa, who has stayed in her office to eat a salad, accompanied by the general staff of Gráficas Adell, tries to make light of Cosette's disappearance with similar arguments to those Blai used a few minutes earlier, or that seem similar to Melchor.

"Do you want me to go with you to the station?" Rosa finally asks.

"No, don't be silly. I'll call you if I need you."

Ten minutes later, accompanied by Elisa and her mother, Melchor parks his car beside the playground in front of the entrance to Terra Alta police station. In the past decade a lot of buildings have gone up in the area, but the place has still not lost its desolate outlying air, beyond which the town disintegrates into a succession of empty spaces that seem to stretch out as far as the Sierra de Cavalls, between marshes, mounds, stones and weeds. Melchor doesn't recognise the officer on guard at the reception desk – a rectangular prism of bulletproof glass known in the station as The Fishbowl – but the officer does recognise him and, despite that, asks to see his identity card and those of his two companions.

"Sergeant Poch is expecting you," he announces, returning their documents. "I'll call her right now—"

"No need." Melchor doesn't let him finish. "Is she in her office?"

The officer says yes and Melchor says he knows where it is

and asks to be allowed through. After a moment of doubt, the officer presses a switch and the reinforced door that connects reception to the police facilities opens with a metallic click. Melchor goes into the station followed by the two women, walks as fast as he can down an open corridor along an interior courtyard that spreads clear daylight through the whole building, jogs up the stairs to the first floor and, after knocking on the door of the chief of the Investigations Unit, opens it.

Paca Poch stands up from her desk to receive them.

"Come in, Melchor," she says, walking around the desk piled with papers and holding out her hand. As she greets Elisa and her mother, Sergeant Poch explains that she has spoken to Inspector Blai and he has brought her up to date on the matter; then she points to two chairs: "Sit down, please."

The two women each take a seat while Paca Poch summons a blond officer with a three-day beard who is working at that moment in the unit's shared office, on the other side of a big window, and motions for him to bring in a chair.

"Leave it, Paca," Melchor tries to dissuade her. "I'm fine standing up."

Paca Poch pays him no mind, sits back down at her desk and, without more ado, begins to type on her computer while announcing that she is going to write up a missing persons affidavit and the officer from the shared office barges in with a chair.

"Put it there, Artigas," the sergeant orders, pointing to Melchor without taking her eyes off the screen. "And don't go anywhere, I'm going to need you."

Melchor can barely recognise, in the urgent gravity of the Investigations Unit chief, the chatty, witty and teasing thirty-year-old he'd seen several times at the library. Paca Poch is as strapping as Blai, and it's obvious that, like Blai, she has sculpted her athletic musculature in long hours in the gym. She has long hair combed back with gel, and her eyes, an arrogant green, dominate a face with very strong features: full lips, prominent cheekbones, steep nose, hard chin. She's wearing a pair of very tight, faded jeans, and a loose red shirt that reveals a deep cleavage between her full breasts.

Still typing, Paca Poch asks:

"We have a recent photo of Cosette, right?"

Nobody answers, and the sergeant turns to Melchor, who has not sat down in the chair that Artigas has brought him and realises that, since he had the hunch or certainty that something has happened to Cosette, he has not been thinking clearly; otherwise, he would not have forgotten that they can't even start to look for his daughter if they don't have a recent photograph to put up on the internet and send to all the police stations, train and bus stations, ports and airports. To Melchor's surprise, at that moment Elisa speaks up.

"We took a lot of photos in Mallorca," she says, timidly. "They're on my Instagram page. I don't know if one of them will work—"

"That'll work," Paca Poch assures her. "Give Artigas the name of your account, please. And, while you're at it, give him the rest of the social media networks you use. We're also going to need to get into your email and your mobile phone, we're going to download the contents so—" The sergeant does not finish her sentence because Elisa has begun to turn pale. "Don't make that face. We're just interested in anything that has to do with your friend."

The statement does not calm Elisa, who turns to Melchor.

"Is it necessary?" she asks. "I've just got my things there."

"It's indispensable," Paca Poch replies, gently but emphatic, before Melchor can answer. "And do me the favour of not looking at him: look at me." Elisa obeys, and the sergeant swivels towards her in her chair, leans her elbows on the desk, clasps her hands together and locks her eyes on Elisa's. "Now listen to me carefully. We don't know where Cosette is. We don't know if something's happened to her or not. We don't know if she's in danger. That's why we have to find her as soon as possible. And you were the last person to see her, so you're fundamental to our finding her . . . You have to tell us everything the two of you did in Mallorca, where you went, who you spoke to, and what you talked about. Everything. Anything might be useful. Also, we're going to go into your social media accounts, we're going to listen to your phone calls and read your messages . . . We can do this the easy way or the hard way. The hard way is a bit more complicated and will take a bit longer, because we'll have to seek a court order, we'd have to download the contents of your mobile in the presence of the secretary of the court and things like that, but we'll do it either way, tomorrow morning at the latest. However, the easy way is much simpler: you give us your passwords, we open everything and start working right now." She unclasps her hands and clasps them again. "That's the only difference. But we are going to do it either way, whether you want us to or not. For Cosette. But also for you: imagine if something happened to Cosette and you haven't helped us to prevent it because you don't want us to read your conversations with your friends or your boyfriends, which we aren't going to read anyway because they're of no interest to us whatsoever. How would you feel then, eh?" Paca Poch pauses while waiting for a reply to her question in Elisa's frightened eyes; then she separates her hands again, lifts her elbows off the desk and leans back in her chair. "Anyway, it's up to you."

"Elisa, please—" her mother says.

The girl holds her mobile out to the sergeant. Artigas, how-ever, is the one who takes it and immediately writes down the passwords she dictates. Meanwhile, Paca Poch fills out a form with Melchor's help about Cosette's disappearance. The ser-geant types rapidly, her expression concentrated and eyes fixed on the screen. When she finishes, she looks at Elisa and then at Melchor.

"OK," she says after a moment of silence, "now tell me exactly what it is that has happened."

5

For the next half hour, Melchor tells Paca Poch what a short time ago he'd told Blai in a few minutes. The sergeant types on the computer keyboard or writes things down in a notebook, and at some point asks if this is the first time Cosette has disappeared.

"Absolutely," Melchor says. "She's always told me where she's going, where she is, who she's with. This is not normal."

"Do you have any idea why she would? I mean—"

"I don't know," Melchor cuts in. "What I know is what I've told you. Yesterday, by WhatsApp, she told me she needed to think. She told Elisa that too, didn't she?"

Huddling against her mother, who has a protective hand on her thigh, Elisa nods.

"Do either of you know what she needed to think about?" Paca Poch insists. "Had she argued with someone? Did she have some problem at home?"

Although aware that it's coming, the question catches Melchor off-guard; not knowing what to say, he looks away from the sergeant, towards Elisa and her mother and then at Artigas, who is attending the interrogation leaning on a filing cabinet, beside the office door.

"I'll tell you when Blai gets here," Melchor finally answers. "I want him to hear it too."

The sergeant, visibly unhappy with the reply, assures him that time is pressing and they should process the report as soon as possible.

"Better wait for Blai," Melchor holds his ground. "He should be just about here."

Paca Poch shrugs and, half-closing her eyes and pursing her lips, complies with his refusal. Then she turns to Elisa, who begins to tell again what she told Melchor yesterday; only that, pressed by the sergeant and the ex-police officer, who interrupts and asks questions and corrects and qualifies, now adds numerous details to her initial tale. She adds, for example, that on the previous Friday, as soon as they landed at the airport in Mallorca, the two friends took a bus that drove them to the Intermodal station, in the centre of Palma, and there they took another bus to S'Arenal. She adds that in S'Arenal they stayed at a little hotel called Caribbean Bay and for the next two days, as well as swim and sunbathe on the beach and go out dancing at night, they wandered around the old quarter of Palma, visited the cathedral, the episcopal palace, the Almudaina Palace and the Parc de la Mar, poked about in the shops on avenida Jaume III, bought a hat (Elisa) and a bracelet (Cosette) from the stalls in the plaza Mayor, and in the city centre bars they ate tapas and ice cream. She adds that, before leaving Terra Alta, they had reserved two nights in a hotel in Magaluf, on the island's west coast, where they were planning to spend Sunday and Monday, but late on Saturday night, while they were having a drink at Tito's, a nightclub in Palma, a girl told them that Magaluf wasn't worth a visit, that it was dirty and packed with tourists, while Pollença, on the other end of the island, was a gem, so they cancelled their reservations at the Magaluf hotel and made a reservation at the Hostal Borràs, in Port de Pollença. She adds that they arrived in Port de Pollença on Sunday at midday, by bus, and for another two days they swam in the sea and sunbathed on the beach, very close to the Hostal Borràs, and wandered around the outskirts, the port and the promenade. She mentions a restaurant called Indian Curry, a bar called Norai and a nightclub called Chivas, where they finished up each night.

Halfway through Elisa's statement Blai shows up. The station chief orders the sergeant to continue with her questioning, makes his way through the chairs that fill up the office – "This looks like a Marx brothers' cabin," he murmurs – and, after giving Melchor's shoulder a fleeting squeeze, he stands behind Paca Poch, as if he wanted to supervise the affidavit she is writing up. Elisa concludes her story spurred on by the sergeant. When they bring it to an end, Paca Poch turns back towards Melchor and, indicating Blai with a slight nod, asks:

"Now are you going to tell us?"

Before the station chief can ask what it is that he has to tell, Melchor turns to Artigas:

"Do you guys still have that disgusting coffee machine downstairs?"

"Yeah." He smiles vaguely, uncrosses his arms, points to the shared office, where one of his colleagues is still working. "But I can offer you something better."

"Offer it to our guests." Melchor means Elisa and her mother, whom he asks: "Could you leave us alone for a moment, please?"

The two women stand up and Artigas opens the office door for them.

"While you're at it get everything off that mobile," Paca Poch orders Artigas, referring to Elisa's phone. "The calls, messages, photos, whatever she has in her social media accounts . . . Everything. Let's see if we can reconstruct the girls' itinerary exactly. And send me a photo of Cosette. The most recent. The best. If you have any problems, call forensics."

As soon as he is alone with Blai and the sergeant, Melchor crosses the office, to the door, checks that it is properly closed and stands there for an instant with his back to the two police officers, his hand on the doorknob, scrutinising it as if it were the dial of a safe the combination of which he was trying to recall. When he turns around, the inspector and the sergeant are waiting expectantly.

"Cosette didn't know that Olga's death was not an accident," he announces. "She found out a couple of weeks ago."

A stony silence follows those words, which had just cracked like a whip in the stillness of the office. Facing him, Blai and Paca Poch do not even blink. Melchor goes on to summarise the story for the sergeant, while, gradually emerging from his surprise, Blai listens to this pressing summary walking back and forth with his hands clasped behind his back, his eyes fixed on the linoleum floor. The ex-cop has not yet finished speaking when the inspector stops, looks up at him and interrupts:

"So that's what it was?"

Melchor nods. The two friends look at each other as if Paca Poch had just left the office, as if she wasn't still there, watching them.

"Well," Blai says. "You've reassured me."

Melchor does not try to hide the confusion this remark produces.

"Now we have a reason why Cosette might not want to be in touch," the station chief clarifies. "Until now, we didn't." Since Melchor doesn't seem to entirely understand, Blai continues: "Fuck, Melchor, her whole life believing her mother died in an accident and now it turns out she was murdered . . . It's natural for her to feel deceived, and to blame you. How is she not going to feel bad? How is she not going to be disoriented and angry? Why would she not want to be alone? Look, I'm not blaming you at all, I'm sure I would have done the same. I'm just trying to put myself in her place. You get it, don't you?" Melchor doesn't answer and, after a silence, Blai turns to Paca Poch, points at the screen of her computer and asks: "What have you put as the cause of the disappearance?"

The sergeant holds out her arms and hands in a gesture of apology.

"Nothing," she answers.

"Well, put family quarrel," Blai orders. "Then close the report and send a copy to the court and another to the Tarragona public prosecutor for juveniles."

"As soon as Artigas sends me a photo," Paca Poch agrees. "In any case, I haven't finished with the girl. I'd like to keep questioning her. And I'd also like, if Cosette does not show up immediately, someone from Egara to come and give me a hand. Someone from Missing Persons."

"Good idea," Blai approves. "I'm sure they can get a lot more information out of Cosette's friend than we could. But meanwhile send the report to the judge and the prosecutor. Then, when there's news, we can bring them up to date on what we're already doing."

"Should we request a tap on Cosette's telephone?" Paca Poch asks.

"No, he won't let us," Blai says. "I know him. Not even twenty-four hours have passed since the girl disappeared. He'll tell us to wait, to keep working. I'll request it anyway: he can't say no till we ask. By the way, who's running Missing Persons at Egara?"

"Here's the photo," Paca Poch announces, ignoring the question.

The sergeant expands the image from Instagram on the computer screen while Melchor and Blai peer over her shoulders to examine it. The colour photograph shows Cosette standing on a promenade; behind her is a strip of beach, a bit of sea, a confusion of sailboats and, beyond, on the other side of something that looks like a bay, an inlet in the deep, rolling, forested land. Melchor's daughter's skin is tanned and she wears a brightly coloured beach wrap tied around her waist; a tiny bikini covers her minuscule breasts. Melchor recognises the hesitant smile (a smile that strikes him as childish, but is not), and notices a wave of heat flooding his eyes. He contains it with difficulty, while Paca Poch asks him if he thinks the photo is good. Melchor says yes and the sergeant, with the help of the inspector, the ex-cop and the notes she has taken by hand, completes the missing persons report. While she's doing it, Blai comments:

"I just remembered something."

Melchor asks him what.

"I have a friend in Palma," Blai answers. "Zapata. I don't know if I've told you about him. He's an inspector with the Policía Nacional."

"The Policía Nacional has no jurisdiction in Pollença," Paca Poch interrupts, stopping her typing and turning towards her superior. "They're under the Guardia Civil, there's a barracks in the port. It's the first thing I found out."

There was a knock at the door while Paca Poch was speaking: a uniformed corporal asks to speak to Blai. The inspector goes out to the corridor and Melchor stays alone with Paca Poch, who immerses herself in the affidavit again: she rereads what she's written, adds or corrects, checks her notes, corrects or writes something else. In the shared office, on the other side of the big window that divides it from her office, Artigas and two colleagues from the Investigations Unit continue to work on Elisa's mobile, concentrating in front of a computer screen. For her part, Cosette's friend waits in a corner with her mother, sitting in silence, each with a paper cup in her hands. While he waits for Blai to come back, Melchor's attention wanders from the affidavit for a second and only then does he become aware that this is the first time in the last five years he has set foot inside that station where he worked daily for more than a decade; he also realises that this is Blai's old office, the first he entered when he arrived in Terra Alta almost twenty years earlier, and that, around him, almost everything is just as it was, from the big window overlooking a patch of wasteland where the town ended and, beyond, the Fatarella mountains – standing out against the afternoon sky, bristling with wind turbines, their white metal blades spinning in the breeze – even the corkboard on the wall where notes, reminders and announcements were displayed. The only thing that has disappeared is the sticker with the Catalan independence flag, which proclaimed: CATALONIA IS NOT SPAIN. For a fraction of a second, Melchor experiences a sort of vertigo, as if those almost twenty years had been nothing but a hallucination or a dream.

But it's just a millisecond. As soon as Blai returns to the office, Paca Poch finishes up the report and asks them both to look it over. Melchor and Blai peer over her shoulders again. The affidavit contains, as well as Cosette's personal details, and Elisa's and Melchor's, a succinct description of the circumstances surrounding the disappearance. Melchor approves the document; so does Blai.

"Send it to 'Personas' and to Missing Persons and PD&RH," the inspector orders. "And then send it to the judge and the public prosecutor for juveniles. And to the Guardia Civil post in Pollença."

Melchor knows the police protocol because his years in the force familiarised him with it, so his friend does not explain what they're doing, although he does remind him, as if trying to make him feel confident or as if his five years as a librarian could have erased it from his memory, that Personas is the police database, indispensable for disseminating a missing persons report and that PD&RH is Unidentified Human Remains, an application of the National Centre for Missing Persons, under the auspices of the Secretary of State for Security, where all reports end up.

"In the blink of an eye Cosette's photo and the report will be everywhere," Blai tells him. "Including the foundations dedicated to looking for missing persons: SOS Desaparecidos, QSDglobal, Inter-SOS. And, through Sirene, all the police forces in Europe will have it. Do you remember Sirene?"

Before Melchor can answer, Paca Poch presses the Enter button on her keyboard, as if playing the last note of a piano sonata.

"Sent," she says. Then she spins her chair towards Blai: "I just have one question. Should we request an Amber alert?"

Blai and the sergeant look at each other without answering. Melchor asks what an Amber alert is.

"A very ostentatious thing," Blai says. "Too much so."
Paca Poch nods.

"It's for missing persons who are in imminent danger," she explains. "And serious. Someone who's confused or dependent on medication . . . Things like that."

"The disappearance is announced on television and radio stations," Blai says. "Cosette's photo would be shown on screens in the airports, bus and metro stations . . . I don't know if that's advisable."

"In order to activate it we'd have to call Egara and request Missing Persons to authorise it," Paca Poch reminds them.

"Who's in charge of Missing Persons?" Blai asks again.

"Cortabarría," Paca Poch says.

"Pol Cortabarría?" Blai asks.

Paca Poch nods. Blai turns to Melchor.

"Do you remember him?"

Although he only worked with Cortabarría for a week, Melchor remembers him. He met him the last time he was stationed at headquarters in Egara, when Blai oversaw the Central Jurisdiction of Personal Investigation and asked him to come and help with the case of the blackmail of the mayor of Barcelona, assigned to the Central Abduction and Extortion Unit, under the command of Sergeant Vàzquez. Melchor had a vague memory of Cortabarría, but Blai, who had been his commanding officer for several years, knows him well.

"Cortabarría, Inspector Blai, calling from Terra Alta." Melchor understands that Blai is not speaking to him, but to his voicemail. "Call me as soon as you can, please. It's urgent."

Blai hangs up and, barely a couple of seconds later, his telephone rings again. It's Cortabarría. After a minimal exchange of greetings, the sergeant confirms that he is in charge of the Central Jurisdiction of Missing Persons and Blai informs him that he has just sent him a report, outlines the case and tells him that Melchor and Paca Poch are with him.

"This is what we'll do," he adds. "I'm going to hang up and call you back from the landline, that way all three of us can talk."

Blai ends the call on his mobile while Paca Poch dials Cortabarría, who answers immediately; now, they all hear the chief sergeant's voice. He says hello to Paca Poch and to Melchor and gets straight to the point:

"Paca, tell me what you've done so far."

The sergeant reads him the report and explains the steps they've taken. Cortabarría offers no objections.

"We called you because we've got a question," Blai interrupts. "We don't know whether to ask you to activate an Amber alert. I think it might be better not to."

Cortabarría does not answer immediately, and through the telephone comes a noise that at first sounds like rain or footsteps on gravel and then traffic.

"Me too," Cortabarría agrees. "If we activate it, all hell will break loose, and it might not be any use at all."

"That's what I said," Blai reminds them.

"On the other hand," Cortabarría argues, ignoring the inspector's comment and following his own, "that alert is meant for other kinds of cases. In our case, it could be counter-productive."

Melchor encourages the sergeant to explain. Cortabarría again takes a few seconds before speaking, during which they hear the unmistakable protest of a car horn.

"Look, Melchor, I'm not going to sugar-coat it," Cortabarría begins. "From what you've said, I also think something could have happened to your daughter. That's what my instinct is telling me. Maybe I'm wrong, let's hope so, maybe nothing's happened and she'll show up as soon as we end this call. But we have to consider the worst."

"Go on," Melchor says.

"Imagine that Cosette has fallen into the wrong hands," Cortabarría continues. "Unscrupulous types that have kidnapped her or are holding her or whatever. Imagine that these people know or suspect they've been seen with her, and get frightened by the fuss the alert raises and, to get rid of the problem, decide to kill her or make her disappear. Forgive me for talking like this, but—"

"Go on," Melchor repeats.

"I would not activate an Amber alert," the sergeant reiterates. "What needs to be done is what you've done: get the investigation underway as soon as possible. That and two more things."

"What things?" Blai asks.

Cortabarría responds to this question with two more.

"What do they have in Pollença? Guardia Civil, Policía Nacional . . . ?"

"Guardia Civil."

"Well, draw up a transfer order and send them all the information you have and everything else you collect. Let them take over the proceedings."

"I don't agree," Paca Poch hurries to object. "We'll lose control of the investigation that way."

"We won't lose anything," Blai corrects her. "Cortabarría is right: the Pollença Guardia Civil are the ones who should be investigating; they're the ones who are on the ground and know what needs to be done. We're working blind from here. Not to mention that we've got no jurisdiction to act over there."

"What's the second thing?" Melchor asks.

Cortabarría asks him to repeat the question. Then he answers:

"Get after the guys in Pollença to start working on this as soon as they can."

Blai agrees with him again.

"I'll call the station chief right now," he announces.

"No, don't," Cortabarría advises. "It's better if I call. The Judicial Police unit is going to take charge of the case, and the

Judicial Police is not answerable to the chief of the post. That's how the Guardia Civil works . . . Leave it with me. I'll call Missing Persons at the Guardia Civil headquarters in Madrid. I talk to them often, I've got friends there. They'll pressure the Pollença crew. And I'll get all my people in gear. You caught me just as I was getting home, but I've turned around and in ten minutes I'll be in Egara. From there I'll call Madrid."

"Great," says Blai. "One more thing. Could you send us someone you trust to interrogate Cosette's friend? We've already got what we can out of her, but I'm sure that a specialist . . ."

"Done," says Cortabarría. "Tomorrow at midday they'll be there."

Then he asks who's going to be his contact in Terra Alta, who should he call or communicate with.

"Paca has taken charge of the case," Blai answers. "But you can call Melchor or me any time you want."

They exchange phone numbers and, before they hang up, Melchor thanks the chief sergeant of Missing Persons.

"Don't mention it," says Cortabarría. "And don't worry: we'll find Cosette."

6

While Paca Poch is writing up the request for a transfer of jurisdiction to the Guardia Civil post in Pollença and Blai is calling the judge in Gandesa to request a tap on Cosette's phone, Melchor looks on the internet for a plane ticket to Mallorca. The judge doesn't answer Blai, who hangs up and says to the sergeant:

"Just in case, when you finish that fill out a request asking the court for authorisation to tap Cosette's phone. They won't give it to us, but . . . Melchor, what are you doing?"

Melchor tells him without taking his eyes off the screen of his phone. He adds:

"The last flight leaves at eight." He glances at his watch, which shows 5:45 and, as if talking to himself: "If I hurry, I can catch it."

"Have you lost your mind?" Blai asks, looking at his own watch. "It takes two hours to drive from here to the airport. You're going to kill yourself on the road."

Melchor ignores Blai's warning and goes on with his search, until a few seconds later he curses his bad luck out loud: there are no seats left on the last Barcelona–Mallorca flight of the day. Congratulating him, Blai takes his friend's arm and drags him towards the door of the office.

"Come on," he says. "Let's let Paca work."

When they emerge into the hallway they bump into Elisa Climent, her mother and Artigas, who have just left the main room of the Investigations Unit. A little pale, both women seem ravaged by the tension of the hours they've spent in the station. Artigas informs Blai that they've downloaded everything from Elisa's phone and are processing the material they've found on it. Blai nods his approval; Elisa's mother asks:

"Are we finished now?"

"For today, we are," says Blai. "Tomorrow morning we're going to need you both again."

The mother asks what for and the inspector explains: he tells her of another interrogation, this one longer and more exhaustive, and of a specialist who will arrive from headquarters in Egara, he says he'll call her when he knows what time they should be back at the station; Elisa's mother asks if the next day Elisa's father could accompany her instead, and Blai says of course. Apart from this dialogue, Melchor is still immersed in his phone, looking for a seat on the first flight to Mallorca the following day, and when Elisa and her mother say goodbye, he asks Cosette's friend if she had tried to get in touch with his daughter again. Elisa says she hasn't.

"Well, please try every once in a while."

Elisa nods and her mother assures him that if there is any news they'll call him immediately, and then the two women head towards the exit escorted by Artigas. As soon as Melchor and Blai are on their own again, the inspector asks:

"Are you really going to go to Mallorca?"

"What do you want me to do?" Melchor answers. "Stay here and do nothing?"

"You're not doing nothing."

"No. But, while Cosette is still there, what am I doing here?"

"She might not be there anymore."

"You're making it worse." Melchor looks back at his phone. "Whatever the case, that's where she was last seen, and that's where we have to start looking."

"You are not the most appropriate person to be looking for her," Blai warns him. "Actually, you're the least appropriate person. And you know it: you're her father, you're confused, in Pollença all you're going to do is annoy people . . . Are you going to let the Guardia Civil do their job? Those people know their territory and know how to work. The best thing you can do to help is leave them in peace."

Blai keeps trying to convince him it makes no sense to fly to Mallorca, until Melchor interrupts him.

"There we go," he announces. "I've just reserved a seat on the flight to Palma that leaves Barcelona at eight." Looking up at the inspector, he asks: "What were you saying?"

Blai clicks his tongue, defeated.

"Nothing," he gives in. "Do you want a coffee?"

Only then does Melchor remember that he hasn't had a bite to eat since, first thing that morning, he had a coffee with Blai at the bar in the plaza, and suddenly feels an almost painful emptiness in his stomach; before he can reply to the inspector's question, Paca Poch's office door opens.

"The file transfer request has been sent to Pollença," the sergeant informs them. Turning to Blai, she tells him that she's just sent all the documentation; then she hands Melchor three printed pages. "And here's a copy of the report for you."

Melchor takes the papers at the same time that Blai's phone rings. The inspector looks at the screen of his mobile.

"The judge," he announces.

Instinctively seeking privacy or quiet, Blai moves away from them. Melchor tells the sergeant what he's just learned from Artigas – that his subordinates have already downloaded everything from Elisa Climent's phone and are working on its contents, and hasn't finished telling her when he receives a WhatsApp from Rosa Adell. "How's everything going?" he reads. "Any news?"

"Sorry," Melchor says. "I have to reply to this."

"Of course." Paca Poch points towards the Investigations Unit's shared office. "I'll be in there."

"We don't know anything," Melchor writes to Rosa. "I'm still at the station. Tomorrow morning I'm flying to Mallorca." Rosa replies with a question mark. "I can't do anything here," Melchor explains. "Over there maybe I could at least lend a hand." He sends the message; but, before Rosa writes back, he adds: "If she doesn't show up first." He immediately changes his mind and erases those words.

"He says no way," Blai announces, coming down the hall and shaking his head. He's referring to the judge, or rather to the authorisation to tap Cosette's phone he's just requested. "He says it's too soon. That there are tons of cases like this and the kids show up in no time at all. That we should wait forty-eight hours and then he'll let us. Anyway . . . I told you that's what he'd say: these young judges are bloody sticklers. At school they've gorged on laws, so the country can be going to hell and they're still hanging on a fucking comma in the constitution. By the time they learn they have to be flexible and that laws have to adapt to reality, not reality to laws, they're ready to retire."

Melchor receives another WhatsApp: "Do you want me to come and pick you up?"

"It's Rosa," he says, reading the message.

"Answer her," Blai says. "She must be worried."

"No," Melchor writes back. "Wait for me at your house." "OK," Rosa agrees. "I'll tell Ana to make us some dinner." Melchor closes the conversation by sending an emoji that shows a yellow face as round as a full moon, with two red hearts instead of eyes.

He spends the rest of the afternoon shut up in his former office at the station, the common room of the Investigations Unit, with Paca Poch and three of the officers under her command, analysing the information contained in Elisa Climent's mobile phone and social media accounts. They examine photos, listen to recordings and decipher messages, and begin to reconstruct Cosette and Elisa's itinerary during their five days in Mallorca; this coincides essentially with what Elisa has sketched out that afternoon, more proof that – Melchor, Blai and Paca Poch all agree – Cosette's friend did not hide information, at least no essential information, and that she is doing everything she can to help them find Cosette as soon as possible. Meanwhile, Blai is constantly coming in and out of the shared office, issuing orders, giving instructions and formulating questions, making phone calls, attending to normal station business, talking to Melchor and Paca Poch. Just before eight, after a couple of failed attempts, Blai manages to speak with his friend in the Policía Nacional in Palma, who is also an inspector and assigned to Narcotics. His friend assures him that in the days leading up to Semana Santa, as the tourist season begins, disappearances increase all over the archipelago and that, even though most of them are quickly cleared up – "tourists have a tremendous tendency to get lost up in the Sierra de Tramuntana," he had said sarcastically – others remain unsolved, something that has mostly been happening for some time now, precisely in the area of Pollença, which is becoming one of the busiest tourist spots on the islands. Blai asks if he knows the commanding officer at the Guardia Civil post in Pollença or anyone in charge of the Missing Persons Department at headquarters in Palma, and his colleague says no and explains that relations between the Policía Nacional and the Guardia Civil in Mallorca are a bit delicate at the moment because of a corruption case, uncovered by the Guardia Civil in the neighbourhood of Son Banya, Palma, that is keeping several police officers in prison awaiting trial, among them a commander, which has poisoned local relations between the two forces. In spite of this, Blai's friend promises to speak to a friend at the Guardia Civil headquarters in Palma to try to put pressure on the commanders of the Pollença post.

It's after ten when Blai tells Melchor that, if he has to get up at four in the morning to catch the first flight to Mallorca, he'd better have a bit of dinner and get to bed as soon as possible.

"Let's go and grab a bite at the Terra Alta," he suggests.

"I've arranged to go to Rosa's house."

"Ah," says Blai.

Melchor, who understands his friend wordlessly, realises the inspector does not wish to be apart from him, so he picks up his mobile and, while he writes a message to Rosa, says:

"A dinner for two can feed three."

"How about four?" Paca Poch joins in. "I'm famished."

Dinner at Rosa's house is wrapped in an abnormal, rather sombre atmosphere. They eat the food that Ana Elena had prepared in the kitchen – a couple of salads, a big tortilla de patatas, assorted cheeses, tomato bread, fruit salad – and the two police officers and Rosa drink two bottles of Clot d'Encís, a Terra Alta red wine. Melchor, who polishes off one of Coca-Cola

Zero, hardly speaks, checks his mobile compulsively and at one point leaves the table to phone Dolors, the colleague with whom he runs the library.

"Don't worry about anything here," Dolors says, after Melchor asks her to cover his shifts while he's in Mallorca. "I'll take care of everything."

When he returns to the table, Blai and Paca Poch carry on bringing Rosa up to date on the procedures they've put into place over the course of the evening, but the subject is soon exhausted, as is the discussion about alternative search methods available to them, and, to avoid uncomfortable silences and perhaps to try to distract Melchor, Rosa brings up the political and media news of the day: Virginia Oliver, ex-mayor of Barcelona and current president of the Generalitat, has just announced that, despite her solemn promise not to stay in power for more than eight years, she will be standing in the next elections.

"I bet she said that abandoning the ship now would be irresponsible," Blai says.

"How did you know?" asks Rosa.

"Because it's what they all say." The inspector smiles. "I'm sure she also said that she didn't want to leave her political project half-finished, that in these moments of crisis her ethical obligation is to sacrifice her private life for her country and blah, blah, blah. What a bunch of clowns: always virtue-signalling."

"The same thing happens to me," confesses Paca Poch, speaking to Rosa. The two women have just met, but, in spite of the age difference, or precisely because of it, they immediately hit it off. "When I hear a politician talk about morals, I grab my purse. By the way –" the sergeant turns back to Blai – "is it true that you and Melchor took care of the case where they tried to blackmail her when she was mayor?"

71

"It's true, but everything they say about that case is untrue," Blai answers. "And how do you know it was our case, anyway?"

"How do you think?" Rosa jumps in. "Because she read it in those Cercas novels."

"Is it also a lie that they tried to blackmail her with a sex tape?" Paca Poch insists.

"That's almost the only bit that's true," Blai says. "That and the fact that they assigned me to the case when I was at Egara. It was just before I came back here, fed up with getting lumbered with all the shit. Right, Melchor?"

Melchor nods, but doesn't say anything, and, while they eat the fruit salad Ana Elena has prepared, the two cops and Rosa talk about the case. It had been much talked about, not so much because of the matter itself but because it had been solved at the same time that the mayor's ex-husband, her right-hand man, and the leader of the conservative opposition died in a house fire in Cerdanya, as well as the chief of the mayor's pretorian guard and another person whose body was never identified. Those five deaths happening simultaneously with the end of the blackmail set off speculations, the most insistent of which claimed that the massacre had been the result of a gangsterish struggle for power in the Catalan capital, that the dead men had tried to extort the mayor to topple her and she had taken advantage of the situation to get rid of them by ordering that massacre disguised as an accident.

"That's not how Cercas tells it," Paca Poch says.

"Pay no attention to Cercas," Rosa recommends. "He makes it all up."

"I don't know what Cercas says, but the murder version is the one that has taken hold," Blai says, with a condescending sneer. "And it's false. That was an accident, not a murder. What actually happens always seems too prosaic to people.

They prefer to invent a conspiracy, which is more entertaining. Reality bores us, that's the sad truth. We prefer fantasy. There's no hope for us, Paca: we're a bunch of idiots."

As soon as they finish dinner, Melchor announces that he's leaving.

"Aren't you sleeping here?" Rosa asks.

"No," Melchor answers. "I need to change my clothes and pack a bag. Also, I have to get up really early tomorrow."

Melchor drops Blai and Paca Poch at the station and, after driving around the old part of town a couple of times which at that hour of the night resembles a deserted fortress or one inhabited only by an army of ghosts, finds a parking place in the plaza of the iglesia de L'Assumpció, beside the monument to those who fell in the Civil War, and walks home without meeting a single soul. When he gets home he puts his laptop into a backpack, along with the missing persons report on Cosette and a couple of changes of clothes; also, his copy of *Smoke*. While he's brushing his teeth, his phone rings. It's Cortabarría.

"I've just spoken to the chief of Missing Persons at Guardia Civil headquarters in Madrid," he says. "He told me he's going to try to talk to the people at the Pollença post tonight. With the Command in Palma as well. I told him who you are and he has assured me that he's going to try to pull out all the stops. He said you should keep calm. They'll do everything they can."

"Great," Melchor says. "I'm catching a flight to Mallorca tomorrow morning."

"Are you going to Pollença?"

Melchor says he is. On the other end of the phone there is silence.

"You're doing the right thing," Cortabarría says at last. "I'd do the same."

73

Melchor is not sure his former colleague truly believes what he's just said, but he is silently grateful.

As soon as he gets into bed, Melchor realises he won't be able to sleep. He considers turning on the lamp on his bedside table and reading a bit of *Smoke*, but, sure he won't be able to concentrate on Turgenev's novel – and that, if he could, it wouldn't help him fall asleep – he resolves to stay in the dark, lying in bed with his eyes closed. In his head spins a furious whirlwind of ideas, feelings and images associated with Cosette or with Cosette's disappearance, a chaos he does not manage to put in order and which at some point leads him to regret not having stayed to sleep with Rosa, who might have managed to calm him. Wide awake, on one occasion he gets up to urinate. On another, to drink water. The last time he looks at the clock it is half past two. He has already decided to give up when he falls asleep.

Part Two

Pollença

A short time after her father gave up the habit of reading books to her at night – the last one, *Les Misérables* – the two of them spent a weekend in Barcelona, in the flat they'd inherited from Vivales. They arrived as usual on Friday night and got up late the next morning, took a stroll down the Rambla and then went to the Frenchman's internet café in the Raval. They found it closed. They asked the neighbours, who told them the business had been inactive for weeks and they didn't know where the owner was. Her father didn't have his old friend's phone number and didn't know where he was living in Barcelona, assuming he hadn't moved, so he resigned himself to the Frenchman's disappearance, and that night, while the two of them were having dinner in a pizzeria, he said that the city had ceased to be his and announced that he was going to put the flat the lawyer had left him up for sale.

Cosette didn't raise any objections. Her father sold the flat easily and used the money to buy the apartment where the two of them lived in Gandesa, the same place where her mother had been living when she met her father. That double transaction left him with a significant amount of money left over, and he decided to spend it on remodelling the bathroom and the kitchen and taking Cosette on a trip. Neither of them had ever been out of Spain, and for months they were discussing where they should go, until they finally decided, for reasons neither of the two could explain or that they forgot over time, to travel around the United States. So at the beginning of August that year they flew to New York, where they stayed for the better part of a week, after which they took a train to Boston and then to Washington. Two days later they rented a car and drove to Chicago, and from there they took Route 66. They spent a little over two weeks following it through the states of Illinois, Kansas, Oklahoma, Texas, New Mexico, Arizona and California, until they reached the end of their journey in Los Angeles. They took their time, sleeping in motels along the highway and stopping where they felt like it. An incident occurred during the trip that Cosette never forgot, despite the fact that neither of them ever mentioned it again, as if it hadn't happened or as if they'd both dreamed it.

It was in a small town near Phoenix, Arizona, towards the end of the journey. In the very modest motel where they were getting ready to spend the night, there was no room service, the restaurant was closed and the desk clerk explained that the only place they could find anything to eat at that hour was the diner at the gas station, on the outskirts of town. They were very hungry so they drove over there, and when they arrived ordered hamburgers with fries from the Mexican waitress at the bar. Hearing them talking to each other, she asked in Spanish where they were from, told them she was from Ciudad Juárez, México, invited them to sit at a table beside the big window that overlooked the parking lot, and a few minutes later brought their order. In the restaurant, a country station was playing very quietly, and just a few solitary customers remained scattered along the bar and at one or two tables. They hadn't finished their meal when a pair of young men burst into the place – they looked like drunken cowboys – having left their car badly parked outside the door, with the headlights still on, and both pulled out big pistols. One of them clambered up on the bar and shouted some words that neither Cosette nor her father entirely understood, but that they didn't need to understand either. Then her father took Cosette's hand, held it on top of the table and murmured without letting go:

"Don't move. Don't worry. It's OK."

Everything happened very quickly, as if the two drunken cowboys were not drunk and had carefully rehearsed the robbery. The guy who hadn't climbed up on the bar forced the Mexican waitress, who was sobbing and terrified, to open the cash register; then, pointing his gun at her head, went into the kitchen with her and further back into the depths of the building. They came straight back out, and then that same cowboy, carrying an industrial garbage bag or something that looked like an industrial garbage bag, went around collecting the customers' wallets, one by one, until he arrived at Cosette and her father. He, as the others had done, deposited his wallet in the bag, without protesting or making a face, but the man stayed for a second scrutinising Cosette, who held his gaze with her eyes wide open, as if she were facing a venomous snake about to bite her. He was a dirty, sweaty guy, with very blue eyes, long, tangled hair, a week's stubble, and a rancid stench. For an instant, the guy seemed to smile, and Cosette noticed he was missing a front tooth; then she heard her father say in an icy voice in his broken English, ten forgettable words that nevertheless remained forever etched in her pre-teen memory.

"Don't touch her," he whispered, as if he didn't want anyone else to hear. "If you touch her, I'll kill you."

The cowboy turned towards Melchor and stared at him for an instant, until the second cowboy, who had in the meantime sat on the bar, said something that sounded like an order, jumped to the floor and took off. The other followed him, first touching his forehead with the tip of his pistol as if saluting, while broadening his gap-toothed smile. The two fugitives jumped into the car and, skidding noisily out of the parking lot, disappeared into the darkness of the highway.

That night they got back to the motel very late – they had to make statements at the local police station, where they also had to report the theft of Melchor's wallet – and when they got back to their room, they had trouble falling asleep. While they stared at the darkness, each in their own bed, Cosette asked her father:

"Were you really going to kill him?"

Her father asked her to repeat what she'd said, and Cosette understood that he wasn't expecting the question and that, to give himself time to prepare an answer, he was pretending not to have understood. She repeated her question and he asked in turn:

"What do you think?"

"You weren't."

"You're right."

"Then why did you say it?"

Silence.

"Why do you think," her father said. "To scare him. So he'd leave us alone."

Another silence. Cosette insisted:

"But, couldn't he have got mad and hurt us?"

This time the silence was shorter.

"No," her father answered. "He was just a thug. And thugs are cowards who are afraid if they think you're not."

"And you're not afraid?"

Cosette turned towards her father and saw him smiling in the darkness.

"Of course I am. But I hold it back. People who aren't afraid are not brave: they're reckless. And I'm not reckless."

Cosette didn't ask anything else, just turned over on her side and fell asleep almost immediately.

A few months after that seminal trip, her father told her that a librarian's position had opened up at the Gandesa library and he was thinking of applying. Cosette was dumbfounded. She knew that her father had been studying library science for years at the Open University of Catalonia, and he had told her himself that, once he finished his degree, he would try to seize the first opportunity that arose to work as a librarian in Terra Alta or around Terra Alta; but her father being a police officer was such a fact of life to her that she always thought that idea was just one of those daydreams we caress over and over again without ever making them real. Of course, he had explained more than once the reasons pushing him to change jobs: he had lost interest in police work, he loved all the tasks at the library, when he left the station and got a job as a librarian he'd have more time to spend with her; nevertheless, Cosette never took these reasons too seriously, and when her father told her the moment had come – when he told her he'd got a job at the munici- pal library and was going to leave the police force – the first thing that came into her head was to ask him the same question she'd asked when she was six or seven years old and he still read her adventure stories at bedtime: "And now who's going to defend the good people from the bad ones?" She didn't ask him, of course: she had turned twelve and understood that was a childish question, unsuited to her age; she neither protested nor demanded explan- ations: she simply congratulated her father and told him she was very happy that he'd got the job he wanted. But, deep down, per- haps without admitting it to herself (or without completely admitting it), Cosette felt that her father's decision was a grave mistake, a sort of dishonour or betrayal, as if he'd given up on himself, or at least the best of himself; she also felt, even more secretly, that this was a posthumous victory for her mother: her father had chosen to be a librarian, which her mother had been, to be in some way with her and enclose himself with her ghost or mirage in the library where they had met and where her mother had worked until the day she died. That's what she felt, without knowing exactly that she felt it: that the mirage had defeated reality, the ghost the man of flesh and blood.

That was the first time she was ashamed of her father. By then Rosa Adell had been part of their lives for several years. Cosette didn't remember exactly how it happened, maybe because it happened progressively and subtly, almost imperceptibly. The fact is that the change was good for both of them, among other reasons because it freshened up a relationship that over the years had become claustrophobic. Cosette felt that Rosa listened to her, that she was sweet, attentive and affectionate towards her, so it didn't take long to transform her into an implicit ally against the ghost of her mother: Cosette imagined that, the more space Rosa took up in her father's life, the less her mother could occupy and the less she would be obliged to combat her spectral presence. Rosa, on the contrary, was a palpable and assiduous but not invasive presence: the owner of Gráficas Adell was intelligent enough not to try to replace her biological mother and, although a frequent visitor to the apartment where father and daughter lived, she never slept over, at least not when Cosette was there; she and her father, however, did sometimes sleep at Rosa's farmhouse, even spent whole weekends there, and often, when Rosa's daughters and their husbands were visiting Terra Alta, they all stayed together, and acted as if Cosette and her father were members of the family. Apart from that, it was obvious to Cosette that Rosa was very much in love with her father (more than her father was with her); it was also obvious that the romantic relationship had improved her father's character: especially at the beginning, it had made him more talkative, warmer and less self-absorbed.

This improvement compensated Cosette over time for the rupture of the exclusive bond of intimacy and the end of the feeling of communion that had tied her to her father when he still read her novels every night. At that point Cosette was no longer a little girl, but nor was she an adolescent yet and, after the shared reading of *Les Misérables* spectacularly failed for both, the literary tastes of father and daughter went their separate ways. He carried on confined to his anachronistic fondness for nineteenth-century novels (which he was only very rarely dragged out of by Rosa's enthusiasm for certain contemporary authors), while Cosette began an enjoyable voyage as an independent reader. Above all, independent of her father. She was still a diehard fan of novels, but for years she did not return to the nineteenth century; nor did she read new books or discuss what she read with anyone, as if reading was an exclusively intimate activity for her, a secret pleasure, the same as it had been for her father before he met her mother. She read what she came across by chance in the school or municipal library, with the only condition being that her father hadn't already read it, or at least hadn't recommended it. And, for some reason, more than books she read authors; when she liked an author, she read all their books, even if she didn't like them all, or even if she didn't understand them (once, in a school essay, she wrote that she liked bad books by authors she liked better than good books by authors she didn't): so before she turned sixteen she read all of Stephen King, all of Ursula K. Le Guin, all of Pere Calders, all of John Irving, all of Eduardo Mendoza, all of Philip K. Dick, all of Roald Dahl, all of Sergi Pàmies, and all of Haruki Murakami.

She was immersed in the work of Dahl when she lost her virginity. She was fifteen and she didn't do it because she liked the boy she lost it to, a classmate she'd known for ever and who had been in love with her for years; she did it because she was impatient to lose it. She didn't enjoy the experience, in fact she found it a bit repugnant, and, to the dismay of her classmate, did not repeat it, at least not with him. The following year, however, she fell in love with a French boy she met in Toulouse during a school trip to the South of

France. The boy, who was a grandson or great-grandson of Spanish emigrants or exiles and spoke funny and approximate Spanish, travelled to Terra Alta several times, and stayed with Cosette, who also went to visit him once in Toulouse, with Elisa Climent. After a few months the relationship ended. The break-up was not the result of a fight, or even an argument; they simply lost interest and stopped seeing each other. Since then, Cosette hadn't gone out with anybody: she'd had three or four pleasant but trivial adventures, which had never lasted longer than one night.

It was during that time she found out that her mother had not died by accident, as she had always believed, and that was when she was ashamed of her father for the second time. She had just turned seventeen and it was only a few months before she would go missing in Pollença.

1

Melchor wakes up in the middle of the night on Thursday panicked by the feeling that Cosette has died. They murdered his mother, murdered his wife and now they've murdered his daughter. He is soaked in sweat.

Tearing the remnants of that poisonous premonition out of his head, Melchor showers, gets dressed, walks down to calle Costumà, gets in his car and drives out of Gandesa while it's still dark. At that hour, he barely meets any traffic on the roads of Terra Alta and, once he crosses the Ebro by the bridge at Móra, the night is a grey bubble, which gradually begins to crack as he drives up the motorway and by Vendrell has broken completely, transformed into a tattered red dawn.

He reaches Prat airport before seven. He parks his car at Terminal 2, passes through security with his digital boarding card and is soon sitting at a table in the Starbucks across from boarding gate B22, with a double espresso and a blueberry muffin. It's the first time he's ever been to Mallorca, and he spends the next half hour looking at photographs and reading about the island in general and Pollença in particular on the internet. When he looks up from his mobile, a queue of passengers stretches in front of gate B22, and the screen announces the imminent departure of the flight.

During the flight, squeezed into a window seat, Melchor opens his copy of *Smoke*, but is unable to concentrate and decides to seek distraction in the spectacle of the sky and sea. That night he had slept for just over an hour, so the sun immediately begins to weigh on his eyelids; he reclines his seat, and, while he balances between sleep and wakefulness, he remembers the nightmare that woke him, though he manages to keep its poison at bay. When he emerges from that vigilant nap, the sea has been replaced in his window by a vast expanse of flat, checkered, multicoloured land, spattered with little white and brown villages, trees and isolated houses. A sky so pure it looks like crystal gleams in the airplane's fuselage.

The plane lands punctually at 8.55 at Palma airport, which does not look like the airport of a small Mediterranean island but more like that of a metropolis in the United States. Or at least that's what it seems like to Melchor as he walks at a quick pace through a futuristic labyrinth of corridors stuffed with sophisticated shops, moving walkways and gigantic television screens while answering the three WhatsApps he's received during the flight: one from Rosa, one from Blai and one from Paca Poch (the sergeant tells him that she and her men are still processing the information from Elisa's mobile and social media accounts, and that the Missing Persons specialists Cortabarría was sending from Egara would arrive at the Terra Alta station at noon, to interview Cosette's friend again). Melchor rents an electric Mazda from Sixt, and the first thing he does when he gets in the car is turn on Bluetooth and type the address of the Hostal Borràs into the satnav: plaza Miquel Capllonch, 13, Port de Pollença. While the satnav calculates his route, itinerary and journey time, Melchor fastens his seat belt and starts the car, and when he pulls out of the car park, the device indicates that, if he doesn't run into any accidents and he drives at the speed limit, it will take him fifty-three minutes to reach his destination.

The prediction proves exact. Guided by a tinny woman's voice, as he leaves the airport Melchor takes a ring road around Palma and a short time later, after several roundabouts and passing a Decathlon, a Leroy Merlin and an Alcampo, he merges onto the Palma–Alcúdia motorway. The traffic has the unmistakable density of a suburban workday morning, a practically summer sun falls like lead on the gleaming asphalt and only a few thread-like clouds or white brushstrokes disturb the perfect blue of the sky. On the right the Mazda leaves behind a succession of industrial estates, while, on his left, the Sierra de Tramuntana mountains – a rocky scar that, as Melchor has seen on maps, stretches from one end of the island to the other – block the horizon. But then, after a while, the landscape begins to change, becomes more rural and more arid, almost like the meseta: on either side of the motorway, in the horizontal vertigo of the plain, wheat fields, barley and rye, olive groves and solid rows of palms. The traffic is lighter now, and every once in a while Melchor overtakes a peloton of cyclists. He leaves behind exits for municipalities with unfamiliar names: Santa Maria, Consell, Binissalem, Inca, Sa Pobla. More or less at the level of the penultimate, the landscape transforms again: the vegetation turns green and lush, here and there remains of agrarian archaeology seem to sprout from the brown earth and, a few kilometres before reaching Pollença, when the motorway comes to an end and the ordinary road begins, for a moment Melchor glimpses a distant fragment of the sea between the rocks. The road runs through pine and holm oak woodlands and, always guided by the satnav, Melchor drives past the town centre of Pollença. Five minutes later he arrives at the port, through a couple of roundabouts (one of which displays a metal sculpture of a seaplane), takes a right off the third and enters a grid of narrow streets and tourist buildings from the sixties and seventies, until, just after the satnav announces the end of the journey ("You have arrived at your destination"), he parks beside the plaza Miquel Capllonch.

The place is a cobbled square, with wooden benches and meticulous flower beds, wrapped by a ribbon of tourist shops and the terraces of bars, restaurants and hotels. Melchor sees the Hostal Borràs on one corner, a three-storey building, with white walls and green blinds, with large balconies and a terrace packed with tables and chairs protected by white parasols, shaded by the leafy branches of two hackberry trees and watched over by a camera that sticks out above the door's lintel. The reception desk is to the right of the entrance. A guy in his sixties, with bulging eyes, a beard streaked with grey and an overhanging belly, wearing jeans and a Dropout Kings T-shirt with a skull and tattered Union Jack and Star-Spangled Banner is leaning on the counter. Behind him the morning sun pours in through an open window.

The guy looks up from the counter covered in bills and scribbled-on bits of paper, and Melchor introduces himself and mentions the fleeting telephone conversation the two of them had yesterday at midday.

"Of course," the guy remembers. "Has the girl shown up?"

Melchor shakes his head and asks in turn if he's heard anything; the guy says no. Melchor then asks if the Guardia Civil have been there, making inquiries, and the guy answers no again.

"Are you sure?" Melchor asks, surprised.

"Completely," the guy says. "As soon as the season starts, I don't move from here all day. I'm the concierge, the manager, everything."

Melchor nods and, for a couple of seconds, glances around the reception, a vast room with very high ceilings and a tiled floor, which looks like a dance hall, a theatre or an old-fashioned cinema: a grand piano occupies the far end as well as a white screen that runs almost the entire length of the wall. On the right is a marble bar and, behind it, several modernist oval mirrors, with borders and mouldings; large windows open at street level illuminate the room, which has big, round, copper lamps hanging from the ceiling. Everything feels old and cosy, like an improbable hybrid of a nineteenth-century casino, a cultural centre and young gentlemen's club commandeered by a popular uprising. After this quick inspection, Melchor asks:

"Could I see my daughter's room?"

"I'm sorry," the manager responds with a gesture of annoyance. "I've had it cleaned. As I told you, we needed it."

It's true: Melchor remembers that yesterday at midday, when they spoke on the phone, the guy warned him; now he curses himself for not requesting that the room be kept as Cosette left it: that would have been very useful for investigating his daughter's disappearance.

"By the way, she left it unpaid," the manager informs him. "The room, I mean." Immediately, as if regretting those words, he opens his chubby arms in apology. "But don't worry about that: you can pay me once the girl shows up."

Melchor puts his credit card on the counter and tells the manager to charge him. The manager tries to say there's no need, but Melchor doesn't let him finish and, without putting up any more resistance, the other gets out the machine and the ex-cop types in his code. When the manager hands him his receipt, Melchor asks:

"And my daughter's things?"

The manager looks perplexed for a second.

"Oh, sure," he rushes to say, before Melchor clarifies what he's talking about. "I'll go and get them."

The Dropout Kings fan walks heavily away from reception and, a couple of minutes later, returns carrying Cosette's suitcase and puts it on the counter. It is a lilac-coloured suitcase, with wheels, an extendable handle and a flap closure, and it's full to bursting.

"We packed everything up," the manager explains. "You can open it if you want, but you can't take it."

Melchor looks at him questioningly.

"I'm sorry," the guy says. "I had a problem one time: I don't plan to repeat the mistake. I know you're the girl's father, but I don't want any hassle."

Melchor realises he's right: without an order from a judge or police officer, the hotel is obliged not to hand over his daughter's belongings. Annoyed, he checks the outside of the suitcase, which still has the Vueling check-in tag tied to its handle and resists the impulse to open it and go through it right there, on the counter: since Cosette's room was cleaned, that suitcase is the main clue to his daughter's disappearance, and Melchor knows from experience that, if he opens it and starts to search for clues to Cosette's whereabouts, he runs the risk of damaging evidence and harming the investigation. It's better for the Guardia Civil to take charge of doing it, he thinks. Then he subjects the manager to an interrogation only halted twice, once by a couple of backpackers and the second time by a child with olive-coloured skin who wanders behind the counter and, Melchor deduces, must be a relative of the man he is questioning, whose replies do not initially contradict Elisa Climent's account. At a certain moment, Melchor asks if he noticed anything abnormal in the girls' behaviour, and the guy says he didn't. Then he asks if he saw them interacting with any other people and the guy says he only saw them with each other.

"Didn't you think it strange when my daughter stayed on in the hotel and her friend left the day before yesterday?"

The manager says no.

"The truth is I didn't even know the other girl had left," he admits. "I simply saw that on Tuesday your daughter came and went on her own, instead of with her friend. But, even if I had known she'd left, why would I think it strange that your daughter stayed? My customers do whatever they want and, as long as they don't bother anyone else, I don't get involved. That's normal, don't you think?"

Then, straining his memory at Melchor's insistence, the manager remembers that on Tuesday, the day Cosette disappeared, he saw her three times, once in the morning, once around noon and again at night, when she went to her room after dinner.

"And she didn't come out again?" Melchor asks.

"No. Not as far as I know."

"Sorry, but I don't understand. Didn't you tell me that my daughter didn't sleep in her room that night?"

"And she didn't."

"How do you know?"

"I already told you: because the beds were still made."

"Could she not have slept in her bed and made it before going out in the morning?"

The manager shakes his head again; but this time, as well, he smiles with a touch of professional smugness.

"People don't make their beds when they leave a hotel," he assures him. "If your daughter had slept in that room, we would have noticed. Not to mention that yesterday she didn't show up for breakfast or at noon, which is check-out time."

His argument seems persuasive to Melchor, but it also seems to open a crack in the manager's account.

"If Cosette went up to her room after dinner, but didn't sleep there," he reasons, "the only explanation is that she left the hotel without you seeing her."

"That may be," the manager admits, shrugging and half-closing his eyes. "One thing is me being here at all hours of the day and night, and another is seeing everyone who goes in or out. So yes, she could have left without my seeing her. And, if she got back late, I wouldn't have seen her come in."

Melchor asks why not and the manager points to the main door.

"Because, at midnight, that gets locked," he says. "Guests have a key and let themselves in through the side door."

Melchor glances at the door, which is still open, looks back at the manager and notices that behind him, built into the wall beside the picture window, there is a pendulum clock, a corkboard covered in notices in English, Catalan and Spanish, a child's bicycle and a skate board; then he looks at the clock face and realises its hands are stuck at an impossible hour: ten to ten.

"But as I said your daughter did not sleep in her room on Tuesday," the manager insists. "You can be sure of that."

His insistence jolts Melchor out of his abstraction, and he writes his phone number on a piece of paper and hands it to the manager and thanks him.

"Call me if there's any news," he adds.

He is already on his way out when he hears at his back:

"Hey, listen? What do we do with this?"

Melchor turns around: the manager is holding Cosette's suitcase up in the air, as if it were a trophy.

"Hang on to it," he says. "The Guardia Civil will be coming to collect it soon."

2

When he comes out of the Hostal Borràs, Melchor spies the seafront promenade on his left, at the end of a very short alley full of shops, and beyond that the peaceful blue of the sea. While he walks towards the place where he has parked the rented Mazda, he sees an unlit sign on the opposite side of the street, that says: CHIVAS. He remembers that was the name of the nightclub where, according to Elisa Climent, she and Cosette finished up their nights in Pollença, so he crosses the street and approaches the entrance. It is closed and, beyond the metal bars, all he can see is a wooden door, also closed. Above the door there is a security camera; above the entrance, a bas-relief the colour of mud composed of figures that suggest musical instruments and, between the bas-relief and the entrance, a sticker of a security company: Trablisa. The nightclub is barely thirty metres from the Hostal Borràs.

He gets into the rental car and types the address of the Guardia Civil post into the satnav: plaza Joan Cerdà, 1. The satnav calculates the route; which it says should take four minutes. Before setting off, Melchor sends a WhatsApp to Cortabarría. "I'm in Pollença," he says. "Who should I ask for at the Guardia Civil?" Following the satnav's instructions again, Melchor turns down one narrow street and then another, drives parallel to the promenade a block inland – on his left the sea appears here and there between the buildings, sparkling like quicksilver under the midday sun – and after one kilometre he arrives at a little square in front of the beach, with a playground nestled under some pine trees. There, the satnav again announces the end of the journey, during the course of which Melchor has received two WhatsApps. After parking the car, he sees they're both from Cortabarría. "I was just about to write to you," says the first. "My contact in Missing Persons says to ask for Sergeant Benavides. He's the chief of the Judicial Police. He just spoke to him." The second carries on from the previous message: "He's also spoken with command headquarters in Palma. He told me they're going to do whatever they can." Melchor answers with two emojis showing two yellow hands with two fingers crossed.

The Guardia Civil post is in an old, elongated and slightly dilapidated building, surrounded by latticed brickwork, with yellow walls speckled with green blinds, air conditioners and security cameras, and occupies an entire block on the seafront. Melchor walks under a brickwork arch flanked by orange trees, crosses a patio and opens a glass door with the Guardia Civil emblem above it: a crown beneath which an angled sword crosses a fasces. In the Citizens' Assistance Office he asks the guard at the door for Sergeant Benavides, and the officer asks in turn why he wants to speak to him. Melchor explains. The officer points to a row of metal chairs in the empty vestibule and asks him to wait for a moment. Melchor takes advantage of the wait to reply with an emoji to a WhatsApp from Paca Poch informing him that the agents Cortabarría sent to interrogate Elisa Climent have arrived in Terra Alta. Once he's answered the message, he checks out the notices that paper the walls of the vestibule; on the lintel of one of the doors he reads: "Honour – principal motto of the Guardia Civil."

After a few minutes a uniformed officer appears and asks him to come with him. They go through a door that leads to a second patio, cross it and reach another door; nailed to the wall beside it, a sign announces: JUDICIAL POLICE TEAM. On the other side of the door is an office lit by LED lights and furnished with six desks; only two are occupied at that moment, one by a man and the other by a woman, both very young, both in plainclothes, both so engrossed in their computer screens that they barely look up for a second to examine the recent arrivals. At the back of the office is another separated from the main one by a translucent partition. The officer who is guiding Melchor knocks at the door, requests authorisation to enter and, when he receives it, ushers in Melchor, who walks into a smaller room, with just one desk behind which sits a man who welcomes them with an expression midway between surprised and inquisitive. The uniformed Guardia Civil tries to introduce the recent arrival, but the occupant of the office – Sergeant Benavides, Melchor infers – seems to suddenly realise something and gestures for him to withdraw. Then he pleasantly asks Melchor to sit down.

"Thank you for seeing me," Melchor begins, taking a seat opposite the sergeant. "I've come from Gandesa, in Tarragona. I suppose you'll have read the report on a girl's disappearance that they sent you last night from the Terra Alta police station. The missing girl is my daughter."

"I'm sorry, I haven't been able to read it yet," the sergeant apologises, pointing to the computer screen on his desk. "But I know we've received it."

"You haven't read it yet?"

"No," the sergeant replies. "I was just about to. I just came in. In any case . . ."

"At least you've talked to Missing Persons headquarters in Madrid."

"I haven't heard anything from headquarters."

"No?"

"No."

Melchor looks at the sergeant uncomprehendingly. Had he misunderstood Cortabarría? Was Benavides lying to him? This man is, perhaps, a little bit older than him, gaunt, long-faced, with fine features and metallic eyes, wearing a white linen shirt and good-quality grey jacket. A very slight smile floats on his lips, maybe an attempt to calm Melchor but which strikes him as a bit out of place; the fingers of his right hand, long and delicate, hold a sharpened pencil that he is gently drumming on a blank piece of paper, producing an almost imperceptible noise. On the wall behind him hangs a portrait of King Felipe VI, with a beard and in dress uniform.

"I already told you I just came in," the sergeant says.

Melchor quickly sets aside his initial bafflement and decides to get to the point: trying not to omit any relevant details, he sums up the case; he emphasises that the missing persons report has been transferred from the Terra Alta station to the Pollença post and therefore the Judicial Police team under the sergeant's command should take charge of the investigation; he tells him what happened at the Hostal Borràs and that, even though the staff had cleaned Cosette's room and the traces of his daughter's stay there will have disappeared, her suitcase is still there; he says he didn't want to open it so he wouldn't destroy any evidence and that it is imperative to examine its contents as soon as possible; he informs him that he has seen security cameras at the entrance of the Hostal Borràs and the Chivas nightclub; he says it's imperative to request all the recordings that might contain images of his daughter and Elisa from the owners of both places and all those the adolescents might have walked past. He is still listing possible places of interest to the investigation when the sergeant interrupts him:

"Sorry." The smile has disappeared from his face some time ago. "What did you say your name was?"

After asking him to repeat the question, Melchor tells him his name again. Then the sergeant drops his pencil on the blank piece of paper, leans back in his seat and, although it is not cold in his office, rubs his hands as if it were.

"May I ask you a question, Señor Marín?"

"Of course," says Melchor.

"Don't take offence, but could you tell me what you're doing in Pollença?"

One part of Melchor understands immediately where the sergeant's question is leading, but another refuses to accept it.

"What do you mean what am I doing?" he replies, a little anxiously. "I told you already: my daughter has gone missing here, I don't know what's happened to her, I don't know who she's with, I don't know anything. I don't even know if she's alive or dead. What do you want me to do? Stay at home and pray that you people will find her?"

Melchor is not speaking heatedly, and his questions are not aggressive, or don't mean to be, although he is aware that they could be interpreted that way. The fact is that a frown has displaced the initial expression of professional courtesy on Benavides' face. The sergeant sighs.

"You told me you're in the police, right?"

"No," Melchor says.

"But you are."

"I was. I'm not anymore. What does that have to do—?"

"It has a bearing." The sergeant adopts a didactic, almost paternalistic tone. "If you have been in the police, you know you shouldn't be here, much less be investigating the disappearance of your own daughter. Supposing she is missing, of course." He pauses, and a suspicious or alarmed gleam suddenly sparks in his pupils. "Tell me, do you get along well with your daughter? I'm asking because maybe the girl has not gone missing but has run away. Maybe she doesn't want anything more to do with you, or doesn't want to see you for a while, or maybe she's found a boyfriend . . . Who knows, at that age it's something that tends to happen. Do you have any idea how many adolescents disappear and show up again after a few days in this country?" To imply that the number he's talking about is very high, the sergeant shows Melchor his hands rapidly tapping the tips of his fingers together. "But it doesn't matter: if your daughter really has gone missing, even worse. There is no way you should be investigating, her disappearance affects you too much . . . It's normal that you're nervous, confused, having a tough time. And we can't work that way. You should know that." The sergeant pauses, smiles again and, since Melchor remains silent, adds, recovering his affable disposition: "Anyway. What you should do is go home and leave us to do our work in peace."

"You're not doing your work," Melchor hears himself say.

He instantly realises that he has made a mistake, that he should not have said what he has just said. But he also realises that he has said what he thinks and most of all that it's too late to take it back. The sergeant says:

"Pardon?"

As if another person were speaking for him – someone who is and isn't him at the same time, someone looking for an insidious way to harm him – Melchor reiterates to the subofficial that he's not doing his job.

"As for leaving you in peace . . ." he adds, unable to contain himself. "Look, time is passing and you know better than I do that the first hours of a disappearance are decisive. There are lots of things to do, I've already told you some of them, and they have to be done very quickly, you should have started doing them several hours ago. In the hotel someone might open the suitcase and touch things inside, or throw them out, the images the security cameras recorded might be erased, people who were working at the nightclub last night might not be working there today . . . I repeat: there's no time to waste, and you are wasting it. You understand, don't you?"

Benavides' second smile turned into a sour and perplexed grimace. Visibly uncomfortable, the sergeant picks up his pencil again and goes back to drumming its sharpened tip against the piece of paper.

"Of course I understand," he responds. "You're the one who does not understand."

The sergeant leaves the pencil on his desk, stands up, walks over to the open window on his left and, plunging his hands deep into the pockets of his tailored trousers that match his jacket, watches the inner courtyard as if looking for someone or something. From the back, his body outlined by the radiant morning sun, he looks taller, brawnier and leaner than he'd seemed sitting down. Melchor is about to ask for an explanation when the other man turns back to him.

"How do you know I haven't begun to work?" he asks without aggression, switching unexpectedly from the formal *usted* to *tú*. The grimace has disappeared from his face and he stares at Melchor, as if trying to scan him. "Tell me, do you know what the Mirador del Colomer is? You don't, do you? Well, I'll tell you: it's a precipice where suicidal people kill themselves on this island. Right now there are two guards on their way there, in case your daughter threw herself into the sea . . . We are also sending a search party up Sierra de Tramuntana."

"My daughter does not climb mountains," Melchor objects. Then, repressing the feeling of the nightmare that woke him that morning, adds: "And she has not committed suicide."

"How do you know that, eh? Tell me, how do you know?" Melchor keeps quiet, impotent in the face of the unexpected aggression from the sergeant. "And another thing," the other man continues mercilessly, "a person doesn't have to be interested in mountain climbing to get lost in the sierra. All they have to do is go for a hike up there without knowing where they're going. Do you want me to go on telling you things you don't know?"

Stunned and defensive, Melchor forces himself to respond, albeit with a question of his own.

"Why haven't you sent anyone to the Hostal Borràs?" he says. "It's the first thing you should have done."

Now the sergeant stares at Melchor with a mocking condescension, slightly intrigued. Then, as if he has just understood something obvious, which had escaped him up till then, he seems to be about to burst out laughing, or that's the impression Melchor has. Finally, he simply shakes his head, clicking his tongue.

"Do you know how long I've been doing this job?" he asks without bothering to disguise his scorn. "Almost twenty years. Are you really going to tell me how I have to do it? And, now that we're on the subject, tell me something else." He takes his right hand out of his pocket and points to a cardboard box overflowing with papers, at one edge of his desk. "See that pile there? Those are unsolved cases. Some are missing persons . . . See how many there are? And now you tell me something: What do you want me to do? Leave them aside because you've got a nice face, because you're a cop like me, or because you were, or because you're a friend of who knows who in Madrid, because you've got connections? What's going on? Your daughter's more important than the rest?" He shakes his head again, puts his hand back in his pocket, smiles. Then, in a tone of voice as pacifying as it is condescending, concludes: "No, my friend. Your daughter is just one more. No more or less important than anyone else. So do me the favour of calming down, get the first flight back to Barcelona and let us work. Believe me: it's the best thing you can do for your daughter."

3

Melchor leaves the Guardia Civil post in a rage and, as he's walking across the plaza in front of it, towards the sea, he phones Blai and tells him what happened in Sergeant Benavides' office.

"The guy's a jerk," he concludes. "I felt like punching him in the face."

Blai tries to calm his friend down by playing devil's advocate: he tells him it's not true the sergeant has done nothing, reminds him of the procedures he'd ordered, repeats the names Mirador del Colomer and the Sierra de Tramuntana, adds without conviction:

"He's done something."

"That's the same as nothing."

"Maybe it's what they need to do first."

"Bullshit," replies Melchor. "You know better than I do that the first thing they need to do is send someone to the Hostal Borràs and follow any leads Cosette has left there, starting with her suitcase. And a whole lot of hours have gone by since the report arrived and they still haven't done it. And on top of that he lied to me."

"Are you sure?"

"He told me he hadn't received a call from Madrid, but Cortabarría says that Missing Persons Headquarters have spoken to him. Also, how did he know I was a police officer if they didn't tell him?"

Blai has no choice but to admit that he's right.

"Maybe we were wrong to transfer jurisdiction," he accepts.

"We weren't wrong." Melchor has come out onto the beach and, without stopping, begins to walk on the sand towards the sea. "From over there you can't do anything. It's these people who have to get down to work. And I have to get someone to take this seriously and tighten the screws on that prick of a sergeant."

Melchor walks along the beach while continuing to think out loud, or simply venting, until Blai interrupts him.

"What do you think you'll do?"

The ex-police officer stops short, with his shoes half-buried in the very fine sand. Barely thirty metres in front of him, the surface of the sea looks like a trembling and dazzling sheet of aluminium; even closer, groups of swimmers are tanning under the vertical midday sun.

"I don't know," Melchor answers. "I could go to the command headquarters of the Guardia Civil in Palma. Cortabarría told me he had also talked to them. Maybe I'll be in luck and—"

"They won't give you the time of day," Blai discourages him. They'll take you for a hysterical father and tell you the same thing the sergeant did: that you should go home and leave their colleague in peace, that he knows how to do his job. They won't take your side against him even in jest. It's called esprit de corps, remember? We've got it too."

"Then all I can do is go and see the judge."

Melchor hears silence and deduces that they've been cut off.

"Blai?"

"Try it," the inspector encourages him, as if he'd fallen asleep for a fraction of a second and just woke up. "You've already had a no. Besides, the courthouse is closer."

Melchor asks where it is.

"In Inca," Blai says. "Less than half an hour from there."

Turning on his heels and retracing his steps in the sand, Melchor announces:

"I'm on my way."

"And I'm going to pester the judge over here again," Blai reassures him. "See if he can give us a hand. By the way, the people Cortabarría sent have been interrogating Cosette's friend for quite a while."

"Paca told me. Any news?"

"Not that I know of. If there is any, I'll tell you."

Twenty minutes later, after going back part of the way he had driven first thing that morning from the Palma airport, first along the main road and then the motorway, Melchor reaches Inca and, always obeying the satnav's instructions, drives through the city's streets until he parks in a large, rectangular and deserted plaza, the centre of which is occupied by a playground with swings, see-saws and stone benches surrounded by a double ring of sickly plane trees. The courthouse is on one side, in a three-storey building, yellowy-grey walls, rounded corners and windows protected by wooden blinds, with thick columns at the entrance and the glass of the doors covered in posters. Melchor walks into the vestibule and, observed by a security guard, places his phone, wallet and car keys in the scanner tray, steps through the metal detector and picks up his belongings. This done, he gets to the security guard, who is seated behind a desk, and asks for the presiding judge.

"Investigative court number one, third floor." The man

points without looking at a staircase beside him, and Melchor has already started up when he is warned: "But the judge just left."

The guard has stood up. He must be more than two metres tall, wears a uniform that's too tight and has hair so blond and skin so pale he resembles an albino; his eyes, also very pale, look with an apathy that borders on disdain. An end of work-day silence reigns in the empty vestibule.

"Do you know when he'll be back?" Melchor asks.

A slight sarcasm tinges the guard's reply:

"Tomorrow, for sure."

"Not this afternoon?"

"Maybe, maybe not. In the afternoons the presiding judge only has to be reachable. But, if you want, try to speak to his secretary. She should still be in the office."

Melchor takes the stairs two at a time up to the third floor, where he immediately finds investigative court number one. At that moment he receives a WhatsApp from Rosa: "How's it going?" "All fine," Melchor lies. "I'll call you later." He knocks on the door, but no-one answers, so he opens it and leans into a spacious empty room, with wood-panelled walls and several desks, computers and chairs. At the back are two more doors, one closed and the other ajar; through the latter comes a muffled sound of voices. Melchor crosses the courtroom and pushes open the door. Inside the office, a woman and a man look up at him: the woman is sitting behind a desk; at her side, the man leans over with some papers in his hands, as if showing them to her or getting her to sign them.

"We're closed," the woman says.

Melchor says he knows and apologises.

"It's an urgent case," he explains. "My daughter went missing yesterday in Pollença."

Then he approaches the desk and, without having received any encouragement, summarises the details of the case.

"Here's the report," he finishes, holding out a copy of the missing persons report that Paca Poch gave him yesterday. "It should have reached you this morning."

With a frown of annoyance (or surprise), the secretary takes the report and gives it a glance; the man, however, does not even look at the document: with his papers in his hand, he remains standing beside the woman, observing the intruder as if trying to recognise him. He's quite a bit older than the secretary, has an unhealthy look to him, like an old bachelor with halitosis, greyish skin, badly shaven cheeks, overhanging belly and sad glasses; Melchor hadn't noticed at first, but with one hand he leans on a walking stick with a wooden handle. With no idea why, the civil servant's gaze casts Melchor into a sudden despondency, and for the first time he wonders if it's true that being Cosette's father disqualifies him from investigating her disappearance, if Sergeant Benavides might be right and he should give up the search and leave it in other hands.

The woman hands him back the report and says curtly:

"We didn't get this."

Melchor does not take the document: overcoming his discouragement, he asks the woman if she is the court secretary. She says she is.

"Could you do me a favour and call the judge to explain what has happened? Or let me explain it to him."

The secretary moves her head to the left and then right, almost scandalised.

"Absolutely not," she answers. "Do you think the judge is going to see anyone who has a problem? That would be a fine thing . . . You should talk to the Guardia Civil in Pollença. If

106

the report reached them, they will be carrying out the necessary procedures. They'll advise us when the time comes."

"The report reached them, but they haven't done anything," Melchor replies. "I've already been there, that's why I'm here, so that you people might help me make them get their act together. Everyone knows the first hours of a disappearance are the most important, and they are wasting them."

"I'm sorry, we cannot—"

"I'm begging you, please," he interrupts, both hands on her desk, leaning in close and looking into her eyes: they are dark, suspicious; the woman has jerked her torso back, a bit intimidated. "Help me find my daughter. At least speak to the Guardia Civil."

Reluctantly, after a second of suspense, the secretary hands the report to the court official, asks him to photocopy it, picks up the telephone while the man leaves the room supporting his unsteady steps with the cane, dials a number and asks to be put through to Sergeant Benavides. For the next three or four minutes, the secretary speaks with the sergeant; or rather listens, nods, asks a couple of generic questions, always avoiding the scrutiny of Melchor, who tries to catch her eye with the photocopier rumbling in the background from the room next door. The secretary is under forty, but her imperious manner, severe expression and slightly horsey face, framed by a blond bob, make her look older than she is; knotted at her throat a pale blue silk scarf contrasts with her jet-black shirt.

The secretary is still talking to Benavides when the official returns, places a copy of the report on her desk and hands the original back to Melchor. Shortly, hanging up the telephone with an air of satisfaction, the secretary assures him:

"Just as I said, they're on it."

"They're on what?" Melchor asks.

107

"Doing what they have to do to find your daughter," the woman answers, with renewed aplomb. "They're searching the Sierra de Tramuntana, the Formentor headland, everywhere. That's what the sergeant told me . . . Look, I understand that you're worried, I would be too in your place. But, believe me, the Guardia Civil know what they're doing, they are professionals. Why don't you go home and let them do their work? Trust me, you won't regret it."

Melchor listens to the secretary with growing exasperation, and is about to tell her she's mistaken, that he used to be a cop and he knows that what the Guardia Civil de Pollença is doing is not what should be done in a situation like this one, but all of a sudden understands that anything he says will be futile or counterproductive and feels an unfathomable fatigue, as if the accumulated tension and lack of sleep were about to overcome him. He looks away from the secretary and notices the court official, standing beside her again, old, downtrodden and leaning a bit on his stick, looking as if he would like to say something but is incapable of saying it.

"I'll leave you my phone number." Melchor overcomes his dejection once more and writes down his mobile number and email address. "I'm going to get a room at the Hostal Borràs, in Port de Pollença. If you find anything out, please, call me."

He runs down the courthouse steps, past the security guard in the vestibule and, when he comes out onto the plaza, fills his lungs several times with the dusty scent of the plane trees. Then, as he starts walking towards the car, he calls Rosa and, before he can even consider the possibility of telling her the truth, his instinct makes him lie to her again: he assures her that the Guardia Civil are doing all they can to locate Cosette, that they will uncover clues, that sooner rather than later they'll find her.

"Don't worry," he concludes, finding a tiny consolation in the fact that Rosa swallows this blend of bullshit and wishful thinking without protest. "She'll show up."

He gets into the Mazda like an automaton, starts the engine and immediately realises he doesn't know where to go or what to do, so he turns it off again. Gripping the steering wheel, he tries to reflect, but the paralysis and frustration cloud his judgement, and suddenly his empty stomach reminds him that many hours have passed since he last ate anything. He looks around and spots a café on the other side of the plaza. He gets out of the car, crosses the plaza and goes in.

The café is an oblong place with a long zinc bar and several formica tables occupied by solitary diners who are just finishing lunch or drinking coffee in silence, ignoring a flatscreen television where a woman is gesticulating in front of a map of Spain crisscrossed by a labyrinth of isobars. Melchor sits at the bar and orders a Coca-Cola and a tuna sandwich, and, while he's waiting, takes a call from Blai, who tells him right off the bat that he's just been in touch with the Terra Alta judge.

"He says he's spoken to the Guardia Civil in Pollença and that they're working on the case," Blai assures him.

"They are not doing what they need to be doing," Melchor replies, with the impression that he has spent the whole morning repeating the same thing, as if he were in a circular nightmare. He has just stepped out of the café to talk without being overheard. "Has he spoken to the judge in Inca?"

"That's the first thing I asked," Blai says. "And he told me there was no reason for him to do so. That we should be patient. That we should wait and see what the Guardia Civil turn up. That they know what they're doing and we should let them work. Truth is, Melchor: I think he's right."

Melchor answers by hanging up on him. He goes back into

the café furious and sits back down at the bar. Blai calls him again, but he doesn't pick up and his friend sends a WhatsApp with three scarlet heart-shaped emojis.

For the next fifteen minutes, Melchor is able to keep his mind blank and eat his tuna sandwich and drink his Coca-Cola as if he had prescribed himself a Zen exercise. Then he orders a double espresso and, as he pays for his meal, decides that, if the Guardia Civil and the judge are not going to do what needs to be done to find his daughter, he will do it himself.

4

Back in Port de Pollença, Melchor parks again next to the plaza Miquel Capllonch, takes his knapsack and enters the Hostal Borràs. The manager, stationed behind the desk, looks up from his papers and asks if there is any news. Melchor says no.

"Has the Guardia Civil been here?"

The manager shakes his head. Neither furious nor perplexed – deep down he expected that answer – Melchor is about to ask if there are any rooms available in the hotel when the other man gets ahead of him.

"I've been thinking," he says. Melchor's silence encourages him to continue. "You know? It's not the first time someone's gone missing around here."

Remembering the stack of files Benavides showed him in his office, Melchor observes:

"People go missing everywhere."

"Yeah, but here, more. Ask the Guardia Civil. All kinds of people, mostly teenage girls. Most of them turn up, but some don't. Some get lost in the Sierra de Tramuntana."

"I've heard that."

"The sierra is deceptive. It seems like one thing, but it's something else."

"What do you mean?"

"That, if you go up there without taking the necessary precautions and without knowing where you're going, you can get lost. And in lots of places it doesn't matter what kind of mobile you've got, because there's no coverage. Especially up there, the sierra is very tricky. I'm telling you, and I'm from here."

"My daughter is no fan of mountains."

"Even worse. Mountaineers aren't the ones who get lost. It's the others who do."

Melchor nods unconvinced. The man seems worried now, anxious to help; behind him, the window is still wide open to the street, and the pendulum clock remains stopped at ten to ten.

"The Guardia Civil are looking for my daughter there," Melchor says, in an attempt to reassure him. "Up in the sierra, I mean."

"That's what they do: when someone goes missing around here, the first thing they do is look in the sierra. Maybe the girl slept at someone's house and the next morning they went for a hike up there. Has anyone else been reported missing?"

Melchor says no. He adds:

"They're also looking for her at the Mirador del Colomer, in Formentor.

"Oh, that's a classic." The manager sighs, half-closing his bulging eyes. "Have you ever been there?"

"No."

"It's beautiful. The prettiest place on the island. You can see people like a dramatic setting to kill themselves." As if it just occurred to him that Melchor could take his words the wrong way, he tries to rectify: "Anyway, I don't mean to say . . ."

112

"I know what you mean," Melchor comes to his aid and, to overcome the discomfort of the moment, asks his thwarted question: "Tell me, have you got a free room?"

"You've hit the jackpot." Relieved by the change of subject, the manager takes out a printed form and puts it on the counter. "This morning I had a cancellation."

Melchor fills out the form and the manager hands him a slip of paper with the wi-fi password written on it.

"Let's go," he says, coming out from behind the counter with some keys in his hand. "I'll show you your room."

As they climb a narrow staircase up to the second floor, the manager explains that his hotel is meant for customers without huge economic resources, sightseers who just stop to sleep and have breakfast and explore the island by bus, bicycle or motorbike, or twenty-somethings who spend their days on the beach and nights at the clubs.

"Is that what my daughter and her friend were doing?" Melchor asks.

"I think so," the other man answers.

The room, as austere as a monk's cell, smells clean. By the entrance is a washroom with a shower, and beyond that a double bed, a full-length mirror, a flatscreen TV and a couple of armchairs; the blades of a ceiling fan are still. There is a wardrobe with sliding doors and a balcony with white curtains, a wooden door and green blinds.

"The girls' room is just like this," the man assures him. "It's on the floor below. The only difference is that, instead of a double bed, it has two singles."

They go out onto the balcony, which overlooks the plaza Miquel Capllonch. On the left, down a narrow street, Melchor glimpses the promenade and the sea; to the right is the church, and in the distance, standing out against the late afternoon sky, the silhouette of the last dry steep spurs of the Sierra de Tra-muntana, which, as the manager explains, ends at that tip of the island, at the shore. Beneath them, the tops of the cypresses, palms, plane and hackberry trees partially hide the evening rush on the plaza.

"Well then," says the manager handing Melchor the room key, "if you need anything, you know where to find me."

Once he's alone, Melchor drinks water from the bathroom tap, washes his face, hands and neck. Then he unpacks his knap-sack, turns on his laptop, connects to the internet and opens his email. There are several unopened messages in his inbox; all relating to the library, so he doesn't answer any of them. Sitting on the bed, he phones Paca Poch. Replying to Melchor's questions, she tells him that her team is still working on what they found in Elisa's mobile phone, email and social media accounts; she also tells him about Cortabarría's officers, who, after a break for lunch, are continuing with the interrogation of Cosette's friend. Then the sergeant asks Melchor how things are going in Mallorca, and he brings her up to date on what's happened since he arrived that morning. When he finishes, Paca Poch asks:

"And what do you think you'll do now?"

"What that dickhead Benavides didn't want to do," the ex-police officer says. "First, get Cosette's suitcase. And then, find all the cameras around this hotel and get the tapes from the last few days. I'm sure Cosette and Elisa will turn up on some of them. That's the most urgent, later we'll see. And I'm going to give it to Benavides, so he can't keep skiving."

"I think you're right," says the sergeant. "The question is how do you think you'll do it."

"That's why I called you, Paca," Melchor says. From the Hostal Borràs terrace, muffled by the glass of the window, comes the sound of laughter and conversations. "I need you to send me warrants so they'll hand over Cosette's suitcase and the video recordings."

"Are you talking about police warrants?"

"Of course."

"That's illegal," the sergeant reminds him. "A warrant can only be presented by a police officer."

"And how are they going to know that mine is illegal, if I present it with an authentic stamp?" Melchor reasons. "Nobody's going to make a fuss. And, if anyone has any doubts, I'll find a way to resolve them."

Paca Poch says nothing. Melchor looks at the plaza through the balcony window.

"Can you think of any other way to do it?" he insists. "If you can, tell me. Nothing else has occurred to me."

"Yeah . . . Tell me something else. Have you talked to Blai about this?"

"What do you think?"

Another silence, this one longer.

"OK," Paca Poch finally decides. "I'll be in my office writing up the warrants as you call them in to me. If anyone doesn't cooperate, put me on the phone with them and we'll sort it out."

The rest of the evening is frenetic. Melchor comes and goes around the Hostal Borràs, trying to reconstruct Cosette's possible itineraries in Port de Pollença. First he finds the security cameras that might have caught images of her and, once he's identified each of the places that have those cameras, asks Paca Poch for a warrant requesting the recordings that interest them; then, with the warrant in his email, goes into the places, speaks to the people in charge, shows them the warrant and a photo of

Cosette and requests the images. Only one manager of a wine bar – the Norai – and one waiter at a restaurant – the Indian Curry – recognise Cosette in the photo, although neither of the two remember any relevant or significant detail about her, apart from the fact that she was with, in both cases, a girl who fits the description of Elisa. Melchor cannot request the recordings from the cameras at bank machines, because the branches are closed until the following morning, but he can from the nightclubs, bars, restaurants and hotels; also, those of two hair salons, a launderette, a supermarket, a karate school (Dr Nicks Academy), a Little Britain, and even those on a bus stop. Of the fourteen people he requests video footage from, six hand it over that very evening: some in person, saved on a memory stick or a disc; others, like the manager of the Hostal Borràs (who also hands over Cosette's suitcase), send the footage by email. The rest promise to do so by the next day. Only a couple of people resist sharing the footage, but Melchor overcomes their reticence by calling Paca Poch, who gives them all sorts of guarantees and orders them, by way of an email with the emblem of the Terra Alta police station, to hand the material over to the ex-police officer.

The only one to refuse outright to help Melchor is the manager of the Chivas nightclub, a short, grim-faced and haggard-looking guy who turns out to be the only one who knows the exact legal requirement that he is only obliged to release the recordings from the security camera of his establishment to a police officer who presents a warrant and identifies himself as such. In fact, that's what he replies to Melchor when he approaches him at the door of the club.

"Come back with the Guardia Civil and I'll give you all you need," he promises Melchor as they both walk down into the place and cross paths with a cleaning woman coming up the stairs carrying a bag of rubbish. "Until then, forget it, my friend."

Melchor insists, tries to get him to speak on the phone with Paca Poch, but the manager brushes him off.

"I don't have to talk to anybody," he blurts out, taking off across the empty dance floor while waving his arms around as if shooing away a swarm of insects. "We'll talk when the Guardia Civil get here."

Melchor knows he needs the footage from the nightclub, because Cosette and Elisa were in there every night, but he decides to continue on his route. After a while, just at the moment he's handing a hotel desk clerk a warrant issued by Paca Poch, it occurs to him how to convince the nightclub manager to give him the recordings. So, when he leaves the hotel (it's the Daina, on a corner of the promenade, very close to the Hostal Borràs), he phones Blai and, combining truths and lies, deceives him: he tells him what he's spent a while doing, but not that he's doing it thanks to the warrants Paca Poch has been writing up with the emblem of Blai's station, committing, therefore, the crime of impersonating a police officer. Blai does not reproach him for hanging up on him last time they spoke; he just asks:

"What about the Guardia Civil?"

"They're still doing nothing."

"It's incredible."

"That's why I have to do it for them. And, to tell you the truth, people are taking it well: as soon as I tell them why I need the footage, they give it to me."

"People tend to be good," Blai says. "As long as you don't put them in a position to be bad."

"Yeah, but there's one guy who refuses to give me the videos," Melchor continues. "And the worst thing is that he's the manager of the nightclub where Cosette and Elisa went dancing each night. Chivas, it's called. I need that footage, and I don't want to ask the Guardia Civil for them."

"So, then?"

"I was thinking about your friend in the Palma High Command. The National Police inspector, wasn't his name Zapata? Do you think you could ask him for another favour?"

"What favour?"

"That he talks to someone who knows the manager or owner of that nightclub. I bet your friend knows someone, or someone who knows someone. A night person. Every station has someone like that . . . Tell your friend the truth, what's going on. Tell him the Guardia Civil aren't doing anything, that we're wasting precious time, that I just need the footage they recorded those three nights, from Sunday to Tuesday. Surely he can do us that favour. We're not asking for anything illegal, you know I wouldn't ask you, we're just requesting . . ."

"Cut the crap, *españolazo*," Blai interrupts. "Let me see what I can do."

That happens at half past six in the evening. Hours later, Melchor shuts himself in his room at the Hostal Borràs and, sitting on the bed with his laptop on his knees, with two Coca-Colas, a bag of potato crisps and another of almonds to hand, he reviews the footage he has gathered while the noise rising from the plaza gradually dwindles as the night goes on. Melchor slows down or accelerates the footage as necessary, and on three occasions recognises Cosette, always or almost always with Elisa at her side; he notices nothing untoward, suspicious or unusual in any of these appearances, but notes down the exact time and place where each was filmed. Shortly after twelve-thirty, he receives a text message from Blai. "I've just sent you an email with the recordings you requested," it says. "Keep me informed and, please, don't do anything stupid." Melchor answers with two consecutive messages. "Thank your friend for me," he says in the first. The second contains an identical message to the one Blai sent him that afternoon, after he hung up on him: three scarlet heart-shaped emojis. Blai's final WhatsApp is another emoji: a round yellow face with a winking eye.

Melchor gets straight to work on the files Blai has just sent. There are three: one contains the footage from Sunday night, another has Monday's and the third, Tuesday's. In the Sunday images, Melchor spots the two friends arriving at Chivas at 23.25 and leaving at 03.41, when the nightclub entrance is not very busy; nobody else is with them. In the Monday images, Cosette and Elisa go in and leave later: arriving at two minutes past midnight; leaving at 04.16. Melchor also notices that, this night, on their way in and on their way out both girls greet the doorman, a guy with his hair pulled back in a sort of topknot and one earring; for a few seconds, the three of them seem to joke around or chat as though they knew each other. Finally, on Tuesday night, which is when she disappeared, Cosette goes in by herself at 22.57, not without first saying hi to the doorman. Melchor writes down her entrance time and, exhausted – it's the second night in a row he has barely slept – guesses that Cosette will repeat the ritual of the two previous nights and accelerates full speed through the preview to save time, until, when the recording's clock shows 02.30 in the morning he goes back to examining what's left of the footage at normal speed; a little while later he reaches the end of the footage without having seen Cosette again. The clock on the recording reads five in the morning: closing time at the nightclub. "She stayed inside," is the first thing Melchor thinks. "She left through another door with someone from the nightclub," is the second. And the third: "Or someone from the nightclub took her."

Suddenly wide awake, he looks up from the computer screen and, thinking of the doorman and the manager of Chivas, he looks in the full-length mirror in front of him, beside the TV screen. He is about to stand up and go out to the nightclub when a hunch stops him, he rewinds as fast as possible back to the moment Cosette went into the nightclub and starts to view what he had skipped. His hunch was spot on: he soon sees his daughter come out; the clock on the recording reads 00.14. In the image, a young woman accompanies Cosette. Melchor pauses the video, studies her; but all he can get from the footage is that Cosette is walking beside the stranger of her own free will and the stranger (slender, with a print dress and shoulder-length hair) seems a bit older than her. With a mixture of anxiety and euphoria, Melchor understands that this is the last image of Cosette, and that he must find this stranger whatever it takes.

Next, he sends Rosa Adell an email with the images in question. "Send this to Lourdes, please," he writes. "Tell her to show her daughter the image of Cosette that appears in the recording at 00.14 on Tuesday. There's a girl with her. See if Elisa recognises her." Then Melchor sends another two emails: one, collectively to Blai, Paca Poch and Cortabarría; the other, individual, to Sergeant Benavides, although he sends it to the general address of the Guardia Civil post. The first contains a copy of all the recordings he's been sent by email, with annotations indicating the date, hour and minute where, in those he has been able to review, his daughter appears. "Look at the last one, that's the last image of Cosette," he writes. "She's walking with another girl. We have to find out who she is." The second email is practically identical, except that it is addressed to the Chief of the Judicial Police of the Pollença post; finally he adds, also for Sergeant Benavides: "Tomorrow morning I'll drop in and give you the rest of the footage I have. Thanks." He is about to send the message when he feels an urge to delete the last word. He does not delete it.

He goes downstairs and walks to the nightclub. It has just closed. Scattered on the pavement and road, around the door, are plastic glasses, beer cans, cigarette butts, papers, broken bottles and traces of urine. Melchor checks the time on his mobile: it's almost five-thirty. Wakeful due to his discovery, the image of his daughter leaving the nightclub with the stranger running round and round in his head, he starts to walk towards the promenade through deserted streets where his footsteps echo in the yellowish light from the streetlamps. The promenade is also deserted, and its terraces bristling with chairs set upside down on top of the tables; the only sounds are the murmur of waves breaking on the sand, the screeches of seagulls flying along the water's edge and the creaking of the rigging of the boats moored at the marina. Melchor sits down on a bench. A few metres in front of him, in shadow created by the combined brightness of the almost full moon and the streetlamps along the boardwalk, stretches the strip of beach where according to his calculations Cosette and Elisa swam daily, and where now his eyes adjusting to the half-light distinguish, with increasing acuity, a patch of sand covered in parasols of woven palm thatch, swings and sunbeds, to the right of which, in a sort of spur that sticks out into the sea, he catches a glimpse of the Hotel Daina's pool. While tiredness dissolves Melchor's anxiety and euphoria and the damp begins to numb his body, on the other side of the bay the crests of Cap de Pinar stand out against a sky that slowly veers from nocturnal blue to a pearly grey. It is dawn.

5

The next day he is woken by the sound of his phone ringing. "Hello, Melchor, this is Lourdes," he hears, half asleep. "Elisa's mother."

Melchor sits up in bed and leans his bare back against the cold wall: for a second he doesn't know where he is, or what day it is, or who Lourdes is, let alone Elisa; the next second reality comes back to him.

"Good morning, Lourdes." Through the half-open blinds oblique beams of morning light pour in and the buzz of conversation and the rattle of cutlery come up from the terrace of the Hostal Borràs. "Did Rosa show you what I sent?"

"That's why I'm calling," the woman says. "Wait a moment, I'll put Elisa on. She has something to tell you."

Elisa says hello to Melchor and asks if he knows anything about her friend.

"Not yet," Melchor answers. "Have you seen the video footage? Do you know the woman leaving the nightclub with Cosette?"

"I think so," Elisa says. "At first I had trouble recognising her, but later . . . I would say it's a girl we met on Saturday night in Tito's, a club in Palma. I think I mentioned her."

"You mean the one who convinced you to go to Pollença instead of Magaluf?"

"Exactly. Although the truth is it wasn't her who convinced us. We convinced ourselves. She just told us that Magaluf wasn't worth visiting and Pollença was."

"And you're sure it's her?"

"I'm not sure. But I've looked at the images several times and I'd say it is."

"Do you know her name?"

"No. We really only spoke to her for a few minutes. She was with a group of people, and they left straight after that."

Melchor peppers Elisa with questions about the girl in Tito's and about the group with her, but doesn't get anything relevant or anything that seems relevant, and, after talking for a moment about her interrogation by the agents sent from Egara by Cortabarría, he says goodbye to Cosette's friend begging her to call him if she remembers any detail about the unknown young woman. Elisa asks:

"Do you think it's important?"

"It could be," he answers. "As far as we know, she was the last person to see Cosette."

Melchor ends the call and checks the time: it's a few minutes to nine. He has only slept for a couple of hours, but he feels rested and not sleepy. On his mobile there is a new WhatsApp: Rosa asks how everything's going and if her secretary has called. Melchor replies with another blend of lies and truths, then gets out of bed. While he showers, the phone rings again. When he comes out of the bathroom he sees there is a message from Blai.

"I've just watched what you sent last night," the inspector says. "Are you sure that's the last image of Cosette?"

"As far as I know it is." While he gets dressed, Melchor holds his mobile between his shoulder and head. "Nobody has seen her since then. Do you think you can identify the girl with her?"

"Sure," Blai says. "At the station we don't have any face readers or facial recognition programmes, or even a database as we should, but they do in Egara. By tonight, at the latest, we should hear from Cortabarría who she is."

"Call him, please," Melchor asks. "With Paca on the line."

"That's just what we were about to do," Blai assures him. "What are you going to do?"

"Take the suitcase and surveillance footage to Benavides," Melchor says. "What I didn't send him last night. Then I'll start looking for any I haven't got yet and watching what I haven't been able to see yet. Maybe I'll find something else."

"Leave that to Paca and her team," says Blai. "You just look for any more recordings. And, most of all, get that Benavides on the job whatever it takes."

"Don't worry," Melchor says. "He'll get to work."

Carrying his laptop and Cosette's suitcase, Melchor goes down to the lobby of the Hostal Borràs, where the manager is at the desk looking after a couple with a child. He goes to the bar, orders a ham and cheese sandwich and a double espresso, finds on his computer screen the last images of his daughter and, while he eats his breakfast, reviews them again. The day has begun dark and cloudy, so, even though all the windows in the room are open, the ceiling lamps are on.

After a while, the manager comes over to the bar.

"Any news?" he asks.

"Yes," Melchor hurries to respond, turning towards him with a cup of coffee in his hand. "My daughter left the hotel on Tuesday night."

The manager has changed out of his Dropout Kings T-shirt into a checked shirt and a pair of Bermuda shorts.

"I told you she might have," he says.

"She was in the Chivas."

"How do you know?"

Melchor points with his cup to his computer screen, where he has paused the image of Cosette leaving the nightclub on Tuesday night. Then he puts the cup down on the bar and places his index finger next to the image of the stranger beside his daughter.

"Do you know her?"

The manager moves his face close to the screen, wrinkles his brow and squints.

"I've never seen her before in my life," he admits, leaning away from the screen. "Who is she?"

"I don't know." Now Melchor slides his finger across the screen to Cosette. "But this girl beside her is my daughter. The images come from the camera at the entrance to Chivas." Now he points to the time stamped on the recording. Fourteen minutes past midnight. My daughter went into the nightclub just over an hour before that."

The manager leans back in towards the screen, frowns and narrows his eyes again. Leaning back, he reaffirms:

"I recognise your daughter, but not the other girl."

Melchor nods without taking his eyes off the screen. Then he gulps down what's left of his coffee, asking the manager to put breakfast on his bill, closes his laptop and leaves.

"If the mountain won't come to Mohammed, Mohammed must go to the mountain," says Melchor, dumping out the contents of Cosette's suitcase ostentatiously on Sergeant Benavides' desk. "Now you can start working."

The chief of the Judicial Police team has turned pale. In

front of him, in a mess with his papers, Cosette's belongings are spilled out: at first glance a couple of dresses, a pair of jeans, several pairs of knickers, a bikini, a bra, a couple of towels, a toiletries bag, a razor, a pen. Lured by the noise, the officers working in the next office burst into the sergeant's office. Standing in front of the desk, Melchor does not turn towards them.

"Do you need me to tell you what you need to do with this?" Melchor stares at the chaos he has just strewn across the officer's desk. "There's work here to keep you busy for a while: photograph it all, look for fingerprints, analyse biological traces . . ." With one hand he lifts the empty suitcase and with the other holds the Vueling baggage tag looped through the handle with an elastic band. "Look, you've even got proof of what flight she arrived on."

Sitting at his desk, the sergeant halts his officers raising his hand with a minimal gesture and, while Melchor sets the suitcase down on the floor, points at his daughter's things.

"Where did you get all this?"

"Another item," Melchor says, dismissing the question. "Last night I sent you an email to the Guardia Civil post's address. It was addressed to you by name, so I assume you will have received it. Have you received it?"

Benavides does not respond. The two men stare at each other unblinking.

"If you have not received it, do me the favour of requesting it," Melchor continues. "It contains the recordings from several security cameras from the vicinity of the Hostal Borràs, the hotel where my daughter was staying with her friend, yesterday I told you about her, right? Her name is Elisa, they came here together on holiday, they're life-long friends . . . Anyway. I have sent you another file with a list of the moments when my daughter appears on these recordings. In any case, review them, perhaps I've missed something. The most interesting is the last one, from the Chivas nightclub. There you'll see my daughter leaving a little after midnight, accompanied by a girl. In the other footage she's with her friend, but the girl who appears there is not her, by that time Elisa had gone home. I don't know who that girl is. I've shown the image to Elisa and she recognised her, she says they met her on the previous Saturday in a nightclub in Palma, it seems she was the one who recommended they come here, to Pollença. Though she doesn't know her name . . . It doesn't matter, we have to find out who she is. She's the last person who saw my daughter. Since we have her face, it can't be very difficult to identify her. Do that. Identify her. Find her. Interrogate her. That girl can lead us to Cosette." Melchor pauses, adds: "I'm putting it on a plate for you, Sergeant. Help yourself. Make a few notes."

As Melchor has been talking, the pallor has vanished from Benavides' face, and his initial bewilderment has given way to an expression of ironic curiosity with which the sergeant is perhaps trying to save face in front of his subordinates. Behind Melchor, they are silently wondering what to do with the intruder, and the sergeant responds by asking them to get back to work. As soon as his office door is closed, Benavides invites Melchor to take a seat; Melchor remains standing. The sergeant smiles unconvincingly.

"Look, Melchor," he begins. "I can call you Melchor, can't I?"

"Call me whatever you like."

Careful not to touch anything with his fingers, Benavides pushes the disorder on his desk away a little; this done, he rests his elbows on the cleared space, folds his hands at chin level and looks back at the librarian.

"Well, look, Melchor." The sergeant reinforces his smile. "I'm not going to take this Sicilian defence personally. We'll just pretend it never happened . . . But now tell me something." Raising his eyebrows, he gestures again towards Cosette's belongings: "How did you get this?"

Melchor does not answer. Benavides insists:

"And the video footage?"

"What does it matter how I got it?" Melchor finally says.

The sergeant arches a sceptical eyebrow.

"But, what kind of police officer were you?" he asks, stifling a little laugh. He has a cavernous mouth and very white, very pointy small teeth, like those of a rodent. "If you have acquired evidence illegally, the whole investigation will go to waste. Don't you know that?"

"I've acquired it all by legal means," Melchor lies. "But I'm going to be honest with you: I don't care where your investigation ends up. The only thing that matters to me is finding my daughter. I couldn't care less about the rest of it."

"Well, I could, and I'm the one in charge of this investigation." He looks Melchor in the eye. Benavides' pupils look like two match heads. "And, since I'm the one running this investigation, I'm going to run it my way, not yours. Which makes sense, don't you think?"

Melchor keeps silent again, wanting to know how far the other man will take this.

"Very good," the sergeant continues. "And now tell me something: are you not going to leave me in peace? Are you really going to tell me how to do my job? Do I have to repeat what I said yesterday? . . . Because, if you force me to repeat it, I might say it in a different way."

His powers of endurance overwhelmed, Melchor asks:

"Are you threatening me?"

The sergeant unfolds his hands and, still smiling, leans back in his chair.

"Take it however you want," he says.

Incredulous, Melchor looks away from Benavides. First, he looks at the portrait of Felipe VI, in front of him, and then, to his right through the window, at the interior courtyard of the post; but he sees neither of them: the only thing he sees is his own incredulity. When he looks back at the sergeant, Melchor's voice has changed.

"Look, *chaval*, you're the biggest wanker I've ever met in my life," he says. "But, don't worry, I'm not going to smash your face in, which is what you deserve." Benavides holds Melchor's gaze. His face has altered, and the smile seems frozen on his lips; a glint of fury shines in his metallic eyes. "I'm just going to ask one thing. Do your job. Find my daughter. That's all I'm asking. If you do your job and find my daughter, I'll leave you in peace for ever. I swear. But, if you don't do your job, I'll fuck up your life, yours and your family's. Understood? Have you got a family?"

"I should have let them kick you out of here," the sergeant mutters.

A stony silence follows these words; now it's Melchor who smiles. Benavides insists:

"I'm telling you for the last time. Get out of here right now or I'll throw you in a cell for resisting arrest."

Melchor sighs, as if disappointed by Benavides' words.

"I see you haven't understood," he says softly. "I'm going to explain another way." He moves his face in close to the sergeant's and, in a whisper, continues: "Know what? I'm a bad guy. Really bad. People who know me know it. And, as well as being a bad guy, I have nothing to do except look for my daughter. Nothing at all . . . Do you know what that means? It means that, if you don't do your job and find her, I'm going to stay here until hell freezes over. And I'm going to poison your life . . . I'm going to pursue you. I'm going to harass your wife and children. I'm going to fuck you up. You and your whole family." Melchor pauses, and he can hear Benavides' accelerated breathing and see his nostrils trembling. "But you can avoid it . . . Do your job as you're meant to. That's all I'm asking. I'm making it easy for you. Put all your people to work. Look for the girl on the recording. Interrogate her. She can lead us to my daughter, I already told you. Find her and you'll never have to hear from me again. I swear . . . But, if you keep fucking around and my daughter doesn't show up, believe me: you are going to spend the rest of your life wishing you'd never met me. Have you got it now?"

When he leaves the Guardia Civil post, Melchor has two WhatsApp messages on his phone from Paca Poch: one of them includes the report on the interrogation of Elisa written up by the agents Cortabarría sent from Egara; the other describes Cosette and her friend's complete itinerary from the time they left Terra Alta, according to Elisa's statements and the material found on her phone and social media accounts as established by Paca Poch and her team. Sitting on a bench on the promenade, facing the sea, Melchor spends several minutes studying both documents. The sky is still cloudy and a storm is threatening from the other side of the bay, advancing up the Cap de Pinar peninsula; in spite of that, groups of undaunted tourists begin to swarm down to the beach, unwilling to allow the lack of sun to ruin their holidays. When he finishes his reading, Melchor gets in the car and, while he's driving back to the Hostal Borràs, calls Paca Poch. The conversation is brief: they agree the two reports are not contradictory, neither of them contains anything substantially new and the best clue they have so far is still the image of Cosette leaving the Chivas with the stranger.

"We have to find out who she is," Melchor insists.

The sergeant also agrees with him on this point.

Melchor again parks near the plaza Miquel Capllonch, gives his computer to the manager of the Hostal Borràs, to hold on to for him at reception, and begins to make the rounds of the places that promised him security camera footage the previous night; he also goes into the bank branches, which had been closed. He is in a queue at the Deutsche Bank when he receives two consecutive WhatsApps and his heart skips a beat.

They are from Cosette. The first one contains a location: the plaza del Duomo, in Milan; the second, a message. "Papá, I know you're looking for me," it says. "Leave me alone, please. I am fine, but I don't want anything more to do with you. I have met someone and I am not planning on coming home. Don't call me or write to me again, because I won't answer. Goodbye." Melchor rereads the text and then reads it again. When he has absorbed it (or when he thinks he has absorbed it), he leaves the branch and phones Cosette. No-one answers. He calls several more times, always with the same result. He writes a WhatsApp. "Cosette, answer the phone and I'll leave you alone," it says. He sends it and then calls his daughter again: in vain. "Send me a photo," he then writes. "I just want to have proof that you're alright. Then I won't bother you again. I give you my word." Melchor sends it and waits a few minutes, his phone burning in his hand like a jewel. But he receives neither a call nor a message. Nothing. Suddenly he realises it has begun to rain, and he's getting wet.

Almost instinctively, Melchor forwards the two WhatsApps from Cosette to Blai and to Paca Poch, and starts walking towards the beach among people running in the opposite direction seeking shelter from the rain. The downpour has brought a murky stormy light to the morning and the promenade is emptying. Still in swimsuits, some tourists seek shelter under the terrace awnings. Melchor ducks under one of them, while waiting for a reply from Blai and Paca Poch, and simply watches the rain falling on the promenade, the port, the bay, further away, on the Cap de Pinar peninsula. He tries not to sink into self-pity or defeatism; he tries to think in an orderly way. He does not even consider stopping his search for Cosette; not, at least, until he is certain that his daughter is fine and really does not want to see him again. It could be, he thinks. Maybe what Cosette discovered, or what she thinks she discovered – about the death of her mother, about his role in that death, about the relationship between the two of them, about herself – has completely changed her, transforming the love she had into hatred. It could be, he thinks again. He thinks it sorrowfully, because it saddens him that his daughter could hate him, but most of all because he has not forgotten Olga's phrase that Blai reminded him of three days ago, while they were drinking coffee in Hiroyuki's bar (Hating someone is like drinking a glass of poison believing you'll kill the person you hate), and it saddens him that his daughter might poison herself by hating him. Although he hasn't forgotten the reply he gave Blai either, and tells himself, actually, maybe Cosette doesn't hate him, that perhaps she feels the same way he feels about Salom, and simply doesn't want to see him, that she has nothing to say to him and no interest in what he might say to her. It's possible, although, does he really not hate Salom? Does he not feel betrayed by the former corporal as perhaps Cosette now feels betrayed by him?

Melchor has not been able to come up with an answer to this question when his phone rings: it's Blai, from his office in the station. The inspector tells him Paca Poch is also listening and, without even mentioning the WhatsApps from Cosette, asks if he's spoken to her.

"I've tried." Melchor walks away from the terrace where he'd been sheltering and stands under the canopy of a hotel, where he can speak without being overheard. "I've written to her as well."

"And?" Blai asks.

"She hasn't replied. Do you think now you can ask the judge to let you tap her phone?"

"Of course," Blai says. "But I don't know if he'll grant it. Remember we no longer have jurisdiction over the case."

"Have you sent those messages to Benavides?" asks Paca Poch.

"No. Nor do I plan to. In order not to have to move his ass, that bonehead insinuated from the start that Cosette had run away. If I send him Cosette's messages, he'll think he was right."

"That's the same problem we're going to have with the judge," says Blai.

There is a silence, during which Melchor understands that his friend is right, and that, reading Cosette's messages, the judge could reach the very same conclusion Benavides reached without reading them.

"In any case, I'll try," Blai promises. "Although I think we've had a better idea. Have you heard of Sirene?"

"It's a liaison organisation between European police forces," Paca Poch says. "Through them we can ask the police in Milan to look for Cosette in the plaza del Duomo. They just have to review the images the security cameras in the plaza have taken at the time you received the WhatsApps and see if they recognise your daughter in any of them."

"Great," Melchor says, trying to sound enthusiastic. "Could you do that right now?"

"Of course," Blai says. "We have to prepare a warrant with the request and Cosette's photo, and then they'll translate it into Italian and send it to the Carabinieri. Within an hour we'll have an answer. Maybe less."

Melchor says "great" again and asks them to let him know when they have any news. When he ends the call it has stopped raining.

6

Waiting for news from Milan, Melchor fights his impatience by wandering the streets around the Hostal Borràs that come out on the promenade, slippery from the recent rain, and collecting or requesting the remaining recordings that might show Cosette. At one point he speaks to Rosa on the phone and, although only at that moment does he decide to stop lying to her, he soon realises that he hadn't fooled her: Blai must have been informing her of the details of the search. At another point he speaks to Cortabarría, who blames some facial recognition software problems for the fact that they haven't been able to identify the woman with Cosette in the footage from the Chivas.

"It's taking longer than expected to find out who she is," he concludes. "But tomorrow at the latest we'll know."

Melchor talks to Blai as well, who phones to give him one piece of good news and one bad: the good is that they've already sent the Italian translation of the police warrant to the Milan Carabinieri and the Carabinieri have replied that they'll get to it immediately; the bad news is that the Gandesa judge will not authorise them to tap Cosette's phone.

"I did warn you," he reminds him.

"Did you forward the WhatsApps?" Melchor asks.

"Of course," Blai answers. "According to him, that's exactly why he can't authorise the tap: he says he understands that you're worried, but in the messages Cosette has already said all she needed to say. Anyway . . . . Let's wait and see what the Carabinieri say."

At another moment Melchor stands with his mind blank, contemplating the colossal rainbow that starts opposite the promenade, at the far end of the Cap de Pinar peninsula, and seems to end in a sunny patch of cobalt blue sky that has opened between the clouds after the downpour.

Around half past two he returns to the Hostal Borràs and asks the manager for the computer he left with him a while ago. Handing it to him over the counter, the manager tells him:

"The Guardia Civil just left."

"Oh right, now that the horse has bolted," Melchor says.

"Does that mean you're not interested in what they wanted to know?"

Melchor answers that he is interested.

"They asked me several questions about your daughter," the manager tells him. "None that you hadn't already asked. They also asked about you."

"Did you tell them any lies?"

"What do you think?"

Melchor shrugs, walks away from the counter and orders a tuna sandwich and Coca-Cola at the bar. Then he turns on his laptop and checks his email. In his inbox are four messages. Three of them – one from Caixabank, another from Targobank, another from Little Britain – are from establishments he had requested security camera footage from; the fourth is anonymous: "Your daughter" is the subject heading. He opens it immediately.

"Señor Marín, if you want to find your daughter, go to Can Sucrer," he reads. "It is a country house in the woods near Pollença. To get there, take the first road into town coming from Inca. You'll pass in front of the Costa i Llobera school, turn left there and take a mountain road towards Vall de Colonya. They call it the camino de Can Bosch. Follow it. Two or three kilometres later you'll see another road on the left. Take that one too. At the end there is a track and a house. That is Can Sucrer.

"A man called Damián Carrasco lives there. He can help you. Tell him about your daughter. Listen to him. What Carrasco will tell you will sound like madness, but it's true. Listen to him, he's a good man, probably too good.

"Please, delete this message once you've read it, and don't tell anyone you've received it. This is very important. It is also important that you don't ask for Can Sucrer. Nobody should know that you've been there, make sure you're not followed. And, most of all, don't try to find out who I am. I am just a man who has children, just like you. Believe me, I am running an enormous risk by helping you. I beg you not to make me regret it. And I wish you luck."

When he finishes reading, Melchor looks up from the screen and around the room of the Hostal Borràs: everything is exactly the same as before – customers sitting at tables, drinking beer and devouring tapas and pizzas, the waiters busy behind the bar, the manager leaning on the counter, the afternoon light brightened by the rain pouring through the windows – and, at the same time, everything is different, as if the words Melchor has just read have stained reality with a menacing tint, as if, around him, everyone – diners, waiters, the manager himself – know where Cosette is and all are pretending not to, as if everyone were acting in a play and he were the only person in the audience. Melchor banishes that momentary impression of a nightmare and wonders just what that email is. An unfunny joke? A providential message? A trap? Melchor thinks, whatever it is, he has nothing to lose by taking it seriously, so he memorises the directions to the place and the email address they came from, asks a waiter to put his lunch on his bill, takes his laptop and, leaving half his Coca-Cola and the sandwich with a few bites out of it on the bar, goes to find his car.

He hasn't left Port de Pollença when Paca Poch calls and tells him they've just received the results of the Carabinieri's investigation.

"No luck," she says. "At the time Cosette sent her message there were eight people connected to the repeater that provides mobile coverage in the plaza del Duomo, but none of them was her."

"Are they sure?"

"Yes."

"Can we see the images?"

"I've requested them, but they won't send them until tonight or tomorrow. Anyway, I don't think they'll change things."

Melchor realises the sergeant is right. He is driving along the road, glistening with rain, that links Port de Pollença to Pollença, between stands of pines and holm oaks, with the last rocky hills of the Sierra de Tramuntana on his right, imposing like a sleeping giant. After a moment's silence, Melchor asks:

"Tell me something, could the location that Cosette sent me by WhatsApp be falsified?"

Paca Poch answers without hesitation:

"It could."

"So, someone, Cosette or whoever, could have sent the location from Mallorca, or from wherever, to make us believe she's in Milan."

"It's possible."

138

"How can we find out if it's true? I mean . . ."

"Requesting the geolocation of Cosette's telephone from her service provider."

"But for that we'd need the authorisation of a judge."

"Exactly. And he's not going to give it to us. If he wouldn't give it to Blai a couple of hours ago, I can't see him giving it to us now."

"Is there no other way to find out?"

"Legally, no."

"And illegally?"

Now the silence is longer and thicker. Melchor looks for the rainbow on the horizon that he saw a short time ago over the Cap de Pinar peninsula, but he doesn't see it. In the distance he can see profiles of the first houses of the urban centre of Pollença.

"Let me try something," the sergeant says.

"Paca," Melchor interrupts, before hanging up. "I have to ask you for another favour. I need you to find out who has created an email account." Melchor spells out the address of the email he has just received. "Do you think you can do that?"

Paca Poch says that she'll try.

Minutes later, following the instructions of his anonymous informer, Melchor turns in towards Pollença by the last road – the first, from the direction of Inca – he soon sees the Costa i Llobera school, turns left and drives past a gothic chapel his informer had not mentioned, which he finds a bit odd. Despite that, he drives up a narrow, lonely and sinuous road, which goes through a valley between stone walls, olive groves, fig trees, holm oaks, prickly pears and carob trees, until, after a few kilometres, almost at the same time as he catches sight of a wall of bare rock and wonders if he is lost, he sees a turn-off to the left and a sign that says CAMÍ DEL RAFALET, and follows it until taking a dirt track that leads to an old farmhouse concealed by a forest of cypresses and holm oaks.

Melchor deduces that it must be Can Sucrer and parks the rented Mazda by the entrance, in front of an old gate. When he gets out of the car he notices the silence of the valley, barely broken by the last of the rain dripping off the trees, and, as he opens the gate and walks across the yard carpeted with pine needles where there is an ancient oven and a stone table, a dense and very robust pine tree and an ivy-covered wall, Melchor feels that, although that place is very close to Pollença, in reality it's very far away, as if in another dimension. Under a vine arbour, the door to the house is ajar.

Melchor pushes it open and the first thing he distinguishes, to the left of the entrance, is a man sitting in a wingback chair, who turns towards him. His demeanour does not betray surprise: the expression is instead rather sullen and annoyed. The man is wearing a blue shirt open over a vest and a pair of striped pyjama bottoms, and seeing him there, barefoot, unshaven, with his hands still on the arms of the chair and his head leaning back against the chair, pictures of old warriors, or samurai come to Melchor's mind.

"I'm looking for a Damián Carrasco," he announces.

One of the man's hands rises but nothing shows in his face.

"Come in," he says.

At that moment Melchor notices that the man is watching a football match; a television is perched on a little table on the other side of that room with thick, whitewashed walls and a stone floor, with a roof supported by beams with protruding iron hooks. The man says something, which Melchor does not understand; pointing to the television with his chin, he speaks again:

"I asked you if you like football."

Melchor says no and the man, without taking his eyes off the game, comments:

"I once heard it said that, of all the unimportant things in the world, the most important is football." For a second he seems preoccupied. "What nonsense. The truth is that football is one of the few important things in this world. All the rest . . . Anyway." The man turns towards Melchor again, as if he'd just remembered he was still there. "I am Damián Carrasco. But, if you want to buy the house, the one you have to speak to is . . ."

"I don't want to buy anything," Melchor cuts him off. "I'm from Catalonia. My daughter went missing here two days ago, and I've been told to speak to you."

Suddenly, Carrasco's face transforms: his eyes look suspiciously into the eyes of the intruder, his brow furrows, his jaw tenses. Melchor stares at him. He must be about sixty. He is a thickset man, with very large hands and a Roman senator's head covered by sparse ashen hair; more than reminding him of an old warrior or a samurai, now he looks like an old boxer, with his flat nose, stubble-shadowed cheeks, stony cheekbones and condescending mouth.

"Who told you to talk to me?" Carrasco asks.

"I don't know."

In Carrasco's eyes curiosity replaces the mistrust. Facing him, on a cherry table he seems to use as a desk, Melchor sees a mobile phone, an iPad, a laptop, a notebook and a couple of pens, several books, a pair of glasses, an empty glass and a dirty plate, with a knife and fork crossed in the middle of it; on the floor, to his left, there is half a bottle of mineral water and, just above him, nailed to the wall, an old ceramic sign that reads: CALLE DEL TEMPLE. Around the cherry table are two wicker chairs.

"You don't know?" Carrasco asks.

Melchor again tells himself he has nothing to lose and, taking one of the wicker chairs and sitting next to Carrasco, he sums up what has happened since Cosette's disappearance up to the point when he received the email that led him to Can Sucrer. While he is talking, Carrasco listens with his eyes half-closed, without looking at him, asking no questions, requesting no clarifications, as if it took a lot of effort to process his words or as if he wanted to absorb them completely or as if he were asleep and dreaming. When he finishes speaking, Melchor insists that the only thing that matters to him is finding his daughter; he also emphasises the negligence or incompetence of Benavides.

"He's useless," he concludes.

The definition seems to awaken Carrasco.

"You're mistaken." Opening his eyes wide, he turns towards Melchor. "He's not useless, he's corrupt."

Carrasco holds his visitor's perplexed gaze for a second and then looks at the television screen; Melchor imitates him against his will: on the screen, a football player is about to take a corner into the crammed area of the rival team. Before the player can kick the ball, Carrasco turns back to Melchor and his pupils stare with an inquisitive clarity.

"Have you heard of Rafael Mattson?"

At first, Melchor doesn't understand the question, as if it's out of place or badly phrased.

"The financier?"

"The financier, mogul, philanthropist, the great man," Carrasco replies. "He has a house near here, in Formentor. A mansion, more than a house. Most likely your daughter is there. Or has been there."

Melchor freezes. For a moment he wonders if the man is in his right mind.

"At least, that's where to start looking," Carrasco says.

Still in shock, Melchor remembers his anonymous informer's warning: "What Carrasco will tell you will sound like madness, but it's true. Listen to him."

"How do you know?" Melchor asks. "How do you know that my daughter—?"

"I don't know." Now it's Carrasco who won't let him finish. "I imagine she is. But I have a very accurate imagination. A cop without a good imagination is not a cop."

"You're a cop?"

"I used to be. But I'm not anymore. Guardia Civil. That's how I know that Benavides is corrupt rather than inept. And that Mattson is a sexual predator."

"Benavides is on Mattson's payroll?"

"You learn fast."

"I used to be a cop too."

"You didn't tell me that."

"You didn't ask. Benavides works for Mattson?"

"Benavides, and I don't know how many more. Among them, the captain of the Inca Judicial Police and two or three magistrates in the Inca courthouse, starting with the senior judge. On this island, those who aren't on a salary from Mattson know there are things it's best not to ask about . . . Mattson has a whole bunch of people by the balls. On this island and off this island. And that's why he does what he likes." Carrasco holds out his palm to Melchor, as if asking for alms: "Have you got that security camera footage? I mean, the one of your daughter leaving Chivas the night she disappeared."

So that both of them can see the images as clearly as possible, Melchor sends the recording from his mobile phone to Carrasco's email address, while the latter opens his computer, puts on his glasses, opens the file Melchor has just sent him and, following his instructions, finds the image of the two girls on their way out of the nightclub.

"Like I said." After a couple of seconds, Carrasco points to the young woman with Cosette. "Her name's Diana Roger. She's one of Mattson's *conseguidoras*."

"*Conseguidoras?*"

"Girls who recruit girls for that son of a bitch. He has a few all over the island. Victims of his, who now work for him. Has Benavides seen these pictures?"

"Of course. I gave them to him myself this morning."

"Bad move. That means Benavides knows that you know. Or might find out."

At that moment, as if alerted by a sixth sense, the former guardia civil takes off his glasses and looks towards the television screen, where a group of football players are celebrating a goal hugging each other euphorically at one edge of the pitch. While Carrasco watches the replay ("Through the whole squad," he murmurs), Melchor again wonders if that man is mad and all that he's told him a delirium and he is the victim of a macabre practical joke that is only going to make him waste time; but then he remembers his informer's warning again and tells himself he has nothing to lose, and is about to ask Carrasco for Mattson's address when his phone rings. It is Paca Poch. Melchor doesn't know whether to answer or not.

"Take it." The old guardia civil stands up from his chair. "It might be important. Would you like a coffee? You and I have a lot to talk about."

Melchor goes out to the yard without answering Carrasco's question.

"The email you received came from the Inca courthouse," the sergeant tells him. "Specifically, from a computer in investigative court number one. The strange thing is that the email

144

account was created this morning and has only been used to send that message, then it was deleted. Does that make any sense to you?"

Before he can say no, Melchor remembers the court official with the walking stick who dealt with him at the Inca court-house, along with the judicial secretary.

"I don't know," he says, suddenly sure it makes sense. "Can I ask you one last favour?"

"Even if it's the penultimate."

Melchor asks her to find out everything she can about Damián Carrasco.

7

"I hope you don't think this is my house," Carrasco tells him when he comes into the kitchen. "The owner is my friend Biel March, who doesn't want to sell it to tourists and rents it to me for a couple of shillings in exchange for looking after it. I'm more of a caretaker than a tenant. But the house is great and a month never passes without some buyer coming by to make an offer on it. That's why I mistook you for one."

Carrasco talks with ease while he makes coffee, filling the filter with ground coffee, fitting it over the water reservoir, screwing the top back on and putting the espresso pot on one of the burners of a camping gas stove. Melchor notices that he still has a bit of hair on the back of his head; he also sees his hard pectoral muscles and flat stomach under his vest, his powerful arms, straight shoulders and robust unwrinkled neck: although Carrasco has an old look in his eyes, physically he's in good shape. Observing his host, Melchor decides that, before taking for granted his hypothesis – according to which Cosette could be in the mansion Mattson owns in Formentor, or could have been there – he should be convinced of what it's based on.

"You were telling me about Rafael Mattson," Melchor reminds him as Carrasco lights the gas ring with a match. "You told me he is a sexual predator. That he has a whole lot of people by the balls."

"A ton." Carrasco blows out the match. "Some of them he keeps on salary. Others get a gift now and then. And everyone knows it's advisable to stay in his good books, or at least not to get involved in anything that does not concern them. You don't need me to tell you that, for Mattson, the money he spends on keeping those people quiet is small change . . ." He throws the half-burnt match into a pristine ashtray and carries on: "But, of course, it's not just about money. Everybody's been to that house: magistrates, ministers, celebrities, top journalists, bankers, presidents . . . The crème de la crème. And, since the house is full of cameras, Mattson has filmed them all. Are you understanding this?"

"I'm not sure."

"What is it that you don't understand?"

"What Mattson films . . . ?"

"It's what you're imagining: the orgies he organises for his guests and his own, of course, since he's a textbook narcissist." Carrasco walks over to a cupboard, takes out two coffee cups and two teaspoons and sets them down beside the sink; suddenly, as if he'd just remembered something important, he turns back towards Melchor. "Tell me, has Benavides already shown you the box where he keeps the unsolved cases?"

Melchor nods. Carrasco smiles sarcastically.

"Of course." Leaning against the edge of the sink and folding his arms, he explains: "He should be ashamed of it, but he loves to show it off. Normal, after all it's his great alibi: he does what he can, he's overwhelmed with work, hasn't got the resources . . . Bullshit. The truth is he doesn't want to do anything."

"That was my impression."

"An entirely correct impression. But you got it because you used to be a cop. Most people don't get it and swallow Benavides' song and dance without a second thought." Carrasco uncrosses his arms and, his eyes wide, takes a step towards Melchor. "Look, the only truth here is that those cases are never solved. They get shelved, filed, lost, left to die. It's not just Benavides who takes care of that, of course, the courtrooms of Inca help him, a lot . . ." Carrasco rubs the knuckles of his right hand across the tip of his nose, as if it was itchy. "Don't misinterpret me. I'm not saying that all the girls who go missing in this area get lost in Mattson's house. What I'm saying is that some of them disappear there. Not some. Lots."

"And do they reappear?"

"Most of them do, yes." The coffee starts to percolate and Carrasco goes back to the sink and picks up a dish towel. "Some show up after a while. Others stay with Mattson or with Mattson's people, working for him or keeping him company or whatever. The ones who disappear are probably dead. Some of them are from here, from the island, normal, average girls, but the majority are tourists . . . Anyway, that house is a black hole. Do you know why Mattson built it here?"

Melchor doesn't say anything.

"Because he spent his childhood summers here," the former guardia civil answers. "In Andratx. His family had a house in the port. In fact, his father and mother met there, on their summer holidays. His father was Swedish, and his mother Spanish, from Madrid, that's why he speaks Spanish so well, it's actually his mother tongue. And that's why he had that house built in Formentor and turned it into his private love nest. How touching it all is, right . . . ? Of course, his wife and kids almost never come here, they live in New York and tend to summer in the Hamptons where they have a house, or on Fårö, in the Baltic

Sea, he owns half the island . . . But, as soon as he shows up here, whatever the season, his people fan out to collect new girls for him. And Mattson arrived a week ago."

"That's what makes you think my daughter is in his house?"

"Exactly."

The coffee has been percolating for a couple of seconds. Carrasco picks up the coffee pot with the cloth and, his back to Melchor, who feels a clot of anguish rising in his throat, begins to carefully fill the cups he has just taken from the cupboard. Around him, the kitchen gleams; it's a traditional country kitchen, with a chimney and its bell hood, a plane wooden table surrounded by chairs and stools, a trough, a shelf where earthenware jugs and vases, ceramic plates and mugs are lined up, a no-longer-used woodstove, a wall bristling with hooks from which hang kitchen utensils: a frying pan, a colander, a mortar, a casserole pot, a spatula.

"Do you know something a person learns over the years?" Carrasco says, while he finishes pouring the coffee. "That all clichés are true or at least contain a substantial amount of truth. And a person who despises them is an idiot . . . Tell me, how many times in your life have you heard that everyone has their price?" Carrasco spins around with the coffee pot in his hand and, with a sort of satisfaction, says: "Well, it's the honest-to-God truth. That's something people like Mattson know from the day they're born. And that I only learned thanks to Mattson."

Melchor interrupts:

"And what is your price?"

As soon as he asks the question, he regrets it, but it's too late to retract it. In Carrasco's eyes the satisfaction transforms into an interest tinged with curiosity, a slight smile seems to dance on his lips and a profound irony in his eyes, as if that question

149

was not a question but the solution or the key to an enigma that he wasn't even trying to decipher. Carrasco points at the cup of coffee and, in reply, says:

"Do you want sugar?"

Melchor says no, Carrasco hands him the coffee, after swirling it around a little to keep from scalding his throat, he gulps it down in one swallow and leaves the cup in the sink.

"How can I be sure that what you've told me is true?" he then asks.

Carrasco hesitates for a moment, or that's what Melchor reads on his face: the smile and irony have disappeared from it, replaced by a questioning expression, as if now it was the former guardia civil who was evaluating him.

"That's easy," Carrasco replies. He drinks his coffee and leaves the empty cup beside the coffee pot. "Come with me."

Followed by Melchor, Carrasco opens a thick pine door in one corner of the kitchen and enters a low-ceilinged room with a rough stone floor, where Melchor deduces the stables would have been and where he sees a fridge, a manger, two big bottles of olive oil and two earthenware jars the size of a person. When they get to a dark corner, Carrasco feels around in the roof beams, lowers a wooden ladder, which was hidden in the dark, and leans it on the floor. This done, he begins to climb the rungs until he disappears through a trapdoor.

"Come on up," Melchor then hears him say. "Don't stay down there."

Melchor does what he says, climbs up and at the top of the ladder finds himself in an old hayloft transformed into an attic, the sloping roof of which barely allows him to stand up straight. Distributed around the space there is a chest, a cot, a desk, chairs and filing cabinets; but what most catches Melchor's eye are the walls, all of them plastered with photographs, newspaper and magazine cuttings, photocopies, graphs, diagrams, drawings, sketches and all sorts of documents – hundreds, thousands of them – related to Rafael Mattson. Allowing his stunned gaze to slide around him, Melchor feels that the place has the exact shape of one of those breathless nightmares in which the vertigo of lucidity merges into madness.

"Ten years of work," Carrasco mutters as if talking to himself, looking around. But he quickly emerges from his abstraction and, with a flat voice bereft of pride, he says to Melchor: "That's what you have here: ten years of work. Well, work and preparation."

For the next half hour, Melchor listens to Carrasco's story, which he tells with dispassionate precision, wandering around the old hayloft like an animal in his den, as if it weren't his own story but someone else's story, or as if he'd never told it before.

It all begins twelve years earlier, when the former guardia civil was a recently promoted captain who had just been assigned chief of the Pollença post. Since he joined the Guardia Civil his career had taken him from one place to another, driven by very demanding assignments, which he does not specify. At a certain point, however, he fell in love with a woman who set as a condition of continuing their relationship that he give up that haphazard existence. Carrasco, who was head over heels in love, accepted. They got married, settled in Bilbao, had two children.

"It was the happiest time of my life," Carrasco says. "I had my wife, I had my kids, I had a calm posting at the La Salve barracks . . . But a person always thinks things could be better. Major error."

His promotion to captain offered Carrasco the chance to choose a new post. The position as chief of the Pollença post was not a professionally attractive one, or even suited to his

151

new rank – normally the chief of a post of that size would be a lieutenant – but the fantasy of a new life in a little seaside town, far from the world or what up till then had been his world, attracted him like a magnet, and it didn't take any effort to convince his wife that this idyllic place was ideal to spend the next years watching their children grow up.

At first the decision seemed right. His wife and his kids were happy with the move; his work was comfortable; his life in the town, calm. Until he crossed paths with Mattson. Carrasco remembers exactly how it happened. One morning, when he'd been stationed in Pollença for about four months, a woman came to the post to report that her daughter had been raped in the mogul's mansion.

"She was a poor woman, from Ecuador," Carrasco says. "Her name was Ana Lucía Torres, a name I'll never forget. She worked as a cleaner in a hotel, she was separated, her daughter was an adolescent and lived with her. She was crying her heart out."

At that time, Mattson was already one of the richest men in the world but had only recently had the mansion in Formentor built and, according to Carrasco, had not yet finished plotting the network of complicity and bribes in Mallorca that would later make him invulnerable. Nor was it necessary in that case. Even though the post's Judicial Police team opened an investigation, it was soon closed because the lady withdrew her complaint. That didn't trouble Carrasco: in such cases, those kinds of underhand arrangements were often made. It didn't trouble him, but it put him on guard.

A little while later the episode was repeated with few variants, and almost at the same time a girl disappeared who had been last seen on the terrace of the Hotel Formentor, in the company of a group of guests who were staying in Mattson's house. On this occasion the investigation was more complex and longer, and Carrasco began to detect irregularities: inexplicable slowness and ineptitude, evidence that was not examined or examined badly or too late, witnesses who didn't want to testify after having offered to. The head of the Judicial Police team's justifications – a warrant officer called Martín, who had been stationed at the post for twelve years – were not convincing, and he took up the case to his superior officers in Inca and in Palma.

"At first they paid no attention to me," Carrasco says. "They brushed me off . . . But I insisted and insisted again, and finally managed to get them to strip Martín of his command of the unit. Guess who I proposed should take his place?"

Melchor remains silent.

"Benavides," Carrasco says. "He worked with Martín, though he wasn't his natural successor. But he seemed like a capable and decent guy. And I got along well with him." Carrasco smiles joylessly. "I fucked up. Don't trust people who seem decent."

Benavides didn't find the missing girl, but Martín's dismissal earned Carrasco the animosity of the whole squad, who considered it unfair. Also, as soon as he took charge, Benavides began to conspire against him ("There are people who can't tolerate having a favour done for them," Carrasco says), and he began to suspect that his subordinates knew things he didn't, that they were hiding information from him and that, one way or another, that information always led to Mattson or had to do with him. Carrasco was no longer in a position to request Benavides' replacement, and in the following months there were more aborted abuse allegations or complaints that ended in dead ends. Finally, fed up with so much negligence and so much ineptitude (or what he still considered ineptitude and negligence), when another girl went missing Carrasco took personal charge of the case and command of the investigation, short-circuiting Benavides and his team, who should have been in charge of it.

That was when things really got complicated. One day his wife mentioned that she thought she saw two men following her coming and going around Pollença. Carrasco downplayed the importance of the incident, but another day his wife told him that a man had come over to her, while she was sunbathing with their kids in Cala Sant Vicenç, and threatened her: he had asked her to tell her husband to be very careful and keep his nose out of matters that didn't concern him. This second episode worried Carrasco's wife greatly and, after a marital discussion that ended in tears, she begged him to request a transfer as soon as possible so they could leave. Carrasco refused: he promised his wife that would not happen again, assigned bodyguards to his family and ordered some trusted men, or men he thought he could trust, to investigate. They had still not found out anything when one afternoon a woman showed up at the post and asked to speak with him. Carrasco remembered her very well: older, slim and silver-haired, impeccably dressed, with a vague swan-like air. She introduced herself as Mattson's lawyer; she claimed she had come from Barcelona expressly to talk to him.

"Her name was Font," said Carrasco who received her in his office. "At first I didn't understand what she wanted, or maybe I understood, but couldn't quite believe it. Then the woman stopped beating about the bush. She told me to leave Mattson alone. That, if I left him alone, I would be duly rewarded, but, if I annoyed him, he'd ruin my life. She didn't put it like that, naturally, she told me without saying so, not in words, but as clear as day. With complete courtesy. Complete calmness. As if she weren't suggesting I commit a crime but rather contribute to the well-being of humanity."

"And what did you answer?" Melchor asks.

"A piece of stupidity," Carrasco says. "Or at least a piece of insolence. I told her to leave my office immediately or I'd have her locked up. And do you know what she said?" Carrasco pauses. "Nothing. The only thing she did was smile. She smiled, stood up and left . . . Ah, that smile. That's another thing I'll never forget in my life."

"Why didn't you press charges?"

"What a question! The same reason I couldn't have locked her up. How was I going to demonstrate that she had said what she said? It was her word against mine . . . Anyway, the fact is the woman went through with her threat. But, to tell you the truth, that's not the worst of it. The worst is how they did it. Or, rather, how I let them. With the oldest trick in the book." Carrasco clicks his tongue and smiles joylessly again. "The truth is I behaved like a naive fool."

At the time the Guardia Civil and the National Police of Mallorca had been investigating for some months a cartel of drug traffickers that was operating throughout the archipelago and, not long after the visit from Mattson's lawyer, an operation was launched against that network, resulting in twelve people being arrested, one of whom declared during the subsequent interrogations that the chief of the Guardia Civil post in Pollença was linked to the organisation. That same day, Guardia Civil agents from headquarters in Palma burst into Carrasco's house and found two hundred grammes of cocaine and three hundred thousand euros in fifty-euro notes in a wardrobe. Carrasco was arrested, interrogated and tried and, even though he kept telling them that neither the cocaine nor the money was his and that he was a victim of a plot concocted against him for not having given in to Mattson's expectations, he ended up expelled from the Guardia Civil and sentenced to eight years in prison, of which he only served two and a half.

"The rest you can imagine," Carrasco concludes. "My wife couldn't handle what happened and left me. I don't blame her, I probably would have done the same. My children live with her. Sometimes they come and see me . . . As for Mattson –" Carrasco takes in the whole of the hayloft with a gesture of sarcastic ostentation – "here you have him, campaigning for your respect."

While Carrasco was talking, Melchor has been trying to imagine him cloistered away for years in that big old house lost in the woods, thinking constantly about Mattson, investigating him full time, stewing in the neurosis of his rancour and his obsession. When he stops talking, Melchor still hasn't been able to imagine it, or not entirely, but he stands up and Carrasco asks:

"Where are you going?"

"To Mattson's house."

"Don't talk nonsense." Carrasco stops him with a hand on his chest. Melchor looks at the hand, not at Carrasco. "Do you think you'll be able to get in? You and how many others . . . ? Another question: what if your daughter's not there anymore? Or she is, but they tell you she isn't? Or she is, but she wants to be and doesn't want anything to do with you? Are you going to drag her out?"

Melchor looks up at Carrasco.

"Don't be naive," the former guardia civil says. "There's only one way to get your daughter back, and that's by destroying Mattson."

"I don't want to destroy Mattson. I just want to get my daughter back."

156

"You can't get your daughter back without destroying Mattson."

Carrasco's statement echoes around the hayloft with the certainty of a verdict. At that moment Melchor's mobile rings, and a quick glance reveals that it is Paca Poch. This time Carrasco does not encourage him to take the call; feeling that this man's story has disintegrated the clot of anguish that had been caught in his throat, Melchor does not take it. He's already decided that, whatever Carrasco says, as soon as he leaves there he is heading to Formentor, to the tycoon's house, but he hears himself say:

"So tell me how to destroy Mattson."

In the half-light of the renovated hayloft, Carrasco looks deep into Melchor's eyes and his lips turn up in a hint of a smile.

"Do you know something?" he says. "I've been waiting for years for someone to ask me that question."

"And what's the answer?"

Carrasco takes his hand off Melchor's chest.

"Do you want another coffee?"

8

"There's only one way to destroy Mattson," Carrasco maintains. "That's by getting inside his house and taking his archive."

Once again in the living room, Carrasco has sat back down in his wingback chair and offered Melchor one of the chairs encircling the cherry wood table, but Melchor prefers to stand. They each have a cup of reheated coffee in their hands. Opposite Carrasco, on the other side of the table, a reality show has taken the place of the football match on the TV. A wide strip of golden light filters in through the door that leads to the patio and tints the former guardia civil's thick, veiny hands a copper colour.

"We have to break in, of course," Carrasco continues, after taking a sip of coffee. "It's not easy. The house is very well protected, and the archive even more so, it's actually an armour-plated room. They've installed the most sophisticated security systems all around, and there's a battalion of people guarding it day and night, three hundred and sixty-five days a year. It's complicated getting in there . . . But I've spent a lot of time trying to figure out a way to do it and I have discovered it. At least, I've discovered that there is a chance. One and only one, truth be told: if it fails, it's over. So we have to choose the moment very carefully." He raises his free hand and shows three fingers. "To succeed all it'll take is time, people and money . . . But don't be scared, we don't need a lot of time, or a lot of people, or a lot of money. With ten or twelve people I can be up and running, and with forty or fifty thousand euros too, maybe even less, it all depends who does it. As for the time, it could be a couple of weeks, just enough to prepare the operation and find the perfect moment to carry it out. In reality, what we mainly need is the will. The desire to finish off that son of a bitch once and for all."

Melchor is about to repeat that he doesn't want to finish off Mattson, he just wants to get his daughter back, when his phone rings once more. Paca Poch again.

"Let me finish," Carrasco begs, pointing to Melchor's mobile. "Then answer it."

As if immersed in one of those nightmares where a person acts against their own will, Melchor puts out of his mind the bunch of ideas besieging him – he is wasting precious time, his daughter is still missing, whatever this man says he must leave immediately for Mattson's house – and, after drinking the rest of his coffee, says:

"Tell me, what's in Mattson's archive?"

"I call it the treasure chamber." Carrasco also empties his cup, leaves it on the floor, beside him, and places his hands back on the arms of his chair; Melchor thinks again of an old warrior, or a samurai. "Mattson is a sexual predator, so you can imagine what he keeps in there. Photos, films, papers, trophies of his victims . . ."

"Trophies?"

"Sure, knickers, bracelets, earrings, pubic hair, chewed gum, all sorts. It's also possible he keeps body parts preserved in

159

formaldehyde, things like earlobes, teeth or nipples . . . Whatever a predator needs to relive the moment when he abused his victims." Carrasco rubs the knuckles of his right hand over the tip of his nose again. "What we have to do is get into that room, take the hard drive of the computer where Mattson stores the photos and videos and, if possible, photograph the rest. And then we have to make it all known, show the world, so it's clear what kind of individual Mattson is." Carrasco lifts his hands from the arms of the chair and, almost noiselessly, sets them back down again. "That's the way to finish that man off once and for all."

Carrasco scrutinises Melchor as if trying to read on his face the effect of what he has just explained, or as if waiting for his reaction; but Melchor does not react, and his silence merges with the silence of the house and the forest that surrounds it. Until, suddenly, Carrasco stands up from the armchair, rips a piece of paper out of the notebook lying on the cherry table, picks up a pen and writes something on it.

"Think about it." The former guardia civil folds the page in half and holds it out to him. "Do me that favour. And, if you decide to give me a hand, here's my number. Call me and we'll talk. I've been waiting for an opportunity for a long time." Carrasco puts the piece of paper in his hand and closes it. "You decide if that guy should keep getting away with what he's doing or not. But remember what I said: you're not going to get your daughter back without destroying Mattson."

As soon as he leaves the house, Melchor phones Paca Poch.

"Cosette has been trying to deceive us," says the sergeant. "She was not in Milan when she sent you that WhatsApp."

"Are you sure she was the one who sent it?" Melchor replies, with Carrasco's words ringing in his ears while the pine needles that carpet the garden of Can Sucrer crunch beneath his feet. "Where was she?"

"In Pollença. Well, next to Pollença."

"In Formentor?"

"How do you know?"

"I'll tell you later." He pushes open the gate. "Tell me one thing: has she got her telephone switched on?"

"I don't know about now, but five minutes ago she didn't. In fact, the last time she connected was to send you that WhatsApp. She connected in Formentor."

"Thanks, Paca."

"One more thing," the sergeant says. Melchor opens the door of the Mazda and gets in behind the wheel. "That guy you asked me about, a certain Damián Carrasco. I've sent you an email with a ton of information about him."

"Shoot."

"Quite a character. Nine years ago he was chief of the Pollença Guardia Civil. Up to that moment he had an impeccable record. Well, more than impeccable. He'd spent a lot of years in the SIU."

"The Special Interventions Unit?"

"Exactly. A tough guy. But the good life on the islands or whatever made him go soft. The thing is they caught him with a big pile of drugs in his house. It seems he was collaborating with a drug cartel who operated all over the Balearic Isles. He went away for a long stretch. Does Cosette's disappearance have something to do with this character?"

"Could be," Melchor says. He starts up the car and goes on: "I'll tell you about this later too. For now, can you do me another favour? You know who Rafael Mattson is, right?"

"Who doesn't?"

"He has a house in Formentor. Look it up and send me the address."

"Roger that. But you're not telling me Cosette's there?"

"That's what I plan to find out right now."

Melchor hangs up, calls Blai and, while he's driving, notes a resistance in the steering wheel, but attributes it to the fact that he's driving on a dirt road.

"Have you seen Cortabarría's email?" is the first thing the Terra Alta station chief says.

"No."

"Look at it. He just sent it to us. He's identified the girl coming out of the nightclub with Cosette. Her name's Diana Roger."

Melchor tells his friend he already knew that and starts to tell him about the conversation he's just had with Carrasco when, coming around a bend, right after turning onto the Vall de Colonya road, he notices that the car is pulling towards the ditch.

"Fucking hell," he swears, as he brakes. "I think I've just blown a tyre. Give me a minute, Blai."

He hangs up, gets out of the car and sees that, as he thought, the front right tyre is flat against the asphalt, like a squashed reptile. While Melchor gets ready to change the tyre, swearing again, a car stops behind the Mazda, which is almost blocking the road. From inside it emerge a man and a woman; they're young and approach smiling.

"Need some help?"

He wakes up lying in front of a large picture window over-looking the open sea. An intense pain fills his whole head and spreads, compact and vibrant, through his entire body, as if

162

someone were operating a silent jackhammer inside his brain. The sun is setting on the horizon. Nearer, a few centimetres away, he can only see, through the slits of his eyelids, the shiny surface of a parquet floor and the worn leather of a purple mat.

With an excruciating effort, Melchor sits up a little and leans his shoulder blades against a backrest. At that moment someone puts a glass of water and a blister pack with two tablets in front of him; Melchor looks up: a woman with Amerindian features, wearing a maid's uniform, is bending towards him.

"Take these," she whispers in a singsong Spanish, encouraging him to take the tablets. "They'll make you feel better."

Melchor reads the brand name Gelocatil on the blister pack, takes out the two tablets, swallows them with the help of the water and tries to deal with the headache while becoming aware that the place he has ended up is a gym: stationary and elliptical bicycles, treadmills, weights of all shapes and sizes, abdominal wheels, rowing machines, muscle stimulators, traction bars and pilates balls. He doesn't understand what he's doing there, and, as hard as he tries, he doesn't remember anything that happened after the young couple offered to help him after he left Can Sucrer.

Twenty-five minutes later, when the pain is just a distant echo in his head and he has verified that he cannot get out of that rectangular room lit by tiny points of light embedded in the ceiling (on the other side of the window, a remnant of violet light still floats on the horizon), one of the doors opens and a man walks into the gym who Melchor recognises immediately, not because his image has been all over the media for years, but because that very afternoon he has seen his face repeated ad nauseum on the walls of the hayloft in Can Sucrer.

"Welcome to my house, Señor Marín," the man greets him

cheerfully, opening his arms in a gesture of hospitality. "You can't imagine how much I regret this misunderstanding."

All of a sudden, when it seemed he was going to shake Melchor's hand, the recent arrival stops short, a metre and a half away, as if afraid of catching some contagious disease. In person, Mattson displays the same radiant and kind smile and the same air of a catholic cardinal as in so many photos, although, as in so many photos, his outfit looks more like that of a Harvard professor emeritus on vacation: trainers, beige chinos and a violet angora v-neck sweater showing the collar of a very white shirt. His features are smooth, as though eroded by age and, behind the elongated lenses of his red-framed glasses, which the media has made iconic, his very blue eyes express a speck of alarm.

"Tell me, how are you feeling?" he enquires, with concern. "Alexandra told me you had a bad headache. I'm not surprised, considering the blow you received from those lunatics . . . Alexandra is the housekeeper here, without her nothing would work, did you take the analgesics she gave you? Are you feeling better?"

Melchor responds to these two questions with a third:

"Where is my daughter?"

Mattson looks surprised.

"Your daughter? Not here, that's for sure. I think she left last night. Or maybe this morning. I've been away and . . ." The man exchanges his surprised expression for one of ironic benevolence. "Ah, so it's true that you have been talking to the guardia civil . . . What a nightmare, good God." There is no longer irony in his voice, or on his face; just a mixture of irritation and sorrow. "I don't know what barbarous stories he'll have told you, but, believe me, that poor man is not in his right mind. I beg you to ignore him."

164

"Where is my daughter?" Melchor repeats.

"You see? He's already prejudiced you against me . . . Tell me, who told you about him? How did you know where he lived?"

"I asked you a question."

"And I've asked you two." Now Mattson smiles with a mischievous glint in his eyes, as if the exchange of demands has amused him, and his smooth face fills with wrinkles on his forehead and at the edges of his mouth; then, still smiling, he is serious again. "Hey, let's behave like reasonable people, shall we?"

"Tell me if my daughter is here or not."

Mattson sighs and, as if arming himself with stoicism, he shakes his head back and forth.

"Of course not. She was, but she's not anymore. When did she arrive? Tuesday, Wednesday? I don't remember. She showed up with a friend . . . Poor thing. She was a little nervous, a bit disoriented. It's what happens to so many teenagers, I have daughters too, you know? . . . She told us that she'd been left alone, that the friend she'd come to Mallorca with had left and she didn't have enough money to pay for her hotel. So we took her in as best we could. It's what I do with lots of girls in her situation. Help them. Give them a chance. I bet that's not what the guardia civil told you."

"Where is she now?"

"Your daughter? I don't know. Not here, for sure. I think she left last night. Or maybe this morning. I've been away and . . . Have you lost your phone? Here, call her from mine."

Melchor takes the phone and walks away from Mattson and calls Cosette. Her mobile is still off.

"No answer?" Mattson asks. "I told you she's a bit disoriented. I don't know your daughter very well, but I thought she was a great girl. What if you try calling her hotel? It's the same one you're staying at, isn't it?"

Melchor uses the internet connection on Mattson's phone to look up the phone number of the Hostal Borràs.

"I'm sure she'll be there, you'll see," the Swedish-born tycoon says. "Do you know why I had you brought here? To apologise. Although the truth is what has happened is not my fault . . . Taking you by force, who would even consider such a thing. But you can imagine how these things go, there are always people too eager to please and they go overboard."

"You mean Benavides?"

Mattson arches his eyebrows inquisitively while Melchor, who has just dialled the number of the Hostal Borràs, waits for his call to be answered with the phone glued to his ear.

"The other guardia civil," Melchor clarifies. "Was it his people who kidnapped me?"

Mattson half-closes his eyes, nodding with resignation.

"Who knows what he was thinking," he laments. "What stupidity, I sometimes think that man's not playing with a full deck . . . The thing is that, as soon as I found out what had happened, I demanded they let you go and told them to bring you here, to apologise personally. It's the least I could do."

"Your daughter showed up," the manager of the Hostal Borràs tells Melchor, as soon as he identifies himself. "I've taken her to your room."

"Is she OK?" Melchor asks.

"I don't know. I suppose so."

"You suppose?"

"I'm not a doctor. She seems tired, that's all. But she's not injured and not complaining of anything."

"Don't let anyone else in that room," Melchor says. "Put

someone outside the door and wait for me at the entrance of the hotel. I'm on my way."

"You see how she's where I said she was?" Mattson takes his mobile from Melchor's hands. "You see how that idiot told you nothing but nonsense? And tell me: how is your daughter?"

Walking towards the door Mattson had come through, Melchor does not answer any of his questions. He opens the door to leave the gym, but a couple of large inexpressive men block his way.

"No, no, please," Mattson intervenes behind Melchor, while he stares down the two strangers. "Leave if you want, Señor Marín. Of course. You are my guest. I just wanted to apologise and perhaps chat a while, I've just been hearing about you and, believe me, I feel a great admiration for what you did. I'm referring to what happened in Cambrils, of course . . . Killing four terrorists at a single stroke is not within most people's capabilities. Do you know how many lives you might have saved? I suppose you'll have been asked many times, but . . ."

"Tell your two thugs, if they don't let me by right now, I'll smash their faces in."

Behind Melchor, Mattson lets out an affable laugh, and the two bodyguards stand aside.

"You're just like they told me you are." He adds: "Would it be too much to ask you to grant me a second, now that you've found your daughter thanks to me?"

Melchor turns around. Mattson has come over to him, though without violating the safe distance; in his hand he still holds the mobile Melchor has just given back to him.

"Look, there are all sorts of legends going around about me, each crazier than the next. You know, don't you? I mean, apart from organising the attack against the Twin Towers, I've been accused of everything . . ." A pause: again, fleetingly, the mischievous smile. "Well, now that I think of it I've been accused of that too . . . Anyway, what I mean is that people get very bored and, to entertain themselves, they need to invent things. To entertain themselves and to make sense of what they don't have, and most of all to alleviate their own frustrations. In that sense I am ideal . . . People like me have existed as long as human beings have existed, they call us scapegoats, and we are created so others can blame us for all the evil in the world and therefore not take responsibility for their own. For example, look what happened to that man, that guardia civil . . . What's his name?"

"Carrasco."

"Carrasco, that's it, I always forget . . . Look at him and tell me something: why does he blame me for all the things that have gone wrong for him? Who told him to get involved with drug dealers? He didn't tell you about that, did he? I bet he didn't tell you he was in prison for I don't know how many years for drug trafficking either? Or, if he did tell you, I'm sure he also blamed me for that . . . It's grotesque. That good man has decided that I am the devil and this house is hell and there is no way to get that out of his head, he's convinced that all the girls who go missing on the island are here. It's madness, don't you see?"

Mattson pauses again, but doesn't take his eyes off Melchor. Behind him, night has turned the picture window looking out over the sea into a perfectly black rectangle.

"I am not as that man paints me," Mattson continues. "As he paints me and so many others like him . . . I am just a man who has had a lot of luck in his life and tries to help those who haven't had as much. I know that's not so fascinating, but it's the truth, which tends to be boring . . . Tell me, do you believe the sadistic monster Carrasco described to you would invest millions of dollars each year in saving children who are at risk of disease and malnutrition in half the world? Or is 'Loving Children' also dedicated to raping missing girls? For the love of God, think about it and you'll realise it's madness."

"Can I go now?"

In just one second Mattson's face shows frustration and then acceptance.

"Of course," he says. "But promise me you won't pay any attention to Carrasco's fantasy films."

"Sure," says Melchor. "If you tell me who wrote the WhatsApp."

"What WhatsApp?"

"The one someone sent me this morning from my daughter's phone. It was sent from here. It was supposed to make me think my daughter was in Milan. Was that Benavides too?"

Now Mattson's expression is one of total ignorance.

"I don't know anything about any WhatsApp. I repeat that I've been out of the house all day. But it doesn't matter." He recovers the kind smile and air of hospitality he displayed at the beginning. "I see I'm not going to convince you that that man has taken against me and tells nothing but lies about me, like so many people . . . Well, you'll figure it out yourself. When you do, call me. Come and see me, we'll talk calmly. I'd really like to be able to help you and your daughter. Tonight I have to leave, but as soon as I can get away again I'll be back, I love coming to Mallorca, it's the only place I can forget my worries and relax a bit . . ." He widens his smile and opens his arms in a priestly gesture. "Anyway, I don't want to hold you up any longer. But, I insist, come and see me and we'll talk. I'm sure I could be of use to you."

*

Melchor drives from Formentor to Port de Pollença in just over ten minutes, with the Mazda's tyres screeching on the curves on the cliffs above the sea, which at this hour is a huge dark canvas speckled here and there by trembling lights. He parks the car in the plaza Miquel Capllonch and, before he reaches the Hostal Borràs, he sees the manager at the door, among the customers who fill the terrace, hopping around on the spot as if he were cold or needed the toilet.

"Thank goodness you're here," the manager says in greeting, holding the door open for him. "Your daughter is upstairs."

"Is she alright?"

"I think so. I think she's gone to sleep."

Melchor starts up the stairs two at a time, with the manager trailing behind.

"I've called your number several times, but you didn't answer." The man is panting, trying to keep up with Melchor. "A car dumped her on the sidewalk. That's what I was told. I didn't see. Poor girl . . . I don't know what happened, but something happened to her."

Sitting on the last step of the landing a girl is engrossed in the screen of her mobile, but when she hears Melchor and the manager she stands up looking startled and lets them pass. Melchor opens the door to the room, which is almost completely dark, and turns on the light. Cosette is lying on the bed, her back to him, in the fetal position. She turns a little, just enough to make out Melchor, who has carefully sat down next to her. Cosette looks at him for a second without opening her eyes all the way, as if she's just woken up or doesn't recognise him; then she sits up, throws her arms around his neck and murmurs:

"Papá."

Part Three

Terra Alta

Cosette had just turned seventeen and for the second time in her life felt ashamed of her father. Only on that occasion, as well as shame, she despised him, felt deceived by him.

It had all started at the beginning of her second year of baccalaureate, months before her trip to Mallorca with Elisa Climent, when a new physics teacher arrived at the Terra Alta High School. In truth, the teacher was not new: she had held a permanent position at the school for years but had been on leave for five years or more; Cosette wasn't in her class, though she did take physics, but was in a class with a different teacher. What happened was one autumn afternoon, on the way out of school with two friends, Cosette crossed paths with her, and, when they had gone by, one of the other girls asked her if she knew who that was. She said yes, of course: the new physics teacher. Her classmate asked if that was all she knew about her.

"What else should I know?" Cosette answered.

The girl pulled a strange face, perplexed or annoyed (as if she smelled something bad), looked at the other classmate, turned back to Cosette, looked one way and then the other as if she wanted to make sure no-one was listening to them and, speaking very quietly, said:

"Her father was in the police. He was convicted in the Adell case and spent time in jail."

"And what does that have to do with me?"

"He was your father's friend," her classmate said. "He sent him to jail. Your father turned him in. It seems he helped the murderer, or the one who paid the murderers. You really didn't know?"

Cosette rushed into a lie: she said she did know, just pretended not to know to see what they knew, she got a bit flustered and, when she and her classmates went their separate ways, she realised they hadn't believed her. "Look it up on the internet," they told her. "It's all there."

Cosette did not look it up; at least, not immediately. In fact, she didn't do anything immediately: she didn't even try to put her doubts to rest by asking Rosa Adell about it, much less her father; nor did she talk about it with anybody. The only thing she did was try to forget that conversation, try to pretend it hadn't happened. However, a few weeks later, after convincing herself that her classmates could not have invented the story and that everyone around her knew it, Cosette ran into the new teacher again. They did not say hello, but she felt sure the woman knew who she was, because they both looked at each other in ways that say nothing and say everything. That same night Cosette decided to find out the truth.

It didn't take her long to find out her classmates were right: that she could find everything she needed to know on the internet. The teacher was called Clàudia Salom and she was the daughter of Ernest Salom, a police officer who had spent some time in prison as a result of the Adell case. Like anyone from Terra Alta, Cosette had heard people talk about the murder of the region's most important business owner and his wife, Rosa Adell's parents, a multifaceted crime that had shaken the country fourteen years earlier, when she was barely three. What Cosette had heard about it were most of all crazy hypotheses, conspiracy theories, senseless legends, half-truths or simple lies; the explanation of this cloud of inventions is that the Adell case had with time turned into more than an event from the police files and the social and political life of Terra Alta, into a sort of myth, the exact point where all the demons of the region's recent history converged and the coagulant or one of the coagulants had given it an identity that, besides, had always been tenuous and precarious, extremely fragile (if not simply made up). In spite of that, Cosette had never been intrigued by that episode: it had never occurred to her to interrogate her father about it, although she knew he'd been involved in it; even less, Rosa, who for obvious reasons (thought Cosette) must not have the slightest desire to revisit the massacre that had sealed her adult life with blood.

So, for several days, Cosette immersed herself in secret in the ocean of information generated over almost a decade and a half about the Adell case, at first seeking simply to establish the facts as precisely as possible – especially, her father's participation in them and her father's relation to the physics teacher – but soon captivated by the case itself, by the intricate labyrinth of suppositions, conjecture and speculations that had been woven about it in the newspapers, on the internet, social media and in popular fantasy. Until one night she found by chance, on a jurisprudence database called Iberley, the sentence handed down by the court on the case. By that moment she knew or thought she knew the fundamental facts of the case: that Albert Ferrer, Rosa Adell's husband, had paid some hit men to torture and murder Rosa's parents (the hit men had also murdered their Romanian maid); that Ernest Salom, Ferrer's childhood friend, corporal at the Terra Alta police station and her father's colleague in the Investigations Unit, had collaborated with Rosa's husband in the commission of the crime and had later tried to cover up clues; that, as well as her father's colleague, Salom had also been his close friend, in spite of which

Melchor had contributed to exposing his part in the triple murder, even if the primary officer responsible for it had been then sergeant Blai, also a friend of her father and currently Terra Alta station chief, who at that time commanded the Investigations Unit of the same station; that Ferrer had been found guilty of inducement to murder and Salom for complicity and concealment . . . Before reading the sentence, all these were or seemed to Cosette to be essential and incontrovertible facts of the Adell case; reading the sentence served to confirm them, but added another much more essential one, not for the Adell case but for her, and that is that Albert Ferrer had also been found guilty of homicide: the court considered it proven that the accused, anxious about Melchor's insistence on pursuing the case when the investigation had been provisionally shelved, had tried to intimidate him by ramming his wife with a rented car, on avenida de Catalunya in Gandesa, the impact of which provoked a cranial fracture resulting in the victim's death.

Cosette had to read that incredible news three times, and for several weeks made an effort to absorb it. She could not. All of a sudden, that her father had sent to prison or contributed to the physics teacher's father being sent to prison for years – and which apparently everyone in Terra Alta knew except her – seemed like an anecdotal fact. Since she was a little girl she had believed that her mother had been the victim of an accident, a misfortune that had caused her death; now, when she was already an adolescent, she discovered that it wasn't true, that her whole life had been built on a fiction: her mother's death had not been accidental but deliberate; her mother had not died: she had been killed. Did everyone in Terra Alta know that as well, everyone except her? Did everyone know that the cause of her mother's death was not just the man who was driving the car and ran her over, Rosa's ex-husband, but also, or most of all, her father? Because it was obvious that, if her father had not insisted on continuing to investigate a shelved case – an

176

investigation that was for the most part useless, since it couldn't bring the dead back to life – if he had not let himself be blinded by his sense of justice as knight in shining armour or adventure novel hero or sheriff or gunslinger, nobody would have run over her mother, and she would still be alive. Did everyone except her know that too? And, even if nobody knew it, why had she had to find it out that way, fourteen years after the events had happened? Why had everyone hidden it from her? Why, most of all, had her father hidden it?

Just as if the earth had opened at her feet, Cosette felt vertigo; she also felt that revelation not only had the power to determine her future, but to alter the past, giving a different meaning to a determining part of hers. Cosette thought she understood, for example, that her father's personality was not cold, evasive, self-absorbed and slightly absent because that was the natural character of heroes, but because he felt guilty about her mother's death. She also thought she understood that, each time her father looked at her in search of her dead mother, he found not only a pedestrian and devalued version of her (as she had always believed), but an incriminatory version, who reminded him of his responsibility for that death. It wasn't just that he had hidden the truth from her about the cause of her mother's disappearance, she thought now; it was that he had hidden it due to cowardice: to not feel obliged to bear the tremendous weight of his error in front of her. She suddenly had the impression, in short, that everything she thought she knew about her father was false, and that all the values her father had embodied until then for her – the values she associated since childhood with knights in shining armour or adventure novel heroes or sheriffs or gunslingers from westerns – were toxic, mistaken: the proof is that, had her father not been guided by them, her mother would still be alive. She suddenly had the impression that everything was an enormous fraud.

Over the following weeks she did not reveal her discovery to anyone. She didn't know what to do with it. She tried to keep it inside but it seared like a burn. To fight the pain, she started drinking beer and smoking marijuana, and a couple of times she threw up when she got home. She neglected her studies. She failed exams. With her father she was sullen and distant, when he asked her if something was up, she said no and asked him to leave her alone. One day, her father spoke to Elisa Climent, who told him that, in fact, something was up with Cosette, but she didn't know what it was, and she told him that her friend had told her that she didn't plan to study in Barcelona, as she'd been planning for years, and that she wasn't even sure she'd take the selection exam, which they had to pass to get into university. After that conversation, her father asked Rosa Adell to talk to her.

"I don't know how to," he admitted. "I feel like she hates me. That she hates me and I don't know her."

"Teenagers are like ailing princes," said Rosa, who had lived with four of them. "But then they get better, and then you're the one missing their ailment." She added: "Don't worry, I'll talk to her."

She did. Or at least she tried.

"Elisa's right: something's up with her," Rosa told Melchor, days later. "But I don't know what. She's keeping her cards close to her chest. One thing for sure is that she's angry."

"Who's she angry with?" he wanted to know.

"I don't know," Rosa admitted. "With you. With school. With her classmates. With the world. Probably with herself. It's natural: she's seventeen. At seventeen sometimes you're mad at everything."

Cosette's father did not know or avoided remembering himself at that age, but he accepted Rosa's diagnosis without contradicting her.

"Leave her alone," she added. "When she wants to tell you what's up, she will."

One night, almost a week before leaving for Mallorca with Elisa, Cosette came home at almost three-thirty in the morning. Her father was waiting up for her in the kitchen, reading a novel by Turgenev called *On the Eve*, but Cosette did not come in to say hello and went straight to her room. It was Saturday, the Coca-Colas he'd drunk after dinner were keeping him awake and the next morning he didn't have to get up early, so, calmed by the arrival of his daughter, he decided to finish the chapter he was reading. After a few minutes Cosette flung open the kitchen door.

"You are a liar," she spat at him, point blank.

She was barefoot and wearing blue pyjamas with white polka dots; she was almost panting, her eyes angry and slurring her words. Her father had an immediate hunch that the moment Rosa had predicted had arrived, and the hope that, whatever it was his daughter had taken that night would help her to confront it.

"What?" he asked.

"Mamá didn't die in an accident," Cosette blurted out. "She was killed. And you were the one responsible."

Standing in front of him on the threshold of the kitchen, Cosette told her father what she had found out about the Adell case, or rather what she'd found out about his involvement in it. She spoke in a gush of words, tripping over them and waving her hands around, and he let her vent. He didn't set her straight: he didn't tell her that, in fact, it had been him and not Blai who had solved the case, exposed Salom and sent him to prison; nor did he reveal who had really been guilty of the crime, or why it had been perpetrated. He didn't even deny that it had been his fault that Cosette's mother had died due to his suicidal insistence on investigating the Adell case. He accepted his daughter's punishment in silence, more or less the way a gladiator accepts the mortal wounds his adversaries inflict on him in the arena, among the howls of the crowd and the stench of blood.

"I'm sorry," was all he could manage to articulate when Cosette finally fell silent, still furious. "I was wrong."

Cosette smiled with a sarcastic grimace.

"Is that all you have to say?" she asked. "Can you not even explain why you weren't brave enough to tell me the truth, why you've kept me in the dark for all these years? And, by the way, what else have you lied to me about? Or, to put it a better way and get it over with, have you ever told me a single thing that was true?"

Melchor remained silent: he found it incredible that he hadn't foreseen that, sooner or later, this very moment was going to come, and that he hadn't prepared to face it. He had no answers to his daughter's questions. He didn't know what to say, and he remembered a long-ago night in Barcelona, when, after spending the evening with the Frenchman, Cosette asked how he knew the former librarian and he did not dare tell her the truth, he was not able to tell her about his prostitute mother, his savage childhood in Sant Roc, his absent father, his furious orphaned adolescence, his stint in reform school or his work as a dealer and gunman for a Colombian cartel, his arrest and trial, his time locked up in Quatre Camins prison and his friendship with the Frenchman and his discovery of *Les Misérables* and his police vocation. He regretted not having told her then (or having told her merely a falsehood interlaced with truths), because now it would have been much easier to explain everything and not have the paralysing sensation that it was too late. Was it? Cosette waited for a few seconds, staring at her father with rage, and then muttered something, which he didn't understand, and went to her room.

They didn't mention the subject again that whole week and barely spoke to each other. Her father relayed the conversation to Rosa, who advised him to wait until Cosette returned from her trip to Mallorca to give her an explanation; Cosette, on the other

180

hand, didn't mention what had happened to anyone, not even Elisa Climent.

That Friday morning, the two friends took the first bus to Barcelona, and just after midday landed in Mallorca.

1

The first days after Melchor and Cosette's return to Terra Alta are nightmare days, or at least that's how Melchor will always remember them.

Now that Semana Santa is past, classes resume at the Terra Alta High School, but Cosette does not attend any. Nor does she leave the house or see her friends, some of whom try to visit without success, because Cosette tells her father she does not want to see them; Elisa Climent tries three times, all in vain. In fact, Cosette spends those days shut up in her room, lying in bed, most of the time sleeping or staring at the ceiling or curled up in the same fetal position Melchor found her in when he got back to the Hostal Borràs after he left Rafael Mattson's mansion, occasionally reading or sending WhatsApps or watching television programmes or series on her tablet. She eats badly and rarely, and seems to be a victim of permanent exhaustion and fathomless sadness, growing increasingly thinner, paler and more turned in on herself.

Her impenetrability is absolute. The day after the father and daughter reunion, during the trip back from Mallorca on a flight Elisa Climent's mother managed to book for them on Rosa Adell's instructions and which they caught at the last minute, Melchor tried to get his daughter to tell him what had happened during the two and a half days she was missing, but the only thing he could get out of her is the fact that she had been in Mattson's house; he did not manage to get a single word out of her, however, about what had happened there. After that initial failure, Melchor has tried over and over again to coax her, always with the same result. Curiously, despite this he doesn't have the sensation that his daughter does not want to communicate with him, that she hates or despises or rejects him, which is what he was thinking before her trip to Mallorca; this is something different: it's as if an insanely thick wall has been put up between the two of them, so that, as hard as she tries, she cannot hear what he's saying to her, or she can hear, but cannot understand. This first sensation is joined by a second even stranger, and even more worrying one: the sensation that he has never loved his daughter the way he loves her now, or that only now is he beginning to truly love her.

Finally, Melchor again asks Rosa Adell to speak to Cosette and, when she has carried out his request, Rosa again tells him more or less what she told him a few weeks ago, when she talked to her the first time: something's up but she doesn't know what's going on. Though on this occasion she adds:

"If I were you I'd take her to a psychologist."

Rosa recommends a specialist in Reus who years earlier saw two of her daughters. Melchor accepts the recommendation and, after a bitter tug of war with Cosette, which lasts for a couple of days, he gets her to agree to visit the psychologist. She has an office in a building on paseo Jaume I in Reus, very close to the bus station. Melchor goes with Cosette and, for half an hour, father and daughter converse with the woman and respond to her questions, none of which have anything to do with what happened in Mallorca. Then the psychologist, a skinny and smiling older woman, with white hair pulled back in a bun and a reedy voice, called Roser Pallissa, asks Melchor to leave her alone with his daughter and come back and pick her up in an hour. Melchor obeys and, to his surprise, Cosette comes out quite happy after an hour alone with the psychologist, although during the drive back to Terra Alta he does not manage to find out why. Two days later they repeat the visit, except that this time Melchor does not go up to the office and spends the hour of the appointment drinking one espresso after another in a nearby café. The third time Melchor goes alone, at the request of the psychologist.

"Your daughter is suffering from depression brought on by an episode of sexual abuse – the woman decrees; she is still smiling as on the first day, but she alternates the smile with a grimace that makes her look younger. "She's also anaemic."

As soon as he hears this diagnosis, Melchor realises he was expecting it. This, or something very similar.

"Was she raped?" he asks.

"It depends how you define rape," the psychologist answers. "There was no violence, if that's what you mean. But for two and a half days she was subjected to abuse and indignities."

"She told you this?"

"More or less. Actually, she doesn't know exactly what happened to her. But that's what happened. I have no doubt at all. Several men took advantage of her. And not once but repeatedly. Luckily this was not her first sexual experience, but, whatever it was exactly that went on in that house, it has left her in a state of shock."

The psychologist remains silent waiting for Melchor's reaction. He does not react: he doesn't move, asks no questions, says nothing; a ball of anguish blocks his throat. In response to her interlocutor's silence, the psychologist slides a card across the surface of the desk between them, until placing it in front of him.

"The best thing would be for Cosette to spend some time there," she says, while Melchor reads a name on the card (Mercadal Clinic) and, underneath it, a postal address in Vallvidrera, an email address and two phone numbers. "It's an institution devoted to curing victims of depression and nervous conditions owing to sexual mistreatment or abuse. It's not cheap, but it's very good. If there's any way you can afford it, have your daughter admitted. They'll help her there."

"The problem is I can't afford it," says Melchor, who has just summarised for Rosa the conversation with the psychologist and the call he's made to the clinic to find out the cost of the hypothetical admission. "So I'll have to get a loan."

It's mid-morning and they are in Melchor's office in the library, where Rosa has just arrived with a couple of cappuccinos in cardboard cups and mini-croissants filled with cream, chocolate and cheese, all just purchased in Can Pujol.

"Don't be silly," she answers, sprawling in the room's only armchair and crossing her legs. "Do you want to make bankers richer than they already are? I'll pay the clinic. You can pay me back when you have the money."

Melchor refuses her offer and Rosa doesn't argue, but later that morning she deposits twenty thousand euros in his bank account. Three days later, after the psychologist in Reus has spoken to the administrators of the Mercadal Clinic and convinced Cosette with unexpected ease that she should be admitted into that institution for a while, Melchor drives his daughter to Vallvidrera.

The Mercadal Clinic turns out to be a beautiful modernist pavilion with well-maintained grounds full of trees, located in the heart of the Sierra de Collserola and run by Dr Mercadal, a psychologist and psychiatrist specialised in treating patients suffering from depression and nervous conditions brought on by accidents, mistreatments and various traumas, such as anorexia, alcoholism and drug addiction. It is the director himself – a man in his sixties with Oxbridge manners, a bowtie and braces and hair like Beethoven's – who receives them in his office, outlines how the clinic functions and shows them around the facilities. At the end of the tour he introduces them to Dr Ibarz, a petite, young, smiling woman, with intellectual-looking glasses who, as the other doctor explains, will be in charge of Cosette's day to day progress. The young doctor says no more than she has to, then leads Cosette to her room while Dr Mercadal accompanies Melchor to the exit.

"Rest easy," he says at the door, shaking Melchor's hand. "Come back in a week and we'll update you."

Melchor cannot rest easy, but at the end of a week he returns to the Mercadal Clinic and finds Cosette a little better, less sad and with improved colour. Or that's what he wants to think. For exactly one hour, father and daughter converse without leaving the enclosure, walking along gravel paths between boxwood hedges; at the end they sit on a stone bench, at one edge of the grounds. Cosette tells Melchor about life in the clinic, where she goes to bed and gets up very early, does a lot of exercise, eats at regular hours and talks to lots of people, other patients and doctors and nurses. She also asks about her friends and Rosa.

"They're all fine," Melchor answers. "Waiting to see you."

"Do they know what's up with me?"

"How do you expect them to know if you don't even know yourself?"

They give each other sidelong glances and Cosette smiles weakly: it's the first time Melchor has seen her smile in a long time. His daughter has cut her hair, is wearing white clogs and tracksuit trousers and a flannel shirt the tails of which hang down from under a brown jumper.

"I'm causing you a lot of pain, aren't I?" Cosette says.

"That's a question from a sentimental novel," Melchor answers. "And you don't like sentimental novels."

Cosette smiles again, this time to herself. They are both looking straight ahead, at the bougainvillea growing on the other side of the path by which they reached this tucked-away corner. Although it is spring, the sun is shining energetically, almost with its summer strength; the dense foliage of an oak shades the bench.

"What you have to do is get better as fast as you can," Melchor adds.

Cosette nods.

"You haven't answered my question," she says afterwards.

"Suffering doesn't improve anyone," Melchor says. "And it doesn't do any good. So I try to suffer as little as possible. I don't always manage it, but . . ."

When lunchtime arrives, he says goodbye to Cosette and heads to the director's office, who receives him immediately and offers him a cup of coffee while they wait for Dr Ibarz. She arrives a short time later, carrying a notebook, and, without any preambles, gets straight to the point, both specialists seated opposite Melchor, on the sofa of the three-piece leather suite that presides over that room illuminated by a large picture window overlooking the grounds.

"We still have yet to reconstruct exactly what happened in those two and a half days," Dr Ibarz says with her hands on top of the notebooks closed on her lap. "We know she was in Rafael Mattson's house and was abused, but we don't know much more. Actually, not even Cosette herself knows. Or she doesn't remember."

"That's what Dr Pallissa told me," Melchor interrupts.

"Cosette has flashbacks, she remembers things, scenes," Dr Ibarz continues. "But nothing else, she doesn't have the whole story. That she was the victim of an abusive situation, I insist, is beyond doubt, but we don't know what it consisted of. Our impression right now is that, during those days of captivity, Cosette imagined a parallel reality to protect herself from what she was undergoing, and having constructed it, she went to live in it and buried the authentic reality deep within herself. And what really happened is still in there, as if she were afraid or ashamed to bring it to light. Or as if she were not able to dig it up."

"That's the first thing that needs to be done," Dr Mercadal says. "Uncover what happened, make Cosette aware of it, make her understand that what she suffered was a situation of brutal abuse and not something else. That's our first task, and it won't be easy for your daughter to carry it out." The doctor runs one hand through his grey and messy hair, straightens up a little and sits on the edge of the sofa, with his hands now folded above his spread knees. "Look, in a situation like the one she experienced, Cosette only had three possibilities: escape, confrontation or mental block. Given the circumstances, surrounded by people and isolated in the house of a multimillionaire, the first two options were out of the question. And thank goodness she did dismiss them, because had she opted for confrontation the consequences could have been much worse . . . So she chose the sensible option, blocking it out. It's an ancestral survival mechanism that we humans can activate in a situation when we're pushed to the limit. And that's what your daughter did: to endure the brutality she was suffering, she closed herself up inside herself, she immobilised herself, dissociated."

"Dissociated?" Melchor asks.

"She separated from herself, evaded reality," Dr Ibarz explains. "The pain was so great that her mind went one way and her body another; to put it a better way, her mind abandoned her body to its fate, so the body was suffering alone, as if she unplugged her mind from her body so she wouldn't have to suffer along with it . . . It's the extreme form of blocking. We're sick of seeing it here." The doctor stretches an arm towards the ceiling, opens her hand and holds it as if it were a camera focussing on her. "There are women who tell us that, while the abuse is going on, they see themselves from above – an aerial view – as if it wasn't them being mistreated but another person." She lowers her hand back to the notebook, returning her arm to its natural position. "That's what we call dissociation. And that is probably what happened to your daughter: the trauma dissociated her. It split her in two. In that moment, it was good, it protected her, maybe saved her . . . But now she has to reintegrate herself, she has to go back to being a single person, she has to reconcile with herself, with her own body, which has forgotten nothing and is still suffering."

"Yes, but we haven't got to that stage yet," Dr Mercadal says. "Integration will come later and will be a slow and painful process. When it's completed, your daughter will be cured. Meanwhile what we have to do is something much more elemental. It's just about getting her to know what happened to her. That she becomes aware of it. From here to her understanding it, digesting it and getting cured is a very long road . . . But we have to start there to reach the other side. It's a complex process and a very simple one at the same time. As I always tell our patients: if you know what happened to you and you understand it, you can overcome it; if you don't know and don't understand, then it will overcome you. And eat you up inside."

"That's what's happening to Cosette," Dr Ibarz says. "That terrible experience is eating her up. We're not saying that the other things have no influence, but . . ."

"What other things?" Melchor asks.

"That you hid what happened to her mother," the doctor clarifies. "It's the first thing Cosette told me about, I think to avoid talking about the other . . . You know? Your daughter has a very high opinion of you, it's possible she's afraid of not being as good as you, or as good as you expect her to be."

"I don't expect anything of her."

"That may well be, but Cosette doesn't feel it that way," the doctor objects. "It's a common feeling among some adolescents in relation to their parents: they feel they cannot live up to all the expectations deposited in them, that they won't be able to pay back all they've been given, and that feeling can manifest in many ways, some of them very destructive, or rather self-destructive . . . But, in your daughter's case, this is mixed with the disappointment of knowing that you had lied to her, and that you lied about something so transcendental for her."

"She feels that I've failed her."

"Exactly," says the doctor, pointing at him with an approving emphasis. "And now it's possible that she feels she has failed you."

"You mean she feels guilty about what happened in Mallorca?"

Dr Ibarz is about to reply, but turns to Dr Mercadal, who has been following the exchange between her and Melchor leaning back again against the back of the sofa, and she contains herself, as if they had arrived at the crux of the problem and judges that she is not authorised to reveal. The senior doctor sits up again.

190

"It's very possible she feels guilty, yes," Mercadal says, once again on the edge of the sofa. "You failed her and she failed you. In short, her whole world has collapsed, and now she has to reconstruct it. Perhaps . . . That's what we have to find out . . . But the essential thing in any case is the other thing, what happened in Mallorca, that is the experience your daughter needs to assimilate in order to move forward and keep it from destroying her, or so she doesn't have to carry it for her whole life. And she feels guilty about that too, probably. Without a doubt she is ashamed of what happened, after all she went to Mattson's house voluntarily, and it's very possible she might think she didn't do enough to stop it, or that she was naive, or that she didn't resist and let things happen . . . Anyway, she needs to dig it up, as the doctor said. Confront it. Confront what happened to be able to reconcile with herself and with her own body, to become integral again, go back to being who she was . . . At first it will be difficult for her, it's very possible she'll have a hard time, but that will last only a short while, and in any case she has no choice but to go through it, if she really wants to overcome it . . . This is the ideal place to do it, we'll help her . . . Anyway, I don't want to sound pessimistic. Neither of us are. Cosette is stronger than you think, and this will make her even stronger. It will take a long time, or it might take less, but she will prevail. I have no doubt."

Beside Dr Mercadal, Dr Ibarz is nodding.

2

As he drives back home, Melchor does not stop for one second replaying his conversation with Cosette and what Dr Mercadal and Dr Ibarz had said to him, and when he leaves the Tarragona motorway and takes the road that leads to Terra Alta he wonders if he should press charges against Rafael Mattson.

It's the first time he has wondered that. When he returned from Mallorca he was too absorbed in Cosette's upheaval and too focused on finding a way to help her out of her paralysis to worry about doing it; in fact, he wasn't even sure then that Mattson or someone close to Mattson had abused his daughter. Now, however, he is sure, or at least he has Cosette's testimony, or at least he could get it when Cosette recovers and is fit to testify. Does he want to? Would it serve any purpose? What tangible proof of abuse could Cosette provide, after she voluntarily went to Mattson's house and when Mattson and whoever else abused her were very careful not to leave a single scratch on her? Would Cosette's word carry more weight than Mattson's in a courtroom, the testimony of the doctors who were treating his daughter or the witnesses the tycoon might produce? And where would Melchor press charges? At the Guardia Civil post in Pollença, which would be the natural place to go, so Benavides could tear the testimony to shreds or stick it in a drawer? The Inca courthouse? Or the one in Palma de Mallorca? Was Carrasco right and all these organisations were protecting Mattson's impunity? And, supposing the truth came to light and, thanks to the charges he brought, Mattson could be indicted, how long would that take? How many obstacles would he have to overcome and how much hardship and humiliation would Cosette have to undergo before achieving it? Are you prepared to allow your daughter to endure that, without the slightest guarantee that justice would eventually be done and Mattson found guilty? Was it worth it for her to go through that? Would that ordeal not end up ruining Cosette's youth, perhaps her life? And what about the lives of the other girls Mattson and his friends had abused? Had they also been ruined? Because, if Cosette had been mistreated in Mattson's mansion, which was now not in any doubt, there was no reason the rest of what Carrasco had told him shouldn't be true, and therefore there must be dozens or hundreds of girls who had been Mattson's victims, dozens or hundreds of girls who could be in the future, dozens or hundreds of fathers who had suffered or would suffer for their daughters the way he was suffering now for Cosette. "That house is a black hole," he remembers Carrasco saying in Can Sucrer. And also: "Mattson has a whole lot of people by the balls. On this island and elsewhere." Was Carrasco also right when he predicted that he could only truly recover his daughter by destroying Mattson? Could Cosette ever completely return to her true self if Mattson didn't pay for what he'd done to her? The idea of finishing off Mattson by turning to the courts seemed remote or impossible, or too onerous, but, what about finishing him off another way, as Carrasco had proposed? Was it not an even crazier and more

193

unrealisable idea, one that could only be the desperate fruit of a sick mind?

Melchor tries to get it out of his head.

But he cannot. That night, when Rosa calls from Córdoba, Argentina – where she has gone to visit the subsidiary Gráficas Adell has had for years in that country – Melchor does not tell her about it, but then he lies awake all night, tossing and turning in bed and reading up on Carrasco on the internet. He doesn't find too much information, not much more than what Paca Poch sent him by email when he asked her for it from Pollença, and then barely read. Now he reads it carefully. Essentially, the information is divided in two parts: one dedicated to his arrest and trial in Mallorca, which is scant, the other to his previous life, scanter still. In fact, what Melchor finds out in essence about Carrasco's wanderings before his fall from grace is that he was born in 1978 in the Madrid neighbourhood of Vallecas – he is, therefore, fifty-seven – and was admitted at eighteen into the Officers' Academy of the Guardia Civil, in Aranjuez, graduating five years later third in his class and then being posted to various different places – Madrid, La Línea de La Concepción, Brussels – until he went to the Special Interventions Unit, when traces of his activities disappear. Only to reappear fifteen years later, when he is posted to the La Salve barracks, in Bilbao, where he remains for another three years until being assigned the command of the Pollença post. Carrasco is forty-seven years old then, and up until that moment his professional trajectory has been marked by training trips, specialisation courses and promotions up the ranks; also, or especially, by being awarded the highest medals and decorations of the corps, all of which correspond to the extensive time he spent in the SIU. Reading those dates and facts, Melchor finds that none of them contradict the autobiography Carrasco improvised for him in Can

Sucrer's secret attic; he also finds that, in the course of that tale, Carrasco did not omit his flaws, but he did omit his achievements, and they say a man who hides his achievements can only be trustworthy. Carrasco's tale does not contradict the information Melchor finds out about his arrest and trial either, but only because he reads it in the light of the former guardia civil's own tale: in fact, only Carrasco's revelations explain, in Melchor's judgement, that he was sentenced to eight years for perversion of justice, belonging to a criminal organisation and narcotics trafficking (as well as being expelled from the corps and stripped of all his distinctions) on the sole testimony of two narcos and the only incriminating evidence being the two hundred grammes of cocaine and three hundred thousand euros found in the family home, especially taking into account that, against the advice of his lawyer, Carrasco refused to accept a plea bargain and continued proclaiming his innocence until the end of the trial and that he had been the victim of a conspiracy orchestrated by Rafael Mattson to prevent him from investigating him for sex crimes.

That night, Melchor barely sleeps a couple of hours, and before dawn he is up and looking for Carrasco's telephone number. He doesn't find it among his papers or his clothes, or on the internet, so he asks Blai to look for it while they are having their morning coffee at Hiroyuki's bar, before they each go to their separate jobs. The inspector asks him who Damián Carrasco is and Melchor tells him he's an old friend he's lost track of.

"Yeah, right, and I'm fucking Mahatma Gandhi!" Blai says. "Tell me, what are you cooking up?"

"Nothing," Melchor answers; he instantly realises he shouldn't have asked this favour of Blai, but of Paca Poch, who already has Carrasco in her sights. "But it doesn't matter: you don't have to look for him."

"And you don't have to get like that over a joke, for fuck's sake," Blai replies. "When do you need it?"

"As soon as possible."

"You'll have it today. And, by the way, how was Cosette yesterday?"

Blai knows that Cosette is staying at a clinic near Barcelona due to depression, but he doesn't know what caused her depression; nor what happened in Pollença: the explanation Melchor has given him is vague and confusing, but, except for Rosa Adell, who demanded the truth and got it (at least part of the truth), everybody has settled for it. Armed with his experience as a father of two daughters, Blai for his part is convinced that the depression was the cause of Cosette's disappearance, not its consequence.

"Good," Melchor replies without lying. "Soon she'll be back home."

It's not even midday when Melchor receives a WhatsApp from Blai with Damián Carrasco's number, to which he replies with an emoji that shows a yellow fist with its thumb raised. An hour later he closes the library to the public and calls Carrasco from his office phone, but he does not answer. Melchor calls him again, with the same result. He is about to leave the library when the phone rings; he goes back into his office and answers.

"Carrasco here," says a decisive voice. "Who's calling?"

"This is Melchor Marín," he hurries to identify himself. "I don't know if you remember me. I was at your house last month. My daughter had gone missing in Pollença and I was told to go and see you."

Carrasco remains silent, as if he didn't know what Melchor

is talking about or as if he were trying to remember, and the librarian hears his breathing over the phone."

"I'm pretty sure you remember me," Melchor insists, surprised. "We were talking for quite a while."

"You're in luck," Carrasco finally says; his voice has turned slow and hoarse, mistrustful. "I never answer the phone if I don't know who's calling."

"You do remember me, don't you?"

"Of course I do," Carrasco admits. "I heard your daughter showed up."

"It's true. How do you know?"

"This is a small town, everybody knows everything."

Melchor didn't expect Carrasco to respond to his call in such a detached way; or that he'd try to deceive him. Almost twenty years before, when he arrived in Terra Alta as an unrepentant urbanite, he often heard that everyone knows everything in small towns; now he knows that it's false: there is no town, no matter how small, where everything is known; also, Cosette's disappearance in Pollença lasted less than seventy-two hours, was not picked up by the media and very few people knew about it. How had Carrasco found out about her reappearance?

"Tell me, why were you calling?" he asks.

"Why do you think?" Melchor answers, aware that something has happened and the man he's talking to now is not entirely the same man he met a few weeks ago in Can Sucrer. "About what you told me in your house, of course. You don't remember that either? We were talking about Rafael Mattson. You told me that—"

"I remember perfectly well what I told you," Carrasco interrupts. "What I can't believe is that you believed it. Is it really possible you're that naive?"

"Pardon?"

"You heard me." Carrasco has recovered his efficient self-confidence, only corrected and augmented. "That I don't understand how it's possible you believed what I told you the other day. For God's sake, it was nothing but a pack of lies! How is it possible you didn't realise?" Carrasco pauses, perhaps allowing for Melchor to answer his questions; but Melchor doesn't know what to answer and does not reply at all. "Listen, do me a favour, OK? Forget everything we talked about. Rafael Mattson is a decent guy, everybody knows it, and I am a poor wretch who fucked up his life on his own and that's why I sometimes go off the rails . . . That's what happened with you. Should I apologise? Well, I'm sorry. Either way, you shouldn't have paid me any mind. What I told you has no rhyme nor reason. I made it all up."

"But, listen . . ."

"No, you listen to me. I repeat: Mattson is a good person, one of those rare beings that make this world less horrible than it is. I know I'm not saying anything new and this is something we all know, after all it is in the newspapers and on television every day, but I'm saying so from experience . . . Although, sure, lots of people hate Mattson precisely for what he is. For that and because, thanks to his efforts and his talent, he has achieved what he has achieved. Things like that are unforgiveable, especially in our country, where success is always looked down on. So, forgive me for what I said about him and take it as the inoffensive venting of a man who is still resentful of his own errors . . . Forget it, please, leave Mattson alone, look after your daughter and pretend we never met. And now excuse me, I have to hang up."

Melchor stands with the phone in his hand for two, three seconds, staring at the device as if it weren't a phone but an indecipherable enigma or as if it were about to come to life, and then he looks up and the first thing he sees is a poster for the antiquarian book fair in Barcelona showing a stretch of the Rambla alive with flowers and books and, at the end, the statue of Christopher Columbus pointing in theory at America. He cannot believe what he's just heard. Was all that Carrasco told him in Can Sucrer really false? And what purpose could all those lies serve? Why had the former guardia civil told them to him? To alleviate his feeling of failure by attributing the responsibility to someone else, as Mattson had said, turning him into a scapegoat and blaming him for his disgrace? He couldn't believe it. Besides, if all that Carrasco had told him was a lie, why had a court official taken the trouble to give him his address, running a risk he didn't have to run? What sense would it have if not that the court official was certain that he was not lying – "what Carrasco will tell you will seem like madness, but it's the truth," he had written, "listen to him" – and could help him find his daughter? Was it not true that Mattson or someone connected to Mattson had abused her? Was that abuse an isolated episode or part of a chain of abuse? Had the horrors Carrasco had told him about Mattson in Can Sucrer not had the unmistakable ring of truth, and had he not recognised the no less unmistakable clang of lies in the hagiography of Mattson Carrasco had just foisted on him, and which was the exact opposite? And, then, what was that hay-loft in Can Sucrer, with its archive about Mattson and its walls covered in photographs, documents, notes and diagrams about the tycoon? Without doubt the evidence of a long, drawn-out obsession, but what kind of obsession? An obsession arising out of lucidity or exuded by madness? When he went up to that attic he didn't know which of those options to believe. Which one now?

"I don't see why Carrasco would lie," Rosa says on her

return from Córdoba, after Melchor tells her about his conversation with the former guardia civil, while they have dinner at her house. "He had no reason to."

"And what reason did he have to lie to me in the first place?"

"Didn't he tell you? Didn't he say they were the lies of resentment? Did he not admit he sometimes loses his marbles? There are people like that: they go mad and then recover their sanity. And there's nothing as maddening as failure . . . Anyway, I didn't want to say anything when you told me about him, but the truth is that what you told me doesn't fit."

"What doesn't fit?"

"That a man had been abusing so many girls for so many years without anyone reporting him. And on top of that a man as well known as Mattson."

"Precisely because he's so well known people don't press charges. Did I report him?"

"No, but you'll press charges as soon as Cosette recovers."

Melchor looks at Rosa with surprise.

"And how do you know?"

"Because that's what I'd do. And because I know you."

"Well, I'm not so sure. Tell me, what price is Cosette going to pay for reporting Mattson? Am I going to make her go through another ordeal after just coming out of one? And what guarantees do we have that, even if she pays that price, the guy will be found guilty?"

"I don't know. You're the cop."

"Well, I'll tell you, even though I'm not a cop anymore: none. It's unbelievable that Mattson has spent years abusing girls without anyone getting to him. Of course it's believable . . . First, because it's not true that nobody has reported him. People have reported him, but then they've dropped the charges. Guess why. And second, and most of all, because Mattson has enough

200

money to buy, intimidate and extort whoever he needs to. In fact, that's what Carrasco told me the first time. And it's plausible, I definitely believe it's plausible. Mattson has more than enough money to buy the whole island of Mallorca, what difference can it make to him to buy a few witnesses, a few cops and a few judges . . . ? No. Carrasco might be mad, but what he told me makes total sense, especially knowing what happened to Cosette. What's implausible is a madman recovering his sanity."

"Don Quixote did."

"Don Quixote wasn't mad either."

Rosa smiles a delicious smile.

"You haven't read Don Quixote, Melchor."

"No, but you don't have to read it to know that Don Quixote wasn't mad. He only pretended to be mad. Maybe Carrasco's doing the same thing."

Rosa shrugs.

"Maybe. Whatever the case, that man is right about one thing, and it's that the most sensible thing for you to do is forget about Mattson. About Mattson and about him . . . The essential thing now is for Cosette to recover. After that we'll see whether we bring charges against Mattson or not."

Melchor is silently grateful for the plural.

3

During the following days, Melchor tries to take Rosa's advice and forget about Carrasco and Mattson. Unexpectedly he achieves it. He sleeps at Rosa's house three nights in a row, something he's never done before, and at some moment wonders if he needs to replace Cosette's absence with Rosa's presence; in another moment he wonders why each time Rosa has suggested that he and Cosette move into her farmhouse, where there is more than enough space for three, he has refused to take her up on the invitation. He does not have a clear answer to the first question; nor for the second: since he is certain that Rosa and Cosette would live quite happily under the same roof, he sometimes tells himself that he doesn't want to live with Rosa because he fears disappointing her, and other times he thinks it is because he's sure he could not repeat with her the heights he experienced with Olga. In any case, that reiterated refusal now seems a bit more incomprehensible since those three days and nights have afforded a hint of the happiness that could come from sharing a home with Rosa.

On the fourth day, while weighing up the possibility of suggesting to Cosette that they both move to Rosa's house, with the hope that such a change would serve as a catalyst to accelerate her recovery, Melchor receives a letter at the library with no return address, with his name written by hand and postmarked in Palma de Mallorca. He doesn't remember when he last received a personal letter, so his curiosity drives him to open it immediately.

The letter is from Damián Carrasco. It is also written by hand, clearly and with nothing crossed out, as if it were the final result of numerous drafts. It consists of five pages front and back and begins like this: "Dear Señor Marín, first of all, I beg your forgiveness for our telephone conversation the other day. Your call made me very happy, but I had no choice but to behave the way I did and hide my delight behind a string of lies. I'll explain why." Carrasco tells him that, the day after their conversation in Can Sucrer, a group of Mattson's thugs showed up. *Sicarios* is what Carrasco calls them, who adds: "They caught me off-guard, but, believe me, it won't happen again, next time I'll be expecting them. The fact is, although some of them went home quite done in, they beat the shit out of me, smashed up Can Sucrer and left saying that if I ever talked to you about Mattson again, they'd kill us both. I know how those people work, so I'm sure they meant it. In any case, the truth is I was lucky. I only spent a few days in hospital in Inca, and when I got home my friend Biel March helped me to recuperate and set Can Sucrer to rights. I was also lucky in another way. Do you remember the archive about Mattson I showed you? Well, the *sicarios* didn't discover it. If they had found it, things would probably have been quite different.

"Anyway, I'm telling you all this so you'll understand why I answered you the way I did the other day. And to ask you not to call that number again. This is important. The telephone is almost certainly bugged by Mattson's people, yours might be too, but mine for sure. And I'm not ruling out that they're watching you the way they're watching me, so watch your step, Mattson has a very long reach, he can get anywhere, including Terra Alta." Then Carrasco asks Melchor, in future, to call him at a telephone number that he'll only use to communicate with him, and suggests that he also buy a phone that he'll use in the same way, only for communications between the two of them. Then he gives him the new number and begs him, when he replies to his missive, to send his new phone number. Next he writes: "For the moment we should continue to communicate like this, by letter, and only when absolutely necessary, it is safest. If there is something urgent, we have WhatsApp. It's best to use the phone only when strictly essential. All this will seem like an exaggeration to you, but it's not, believe me, we can't be too careful.

"But moving on to what really matters," continues Carrasco. "I said before that your call made me happy, although I had to swallow my delight. Well, I was downplaying it, in fact your call made me euphoric. I suppose you don't need me to explain why – I already told you I've been waiting years for this chance, the opportunity to finish off Mattson, and I understand that your call means the moment has arrived. You can't know how jubilant it makes me. I imagine that speaking to your daughter has made you realise that everything I told you was true and it's not just about settling a score with Mattson, deep down that doesn't matter much, and besides it only matters to me, but there is really something much more important, and that is that your daughter and all the other girls who have been victimised by Mattson need justice to be done, even if only so that no more girls like them fall into Mattson's hands. That's what this is about here, justice and not revenge, that's what we're talking about, you used to be a cop like me and I'm sure you understand better than anybody. The girls who have been victims deserve justice, and the girls who are going to be victims deserve not to be victims. And you and I can prevent it.

"But, of course, your call also made me euphoric for another reason, and that's because it means you have understood that the only way to stop Mattson is by doing what I explained. There is no other way, believe me about this too, after so many years going over and over this matter I am sure any attempt to bring Mattson to justice is destined to fail. I don't know if I said this the other day, but that's the way it is, I guarantee it. And the reason is that, in Mallorca, Mattson is armour-plated, completely untouchable, no room for doubt about that, I know from experience, I told you about that." Next, the letter's prose tilts into an academic or pseudo-academic tone here and there which allows Carrasco to knock out a slightly confusing historical–political digression. At first Melchor doesn't know what it's about or where it's coming from, and as he skims through and reads bits of it, he again starts to wonder about the former guardia civil's mental health. He begins by claiming that, in Mallorca, two societies live practically back to back, as if they each inhabit parallel, independent and almost opposite worlds: that of the foreigners and that of the Mallorcans. For the foreigners, Carrasco maintains, Mallorca is paradise: safe, cheap and cosmopolitan, with an omnipresent and friendly sea, a benign climate, good hospitals and good connections to the whole world. "What more could you ask for?" he writes. "For Mallorcans, however, things are different." According to Carrasco, Mallorcan society has always been a closed one, slightly claustrophobic, almost asphyxiating. "This is an island," he reminds him. "And that imprints a character." Carrasco describes a group of very conservative, hierarchical and endogamous people, a world dominated by agrarian landowners who, for centuries and centuries, until a couple of generations ago, remained almost in the Middle Ages, frozen in time. "This traditional structure, of despots, is what determines the feature that best defines Mallorcan society," Carrasco says. "Corruption. This place is accustomed to it. For eight hundred years, corruption has not been an exceptional thing, it's a natural way of life, the people of Mallorca have coexisted with it for ever. And that explains a lot."

"Where am I headed with all this?" Carrasco continues, just when Melchor begins to guess. "Mallorca is the ideal place for Mattson to do what he's doing without anyone bothering him. Perhaps he chose it for this reason, I don't know, it's possible, after all, he's known the island since he was a boy, and I doubt very much that he would dare to do in his own country or in the United States what he's doing here. Or maybe he does, I don't know and I don't care. The other day I told you that the cliché that everyone has their price is the purest truth, remember? But what I didn't say is that in Mallorca that's an ancestral truth, something ingrained in people's mentality, and everyone is used to living with it. To make things worse, Pollença is a tiny and isolated place in a corner of the island, with a tiny and isolated Guardia Civil post accountable to a tiny and isolated courthouse . . . In short, a piece of cake for Mattson.

"That's why I said that that man, here, is completely untouchable. It's very possible he's untouchable away from here as well; I did explain that very important people go to his house, and that Mattson films them all, so it's probable he could blackmail all of them. Almost for sure. But here in Mallorca he is shielded, and that shield is what we have to break."

Carrasco then reminds Melchor what he told him in Can Sucrer: the way of piercing Mattson's armour and finishing him off. The idea consists of getting inside the Formentor mansion, entering his sexual predator archive – which Carrasco calls "the treasure chamber" – getting their hands on the maximum quantity of material possible and broadcasting it to the four winds. Then he insists, as he did in Can Sucrer, on the fact that, apart from the decision, they only require three things: time, personnel and money. "The time is my department, I'll take care of it, because I designed the plan and I'm the one who says when and how we should execute it," he writes. "So forget about that, it's on me, when the time comes I'll explain everything. But you'll have to take charge of the rest, I have no money and no people, well, except for one person who will be fundamental for us, who I'll introduce when the time comes. But, apart from that, the rest is up to you." Carrasco explains that, to realise the operation successfully, they'll need a force of seven, apart from the two of them and the one person he'll bring: ten, in all. "They should all be professionals. If you still have friends in the force, former comrades who'd be willing to help you, great, although, they would have to be absolutely trustworthy. If not, you'll have to get a move on and hire some. It's not ideal, I suppose you're aware of that, but we might not have a choice, you could resort to any security company, on the internet they're always advertising and lots of them accept this kind of job. If not, you can always look on the darknet. There, with money, you can get anything." Carrasco then enumerates the equipment and weapons they're going to need: the list includes pistols, automatic rifles, ammunition, cartridges, bulletproof vests, laser sights, handcuffs, torches, clips, bala-clavas, two cars, a signal jammer, chainsaws, mobile phones, fake license plates and ID. "To buy all that you'll need money," Carrasco writes. "How much? I don't know exactly, you'll fig-ure it out once you start preparations, but remember that, as well as hiring professionals, if you need to hire some, and getting the weapons and equipment, you'll have to buy airline or ferry tickets to and from Mallorca, you'll have to rent apartments, cars, etc. It's going to cost a fair amount." Carrasco asks Melchor if he can get all this and if he is prepared to carry out the operation. "If the answer is yes, tell me as soon as possible, send me a WhatsApp with the phrase 'Yours is the Earth', so I'll know you're ready and I will complete planning everything and start looking for the perfect moment to act. When might that be? I don't know. It should be soon, as soon as possible, but I wouldn't want to rush either, the important thing as I said is finding the right moment. I have a couple of ideas, but it might take a while to find it, we have to be sure that it's right so we won't run the risk of failure. Be that as it may, if you commit to doing it, you should start preparing as soon as you give me the starting signal. Then, if it gets postponed for whatever reason, it won't matter, quite the contrary, we'll already have everything on the boil. In any case, the sooner we do it the better. Much better . . . Think of your daughter. Remember what's at stake. Remember this is not about revenge, this is justice. And most of all remember that we'll only have one chance. If we fail, there won't be another, of that you can be sure, and then that son of a bitch will get away scot-free. Think it over. And, when you're ready, write to me. Don't forget: 'Yours is the Earth.' As you can imagine, I await with all possible impatience.

"All the best."

Melchor reads Carrasco's letter very slowly, as if it were written in a language he doesn't quite understand. Then he reads it again. After the third reading he puts it in the back pocket of his trousers, and for the whole rest of the day cannot get it out of his head. He rereads bits of it now and then, but that night he avoids mentioning it to Rosa.

The next morning, he and Rosa each leave separately for Barcelona: she, to spend the weekend with her daughters; Melchor, to visit Cosette. He is confident that his daughter will have improved since last Saturday, and his expectation seems confirmed as soon as he sees her in the vestibule of the Mercadal Clinic. When he goes outside and starts walking around the grounds with her, however, he realises that she has actually gone downhill in an alarming manner: her physical appearance is not bad, but she has a lost look in her eyes, she's preoccupied and barely speaks; in spite of that, when he asks her if something bad has happened, she says no. The day has dawned as cheerless as his daughter. An inclement wind rustles the branches of the trees, but does not sweep the clouds from the Collserola sky, parading above them like a funeral cortege. Although it's a bit cold, father and daughter sit on the same stone bench as the first time, in front of the bougainvillea bush, and, feeling the bulge of Carrasco's letter in his back pocket, Melchor starts talking about Terra Alta: about the people who have asked after her, about his work at the library, about a Turgenev short story he'd really liked – it's called "The Dream" and it's about a character who you can't tell if they're alive or dead – about a new priest who has just arrived in the parish, a young Latin-American priest, Colombian or Bolivian or Pana-manian, who is reopening all the closed churches in the region and saying Mass in them. He also talks about Rosa and tells her that, in her absence, he had been sleeping at her house all week. Then he hesitates. He says:

"I've been wondering." Around them only a few distant, indistinguishable voices can be heard and the moaning of the wind in the branches of the trees. "I don't know, I wonder if we should move in with her. With Rosa, I mean . . . Not now, of course. When you come home. When we feel like it. Her house is very big, we'd all fit with space to spare, and she would love it. Would you like that?"

Cosette remains silent. Melchor asks the question in a different way, turning towards her; she finally makes a gesture of indifference. Her arms are crossed and she holds her forearms in her hands, as if trying to get warm; but her father asks her if she's cold and she shakes her head, staring at the bougainvillea tossing in the wind, her gaze turned inwards. Exasperated by his daughter's silence, Melchor is about to ask again if something had happened during the week when he notices that she is moving her lips and murmuring.

"What?" he hurries to ask.

Cosette doesn't seem to hear and does not answer, doesn't even look at him. After a few seconds, however, she murmurs again, just as if she were talking in her sleep. Melchor thinks he understands the word "wolves" but then thinks the word was actually "fools" and asks Cosette if she had any problem with the other residents. Increasingly sunk inside herself, Cosette does not respond. Melchor seems to recall then, vaguely, news or rumours about the presence of wolves in the Sierra de Coll-serola, and he asks his daughter, looking around the parkland surrounding them as if looking for canines among the trees, if it's true there are wolves there. Then Cosette turns towards her father and looks at him as though she doesn't recognise him, while he thinks he sees something in his daughter's eyes, something he's never seen and at first does not recognise. Then he does: it's terror.

"Are you alright?" Alarmed, Melchor puts an arm around her shoulder and takes her hand. It is freezing. "What are you frightened of? Has someone done something to you? Are you having a bad time here? Are they not treating you well? Do you want me to get you out of here? If you want, I'll get you out right now . . . Tell me what's wrong, please."

Cosette drops her head and shakes it back and forth without saying anything, as if saying no or as if something is preventing her from talking, and then her eyes fill with tears and she starts crying without a sound and then directs her lost gaze back towards the bougainvillea. Impotent, his throat clenched and bile rising from his stomach, Melchor presses his body against Cosette, who rests her head on his shoulder and hides her face in his neck. They stay like that for a while during which he wonders if he should go up to Cosette's room, collect her things and take her home or if he should continue to trust the clinic. Finally, he resolves to speak to Dr Mercadal and decide accordingly. In the distance, some residents and their relatives begin to climb the steps up to the pavilion. Visiting hour is over.

4

Dr Mercadal's secretary says that her boss cannot see him at that moment as he has a visitor.

"That doesn't matter," Melchor assures her. "I'll wait."

"Then he has another," the secretary insists.

Melchor answers that he'll wait until the doctor finds a space to squeeze him in and the secretary – an elderly and plump woman, wearing a white nurse's uniform – makes a sceptical grimace of agreement before pointing him towards a line of chairs. Melchor takes a seat and, when he sees a woman coming out of the doctor's office, he takes advantage of the secretary's momentary distraction with her to slip in. Behind the door, the doctor is standing up, looking out at the grounds through the big window on the other side of his desk. At his back, Melchor hears the secretary's annoyed voice:

"Hey."

Dr Mercadal turns around to confront Melchor and the woman, who has burst into the office behind him.

"I just want to speak with you for a moment," Melchor hastens to excuse himself. "It's urgent."

The doctor asks his secretary if his next visitor is waiting;

the secretary says no, and the doctor asks the woman to let him know when they arrive.

"Sit down." He points Melchor to a chair in front of his desk. "And forgive me, visiting days are always complicated."

Melchor does not sit.

"I won't take much of your time." He says: "I just need a moment." Mercadal also remains on his feet. Melchor confesses: "I'm worried."

"If you're worried about Cosette, you shouldn't be."

"I just saw her and she's much worse than last week."

"She seems to be, but she's not." The doctor smiles reassuringly. "On the contrary, she's much better."

Melchor stares at him, perplexed and expectant. Mercadal walks around his desk while brushing a lock of hair away from his forehead.

"Do you remember what Dr Ibarz and I were saying the other day?" he asks. "That Cosette has to get out what she's carrying inside, that she has to dig up what she buried . . . Well, that's what she's doing: confronting the reality of what happened in Mattson's house. And, the truth is, she's doing it much faster than we expected. Your daughter is very brave."

"She was crying."

"Is that bad?" The doctor sticks his hands in the pockets of his trousers and his smile widens and becomes more confident. "I'll tell you the answer: it's not. On the contrary, it's good . . . I understand that you got a fright, but you shouldn't be afraid. Didn't we tell you the process was going to be painful? When she arrived here, your daughter was depressed. She still is, but the depression has surfaced entirely and turned into a powerful urge, into a self-destructive impulse . . . Her self-esteem is very low, her body disgusts her, seems repulsive, she has urges to punish herself, and probably suicidal thoughts. But, do not

213

worry, she is fine here, always under control, and nothing is going to happen to her . . . Quite the contrary. All this means she has come into contact with the pain, with how much she suffered, with what happened to her in Mattson's house . . . It's something that is still overflowing, that she's not yet able to digest, and that's why she's crying. It's normal. It's good. It means she's getting back in touch with her body, that the healing process is beginning . . . A time will come to understand what happened, but for now this is enough."

"Are you sure?"

"Of course. The other day I told you this as well: if you know what happens to you and understand it, you can govern it; if not, that's what governs you . . . Until now, Cosette didn't know what had happened to her, because she had hidden it from herself and enclosed the secret under seven locks. Now she's finding it out. It's a tough and painful process, and that's normal, I warned you . . . But I also warned you it's indispensable, she must do it. In fact, I would almost say, the more it hurts now, the less it will hurt later, because she'll be able to govern it better. And the faster she'll recover. It's like a wound." The doctor takes his hands out of his pockets and rubs his right index finger on the back of his left hand, as if trying to erase something written there. "For it to scar over properly, you have to clean it, cure it and sew it up. And that hurts . . . Tell me something, did Cosette talk to you about the wolves?"

Melchor doesn't answer, but the other man deduces from his silence that she did. At that moment the secretary interrupts: she announces that the visitor has arrived; Mercadal responds that he'll be available in a minute and the secretary backs out.

"It's one of the things we now know for sure, and so does she." The doctor resumes his explanation. "It wasn't just one man who abused her. There were several. She calls them the wolves . . . We still don't know exactly what happened with them, what they did to her or, what they forced her to do to them, but we do know that they terrify her, and that's what she calls them. Wolves . . . Cosette has buried that and buried it deep, she doesn't want it to surface, but we haven't had to use forceps to get it out, she's done it herself . . . Did she also tell you they kept her locked in a wine cellar or a basement or somewhere like that, like an animal in a cage?"

"No."

"Well, that's what happened. Someday she'll tell you too . . . Or not. In reality, it's enough that she tells herself, it's enough that she comes to terms with exactly what happened and why it happened. And that she understands that she is not guilty of anything, that she did what she had to do, to protect herself, and others did all the bad things to her. That those men were the persecutors and she was the victim . . . Anyway, that's where we are. But we need more time. And so does your daughter. Time and tranquillity. Those are the two things your daughter needs most. And the best things you can provide for her right now."

There is another knock at the door and, although this time the secretary does not come into the office or say a word, Dr Mercadal runs a hand through his hair again, takes Melchor by a shoulder and walks him to the door.

"In any case, I repeat what I said the other day," he continues. "You can rest easy. I know it doesn't seem like it now, but Cosette is making progress. I assure you." Before opening the office door, his hand still on Melchor's shoulder, he looks into his eyes. "Your daughter has told me you like to read novels. What was that one? What doesn't kill you makes you stronger, no? Well, maybe it was a film. Or a song. Doesn't matter. It was actually Nietzsche who wrote it, and it's true.

215

An honest-to-God truth . . . What I'm trying to tell you is that what happened to Cosette is horrible, but it's not going to kill her. There are women who die for much less, they keep it all inside and it destroys them, makes then unable to live. That's not going to happen to Cosette. Thanks to your rapid reaction. And most of all thanks to her . . . That's my advice: have faith in your daughter."

Melchor leaves the Mercadal Clinic heartsick, and for several kilometres he drives his car not knowing exactly where he's heading. As he leaves Barcelona, the day doesn't seem like the same one: the wind is dispersing the clouds and clearing the sky for a sun that sometimes dazzles him. His throat is dry and he has an enormous desire to pull over, buy a bottle of whisky and drink the whole thing; he also feels like crying. He doesn't pull over anywhere. Nor does he shed a single tear. But a memory comes to mind of the last time he cried, fourteen years ago, while he swam at dawn off a Barceloneta beach after having spent the night in a suite of the Hotel Arts and having solved the Adell case. Then he wept for his wife and for his mother, both dead, and now he tells himself that in both cases the murderers ended up paying for what they'd done: some, almost immediately; the others, years later; some with prison and the others with their lives. But neither of the two crimes went unpunished. Would Mattson now get away with his crime, he wonders. Is that man not going to pay for what he did to Cosette? Would he pay if they pressed charges? As he drives, Melchor feels the bulge of Carrasco's letter in his back pocket and wonders if the former guardia civil's project is viable. He doesn't actually know it in detail, because Carrasco hasn't outlined it, or he only knows the essential bits, but he knows the man is an experienced cop and not a lunatic, that he has been preparing the operation for years and no-one else is more interested in its successful outcome. What then is more plausible, Melchor wonders. That a police officer and a judge hog-tied by Mattson will do their jobs and send the tycoon to prison, or that a group of resolute professionals carry out Carrasco's plan? Is he in a position to help him bring it off? Is he willing to try?

Melchor stops for petrol at El Mèdol service station, shortly before turning off to Terra Alta. Then he goes into the cafeteria and orders a cheese sandwich and a Coca-Cola. While he eats sitting at a table overlooking the motorway, he carries on ruminating about Carrasco's project. He doesn't know whether Rosa would lend him the money needed to carry it out, but he could deceive her and tell her he needed it for something else; and he also knows that, if Blai agreed to participate, the sum of money would be feasible: after all, as Terra Alta station chief his friend has a considerable quantity of armaments and equipment at his disposal (and could easily have access to more). Would Blai agree to join the operation? Melchor didn't think so. Not, at least, at first. Not, unless he felt obliged to and with no choice but to agree. In his letter, Carrasco made something obvious understood, and that was that, to assault Mattson's house, it would be ideal if Melchor could recruit some of his former colleagues. Was there any possibility that any of them would agree to accompany him? The first name that occurs to Melchor is that of Vàzquez, who was his boss at the Central Abduction and Extortion Unit at Egara, now retired and living in La Seu d'Urgell; the second is Paca Poch.

Still sitting at the cafeteria table, Melchor calls the sergeant.

"You only think of Santa Bárbara when you hear thunder, Mr Librarian," says Paca Poch as soon as she answers the phone. "Which gut have you busted now?"

"None," Melchor says. "Do you fancy a drink?"

"Could there be any doubt?" the sergeant says. "Where shall we meet?"

"Are you at home?"

"Yes."

"I'm having lunch at El Mèdol service station. Give me your address and I'll be there before you know it."

Melchor finishes eating the sandwich as he walks to his car, puts Paca Poch's address in the satnav and one hour and ten minutes later drives into the underground car park at plaza Alfons XII, in the old part of Tortosa. From there he walks to the building on calle Argentina where the sergeant lives; she answers the intercom, unlocks the main door and waits for him leaning on the doorframe of her apartment.

"To what do I owe the honour?" she says in greeting.

Melchor says he's on his way home from visiting Cosette in Barcelona; Paca Poch asks how his daughter is and he says fine: soon she'll be back home.

The sergeant's apartment is minuscule and impersonal, as if its tenant didn't plan to live there for long, but it has a large kitchen-dining room, divided in two by a breakfast bar and lit by a big picture window overlooking the river, through which pour torrents of afternoon light. In the centre is a table surrounded by several chairs, and beyond that a switched-off television, a couple of almost bookless shelves, a white leather armchair and matching sofa with a couple of piles of clean and folded clothes; between the sofa and television a steaming iron sits on an ironing board.

"It's laundry day," Paca Poch explains, carrying a huge pile of clothes. "Give me a minute and I'm all yours."

While the sergeant clears up the room, coming and going from her bedroom (she's wearing a baggy white shirt, tracksuit trousers and old slippers; her hair is bunched in a chaotic bun held by a tortoiseshell clip at the nape of her neck), Melchor looks out of the window and stares for a few seconds at the sparkling reflection of the sun on the whirlpools in the river and on the facades of the buildings on the opposite shore. Then he starts to nose around her shelves, where he only sees a couple of novels: *Even the Darkest Night* and *Prey for the Shadow*, by Javier Cercas.

"I went down to the supermarket to buy Coca-Cola and whisky," he hears at his back. "Whisky for me and Coca-Cola for you . . . On the rocks or straight up?"

Paca Poch takes two glasses out of a cupboard, fills one with ice cubes and Coca-Cola and hands it to Melchor; in the other she pours two fingers of Famous Grouse. Sniffing the whisky and peering at Melchor over the rim of her glass, she asks:

"Is it true that you go mad if you drink?"

"Who says that?" Melchor points at the shelf with his glass brimming with Coca-Cola and asks: "Cercas?"

The sergeant glances at the shelf for a second.

"Have you read him?"

Melchor shakes his head.

"Should I?"

Paca Poch shrugs. Then she raises her whisky towards him: "To Cosette's health."

For the rest of the afternoon they talk sitting in the dining room while the daylight gradually fades on the other side of the window. The conversation dissolves Melchor's anguish, and he doesn't find or doesn't seek a moment or a way to talk about Mattson and set out Carrasco's project for the sergeant, in part because he fears she'll turn him down, in part because he suspects that, as soon as he hears himself talk about Carrasco's plan out loud, he will judge it to be unrealisable madness. At a certain moment the sergeant asks him why he left the police force.

"That's easy," Melchor answers. "Because I find it a thousand times better to live among books than to live among cops and robbers. What about you?"

"Why did I become a cop? That's even easier." Paca Poch winks at him. "Because I love cops."

"And robbers?"

"Even more."

At another moment, when Paca Poch has already had a couple of whiskies, she asks him about the Cambrils attacks, or rather his role in the Cambrils attacks. He tries to avoid the subject, but the sergeant insists:

"Just tell me one thing. Were you scared?"

The question surprises Melchor, perhaps because he'd never asked himself, which surprises him even more.

"I don't know," he says. "I don't remember."

"You're a lying librarian." Paca Poch smiles. "Come on, tell me the truth."

Melchor makes an effort to relive the moment that changed his life. It's been seventeen years since it happened, but suddenly he realises it's as if it happened last night; more than surprise him, it disconcerts him.

"I don't know," he repeats. Maybe contradictorily, he adds: "It all happened so fast I don't think I had time to feel it."

"What a cliché," Paca Poch says.

Melchor reflects for a moment: not wanting to disappoint the sergeant, he searches for a better response. But he doesn't find one, so he shrugs.

"I don't know," he says, for the third time. "Maybe all clichés are clichés because they're true."

Around eight, when night is falling, Paca Poch suggests going to watch a football match with some friends.

"What match?" Melchor asks.

"What match do you think?" the sergeant says. "Barça-Juve. The semi-final of the Champions League. The winner plays Madrid in the final."

Melchor says nothing. Paca Poch asks:

"Don't you like football?"

"Not much."

"You'll like this match. You'll see."

Melchor, who even Cosette's youthful passion for football did not manage to ignite his interest, turns down her invitation and says he's going home.

"Is Rosa expecting you?" Paca Poch asks.

"No," Melchor answers. "She's in Barcelona."

The sergeant's face lights up as if a lamp has switched on inside her.

"So, what's your hurry?" she asks and, before Melchor can answer, stands up from the sofa and suggests: "Stay the night. We'll have a good time, you'll like my friends. Later, if Barça wins, we'll go out dancing. And if they lose too, to drown our sorrows. This city is not much, but there are a couple of great places to go. Tell me the truth, how long has it been since you've been out partying like God meant you to?"

Melchor doesn't answer, but at that moment he feels that those hours of conversation, Coca-Cola and whisky have turned Paca Poch into a friend, and the moment he was waiting for has arrived. With a sigh, he looks away towards the window: the lights on the opposite shore tremble in the waters of the river.

"I lied to you before," he admits, turning back to look at the sergeant. "The truth is I have a problem."

Paca Poch sits back down on the sofa; the lamp in the interior of her face has switched off, and her features express a sort of mocking disappointment.

221

"I knew it. What kind of problem?"

"It's not really a problem. It's something I have to ask you for."

"Important?"

"Yes."

"Granted."

Melchor arches his brows.

"I haven't told you what it is yet."

"Doesn't matter. Granted."

"It's dangerous."

"Even better."

"Dangerous and illegal."

"You're making me horny."

Melchor smiles; then he points at the half-empty bottle of Famous Grouse. Paca Poch is ahead of him.

"You're the one who goes mad when he drinks," she says. "Not me."

Melchor does not correct the sergeant, and immediately pulls Carrasco's letter out of his pocket, unfolds it and hands it to her, starts telling her what happened to Cosette in Mattson's house, or what he knows happened. Paca Poch listens carefully and then reads the letter and asks Melchor three or four very concrete questions about Carrasco, about what he knows of Carrasco's plan, about Mattson and what happened in Pollença, questions he answers with as much precision as he can. Then the sergeant folds the letter and, smiling as if her interior lamp was on again, she hands it back to Melchor and asks:

"When do we leave for Pollença?"

5

Melchor spends the night on Paca Poch's sofa, and the next morning, before leaving, he tidies up the room a little, takes a shower, gets dressed, drinks a coffee and leaves a note on the breakfast bar for the sergeant, who is still sound asleep in her room. "Thanks for everything," he writes. He already has his hand on the doorknob when he remembers how last night, once they decided to go out and have some dinner, his hostess disappeared and, a quarter of an hour later, returned freshly showered and made up, her damp hair falling over her shoulders, wearing high heels, tight jeans and a leather jacket over a T-shirt that emphasised her breasts. "What do you think?", she asked him; she had her hands on her hips, eyes defiant and a provocative smile. "Gorgeous, right?" Now Melchor turns around and walks back to the counter. "And by the way," he adds to the note, "it's true: you are gorgeous."

He finds his car in the underground car park, types an address in La Seu d'Urgell into the satnav, drives up to the surface of the plaza Alfons XII and, instead of taking the Xerta road towards Terra Alta, to go home, he heads off towards Tarragona. It's a splendid day, spring sunshine and clear blue sky, and the traffic on the Mediterranean motorway is light on this Sunday morning. Shortly after taking exit 35 and the road to Reus, he calls Rosa, with whom he'd spoken for a moment last night from the Irish pub in the old quarter where Paca Poch took him out for a hamburger.

"How was the binge?" Rosa asks.

"Great," Melchor answers. "I got three hours' sleep."

"At Paca's place?"

"Of course. That girl is a great signing."

"Should I be jealous?"

Melchor doesn't even answer the question: he tells her about the Irish pub where Paca Poch seemed to know everybody and where they had dinner and saw Barça's victory over Juve in the semi-final of the Champions League on television; he also tells her about a nightclub a few kilometres from Amposta where the sergeant apparently goes out on the pull every weekend ("You know what Saturday means: a new shirt and a roll in the hay"), a place that from outside looks like a transatlantic ship stranded in the middle of the night and from the inside a swarming and ramshackle garage riddled with strobe lights. Then he asks Rosa about her weekend in Barcelona. She sums it up with a few broad strokes and then explains that something has come up and, although they had planned to have lunch together at her house, if he didn't mind she was thinking of having it in Barcelona, with her daughters, grandchildren and sons-in-law.

"I don't mind at all," he assures her. "In fact, I was going to tell you that I can't have lunch with you today."

"And?"

Melchor feels tempted to tell her where he is going at that moment, to tell her about Carrasco's letter and Paca Poch's unreserved support for his plan; but he tells himself it is premature and maybe by the end of the day things will be clearer.

Also, he remembers Carrasco's warning about the possibility that his phone might be bugged ("Don't rule out that they might be watching you the way they're watching me, so take care"), and he thinks, in any case, it's better to explain the whole thing to Rosa face to face.

"I'll tell you tomorrow."

Two and a quarter hours later, after leaving behind Tàrrega, Cervera and Guissona, Melchor reaches La Seu d'Urgell and, following the instructions of his satnav, stops to fill up at a service station he finds on the way out of the municipality, on the road to Puigcerdà. While he's paying for the fuel at the cash register, he asks about a dog breeder called Canis.

"It's very close," the woman tells him, giving a few directions and adding: "You can't miss it."

Now following her instructions, Melchor drives a couple of kilometres up the road towards Puigcerdà, until he turns right onto a dirt road, crosses a bridge over a stream, into a holm oak wood, passes a cluster of houses and after a couple of kilometres parks in a clearing in front of an old farmhouse, beside a wooden sign stuck in the earth that announces the name of the kennel.

Melchor turns off the engine: all he hears in the immaculate quiet of the valley is some dogs barking nearby. The door to the farmhouse is ajar; pushing it, he glimpses a dark entrance hall with several closed doors leading off it and, at the back, a staircase going up to the first floor. Melchor's voice echoes in the space:

"Anyone home?"

He waits a few seconds, but nobody answers and he walks round the house, and at the back opens a patio door taking him into a yard; to his left, a string of cages occupied by dogs is lined up there. As soon as he goes through the patio door, the pitch and intensity of the barking increases until it is scandalous and from one of the cages, a little bent over, a man emerges, with a metal bucket in one hand who, seeing Melchor walking towards him, puts his forearm to his brow and scrutinises him through half-closed eyes.

"Seeing is believing," ex-sergeant Vàzquez mutters. "But if it isn't the hero of Cambrils in the flesh."

Melchor stops a metre from Vàzquez and the two men stand for a moment face to face, observing each other amid the dogs' deafening racket, until the former sergeant leaves the bucket on the ground and gives his ex-colleague a bear hug. As he feels Vàzquez's body against his, rock-hard under clothes that smell of dog food, Melchor's brain summons up two fleeting memories or rather two images.

They are both from long ago. Melchor met Vàzquez shortly after his wife died, when he left Terra Alta for a while fleeing that poisonous memory and ended up assigned to the Central Abduction and Extortion Unit in Egara, on the outskirts of Barcelona. Vàzquez, then in his forties with a shaved head, muscular and hyperactive, with the air of a bulldog and a reputation as a strict and combative officer, ran the unit, and Melchor worked under his orders for two years; until, not long before his return to Terra Alta, the unit fell apart owing to an episode that ended with Vàzquez in hospital for a week and later transferred at his own request to the station in La Seu d'Urgell, his hometown. The episode was the kidnapping of a Venezuelan drug trafficker by a rival gang. For months, the whole unit worked the case with Vàzquez as the main negotiator between the narcos. It was a tough, complex and nervous negotiation, during which the Venezuelan received in his house, one after another, three small fingers amputated from his daughter, who had just turned five. Finally, Vàzquez thought he'd found her in a warehouse on the

226

outskirts of Molins de Rei and pulled together a rescue squad of eighty people, including Guardia Civil and National Police. The operation failed. There were three arrests and one man was killed, but the police did not manage to save the narco's daughter, and the most vivid memory Melchor retains of that terrible day is Vàzquez sitting in a pool of blood on the cement floor of the warehouse, with the little girl's severed head in his lap, his eyes popping out of his head, trembling and shrieking like a man possessed.

That's the first image of the former sergeant that now, while he hugs him in the farmyard, comes into his memory. The second is from three years later, when Melchor rejoined the same unit for a few days to help resolve an attempt at sexual extortion against the mayor of Barcelona; he did so at the request of Blai, who was in charge of the Central Jurisdiction of Personal Investigation at Egara, and he found Vàzquez back in his post. He went back to working under the sergeant's orders for a couple of weeks, from which he also conserves a very vivid memory which now revives unbidden: the image is of Vàzquez sobbing in his arms, like a dirty, feverish and foul-smelling child, in a darkened room in his post-divorce apartment in Cerdanyola, the morning Melchor discovered that for many years the toughest guy he'd ever known was prey to a bipolar condition that plunged him into alternating periods of euphoria and depression, during which he was obliterated as a police officer and as a person.

When the two men come out of their hug, Vàzquez asks Melchor what he's doing there. Melchor smiles and shrugs; then asks about Verónica.

"She's gone shopping in town," Vàzquez answers, picking up the bucket and adding: "Come on, come with me while I feed this gang."

The cages teem with dozens of dogs of different breeds, most of them very young, who go crazy with joy when Vàzquez enters their cubicle and gives them food. The former police officer treats his animals with familiarity but without fuss, he gives them orders and scolds them while talking about them to Melchor. Seven years earlier, when he was still stationed at Egara, Vàzquez had succumbed to a new onslaught of his illness and had been forced to end his police career. By then he had been going out with Verónica Planas for a while, who at that moment was the force's chief press officer. Verónica helped him overcome the depression and left her work in Barcelona to move with him to La Seu d'Urgell, where they eventually got married. The two friends have not seen each other since the wedding day, and that was almost five years ago.

Vàzquez is still feeding the dogs, but, in reply to Melchor's questions, he stops talking about them to talk about the farmhouse he lives in and where he's set up his business.

"It was my mother's," he says while carrying on with his task. "Well, my mother's family . . . My father wasn't from here. He was in the Guardia Civil. From Badajoz. But they sent him here, he met my mother and here he stayed."

Vàzquez asks about Cosette, Rosa and Blai; Melchor tells the truth about the latter two, but not about the former. When Vàzquez comes out of the last cage and closes it behind him, the two men go inside the farmhouse through an ancient stable, where there is a sink and the ex-sergeant strips to the waist and washes his face, hands and torso in cold water. Melchor notices his abdominal muscles without an ounce of fat, and Vàzquez guesses his thought.

"What did you think?" He smiles without irony, pounding his chest with closed fists. "That I'd turn into a flabby old man?

Bollocks to that . . . I go running every day, lift weights, ride a bike, everything. Modesty apart, I'm as strong as an ox."

"I can see that."

"We've got to be prepared, kid. You never know when war will be back." While he dries his shaved head and neck with a towel, he adds: "You know what? I read novels too."

Melchor raises his eyebrows, intrigued.

"Vero makes me." Vàzquez makes a half-resigned half-sly face, as if he's just admitted a bit of naughtiness. "She says people who don't read get cobwebs on the brain. She also says, the less I read, the more I resemble my dogs. I'm not kidding: as if that were a bad thing . . . By the way, I bet you don't know what I've just read?"

Without waiting for Melchor's reply, Vàzquez gestures for him to follow him inside.

"A clue," he says. "Not *Les Misérables*."

Melchor doesn't remember ever exchanging a single word about literature with Vàzquez, so he wonders how he had discovered that, for years, Victor Hugo's novel was his bedside reading. Walking into the shadowy entrance hall he's glimpsed a little while ago, when he peered inside the farmhouse, Vàzquez stops and proclaims:

"The Cercas novels."

Melchor stares at him without curiosity.

"I read the second because Vero told me I was in it," Vàzquez explains. "*Prey for the Shadow*, it's called . . . Then I read the first. And do you know what I say?" In his face, the resignation and naughtiness have turned to scepticism. "They're not bad. At least they're entertaining, not like some of the other stuff I've had to swallow . . . Man, it's true the guy makes it all up. Well, almost all of it: I tell you that bastard has done a lot of research, at least to write the second one, I'm sure he talked to people at

Egara who told him things . . . Now, when it comes to using his imagination, the guy's on his own. I bet you don't know what he says about blackmailing the mayor?"

"No, but I can guess."

"Well, I bet you whatever you like you can't . . . I mean he does not say what everybody says these days, in other words, that the three tenors and Hematomas were bumped off by the mayor . . . He says that you killed them, because you discovered that they had murdered your mother." In the semi-darkness of the hall, Vàzquez smiles with all his teeth, opening his eyes wide and shaking his head from side to side. "What do you reckon? . . . Anyway, as Vero always says: lies sell more than truth, because they're more attractive and easier to tell."

"Blai says that too."

Vàzquez, who had started walking again, stops once more.

"Yes, but Vero knows more than Blai about this," he warns Melchor, poking him with an admonishing finger in the chest. "About that, and about pretty much anything else."

Vàzquez's wife appears a short time later, with two bags of shopping and a newspaper under her arm, and finds them sitting at the kitchen table, having an aperitif.

"I was wondering whose car that was outside." Without repressing her joy, she sets the bags and paper down on the counter and throws her arms around Melchor's neck to kiss him on both cheeks. "What on earth are you doing here?"

Melchor replies without answering, as he did a while ago with Vàzquez, but his friends don't insist and start making lunch all together. Later, while they're eating a tomato and tuna salad, gnocchi with pesto and an apple tart, Verónica explains to Melchor that, after many years in corporate communication, she's gone back to working as a journalist and is very happy writing freelance for several newspapers and spending

230

three days a week in Barcelona, where she keeps a pied-à-terre.

"That way I can see my friends, go to the cinema, the theatre and concerts," she says. "The truth is I'm up to date on everything, kid." Pointing to Vàzquez with her fork, she adds: "Not like this big lug, who is antisocial."

Vàzquez laughs happily, kisses Verónica on the lips, who shoves him away with a giggle. Although they've been married for five years now, they seem like a couple of newlyweds, but Melchor knows it took a lot for Vàzquez to win over Verónica.

In fact, Melchor has known Vàzquez's wife longer than his friend has. When the jihadist attacks happened in 2017, Verónica was already the chief press officer of the Mossos d'Esquadra, and a little while later suggested that Melchor, without revealing his identity, should tell his experience of 17 August in Cambrils before Catalan television cameras, for a special report on the incident. Verónica, who Vàzquez had then barely ever met, and only in passing, argued that Melchor's appearance in the report would help raise his colleagues' morale, which was in the dumps since the head of the force, Major Trapero, had been accused of obstructing justice and disobeying orders during the secessionist attempt in the autumn of that year, when the autonomous Catalan government unilaterally decreed the separation of Catalonia from the rest of Spain. Melchor turned Verónica's suggestion down. However, years later, while he was stationed in Barcelona under Vàzquez's orders, Verónica insisted on reviving her suggestion with the added lure of a documentary made by a prestigious filmmaker. It was then, or shortly after, when the press officer insisted on visiting Melchor in Terra Alta to try to convince him, when Vàzquez fell head over heels in love with her, so he asked his friend to agree to Verónica's visits on the condition that Vàzquez come with her from Barcelona. Melchor agreed. And, even though those visits to Terra Alta did not enable Verónica to persuade Melchor, they did enable Vàzquez to seduce Verónica.

"I'm also planning to write a best-seller," she jokes, turning to Melchor. "Know what it's going to be called?"

"What?" Vàzquez asks, looking at her ecstatically.

Verónica passes a hand in front of her face, in a sort of flamenco flourish, and announces:

"*I Married Cro-Magnon Man.*"

Vàzquez bursts out laughing again and pounds on the table.

"We'll make a killing," he predicts.

Once lunch is over, Verónica announces:

"With your permission, I'm going to have a siesta. Do you take siestas, Melchor?"

He says he doesn't.

"Neither does this savage." She points with her thumb at Vàzquez. "There you go. It's important to have a siesta. A good custom we have in this country that we're losing. The siesta is good for everything. All doctors say so. It should be obligatory, with prison sentences for those who neglect their siestas . . . Don't laugh. I'm serious. In any case, people who work hard, like me, cannot allow ourselves the luxury of not having a siesta. There you have it."

The two men clear the table and wash the dishes; when they finish, they go out for a walk. First, they walk down the farm track but that comes to a dead end after a few metres and turns into a wide mountain path bordered by pines. For a while they walk in silence, listening only to the sounds of the forest and their footsteps on the earth. The valley air is clear and fresh. The afternoon has warmed up a little, with a gentle sun and cloudless sky.

232

"Tell me something, Melchor," Vàzquez says when they've been walking for some time. "You haven't just come to pay us a visit, have you?"

Melchor stops in the middle of the path.

"No," Melchor says. Vàzquez stops a few steps further on and turns to look at him. "I've come to ask you for a favour."

6

First thing on Monday, while drinking coffee with Blai in Hiroyuki's bar ("How is the empire of the rising sun?" the inspector had greeted the Japanese man), Melchor does not tell his friend that last night he was in La Seu d'Urgell with Vàzquez, or that he slept in Tortosa on Saturday night, in Paca Poch's apartment, and simply listens to him vaguely, a bit distracted while he searches for a way to convince him to join the operation as well. He does not find one. Almost twenty years of friendship suffice to enable him to guess that Blai will refuse to support him unless very special circumstances come together and he feels he has no other choice but to do so.

Before he goes to work, Melchor walks to a mobile phone shop on avenida de València, buys a phone in Cosette's name and, while he walks as fast as he can to the library, sends a WhatsApp to Carrasco's mobile. "Yours is the Earth," it reads. As if the former guardia civil had been waiting for that message, Melchor receives an immediate reply. "Hallelujah," it says. "Adelante? Everything ready?" "I'm on it," Melchor responds in turn, noticing that Carrasco is suddenly addressing him as *tú* and not *usted*, as he had done up till then; he replies in the same fashion: "Get everything ready in the meantime, and when you've decided the day, let me know. By then I hope to be ready." "You must be ready," Carrasco emphasises. "I will," Melchor assures him, not knowing whether he will or not. Carrasco's reply is a yellow-handed emoji with two fingers raised in a victory sign.

Melchor spends the rest of his working day stealing time from his job to search the internet for information about the professionals, weapons and equipment they'll need to assault the mogul's house. Especially, the professionals, which is what most worries him. According to Carrasco's calculations, they need ten in total, including himself, Melchor and a person Carrasco will bring; if they add Paca Poch and Vàzquez to those three, who are already committed to the operation, the result is they still need five more people to complete the team. Melchor visits the web pages of several Spanish security companies, studies their characteristics, calls three of them on the phone (Segur, Security Services and Virela) and, using half-spoken words and euphemisms, describes the kind of operation he needs to hire professionals for ("Entrance to a domicile without legal coverage," is the formula he employs). All three assure him they don't provide that sort of services, but someone at the last company calls him back a while later from another phone, insinuating that it could be done and suggesting he come and visit them at their head office in Alcalá de Henares. When Melchor asks how much money it would cost to hire each professional for one or two days, the reply is:

"Depends how complex the operation turns out to be and risk entailed."

"Let's suppose it's complex and the risk is high."

"Seventy thousand euros. Maybe a bit less."

Melchor then decides to turn to the darknet, which he accesses anonymously through a search engine called Tor. It's the first time he's done this since leaving the police force, five years earlier, and he is shocked by the elephantine growth the darknet has undergone in that time; he's not shocked by the absolute gall and absurd abundance with which the consumer is offered all kinds of goods and services, from lots of heavy armaments to snipers specialising in selective assassinations. In spite of that, and no matter how hard he looks, he is unable to find a page offering a professional for a high-risk operation for less than thirty thousand euros. This means, he calculates, the cost of the assault on Mattson's house will climb to a minimum of a hundred and fifty thousand euros, just for the humans; to that they'd have to add, also in the best-case scenario, thirty or forty thousand euros in technical material, weapons and other expenses. Total: around two hundred thousand euros. It's true, Melchor reasons, that, once the operation is concluded (and even if it fails), the weaponry and technical material could be resold somewhere on the darknet, but it's no less true that, at least to start, they would need to get hold of that exorbitant sum of money. Can he get it? He doesn't know if Rosa would give it to him, and much less to spend on what he's planning to spend it on, but he rules out asking her for it. So, how else could he get it? Would his bank give him a line of credit of such pro-portions? He has not yet finished asking himself the question when he again thinks that, if Blai joined the operation, its cost would be substantially slashed and its success would become much more plausible, and an idea occurs to him that, he thinks, might convince him to join the operation, or at least force him to seriously consider the hypothesis of doing so.

At five-thirty, when his shift at the library ends and Dolors arrives to relieve him, Melchor goes home, gets in his car and drives out of Gandesa by the cemetery road, in the direction of Vilalba dels Arcs. Ten minutes later he reaches the town, without seeing a single soul and, after he passes a football pitch, he turns right onto calle de la Bassa Bona. Just before the urban area peters out into fields, he parks in front of a tractor, beside some broken pavement. Melchor gets out of the car, walks back down the street a short distance and knocks on the door of an old, renovated house, from the front balcony of which hangs a sign that says: CAN SALVI. RURAL TOURISM. The iron knocker striking the wooden door resounds through the sub-urban evening calm. There is no wind, and in the distance, on the crests of the Sierra de La Fatarella, the wind turbines stand out against the cobalt blue of the sky, immobile like gigantic sleeping insects.

He is about to knock again when the door opens and Salom appears. The two men stand looking at each other for a few endless seconds, as if they didn't recognise each other. Melchor has not been this close to the former corporal in almost fifteen years, when they used to see each other every day, and he is certain that the last time Salom saw him was the night he solved the Adell case by discovering that his partner was implicated in the multiple homicide, dragged him from his house and forced him to surrender to Blai, who was waiting at the station. And now the two of them are there again, face to face, not knowing what to say. Eventually it is Salom who speaks.

"Would you like to come in?" he asks.

Salom silently precedes Melchor through a semi-dark vesti-bule and dining room that smell clean, furnished in a slightly impersonal way. Until they reach, through a long hallway, a bright kitchen with a window and glass door, a patio; in the kit-chen, which looks recently refurbished, there is a brazier table with a checkered oilcloth, surrounded by Ikea stools and chairs, on one of which is sitting Mireia, Salom's younger daughter, a woman of thirty-some years who stands up when Melchor appears and regards him with a bitter, shocked expression. She and Melchor have known each other for many years, but it has also been many years since they've seen each other. Or, if they do see each other, they avoid each other. Or rather Mireia avoids Melchor, as does Clàudia, Salom's first-born.

"We're doing some accounts," the ex-corporal explains, simulating a poise he has always lacked. "Do you remember Mireia?"

"Of course," Melchor says, turning to the woman. "How are you?"

Salom's daughter is tall and dark-haired, with large black eyes, and is wearing a blue dress. While he awaits the reply to his greeting, Melchor regrets not having called his former colleague before trying to speak to him. To break the silence, Salom asks him:

"Would you like a coffee?"

"I don't want to bother you," Melchor says.

"It's no bother," says Salom.

"Yes, it is a bother," Mireia interrupts.

The woman's words crack through the kitchen like a whip. Mireia observes Melchor without fondness, her expression slightly shocked; her thin lips, hardened by her astonishment (or by disdain), look like knives.

"What are you doing here?" she asks.

"Mireia, please," Salom interrupts.

"Don't you know you're not welcome in our house?" Mireia asks, ignoring her father. "Well, you should know that."

"Don't listen to her, Melchor."

"Shut up, Papá." Salom's daughter does not take her glacial gaze off Melchor. "What are you doing here?" she repeats. "You already destroyed our lives once, was that not enough for you? What do you want? To destroy them again?"

Before Salom tries to intervene again, Melchor stops him with a gesture.

"No," he says. "Your daughter's right. This was a mistake. I should not have come."

He quickly adds an apology, turns around and leaves. Salom does not see him to the door.

As he drives back to Gandesa, Melchor wonders if he shouldn't accept that Carrasco's project is beyond his means and should send the former guardia civil a message saying they should cancel it.

When he gets home he thinks not and goes back onto the darknet. An hour and a half later he has reached the same conclusion he reached first thing this afternoon: to do what they want to do, he needs two hundred thousand euros. A minute later he receives a WhatsApp from Rosa, who tells him a problem has come up and she won't be able to get home by nine as they had arranged. Melchor, who would almost prefer not to have dinner with her tonight, so he won't give in to the temptation of telling her what's going on and asking for her help, asks if it is a serious problem. "No," Rosa answers. "But I won't be finished work until late. One of these days I'm going to close this damned business and run away with you to Bora-Bora. Deal?" Melchor replies with a thumbs-up emoji. "Ana has made us dinner," Rosa continues. "You eat, and I'll get there when I finish." "Don't worry," Melchor answers. "I'm at my place, too lazy to leave. See you tomorrow." Rosa accepts Melchor's decision and he makes himself a salad with avocado, cream cheese, cherry tomatoes, walnuts and balsamic vinegar and eats it standing up at the counter, looking out of the window at calle Costumà wrapped at that hour in the yellow light of the streetlamps. Then he tries to distract himself by reading a Turgenev novel called *A Nest of Gentlefolk*, but he doesn't manage to read any more than the first chapter, which he likes a lot even though for some reason it reminds him of Mattson, which makes him put down the book, pick up his laptop and start looking for information about the tycoon. Only then does he notice that, in spite of the enormous quantity of news about Mattson that shows up on the internet, there is barely any mention of the Mallorca mansion, and he can't even find a single image of it. Melchor interprets this fact as another confirmation that Carrasco is not wrong: Mattson has built a secret or almost secret refuge in Formentor where he can enjoy his pleasures with discretion and entertain his guests at the same time as filming them to be able to blackmail them.

That night he doesn't go to bed until after two, but it still takes him a long time to fall asleep, and before he does he has decided that the next morning he'll call his bank to ask for a loan of two hundred thousand euros.

The next day, when he arrives at the library after having coffee with Blai in the bar on the plaza, Melchor finds Salom waiting for him at the door. The librarian stops in front of the former corporal, who stands blinking on the deserted pavement as if dazzled by the sun.

"I've come to apologise for yesterday," says Salom.

"You have nothing to apologise for," Melchor replies. "Mireia is completely right." There is silence; Melchor hears the scant traffic on the avenida de Catalunya behind him. "Do you want to come in?"

Salom doesn't say no and Melchor opens the door to the library and invites him in. While he checks over the notes

Dolors left behind the customer service counter and carries out his daily routine to get the place ready for the public to come in, Salom glances at the reading room, a vast rectangle with very high ceilings, full of shelves and illuminated by a huge window that takes up the whole facade.

"Do you know this is the first time I've ever been here?" Salom asks.

"That's bad," Melchor answers. The other day I heard a friend say that a person who doesn't read gets cobwebs on the brain."

Salom nods without conviction, examining the spines of the books lined up on a shelf. Melchor opens the library to the public while keeping watch over his former partner out of the corner of his eye. He is only a couple of years older than Blai, though he has always looked older than him. He still does: he still has the same bushy beard streaked with grey that he had fifteen years ago, but he's lost hair on his head, and what little he's got left has turned completely white; he wears the same glasses as ever, large, old-fashioned and plastic-framed, moves in the same laid-back way and it's obvious he doesn't exercise and eats too much, because he has put on weight.

"This is where you met Olga, isn't it?" Salom asks.

Melchor says yes and, when the library has been open for less than five minutes, the first user comes in, an old man called Antoni Bes, who often comes in to read the newspapers, to interrupt Melchor once in a while and snooze a bit in one of the armchairs. Salom says hello to the recent arrival and, as Melchor hears the sound of the two men's conversation, he observes them out of the corner of his eye and at times seems to recognise in the former prisoner the slow, cautious, austere, unlucky and likeable friend he was to him during his first four years in Terra Alta.

241

When Salom escapes from Bes and approaches the library counter, Melchor resolves to try again.

"Come," he says. "I'm going to show you something."

They go into his office and, once Melchor closes the door behind him, he starts telling Salom about Cosette's trip to Mallorca, about Sergeant Benavides, the Inca courthouse, about Mattson and about Carrasco. Salom stands there listening, without interrupting or making any comment; through the thick lenses of his glasses, the expression in his eyes goes from confused to concern and from concern to terror. Melchor has not yet told him the whole story when he shows Salom Carrasco's letter, he puts it down on his desk, among invoices and delivery notes, and invites the former corporal to sit down.

"Take a look at this, please," he says. "Then we'll talk."

Melchor leaves Salom and returns to the reading room. Salom takes more time than Melchor expected to read the letter, or at least to come out of his office. When he does finally come out, he has the letter in his hand and a new confusion in his eyes; before he can say anything, Melchor takes him back into the office and closes the door again. Salom asks:

"What does this mean?"

"It means that I am recruiting people to break into Mattson's house," Melchor answers. "So far I've got two who have agreed to join me. Two sergeants. One is currently on the force and the other is not. I don't think you know them. They're both really good." He pauses and adds: "Can I count on you?"

Now Salom's eyes scrutinise Melchor while his lips stretch into a disbelieving smile.

"This is a joke, right?"

Melchor answers with another question:

"Do you think I would joke about something like this?"

Melchor sees Salom's smile freeze on his mouth, how he

looks away from him and around his office, as if looking for an answer in those disorderly stacks of books and cardboard boxes, some open and others yet to be opened.

"I know what you're thinking," Melchor says. Salom looks back at him. "You're thinking that I am a son of a bitch. That you spent seven years in prison on account of me and the next time I deign to speak to you it's to ask a favour."

"And a half," Salom corrects him. "It was seven and a half years. And it wasn't your fault."

"That's true," Melchor agrees. "But, if not for me, nothing would have happened to you. That is also true . . . So maybe I was a son of a bitch, maybe I should have kept my mouth shut. Could be. We can discuss it any time you want. I don't know what use it would be, but I'm prepared to do it . . . Whatever the case, we've got another matter to deal with now. The fact is there is a much worse son of a bitch than me. A huge son of a bitch. And we have to get rid of him. However we can. It's a simple question: are you going to help me?"

Salom seems to think it over for a moment. Then he clicks his tongue and, almost imperceptibly, his head starts to move left to right. He asks:

"How is Cosette?"

"How do you think she is?" Melchor answers. "At the moment, she's staying at a clinic. Are you going to help me, yes or no?"

Salom's headshake becomes more obvious, but it seems less like a refusal and more like a gesture of pity or resignation.

"You're mad." He puts Carrasco's letter down on the desk and, without looking, puts one finger on it. "This guy's insane and you are madder than he is . . . Look, I am really very sorry about what happened to Cosette. And, if it was Mattson who did it, he should pay." He moves away from the desk and takes a step towards Melchor. "I understand that you feel bad, but what you should do is report what happened right now and let the justice system do their work."

"Reporting Mattson wouldn't be any use." Melchor also points to the letter. "Didn't you read what Carrasco says? Didn't I tell you what happened to me at the Guardia Civil post? Carrasco is right: that guy is armour-plated, it wouldn't be any use . . . And even if it were, have you forgotten how these things go in the courts? Do you think I'm going to put Cosette through an ordeal lasting years for them to finally absolve Mattson? Would you put your daughters through something like that? . . . No, Carrasco is perfectly sane, I'm telling you and I've talked to him, and he's been preparing for this moment for ten years. If he doesn't know how to finish off Mattson, nobody does. And I want to find out if he does know or not. That's all. And I also want to know if you're going to help me find out."

"If I could help you, I'd help you. Believe me. But what you're suggesting is madness."

"It's not madness. And don't kid yourself: of course you can help me. A lot. You have experience. You're a cop."

"I was. But I'm not anymore. And neither are you."

"That's not true. Once you're in the police, you never stop being a cop."

Salom swats at the air, as if shooing away a fly.

"That phrase sounds like Blai, Melchor," he says. "Not you."

"That may be, but it's true."

"Rubbish."

Melchor knows Salom is right, but holds his gaze as if he weren't. Then he pulls out the rest of it.

"Besides," he says, "if what you wanted was a chance to make up for what you did wrong, here it is."

Salom now looks at Melchor with real curiosity. The silence in the office has become more compact, denser.

"Did Blai tell you that too?"

"I'm the one who's saying it."

Now Salom walks over to stand a metre from Melchor; the smile had disappeared from his face a while ago, transformed into a harsh sneer.

"See how mad you are?" he says. "That redemption thing is a tall story. A fairy tale. I don't know about those novels that get the cobwebs out of your brain, but that's how it is in reality. You make one mistake and you carry that mistake for ever. It's called remorse, Melchor. I imagine it rings a bell."

Melchor thinks of his mother, thinks of his wife, thinks of Cosette; but he doesn't say anything and, as if silence were a form of assent, Salom smiles again and walks away until he stops in front of the poster for the antiquarian book fair in Barcelona, with its rambla full of flowers and books and the statue of Columbus. He examines it while Melchor observes his thinning, white, circular hair that, around his crown, forms a sort of tonsure; after a few seconds, during which Melchor searches in vain for an argument to break Salom's resistance, he turns back around towards him.

"Tell me something, Melchor." His tone of voice has changed. "Why are you asking me to do this?"

"I already told you," Melchor answers. "Because I need you. Because I think you can do it."

"Are you sure?"

Melchor detects a little sarcastic sparkle in Salom's eyes; the former corporal asks:

"You think I was born yesterday, or what?"

"I don't understand."

"Sure you do." Salom walks back over to Melchor, who sees

a little cluster of hairs sticking out of his nostrils. "The key to everything here is Blai. You know that, if Blai signs on, the thing'll get done, because Blai is Blai and most of all he's the station chief and has the means and people to do it. I don't know who those two sergeants are who've already said yes, but I'm sure they're not enough to convince Blai. So it occurred to you that I am the weight you're missing to tip the scale in your favour and that, if I join, Blai will come along. Am I mistaken or not?"

Salom is not mistaken, not at least about the key facts, but Melchor has no intention of admitting it, and the question is still floating in the silence of the office when a couple of providential little raps at the door free Melchor from having to answer: it's a history teacher from Terra Alta High School, who is looking for a book by Eric Hobsbawm and can't seem to find it.

"Wait a moment," Melchor asks Salom. And he goes with the teacher to the shelf where the book should be.

Indeed: it's not there. Melchor looks for it in vain in the signed-out books registry and on the returns cart where the books he hasn't yet had time to shelve are waiting, and then eventually finds the volume on a shelf next to the one it should be on, where someone had left it by accident. Melchor signs out the book, deactivates the anti-theft sticker and hands it to the teacher.

When he gets back to his office, Salom has left.

7

Resigned to not being able to count on Blai or Salom, at one in the afternoon, after closing the library, Melchor shuts himself in his office, calls the last physical branch of his bank still open in Terra Alta from the land-line and asks to speak with the manager, a guy called Martí Descarrega who has a son the same age as Cosette and lives in Batea. He has to wait a while to speak to him, but he finally comes on the line and Melchor asks point blank if he thinks the bank would grant him a loan of two hundred thousand euros.

"Wow," the manager answers. "That's a lot of money. Anyway, it depends."

"What does it depend on?"

"On who your guarantor is."

"I have a salary and a house. Is that not enough of a guarantee?"

"The way things are these days, I'm not sure. Maybe, maybe not. If you'd asked five or ten years ago, not to mention fifteen, we would have granted it in a moment without blinking. Now things have changed . . . But, it's not impossible either. I'd have to study the case."

"How long will it take you to study it?"

"A few days."

"And how long before I could have the money?"

"I don't know. Four or five weeks."

"Couldn't it be sooner?"

"I could try. Though it's not easy . . . Supposing we can grant it, as well as the evaluation there's the procedures, the paperwork, you know how these things are. Although I insist: it would all be much easier if someone solvent underwrites you. And faster too."

Melchor knows who the manager is referring to, but he doesn't say anything.

"Anyway," the manager continues, "if you tell me to go ahead and I start looking into it today, I can have an answer for you within the week. Meanwhile, think about the guarantor."

Melchor tells him to go ahead.

The sun is setting when he gets to Rosa's house. He parks on the gravel driveway in front of the house, beside her car, goes up to the first floor and into the kitchen, where Ana Elena is chopping vegetables on the marble countertop.

"The señora is on the balcony," she tells him.

Melchor finds Rosa stretched out on a sofa, contemplating the sunset with a glass of wine in her hand. It's a white leather sofa and it's under a beige awning.

"Come," Rosa calls him to her side, patting the seat while pointing to the west. "Look."

Melchor sits beside her. Facing the sofa, the rocky peaks of the Sierra de Cavalls devour the last remnants of an enormous, round, pink sun, which is turning the sky a soft pomegranate colour.

"You think Bora-Bora is better than this?" Melchor asks.

Rosa gives him a tired smile, and, while she finishes her glass of wine, begins to tell Melchor what's been happening over the last few days: it seems, they have not been easy ones on account of a problem with cardboard supply at the Timişoara factory, that she almost had to fly urgently to Romania. When she stops talking, or when she gets tired of talking, the sky is just violet light and the night is beginning to cast shadows around them. The day had been one of summer heat, but the evening has cooled off and the owner of Gráficas Adell has thrown a cardigan over her shoulders.

"Anyway, I have not yet ruled out the Bora-Bora option," she says. "Meanwhile, tonight I'm going to get drunk." She holds up her empty glass to Melchor and asks: "Why don't you act like a gentleman and pour me another?"

"Sure." Melchor stands up and, taking Carrasco's letter out of his back pocket, he hands it to Rosa. "In the meantime, read this."

On his way inside, he dispels the darkness that has taken over the balcony by flicking a switch that turns on two white globes fitted into a wall. In the kitchen, while Ana Elena pours him a Coca-Cola with ice in a cut-glass tumbler, Melchor refills Rosa's glass and asks the woman about her children. Ana Elena answers without pausing her work, and, after a few minutes of conversation, Melchor returns to the balcony. Several of Carrasco's handwritten pages are scattered on the sofa, but Rosa hasn't finished reading the letter, or perhaps she's reading it a second time. Melchor stops in front of her, and hears her muttering:

"I knew we hadn't heard the last of this man."

He hands her the full glass of wine, sets his half-finished glass of Coca-Cola on the floor, picks up the pages of the letter, folds them and puts them into his pocket again. He sits back down beside Rosa, who takes a sip of wine and says:

"I suppose it's not worth trying to convince you not to do it."

Melchor's reply consists of taking a sip of Coca-Cola. Rosa sits up a little and asks:

"You've already told him yes?"

Melchor nods. Rosa smiles and reclines again against the back of the sofa. Beyond the illuminated terrace, an impenetrable darkness has taken the place of the changing spectacle of the sunset. The owner of Gráficas Adell takes another sip of wine and then holds the glass with both hands and fits it between her breasts, as if she wanted to hide it there or as if it were a baby. She has come directly from work and has not yet had the time or desire to change her clothes: although she is barefoot, she is wearing a purple trouser suit over a round-necked white blouse.

"What I don't understand is why you're telling me," she says.

"Because I don't want to hide it from you," Melchor says. "And because I have to ask you a favour."

"If it's for this, you better not ask me."

Ignoring Rosa's warning, Melchor relates the conversation he'd had that afternoon with his bank manager. Rosa listens with a look of concentration, not meeting his gaze.

"I need you to guarantee the loan," he concludes. "That's all. In the worst-case scenario, if things get rushed, I might ask you to advance me the money for a few days. No more. As soon as the bank gives it to me, I'll pay you back."

"You're going to do it that soon?"

"I don't know . . . It depends on Carrasco. He's the one who has to choose the date. It could be a while, but I want to have everything ready as soon as I can. In case things get rushed."

Rosa's lips curve down and, still staring out at the darkness, she nods. Judging by her expression, Melchor's explanations seem to have convinced her; in reality it's the opposite.

"It's madness," she declares.

"It's not madness," Melchor corrects her. "It's just something that has to be done. If someone had done it a long time ago, Cosette would not be where she is. And all those girls would not have gone through what they did."

"And, since nobody has done it, you're going to do it."

"Somebody has to do it, don't you think? . . . Also –" he sits up a little and, with his free hand, pats Carrasco's letter in his back pocket – "I won't be doing it alone, I'll do it with the guy best placed to do it. That's why I need the money: to do it properly. And that's why it's not dangerous. The worst that could happen is that we'd have to come home empty-handed."

"And if they catch you?"

"Nobody's going to catch us."

"How do you know?"

Melchor does not know, but he answers:

"Because I know."

Still nodding, Rosa raises her glass of wine and stares at it as she swirls the liquid in the creamy light of the terrace, as if looking for something in it; then she takes another sip and turns towards Melchor leaning her glass on her knee.

"The other day you didn't answer a question."

"Which question?"

"Did you sleep with Paca Poch?"

Melchor does not answer straight away, so Rosa repeats the question.

"What do you think?" Melchor asks.

"What I think doesn't matter," Rosa says. "Did you sleep with her or not?"

"Of course not. If I'd slept with her, I would have told you."

"Really?"

"Really."

Rosa looks at Melchor for a second; then she smiles, raises her glass, clinks it against his glass of Coca-Cola and takes a long sip of wine. Melchor then tells her why he went to Tortosa on Saturday and on Sunday to La Seu d'Urgell, and the answers he got from Paca Poch and Vàzquez. Suddenly lively, as if the alcohol had got rid of her fatigue, Rosa asks:

"And Blai?"

"What about Blai?"

"Have you talked to him?"

"No."

"Why not?"

"Because I know I won't be able to convince him."

"That means that what you're going to do is insane."

"That means that Blai is the way he is. Nothing more." Melchor does not even consider telling Rosa that, in part to convince Blai, he had also tried to convince Salom: even though the latter was Rosa's friend long before he met either of them, it didn't seem a good idea to tell her he tried to recruit someone who had spent years in prison as an accomplice and accessory to the murder of her parents. "Anyway, if you know of any way to convince him, let me know."

"I do not. But, now that you're going to do it, you should count him in."

Melchor shows his agreement with her at the same moment Ana Elena appears on the balcony to tell them dinner is ready. Rosa says they'll be right there, drinks the rest of her wine and stands up from the sofa; he remains seated. Only the song of one cricket disturbs the silence of the terrace.

"Well," Melchor asks, standing up as well, "what do you say?"

Rosa wraps her arms around his neck; her eyes are shining and her breath smells of mint and wine.

"I say you're crazy," she replies, "but I am even crazier than you."

The next day, as soon as the bank opens, Melchor calls the manager to tell him that Rosa Adell will be his guarantor.

"Great," the manager says. "You can count on that loan. When the papers are ready, I'll call you to come in and sign them."

A little while later, Melchor is having coffee with Blai in Hiro-yuki's bar, as they do every morning, and when he gets to the library he receives a call from Salom, who blurts out point blank that he'll join the mission. Melchor has not yet recovered from the surprise when he remembers Carrasco and thinks to himself, if his phone might be tapped, the library's might be as well.

"Sorry, Salom," he answers, writing down the number on the telephone screen. "I can't talk right now. I'll call you later."

He hangs up without explaining any further, grabs the mobile he bought yesterday in Cosette's name and calls Salom.

"Salom? It's Melchor again. Sorry for hanging up on you. I'm being cautious. Carrasco thinks my phone might be tapped . . . I don't know if it is, but it would be best that, when you want to talk about Mallorca, call me at this number. I'm not using it for anything else."

"OK. I'll buy a burner phone too."

"That would be best. Keep the receipt and I'll pay for it."

"That's not necessary. Do you want me to talk to Blai?"

Melchor thinks it over for a couple of seconds.

"Let me try first," he answers. "If I can't convince him, I'll let you know. That way, instead of one chance, we'll have two."

"And if neither of us can convince him?"

"We'll do it without him."

At the other end of the phone there is silence. For a moment, Melchor thinks the call has been cut off.

"Salom?"

"Tell me one thing," the former corporal says. "When will we do this?"

"I don't know. As soon as Carrasco finds the right moment."

"And you? Have you got everything prepared?"

"Almost. I have the two sergeants I told you about. I have you. I know where to find the equipment and people we need . . . and pretty soon I'll have the money to hire them."

"If Blai comes in, maybe you won't need to."

"That's why we have to make sure he comes in. I'll try to meet him today."

He does. As soon as he hangs up the phone, he writes a WhatsApp to the inspector inviting him over to his house for lunch. "I can't, I have a meeting," Blai writes back. Since they'd just seen each other barely an hour earlier, he adds: "Has something happened?" "Yes," Melchor answers. "We have to talk." "Is it that urgent? You can't wait till tomorrow?" Blai asks. "I'd rather not," Melchor replies. Blai suggests: "If you want, I could stop by the library after lunch. At four?" Melchor agrees. A little while later, however, he remembers that Salom was in the library the previous day and so much coming and going of former colleagues to his workplace could catch someone's attention. So, telling himself that at that moment he can't be too careful, he calls Dolors and asks her to switch evening shifts: for her to look after the library between four and six and he'll do the six till eight. Dolors agrees and Melchor writes back to Blai. "Let's meet at my house, not in the library. It'll be quieter." Blai answers: "OK."

8

"Hey, Melchor," Blai says, sitting at his friend's kitchen table with Carrasco's letter in one hand and his reading glasses in the other, "this *picoleto*'s off his rocker, isn't he?"

It's four-thirty in the afternoon and Melchor has had time to give the Terra Alta station chief a quick overview of Cosette's actual experience in Mallorca and, in more detail, his own. Then he's told him about the Mercadal Clinic and his daughter's state of health, after which he's handed him Carrasco's letter. Now, while he finishes making the second cup of coffee, as if he hasn't heard Blai's comment he explains that he has agreed to Carrasco's plan, that he is finalising preparations to carry it out, that he has spoken to Paca Poch, Vàzquez and Salom and that all three have said they're willing to help him. Blai has been listening to Melchor for almost half an hour while he leaps from one surprise to another without interrupting his speech except to reproach him every once in a while for not having told him the truth from the start, but now he cuts him off:

"You've spoken to Salom?"

Melchor nods.

"And he has also said yes," he insists.

"I can't believe it."

Melchor takes Carrasco's letter, gives Blai a cup of coffee and, with his own in hand, sits down opposite him.

"I've explained and he understood. The same with Vàzquez and Paca. I hope you understand too. Salom and I have been separated by certain things, but this is going to unite us. I hope the opposite isn't going to happen with you."

"What's this? Blackmail?"

"I'm just telling you how it is. But, if after almost twenty years of friendship you're not able to understand something that even Salom understands, then our friendship is not what I thought it was."

Gobsmacked, the inspector doesn't even seem to have noticed the cup Melchor has put in front of him.

"Let's see if I understand how it is," he says, drilling his blue eyes into Melchor's. "You're telling me you're thinking of breaking into the house of one of the richest men in the world? And you're planning to do so with a nutjob, an ex-con, a sick man and a nymphomaniac? Is that what you're telling me?"

"Three of us are ex-cons," Melchor corrects him. "Carrasco also spent some time in prison."

"Go to hell, *españolazo*."

Melchor responds by pointing to Blai's cup:

"Your coffee's going to get cold."

The Terra Alta station chief throws his glasses on the table and, standing up, starts ranting and raving while he walks up and down the kitchen.

"You're off your rocker too, Melchor," he says. "That fucking guardia civil has sucked out your brains . . . But, how could you even consider something like this? Can you not see it's outrageous? What you should do is press charges against that fucking son of a bitch Mattson and let the Guardia Civil and the judges do their work . . . Really, Melchor, who do you think you are? Superman?"

"I don't think I'm anybody, Blai," Melchor answers. "And what we're going to do is not outrageous. I'll tell you the same thing I told Rosa last night: this is something that has to be done. Simple as that. If someone had done it before now, Cosette would not be where she is. And all those girls wouldn't have gone through what they did. By the way, Rosa is going to help me too."

Blai stops short.

"I don't believe it."

Melchor makes a tiny affirmative gesture.

"You've all gone crazy," Blai grumbles, starting to pace again. "And I should lock you up right now. That's what I should do."

"Blai."

"What?"

"Sit down, please. And drink your coffee."

Huffing and furious, Blai sits back down. There is no sugar in his coffee, but he stirs it vigorously.

"Let me tell you something," Melchor says.

Before he can continue, Blai points with his teaspoon.

"Don't try to blackmail me."

Melchor raises his hands a little, showing his empty palms.

"Calm down," he says. I won't try. I give up, I accept your refusal. Happy?"

Blai does not seem happy. In a single swallow, he downs his coffee.

"Let me tell you what I wanted to say," repeats Melchor, lowering his hands. "Do you know what that guy did to Cosette?"

"It doesn't matter what he did," Blai answers. "That's not the issue. And you know it."

"OK, but, will you let me tell you?"

Blai stares at him, still huffing. Then, coldly and devoid of inflection or dramatism, Melchor recalls his dialogues with the psychologist in Reus, Dr Mercadal and Dr Ibarz, mentions confinement, massages, fellatio and rape, he alludes to the wolves. On the other side of the kitchen table, the inspector listens with an increasingly sombre expression, fiddling with his reading glasses; the tie of his uniform has come loose and he's undone the top button of his shirt, as if he was having trouble breathing.

"That's what we know so far," Melchor concludes. "The doctors say we'll eventually find out the rest, but for our purposes it doesn't matter. What do you think?" He pauses; Blai does not answer. "Seventeen years old. Cosette is seventeen . . . A little girl. And I wonder: how many girls have had things like that happen to them in Mattson's house? Dozens? Hundreds?" Another pause. "And now tell me, what would you do if something similar had been done to one of your daughters? To Glòria, or Raquel. What would you have done, eh?"

Blai looks up at Melchor.

"I don't know," he says in a different, calmer tone. "If I told you I knew, I'd be lying . . . But what I do know is what should be done. And that is report it to the Guardia Civil."

"And if the Guardia Civil ignored you, like they did me?"

"Now they'll listen to you."

"Really? Why? How do you know? How do you know that Mattson doesn't have half the island under his control, like Carrasco says? Because that's the impression I got . . ." Now it's Melchor who's talking with an almost vehement emphasis. "Blai, please, you know how the world works, you know what

Carrasco says is plausible. More than plausible, I don't actually have a single fact that allows me to think what he says is false or that he's mad or whatever. But, well, let's suppose Carrasco is lying or exaggerating, and that what happened to me in Pollença was just bad luck and that, this time, the Guardia Civil and the court will do their jobs like they're meant to and we'll take Mattson to trial . . . Tell me, who is the judge going to believe? A seventeen-year-old girl, daughter of a fucking librarian from Terra Alta, or Rafael Mattson? Do you think Cosette's testimony is going to stand up against the ruses of the world's best lawyers, who are going to be the ones defending Mattson? How do you know I wouldn't be putting my daughter into hell, another hell, only worse, so bad that maybe she wouldn't be able to get out of that one? Is that what you'd do to your daughters?"

Melchor's string of questions hangs in the silence of the kitchen like a toxic gas or a pestilence. Blai's gaze is lost in the bottom of his cup and he has a very serious look on his face; Melchor can hear his breathing.

"No," the inspector admits. "I don't suppose I would. But this is no way to fix things."

"I agree," Melchor instantly accepts. "Give me another and I'll buy it."

Blai says nothing.

"There isn't one," Melchor assures him. "This is the only way. Take it or leave it. If you take it, there is a possibility that Mattson might pay for what he's done. If you leave it, there is none, or it's such a remote possibility that it almost doesn't exist. That's how things stand. That's what Salom understood. And what Vàzquez and Paca have understood. And Rosa. And that's what you should understand too, you even more than them . . . Look at me, Blai." The inspector looks. Melchor leans his elbows on the table and his head towards him. "I'm not saying Carrasco's plan is infallible. I'm saying we don't have any other. And I'm not saying we have to do exactly what Carrasco says . . . What I'm saying is this: that man is not a fantasist, I assure you, have a look at the internet and you'll see he was a real cop. While you're at it you can see how Mattson deals with people who don't dance to his tune, that's why Carrasco was in prison, he got rid of him by accusing him of being mixed up with a cartel . . . But here's what I was getting to. Carrasco has spent years thinking of a way to get rid of Mattson, there is nobody more interested in taking him down. So we should listen to him, we'll prepare everything as he suggests, we'll go to Pollença. And, if we see a better way to do it once we're on the ground, we'll do it that way, our way. I'll tell you another thing: if we reach the conclusion that it's all madness, as you say, we'll call it quits. I give you my word of honour . . . You know me, Blai. I'm not insane. I'm not a kamikaze. But, if we do what I've said, at least we won't have to reproach ourselves for not having tried everything. That's all I'm asking. That we try."

Blai has followed this explanation almost without blinking and, once Melchor stops speaking, looks away from him and around the kitchen: the sink, the drying rack with a couple of plates and a few pieces of cutlery recently washed up, the microwave, the cupboards, the Nespresso machine, the apple-shaped clock on the wall. The inspector furrows his brow, as he sometimes does when considering things, clenches his jaws with such force his chin throbs. When he looks back at the ex-cop, Melchor implores:

"Think it over, please."

Blai sighs, and stands up almost in slow motion while he puts his glasses in his shirt pocket, just below the force's crest.

Before he says a word, Melchor guesses what his reply is going to be.

"I don't have to think it over," he says, in effect, and straightens his tie without doing up the button of his collar. "What you are going to do is outrageous, as I said, and I have no intention of participating. Nor am I going to try to convince you not to carry on. What for, if you've already made your decision . . . But you can rest easy: you are my friend, I'm not going to turn you in, which is what I should do right this moment. You know what you're doing, you're a big boy now. And the same goes for the rest of them, including that loony Paca: if she wants to risk her career, let her. But don't let me hear of her recruiting anyone from her team. Not from her team or any other. Tell her for me."

"Blai . . ."

"Do not insist, this discussion is over, I have nothing more to say. Except for one thing. Don't mention this matter to me again, please. I don't want to know any more about it. Not a word. No message. Nothing. It's as if, today, you and I have not spoken. Got it?"

Blai has been perfectly clear, but Melchor does not give in: for some reason, now more than ever he harbours the certainty that the support of the Terra Alta station chief could be fundamental to the success of the operation and, although he has not detected a single crack in Blai's refusal, for the moment he has not the slightest intention of resigning himself to it, so he pours everything into trying to reverse it. That very afternoon he phones Salom, tells him what happened and asks him to try to convince his former colleague. Salom promises to try.

The next day, Blai does not show up for coffee at the bar in the plaza.

"Your friend has left you on your own?" Hiroyuki asks. "Is he ill? Have the two amigos of Terra Alta had a fight? Friends no more?"

Melchor answers the Japanese man evasively, and during the rest of the morning sends the inspector three or four WhatsApps that are not even answered. A short time before lunch he calls Salom.

"I've just talked to Blai," he says. "We're fucked: he doesn't even want to talk about it. I think we're going to have to do it without him."

"We can't do it without him."

"Well, we're going to have to."

Happy with Salom's determination, Melchor immediately gets in touch with Vàzquez and asks him the same thing he'd asked the former corporal.

"No way," the former chief of Egara's Central Abduction and Extortion Unit tells him a short time later, having just talked to the inspector. "Great to hear from me, great to hear from me, but in the end he told me to go to hell. He's the same as ever: a stubborn fucker. If you want the truth, I don't think we're going to be able to convince him."

Melchor rules out the option of turning to Paca Poch to put pressure on Blai, because he's almost certain it would be counterproductive. And he is starting to reconcile himself to the idea that he won't be able to count on his friend, when Carrasco phones him. The call startles him: Carrasco had warned him he'd only call if he had something urgent to communicate; it's the first thing Melchor reminds him.

"This is urgent," Carrasco replies. "We've got our D-day."

"So soon?"

262

"The sooner the better. You told me you're not into football, didn't you?"

Melchor says he's not. Carrasco insists:

"But even you must know that this year's Champions League final will be between Madrid and Barça."

"I saw the semi-final between Barça and Juve."

"Oh, it cheers me up that I'm going to risk my life with someone who lives in the real world. Tell me, what did you think?"

"About the match?"

"Of course."

Melchor finds the conversation disconcerting. Are they going to talk about football? He answers with the first thing that comes into his head:

"That Juve deserved to win."

"You're wrong. Barça deserved to win. I hate to admit it, but it's a fact. That's the good thing about football: it's nothing like life. In football the better team always wins, even if it doesn't always seem like it."

"Are we going to do it the day of the final?"

"Bingo. Same day and the same time. I had almost decided the ideal moment was the night of San Juan, when everyone's out dancing in the streets, but I've changed my mind. The night of the match is much better. Don't you realise? . . . Something like this has never happened in history. It's a unique event. Everyone will be watching television, the entire country paralysed, the whole world. An opportunity like this does not come around twice. It's not this Saturday, but the one after. That's our day. Have you got everything ready?"

"More or less," Melchor lies, thinking he'd better ask Rosa to advance him the two hundred thousand euros immediately. "I have a few details to tie up, but . . ."

"Don't worry. You've got nine days. Do you think that'll be enough?"

"Hope so."

"I've already told the people we need here, in Mallorca. Actually, it's just one, when the moment comes I'll introduce you . . . One more thing. I told you Mattson's people are watching me, so it's better if you rent the apartments you're going to need from there. It's really easy, have a look at the Airbnb website and you'll find tons of cheap apartments for one night. You won't need more than that. Rent them in different places, though, to avoid raising suspicions. Cars are even easier, maybe it would be best to rent them over there and come over with them on the ferry, though ideally some of you should come on the ferry and some by plane . . . Anyway, it's just common sense, discretion is fundamental, nobody should suspect you're together, you'll see how you manage. If you give me a secure email address, I'll send you all this written out and also a complete list of the necessary armaments and equipment, so you don't forget anything."

"I have the list. You sent it in the letter."

"Oh yeah, I forgot. I imagine you have the men we need . . . You trust them?"

"The ones I have, yes. They're comrades. Well, ex-comrades."

"How many have you got?"

"Four," Melchor says, counting himself. "I'll probably have to hire the rest, but I know where."

"Fantastic. If I were you I'd get them together as soon as possible. The ones you already have, I mean. So they can get to know each other, if they don't already, and to fill them in on the essentials, if you haven't already. I'll give them the details when we see each other."

"Can't you give them to me now?"

264

"Better not. We really shouldn't talk about this over the phone. Just in case. Really, the less we talk on the phone and by WhatsApp, the better . . . Also, I can't tell you some of the essential things, we need a specialist for that, and that's the person I told you about, you'll meet them when the time comes. In any case, the operation is complex but not difficult to execute. You and your friends can rest assured I have prepared it precisely, although we'll have to do it all really well to prevent problems from cropping up. That's why the group has to work very well together, at least the hard core of the group, and that's why it's best that you get them together as soon as you can. Tomorrow's better than the next day . . . You won't need to be in Pollença very long, a couple of days should suffice. The ideal time to arrive would be Friday at midday. In the afternoon I could give you the details of the operation and the next night we'll carry it out. Sunday morning you should all be back in Barcelona."

"Great."

"There is one more thing. The material we remove from Mattson's house: the photos, film footage, everything that can incriminate him."

"What about it?"

"We have to make it known. And it might not be that easy . . . I mean most likely the media won't dare to broadcast it. The ones based in Mallorca, definitely not, as I've told you Mattson has a lot of people by the balls. But I wouldn't trust the media in the rest of Spain either, or even in Europe or the United States."

"Are you sure you're not exaggerating? The media, no matter where, lives off airing shit, and this shit is irresistible. Any of them will buy it."

"You're an optimist, Melchor. When it comes to Mattson,

there is no way to exaggerate. You're forgetting who we're tak-ing on. Do you think it's so easy to mess with this man? . . . But, anyway, let's hope you're right. Although I would start thinking about it, just in case . . . Anyway, this is an important but lesser problem. When we've got our hands on the material, we'll be the ones who have Mattson by the balls. We'll be in touch. Until then, let's get to work."

Part Four

Pollença

The night she disappeared, Cosette was as disoriented as a little girl lost in a forest.

She had spent hours sunbathing on the beach and wandering around the port. At nightfall she went back to the Hostal Borràs and up to the room she had shared with Elisa Climent and which was now hers alone, showered, got dressed and went down to have dinner among the noisy evening activity of the terrace. At some point, while she was going through the photos she'd posted on Instagram since landing in Mallorca and eating a sandwich and drinking a can of 7up, her father phoned. She was expecting the call, but she didn't answer. After a few seconds she listened to the message he'd left. "Cosette," he said, "it's me, Papá. I'm at the bus station with Elisa, she just arrived. Please call me." Cosette had planned her reply very well; but still, she took her time answering. "Papá, don't call me, please," she wrote. "I don't want to speak to you. I'm fine. Don't worry and give me a bit of breathing space." Her father's reply also took its time. Contrary to her expectations, it was not another call; it wasn't a message insisting she come home either: just a simple question. "Have you got money?" it said. "Yes," Cosette lied. "I'll be back when it runs out." The last WhatsApp from her father arrived a minute later and surprised her even more than the previous one: it consisted of a yellow thumbs-up emoji.

She picked up the sandwich again, bit off a piece and, chewing the bite, thought that Elisa had been very persuasive with her father. An instant later she felt she'd made a mistake: she shouldn't have stayed in Pollença; she should have gone home with her friend; she should talk to her father right away, get it off her chest, clarify the situation. It was true that her father had committed a grave error – grave enough to have deceived her for her entire life – and so it was logical for her to be furious with him; but she should at least give him the chance to explain, to apologise, to try to correct his mistake.

She did not call her father, she didn't send him a WhatsApp. Suddenly relieved, she closed Instagram and started looking for plane tickets from Mallorca to Barcelona and bus timetables from Port de Pollença to Palma and from Palma to the airport. She had just found them when the relief disappeared, as suddenly as it had appeared: all at once she knew she couldn't go home. Not yet. She wouldn't have been able to say exactly why, but she couldn't. She was too wounded, too anguished, too confused. She didn't yet feel ready to forgive her father, nor to listen to his explanations, supposing he wanted or was able to give her any. No: she had decided to spend a few more days on the island and she was going to have them. Never before had she felt so lonely and never until then had she felt such a need to be alone. She had to calm down. She needed to reflect. It was better to stay.

She charged her meal to her hotel bill, went up to her room, brushed her teeth, put on her pyjamas, turned on the television and lay down on the bed on top of the covers. For a while she flipped through the channels, but when she didn't find anything that caught her attention, she turned off the television and picked up the Angela Carter novel she'd brought with her. It was called *Wise Children* and, even though she liked it a lot, she couldn't manage to concentrate on it, so she left it on the bedside table and turned out the light. From plaza Miquel Capllonch the sounds of laughter, cutlery and conversations rose up to her room, and in that darkness broken only by strips of light filtering in through the half-closed blinds, a whirlwind of ideas or scraps of ideas spun around uncontrollably in her head. She soon understood she was not going to be able to sleep, so she turned on a lamp, got up, got dressed and went outside.

It was ten-thirty, the terraces were still full of tourists and, under the trees that grew in the centre of the plaza, the nightly booze-up was starting to get underway. She headed towards the promenade and turned right, walking parallel to the sea, illuminated at that hour by the lively coastal glow and by a full moon that allowed her to glimpse, on the other side of the bay, the shadowy profile of the peninsula of Cap de Pinar. The night was warm, and there, too, the terraces of the bars, hotels and restaurants swarmed with people; some shops were even still open, as if they were already in peak tourist season and not just barely at its start. She stopped at an ice-cream shop and bought a two-scoop cone – strawberry and coconut – and was licking it until, near a little plaza that opened onto the sandy beach, the ice cream melted in her hands, at which point she turned around and headed back. She was trying not to think, she was trying to tire herself out after a day of idleness, so she'd be able to sleep; but, when she arrived at the door of the Hostal Borràs, she noticed she was wider awake than when she'd gone out. It was almost midnight, the session in the centre of the plaza was still growing and she crossed the street round the corner of the hostal, until she came to an establishment with a luminous sign: CHIVAS.

The doorman, a beefy guy with his hair pulled up in a sort of topknot and one earring, said hello, asked where she had left her girlfriend and, without waiting for an answer, let her in. She went down some stairs that led to a dance floor where reggaeton was playing; it was deserted: from her experience of the previous nights, Cosette knew it didn't start to fill up until the early hours of the morning, when the session in the plaza broke up, and the cocktail bars in the port closed, and the plaza Miquel Capllonch and the promenade were left empty. She didn't really like reggaeton, or not that much, but she started to move to its rhythm in the centre of the dance floor. She kept her eyes shut, drinking in the music, as if trying to blend in with it or dissolve inside it. She was like that for a while, dancing to whatever they played and noticing that, little by little, the nightclub was livening up. Until, at a certain point, while one song segued into another, someone touched her shoulder. She opened her eyes: in the epileptic light of the strobes, she saw a girl smiling at her as though they were friends.

"You don't remember me?" the stranger asked, shouting in her ear as the music blared out over the dance floor.

She was ten or twelve years older, with short, dark hair and a flowery dress with a full skirt; an insistent smile animated her face. Suddenly, Cosette remembered who she was.

"Of course," she shouted in her ear.

It seemed like an incredible coincidence. She had met her three nights earlier, in Tito's, one of Palma's emblematic clubs; it had been that girl who had convinced her and Elisa to change their initial plan of going to Magaluf for their last two days of holidays and go to Pollença instead. "Magaluf is a shithole full of foreigner tourists," she'd warned them. "If you haven't been to Pollença you haven't been to Mallorca."

"In the end you listened to me," the girl said. She nodded, happy she'd recognised her, almost as if someone had found her in the darkness of the forest. "Where's your friend?"

Cosette answered that Elisa had gone home. Still smiling, the girl looked surprised.

272

"And you?" she asked.

This time the answer consisted in shrugging her shoulders. The other kept looking at her, inquisitively, so she felt obliged to give an explanation that was no explanation.

"I'm going to stay a few more days," she said.

Less surprised than interested, the girl nodded. Then she said something that Cosette didn't catch and, taking her by the arm, dragged her over to the bar and asked her what she wanted to drink.

"Nothing," Cosette responded. "I don't have any money."

The girl interrogated her with an unequivocal look, which meant: "So, how is it that you're staying?" Cosette shrugged again. The other girl laughed inaudibly, and when the waitress appeared behind the bar, she ordered something. A moment later the waitress came back with two mixed drinks; following the girl's instruction, Cosette picked up one of the two and tasted it: it was vodka and orange. They clinked glasses and drank a sip. Then the girl said:

"Wait a moment. I'll be right back."

Cosette saw her go outside and return a few minutes later. Then the girl took another sip and, speaking in her ear again, asked:

"Do you want to earn five hundred euros?"

"What?"

"Do you want to earn five hundred euros tonight." She added: "With that money you could spend a few more days here."

The girl leaned away from her a bit and looked her in the eye. For a second, Cosette thought she was joking; the next second she knew she wasn't joking.

"Have you heard of Rafael Mattson?" the girl asked.

Cosette half-closed her eyes and smiled vaguely, as if saying: "Who hasn't?"

"He has a house near here, in Formentor," the girl explained. "There's a party there tonight. Shall we go?"

"Now?"

The other girl nodded. Cosette was still in shock.

"Is he a friend of yours?"

"Yeah. And he's a great guy. Really normal. Really nice. The first time I was at his house I told him about a friend of mine who was studying in Barcelona and that very night he brought her over in his private plane." The girl moved back a little to measure the impact of her anecdote. "You'll really like it, you'll see." She held out her hand and nodded towards the nightclub door: "If you want, we can go right now."

Cosette furrowed her brow and leaned over to speak into the girl's ear.

"They're going to pay me five hundred euros just to go to a party?"

"Exactly," the other girl insisted. "It's a bunch of old geezers. Politicians, businessmen, people like that. They want young girls, you know, to liven things up, they get bored on their own . . . You don't have to do anything special. Just be there. Have a drink. Chat. Then if they like you, they might help you. Mattson's done that with loads of girls. Sometimes he finances their studies. The guy is like that, generous, you'll see . . ." She turned back to hold out her hand, but this time she didn't wait for Cosette to take the initiative. "Come on, let's go," she said, taking her by the arm. "The house is fifteen minutes from here."

The girl's car, a Ford Escort, was parked very close to the nightclub, beside the corner of the Hostal Borràs. Before getting in, Cosette asked, since they were going to a party, if she could give her a minute to run up to her room and change, but the other said it wasn't necessary, that she looked just fine as she was, and they both got into the car, drove out of town and took a right towards the cabo de Formentor. The road soon became steep and turned into a mountain road zigzagging between the sea and a mass of shadows in which the car's headlights illuminated tall rocky cliffs, pine trees and fan palms. While she drove, the girl kept talking about Rafael Mattson, about luxury and generosity and good humour and extravagances; every once in a while they met a car coming down the road in the opposite direction. A few minutes later, after crowning the crest of the headland, they abruptly began to descend. Now the curves were reversed, the sea was down below on their left, and on the right the darkness grew increasingly intense. The girl had stopped talking, as if the road were absorbing all her attention; all they could hear was the noise of the wind buffeting the car, and every once in a while the sound of the sea crashing against the rocks. At one point Cosette asked if it was much further and the girl told her they were almost there.

"By the way," she added, "my name's Diana."

Cosette said her name.

"Are you French?" Diana asked.

Cosette said no, but didn't explain why she had a French name if she wasn't French – the girl didn't ask either – and, not knowing why, at that moment Cosette felt she shouldn't have accepted the invitation. In spite of that, she didn't dare ask her new friend to turn around and take her back to Port de Pollença; but she decided that, even though she was going to go to the party and spend a few minutes there, she would leave at the first opportunity.

It didn't take them long to reach the foot of the mountain, where the headlights shone on two signs that announced: CAP DE FORMENTOR and FORMENTOR. They took the second turning, passed a beach on the right – silvered by the moon – that spread out beyond a pine forest, turned up a paved lane which ran between wooded hillsides and passed by a huge building spotted with lights that sparked off the girl's loquacity again: as she drove up a dirt road that climbed a hill, with the sea on the right, she said the building they'd just passed was the Hotel Formentor, which was a historic establishment where many celebrities had stayed, mentioning Charlie

Chaplin and Grace Kelly. Finally, just after rounding a curve, the trail seemed to end at a big metal and wooden gate.

"Here we are," announced Diana, who had recovered her initial vivacity. Without turning off the engine she picked up her telephone and, while she typed a message, said: "They'll open it for us now."

A few seconds later, the gate slowly began to open. Once it was completely open, they drove down a ramp illuminated by a double string of lights at curb level, on the other side of which a vast lawn spread down to the sea. Beyond that stood the mansion: enormous, dark, built on the edge of the cliff, with white walls and big windows, a bit spectral. They parked beside an empty level area. Around them reigned a silence so profound that, if it weren't for the nearby sound of waves breaking against the rocks, she would have said the house was submerged in a mine shaft.

"Are you sure the party is here?" Cosette asked.

At that moment, a light switched on above an entrance in a lateral wing of the building; a second later the door opened and a silhouette of a female figure appeared in the doorframe.

"Look," said Diana. "There's Alexandra."

"Who's Alexandra?" Cosette asked.

"Mattson's housekeeper." Diana fixed up her hair in the rear-view mirror. "She lives here all year round, with her husband, they're both Chilean." Pulling the handle to get out of the car, she went on: "You'll see. We're going to have a great time."

1

On Sunday, six days before the night they'd fixed for the assault on Rafael Mattson's Mallorcan mansion, Melchor holds a meeting at his house. The encounter is at three-thirty in the afternoon; present are Paca Poch, Vàzquez and Salom. They still need another four people to complete the team Carrasco considers necessary in order to carry out the operation and, because Melchor does not know if any of his three companions know anyone who might join them, he spends a large part of Friday trying to recruit four experienced professionals from the depths of the darknet. Finally, after exchanging different messages with people advertising themselves with clearly invented names, he arranges a meeting in a place in the Zona Franca of Barcelona with four mercenaries who offer to do the job for a sum total of seventy thousand euros, not including expenses. The meeting is on Wednesday morning, when he should already have deposited six thousand euros into the professionals' bank account by way of an advance. On the afternoon of the same day, Melchor has arranged another meeting, in a flat in Nou Barris, with a guy with a German surname who, in exchange for twenty-five thousand euros, has committed to supplying almost all the equipment and armaments they need. Melchor also rents two cars at the Palma de Mallorca airport, two apartments in Pollença and another three in Port de Pollença. As for the ferry and plane tickets the group will need to get to Mallorca, as with the rest of the team, he has chosen to refine all of that at Sunday's meeting.

On Saturday morning he visits Cosette at the Mercadal Clinic. Melchor gets the impression that his daughter is better than she was seven days ago – her appearance is healthier, she's less sad and more communicative, she does not cry – although he's not certain that this apparent restoration reflects a genuine improvement, because he does not manage to speak with either Dr Mercadal or Dr Ibarz. That night he has dinner at Rosa's house and outlines the preparations he's been making (the only thing he omits, as always, is Salom's participation). He doesn't do this because she requests it, but because, especially after she advanced him the two hundred thousand euros on the bank loan, he considers her for all intents and purposes as one more member of the group, with the same rights as the rest of them to be kept informed. Rosa listens with attention, just as if all her doubts and objections had dissipated, but, when Melchor tells her who is coming to the next day's meeting, she interrupts to make sure Blai isn't one of them.

"I haven't been able to convince him," Melchor laments. "I was sure I'd manage it, but I haven't been able to. It's aggravating. Though I do understand. Anyway, it doesn't matter: we'll do it without him."

To Melchor's surprise, Rosa does not deplore Blai's absence but simply offers her house for the next day's meeting.

"It would be more discreet," she adds. "And you'll be more comfortable than in yours. I'll give Ana the day off and that's that. Also, maybe I could lend you a hand. After all, four heads think better than three."

"Thanks, but no," says Melchor, remembering Salom again. "I'd rather do it at my house. And I'd also rather you kept a bit on the margins. We might need you for other things. Probably not, of course."

Melchor mentions Carrasco's concern about the way to disseminate the incriminating material they should get out of Mattson's residence. Rosa asks:

"Wouldn't it be better to wait till you have it to think about that? Are you not getting a bit ahead of yourselves?"

"Could be," Melchor says. "But Carrasco insists we need to have a plan for it. And he might be right . . . You can't just put that information on the internet, because for Mattson it would be easy to neutralise it, make it pass for one more of the hoaxes that circulate about him. We need to get an authorised media outlet to release it, and I don't know if there are too many in Spain ready to detonate such a big scandal about Mattson. Carrasco thinks not. Neither in Spain nor in Europe, he says. Nor in the United States. Mattson has interests all over the world."

"It's true, but nobody can control the whole world, all the time and everywhere. Not even Mattson. Will nobody dare to bring this to light?"

"Can you think of anyone?"

"Not right at this moment. But let me give it some thought."

The next morning, while having breakfast on the terrace, Rosa asks Melchor:

"Have you ever heard of Gonzalo Córdoba?"

"No."

"He's the president of Caracol Televisión, the most important channel in Colombia. Do you remember the weekend I spent at La Inés, the family farm of my friend Héctor Abad, the writer? Remember I told you we were there with some friends of his? . . . Well, Gonzalo was one of them. We became good friends, I've seen him a couple of times since. He's not the owner of Caracol Televisión, but he's free to do what he wants, and he's a brave and honest man. I'm mentioning him because of what we were talking about last night: about how to air Mattson's dirty laundry, he might be our man. He wouldn't be frightened off."

Vàzquez arrives at two-thirty. Melchor has prepared a tomato and anchovy salad and some spaghetti a la carbonara for the two of them. They eat in the kitchen, talking about Blai, about Blai's refusal to join the group and about the repercussions his absence could have on the outcome of the operation they're organising; Vàzquez also expresses his distrust at the prospective of having to work with mercenaries, his lack of confidence in them.

"It's not that the idea fills me with enthusiasm," Melchor agrees. "But what choice do we have?"

After Vàsquez suggests without much conviction a couple of names of former comrades who he could try to recruit to replace the mercenaries, Melchor is still doubtful:

"I don't know. Let's see what Salom and Paca have to say. Anyway, on Wednesday I'll meet those people and we'll clear up our doubts."

Then they change the subject and Melchor asks Vàzquez if his wife is aware of their plans.

"Are you crazy or what?" Vàzquez says. "If Vero gets wind of this mess, she'll hang me by the balls. And you too. I told her I'm with a friend in Prades, in the south of France, at a sheep-dog competition. And that next weekend I'm going to Mallorca with you and Blai, to talk over old times and stuff . . . Poor girl, she'll believe anything."

Shortly before the agreed time, when both men are still stacking their plates and glasses in the dishwasher, Paca Poch shows up; Salom arrives a few minutes later. None of Melchor's three friends know each other personally, but they have all heard of each other. The host makes the introductions and, with Salom's help, makes coffee. They haven't finished serving it when the buzzer rings; three pairs of eyes converge on Melchor.

"Is someone missing?" Paca Poch asks.

Melchor replies with a frown, but on his way to the front hallway it occurs to him that maybe Rosa has decided to join the meeting. He's mistaken: the intercom camera frames Blai's well-built body, dressed in civilian clothes.

"Open up, Melchor."

The Terra Alta station chief appears on the landing unmistakably fuming.

"What's up with you?" Melchor asks.

Blai doesn't answer until the door closes behind him.

"What do you think's up?" The inspector drills an accusatory index finger into his friend's sternum. "I've spent the whole morning listening to Rosa crying. That's what's up. Can you do me a favour?"

"Whatever you want."

"Wipe that half a smile off your face, go on."

Two very long seconds of silence greet Blai's entrance to the dining room, where Vàzquez, Salom and Paca Poch turn towards him with varying degrees of bewilderment on their faces. The inspector looks at them one by one, shaking his head.

"What a bunch of nutcases," he mutters.

Blai hugs Salom and then Vàzquez, who, as he recalls out loud, he hasn't seen since the day he married Verónica. Paca Poch, however, he only points at with the same finger he'd just been poking into their host's chest.

"You and I have a conversation pending, sergeant."

"Whenever you like, boss."

"Don't call me boss. And, just in case, keep it nice and quiet."

"Yes, sir, boss."

Vàzquez laughs and Paca Poch winks at him, and the four of them are soon caught up in conversation while, repressing a slight sense of euphoria, Melchor finishes serving coffee. A while later they're all sitting around the dining table, Blai and Paca Poch opposite Melchor, Vàzquez on his left and Salom on his right. To bring them all up to date, Melchor recapitulates: he tells them about Cosette, about Benavides, Carrasco and Mattson. When he finishes summing up the dialogue he had with the former guardia civil in Can Sucrer, Blai admits:

"It's possible that what this guy told you might have some substance."

"No shit," Vàzquez interrupts. "Of course it has substance. What do you think we're doing here?"

Melchor asks Blai to explain.

"Do you remember the friend I told you about?" the inspector asks, turning to him. "The national policeman who works in Palma, the one who helped us get the security camera footage from the nightclub . . ." Melchor nods. "Yesterday I phoned him. I asked about Mattson, told him there were rumours about things going on at the mansion in Formentor and he gave me to understand that this was a subject it was better not to touch. That I should steer clear. Truth is, I smelled a rat."

Thinking that perhaps Rosa's tears had not been the only reason for Blai's change of mind, Melchor carries on reminding them in broad terms of Carrasco's plan or rather what he knows of Carrasco's plan, explaining that the former guardia civil will supply the details of the operation on the eve of the assault, in a meeting that will take place in Pollença, reveals the date and time chosen as well as the reasons for the choice and tries to reassure them by repeating what he said to Blai days earlier: even if in principle they are going to follow Carrasco's plan, if once they're in Pollença they didn't like his proposal or it didn't convince them or they thought it too risky or unsatisfactory, as a whole or at either end, then they would carry out the operation as they thought best; ultimately, the final decision would always be theirs.

"In the worst case," Melchor emphasises, seeking the words that will completely reassure his comrades and clear away any shadow of doubt or uncertainty they might still be harbouring, "if we reach the conclusion that his plan is not clear, or not ready, or whatever, we'll cancel the operation and come home. We'll always be in time for that."

"I have no intention of going home empty-handed," says Vàzquez.

"Me neither," Paca Poch backs him up.

"You be quiet," Blai says.

"Who said anything about coming home empty-handed?" Melchor intervenes. "The important thing is that the things come out, whether or not at our first attempt. And sometimes you have to fail partially to be able to triumph later."

"That's true," Salom says.

There is a tense silence. Melchor asks:

"Are we in agreement?"

His gaze jumps from one face to the next in search of signs of acceptance. All of them end up nodding, also with varying degrees of conviction. Melchor then moves on to the subject of equipment, armaments and the men necessary for the attack and, when he mentions the two meetings he's set up for Wednesday in Barcelona, Blai interrupts him again. Melchor was expecting the interruption, but not his friend's categorical tone.

"You can cancel those," he says. "And you can start paying Rosa back her money."

"Money?" asks Vàzquez, to whom Melchor has said not a single word of the bank loan Rosa has given him an advance on, information he has also withheld from the rest of them. "What money?"

"None." Blai points with his head at Melchor. "This guy, who's a punk." Then he continues: "The automatic rifles, pistols, cartridges, handcuffs, balaclavas, clips and ammunition we'll get out of the cellar. Nobody has any reason to notice, and even less on a weekend. The torches we can get at any supermarket and the chainsaws at a Bauhaus or Leroy Merlin."

"What the fuck are we going to need chainsaws for?" Vàzquez asks again.

"What else was there?" Blai asks.

"Nine bulletproof vests, nine sets of laser sights, a frequency inhibitor and two fake licence plates," Melchor enumerates.

"Cortabarría can lend us all that stuff," says Vàzquez, who was the commanding officer of the man mentioned when he ran the Central Abduction and Extortion Unit. "He's in charge of Missing Persons at Egara."

"I had thought of him," Blai admits. "When Cosette was missing he lent us a hand."

"Not one," Paca Poch corrects him. "Both of them."

"He owes me a couple of favours," Vàzquez explains. "So you can count on him."

"We should ask him for the cars as well," Blai adds. "To do something like this I don't want to be driving any old piece of junk. And, now that we're on the subject, I'm not going over there without false papers."

"Cortabarría can get all that for us," Vàzquez insists.

"You see?" Now Blai speaks to Melchor. "The material and weapons are no problem. The problem is the people."

"There's five of us," Vàzquez counts. "Plus the two in Pollença, seven. We're three short."

"I already told you I've got a meeting in the Zona Franca on Wednesday," Melchor says. "They've promised me four good professionals. Instead of hiring four, I'll hire three."

"And I've already told you I don't trust those people," Vàzquez says. "A mercenary is a mercenary."

"Ugh," Paca Poch grunts. "I wouldn't trust guys like that as far as I could throw them."

Melchor reads in the eyes of Blai and Salom that neither of them disagree with the scepticism or outright refusal they've just heard. Acquiescing, he gets things started:

"Any ideas?"

Vàzquez brings up the names of the two former colleagues he mentioned during lunch, but does so with the same lack of enthusiasm as before. And when Melchor is about to sound out Paca Poch about the members of her unit, he remembers that Blai unequivocally forbade the sergeant from involving anyone under her command in the operation and aborts the question. At that moment the inspector speaks up again.

"Maybe we don't need anybody else," he conjectures. "Are seven people who work well together not enough to assault that house?"

"Depends what the house is like," Paca Poch says.

"What ten can do seven can also do," Blai hazards.

"Perhaps," Melchor accepts. "But only Carrasco knows. He's the only one who knows the house, the security systems, the people protecting it and the rest. So, at least for the moment, we have to trust him. If Carrasco says we need to be a minimum of ten, the best idea is to get another three people."

"Or not," Blai perseveres. "Had we not agreed we're going to do this our way, not Carrasco's? Besides, the more we are, the more probabilities there are that someone runs their mouth off and everything gets fucked. I trust the people here in this room. I don't know about any others."

"That's true, Melchor," Salom chimes in. "Are we going to risk our hides with people we don't know?"

"Not me," Paca Poch says.

"Me neither," says Vàzquez.

"It seems riskier to me doing it with those people, no matter how good they are," Salom argues, "than doing it on our own, even if there aren't enough of us according to Carrasco. If he wants to do it with who we've got, we'll do it; if he doesn't, we won't . . . But, after waiting so long for a chance, I bet he'll want to. If he knows what's good for him."

Melchor stares at Salom. Then he looks at Blai, who shows him the palms of his hands in a gesture at once interrogative and conclusive."

"It looks to me like the four of us are in agreement," he says. "How about you?"

Melchor reflects for a moment.

"Fine," he accepts. "We'll do it on our own."

The meeting ends shortly after seven, after they've made all the essential decisions to carry out the operation, or the ones that, at that moment, without yet knowing the details Carrasco will reveal in Mallorca, they judge essential. At the end, Blai sums up what was said and Melchor insists on one matter in which, he suddenly thinks, he hasn't insisted on enough. He reminds them all that it's possible Mattson's men may have tapped his phone, because Carrasco's is tapped, and asks them all to always communicate only over safe lines, and to limit calls to those of maximum urgency or necessity and to restrict communications among themselves. Paca Poch has persuaded them that it's safer to write to each other over Telegram than WhatsApp, so Melchor asks, if they have to send messages, to stick to Telegram.

When Melchor finishes speaking, Blai takes over again:

"Questions? Comments?"

They all look around at each other with questioning looks, but nobody says a word. They are still sitting around the dining table, all except Paca Poch, who has stood up several times during the meeting and has now been on her feet for a while, leaning against the frame of the window that looks out on calle Costumà and through which a dwindling light shines in. The table is covered in the debris of their meeting: two empty bottles of mineral water, five empty coffee cups, five empty glasses, three pens and a notebook with a blue cover with several torn-out squared pages on which Melchor, Paca Poch and Salom have taken notes or drawn diagrams. None of those present smokes, but, after being shut up in there for more than three uninterrupted hours, the dining room is stuffy and needs airing.

"Well," concludes Blai, leaning on the table to stand up, "if there's nothing more—"

Melchor grabs his arm.

"Just one thing," he says.

Blai turns towards him.

"What?"

Melchor looks away from the Terra Alta station chief and at Salom, then at Vàzquez and at Paca Poch; finally he looks again at Blai. Then he says:

"Thanks."

2

On Monday morning, Hiroyuki welcomes Blai to the bar in the plaza jumping for joy.

"What's up, man?" The Japanese man interrogates the police chief, points to Melchor and protects his face like a boxer in the ring. "Two amigos of Terra Alta no longer fighting? I ask your friend for you. He tell you? Where are you? Ill?"

"Where was I going to be?" Blai rests a pacifying hand on Hiroyuki's shoulder. "Chasing your yakuza mates. So they don't make mincemeat out of you."

During the rest of the morning, from the library, Melchor cancels the bank loan for two hundred thousand euros, as well as the reservation for one of the two cars he rented for the next weekend at the Mallorca airport and two of the five apartments where he planned to put up the team, one in Pollença and another in Port de Pollença. He also cancels the meeting with the German arms dealer at the Nou Barris flat and the interview in the Zona Franca with the four mercenaries (this means he loses the six thousand euros of the advance, which doesn't bother him too much). In the afternoon, Vàzquez writes to him on Telegram that, as they'd agreed the previous evening, he has just spoken to Cortabarría, who has committed to getting the material they need and giving it to Blai and Melchor on Thursday night at headquarters in Egara. "I didn't tell him what we wanted it for," he concludes. "And he didn't ask me. I told you he was a decent guy." "Perfect," Melchor congratulates him. "He told me they'll have a car ready for us," Vàzquez goes on. "And he asked me to get each of us to send him a passport-sized photo today. He needs them to prepare the false documents. Meanwhile, he's given me five aliases and five passport numbers, so you can start buying the tickets." In his last message, Vàzquez says he'll ask the other three for photos and send them along to Cortabarría, and he attaches the list of false names and numbers. As soon as he receives it, Melchor starts looking for tickets. At the previous evening's meeting they decided that, Friday morning, Vàzquez, Paca Poch, Salom and he himself would fly on different flights from Barcelona to Palma de Mallorca, but Melchor discovers that there are only three direct Barcelona–Palma flights in the first half of the day and decides that he and Paca Poch will both travel on the last one. As for Blai, Melchor gets him a ticket for the car ferry that leaves the port of Barcelona first thing on Friday morning, and another for the ferry that departs from the port of Palma first thing Sunday morning. Once he's bought all four return tickets, he sends them to his colleagues by email.

In the afternoon Melchor drives to a Bauhaus four kilometres up the Reus–Tarragona motorway, where he buys two Husqvarna chainsaws, and then he drives to Tortosa. There he buys another identical chainsaw at the Leroy Merlin store on avenida de la Generalitat and a set of eight battery-operated torches from the Lidl on avenida de Catalunya; he also gets four passport-sized photos taken in a studio called Gerard Fotògraf. Later, when he gets to Rosa's house for dinner, he scans the photos and sends them by email to Vàzquez.

During dinner he does not fall into the hypocrisy of rebuking Rosa for interceding on his behalf with Blai, but he doesn't thank her either. He simply sums up the decisions they took on Sunday that they've started implementing today. Rosa asks some questions, which Melchor tries to answer, and expresses some doubts, fears and worries, which Melchor tries to allay. Then he asks:

"Have you spoken to your Colombian friends?"

"I've spoken to Héctor Abad," Rosa answers. "I only told him that I might be able to get hold of material that proves Mattson is a sexual predator."

"And?"

"He assured me that if I do, Gonzalo Córdoba will be delighted to fuck up that bastard's life. And so will he."

First thing the next morning, Melchor calls the Mercadal Clinic and asks to speak with the director, but he's told he's busy and is asked to call back in ten minutes. He spends five of those ten minutes phoning Dolors, his co-worker. He explains that something unexpected has arisen and this Friday he won't be able to do his shift at the library because he has to go to Barcelona.

"Is Cosette worse?" the girl worries.

"No," he answers. And, as if formulating a desire, he affirms: "Cosette is recovering. Little by little, but she's getting better." Then he justifies his Friday absence with the pretext of administration tasks, which he does not specify. And he adds: "Could you cover for me?"

Dolors agrees and Melchor calls the clinic again. This time they put him straight through to Dr Mercadal, who Melchor rushes to give a hopeful report of his Saturday visit.

"She's better," the therapist confirms. "I said you should have faith in your daughter. And that she'll get through this."

290

Dr Mercadal enumerates some of the progress Cosette has made and insists that the most important thing is bringing to the surface the events that occurred in Mattson's mansion, to be able to confront and understand them.

"She's a very brave girl," Mercadal repeats. "And that's why she's recovering much faster than we expected. I wouldn't want to be unduly optimistic, but, if things carry on the way they've been going in the last few days, you might have her home in two or three weeks. In any case, we can speak about all this on Saturday, Dr Ibarz also has things to tell you."

"That's precisely why I'm calling," Melchor says, happy with the good news. "I have to be somewhere else on Saturday. Any chance I could see Cosette and speak with you on Friday morning?"

"Impossible," the doctor says. "The rules of this house are what they are, and must be respected. Respecting them is precisely what has allowed Cosette to get better. We're not going to violate them now . . . You understand, don't you? If you want, you can speak to her over the phone on Friday, but only between twelve and one."

Melchor does not insist, seizes the alternative the doctor offers and says goodbye. He devotes the rest of the day to double-checking the preparations for the assault, including exchanging a few messages, only indispensable ones, with Vàzquez, Paca Poch and Salom; he doesn't need to write to Blai, because he sees him every morning in Hiroyuki's bar. Finally, at dusk, he sends a message to Carrasco. "Everything ready over here," he says. "Here too," Carrasco replies. "When can we all meet in Pollença?" Melchor thinks for a couple of seconds. "How about Friday at 7pm?" he types. "Perfect," Carrasco replies. "Send me the addresses of the apartments where you'll be staying." Melchor does as he says. "Only three?" Carrasco asks. Melchor has no intention of revealing in advance that four rather than seven people are travelling with him from Barcelona, so he simply replies: "Don't worry. That'll be enough." A short time later he receives Carrasco's last message. "OK. Let's meet at 19.00 on Friday at the apartment on calle Sant Sebastià," Melchor reads, thinking that Carrasco does not want the meeting before the attack to be held at Can Sucrer. "It's in the old quarter of Pollença. Ask everyone to be punctual."

The next morning, Wednesday, Melchor and Blai take leave of each other in the plaza de la Farola until that night, after having their coffee in Hiroyuki's bar. Melchor spends the rest of the morning and half the afternoon concentrating on library work, which he has almost completely ignored all week, and, when he gets home after his shift, he finishes reading *A Nest of Gentlefolk*, the Turgenev novel he's been reading recently. Later, after eating dinner and starting the dishwasher, he begins to read *A Sportsman's Sketches*, also by Turgenev, which he likes more than the novel and which manages to absorb him completely. Around midnight he leaves home again, gets into his car, takes the Zaragoza road and, once he gets to the detour that leads to La Plana industrial estate, where Gráficas Adell still has its offices and original factory, turns right, follows a paved road and then a dirt road that ends in an empty field. There he stops the car and turns off the engine, but remains sitting behind the wheel. Around him, the silence is dense and the darkness almost total: a moon shaped like a cutlass shines in the sky, and in the distance, on the invisible hills of the Sierra de La Fatarella, tiny red lights blink on the wind turbines. For twenty minutes Melchor does not turn on the radio or listen to music or move from his seat, until, at the end of that period of time, two blurry dots of silvery light appear in the rear-view mirror and approach until they turn into the headlights of a vehicle that parks beside his. Melchor gets out and, while he helps Blai and Paca Poch move the rifles, pistols, magazine cartridges, handcuffs, clips, balaclavas and boxes of ammunition they've just taken out of the station into the boot of his car, asks:

"All in order?"

"All in order," Blai answers. "As long as nothing happens this weekend and nobody misses this arsenal, of course."

"Do you know the first thing Salom told me when I arrived in Terra Alta?" Melchor remarks to Paca Poch.

"What?" the sergeant asks.

"Don't worry," Melchor recalls. "Here in Terra Alta nothing ever happens."

Paca Poch laughs.

"He was right."

"Sure," Blai murmurs. "Nothing ever happens. Until it does."

Melchor and Blai leave for Barcelona at dusk the next day. They travel in Melchor's car, loaded with the armaments and material, but they spend the trip talking of everyday things, as if it were any other day and they were sitting on the terrace of Hiroyuki's bar, drinking coffee; they also talk about Cortabarría, who is expecting them at Headquarters in Egara and who neither of them has seen in the last ten years.

Just before eleven they stop at the entrance to Egara, between Sabadell and Terrassa, on the outskirts of Barcelona, and, after identifying themselves to the guards, one of them says that Sergeant Cortabarría is waiting for them in the garage. Melchor and Blai drive across the car park in front of the complex, where at that hour of the night there are just a few vehicles remaining, they skirt around the main building, drive down into the garage and, without getting out of the car, start looking for the sergeant in the insipid light of the fluorescent bulbs, until they spot a tall and burly guy waving and walking towards them from the back of the underground car park.

"The seventh cavalry of Terra Alta," Cortabarría jokes as they get out of the car. "Welcome home."

The sergeant shakes Blai's hand and hugs Melchor. Physically he's hardly changed — he still has the same blond and messy hair, the same direct gaze, the same muscular vigour — although he has grown a moustache that almost completely covers his harelip. He's wearing a brand-new pair of trainers, old jeans and a worn leather jacket. The three men walk to one end of the garage while, in answer to Blai's questions, Cortabarría tells them that he married a corporal a couple of years ago and they've just had twins. When a black Audi Q7 comes into view, the sergeant points it out.

"That's the car," he announces. "It's mine. Missing Persons', I mean. We confiscated it from a narco, put reserved plates on it and we've been using it for our work. But the plates on it now are fakes, the ones the narco used, I put them back on. So nobody can trace it back to you or to us."

Cortabarría opens a door of the vehicle and shows them the interior: it's empty and recently cleaned; it smells vaguely of lemon.

"And the equipment?" Blai asks.

The head of Missing Persons leads them around to the boot and opens it. It's very spacious, but just as empty as the rest of the car. A teasing spark flashes in Cortabarría's pupils when Melchor and Blai turn to him uncomprehending. Then the sergeant disappears and, a few seconds later, the car's engine starts and the left indicator starts blinking and the sidelights come on while the back of the back seat opens and reveals a false bottom, as deep as a cave, in which Melchor first sees several bulletproof vests.

"It's totally undetectable." Cortabarría has returned to their side leaving the motor running. "When the seat back is in its place, knock on it and it doesn't sound hollow. The narco used it to transport drugs, and not even our dogs could smell what was in there."

"How do you open it?" Blai asks.

Melchor guesses:

"Putting it in reverse and turning on the left indicator?"

"No more, no less," says the sergeant. "Anyway, if you have to take the ferry to Mallorca with all that artillery, I think this is what you need."

The three men spend a moment admiring the car's secret compartment.

"You're a fucking star, Cortabarría," Blai says.

"Inside is all the stuff Vàzquez asked me for," he carries on, impervious to the compliment. "Nine bulletproof vests, nine laser sights, a frequency inhibitor and two false licence plates . . . Oh, another thing." Now he points to a sort of router, with an antenna and a lever. "The frequency inhibitor. It's heavy duty, the strongest on the market. Strong enough to nullify an anti-inhibitor. But don't trust it."

"Does that mean we can't be sure it'll protect us completely?"

"That means don't trust it," Cortabarría repeats. Then he takes five passports out of his jacket pocket and hands them to the inspector. "Your documents. They were made by a friend in forensic document analysis who has a contact in National Police in Canillas. He really is a star."

While Blai examines the fake passports one by one, Melchor goes over to his car, drives it to where the Audi Q7 is parked and, in the blink of an eye, the three men move the weapons and material they've brought from the Terra Alta station to the false bottom of the Audi and restore the back seat to its position, leaving the empty boot visible again.

"OK," Cortabarría says, rubbing his hands. "Now you're going to have to forgive me: I have to take off, as my wife's on duty and the babysitter can only stay till midnight."

Melchor leaves Egara driving his own car, with Blai following him in the narco's Audi Q7, and that night, after eating a dry sandwich in a bar near the Rambla, they both sleep in the flat Rosa keeps on calle Pau Claris, next to plaza Urquinaona. The next morning, Melchor wakes up a while after Blai has already left: the ferry to Palma sets sail at nine o'clock and the inspector had to meet Vàzquez right before embarking, to give him his, Salom's and Paca Poch's false passports, so all three will have the necessary documents to take their respective morning flights. Later, Melchor has a leisurely breakfast in a Café di Roma, leafing through *La Vanguardia*, and, around eleven, he drives to the airport, where he arrives an hour and a half before his flight's departure time. He leaves his car in the Terminal 1 car park, passes through security, locates his plane's boarding gate and stations himself at a prudent distance.

From there, at exactly twelve noon, the time given to him by Dr Mercadal, he calls Cosette. As a precaution, he calls her from the same telephone he uses to communicate with Carrasco and the others, and the first thing his daughter asks is why he isn't going to see her this Saturday. The tone of her question is not complaining but perky, almost festive, and at that moment Melchor makes an irrational decision, which surprises even himself: he tells Cosette the truth. So he confesses he's in the airport, about to fly to Mallorca; he tells her about Carrasco, Rosa, Blai, Salom, Vàzquez, Paca Poch; he explains the project they have in hand. Cosette listens in such complete silence that Melchor has to check several times to make sure the call hasn't been cut off. Meanwhile, the flight attendants arrive at the boarding gate and Melchor watches the queue of passengers gradually grow in front of it, among whom he recognises at a certain moment Paca Poch, who walks past without looking at him, shielded behind a pair of big sunglasses, a low-cut colourful camisole, extremely tight jeans and very high-heeled sandals. When he finishes his explanation, Melchor wonders if, on the other end of the line, Cosette is crying. Then he asks her, and she says no and, to his surprise, instead of asking him any questions or making any comment or criticism, she begins to tell him what she has done during the week. Melchor listens disconcerted, not knowing what to think. In front of him, the boarding gate opens and begins to swallow the first passengers; when it gets to the last ones, Melchor says goodbye to Cosette, promises he'll go and see her next Saturday without fail. He is about to hang up when he hears:

"Papá."

Using his free hand to give his boarding pass to one of the flight attendants, Melchor asks:

"What?"

"Can I ask you something?"

"Of course."

Cosette takes a second to continue:

"Finish him off."

3

Shortly after landing at Palma airport, Melchor takes a bus into the capital on which Paca Poch is also travelling. Twenty minutes later he disembarks at the station, on the plaza de España, buys a ticket for the next bus in the direction of Pollença and, while waiting for its departure to be announced, orders a tuna sandwich and a Coca-Cola at the station bar while at a certain distance from him, on the other side of the room, Paca Poch has a glass of red wine and some tapas sitting at a table. When he finishes eating, Melchor orders a double espresso, and at that moment an excessively combed guy, who looks like he fancies himself a Don Juan, sits down next to Paca Poch. Spying on them out of the corner of his eye, Melchor sees how the man starts hitting on the sergeant and she flirts or pretends to flirt, talks, giggles, waves her hands around, until the guy suddenly goes silent and sits very rigid and looks very serious at the same time as the blood seems to drain from his face and his features seem to slacken. Seconds later, without another word, the guy stands up and walks away.

Twenty minutes later the bus leaves for Pollença. Melchor takes a seat in the back row; Paca Poch, three rows ahead. It's high season now, the vehicle is almost full and Melchor soon

298

falls asleep, with the jagged profile of the Sierra de Tramuntana on his left cutting into the metallic blue of the horizon. He wakes up half an hour later, when the bus makes its first stop, in Inca; then it stops again in the same town, and later in Crestatx, until, at the first stop in Pollença, Melchor gets off along with a handful of passengers, among them Paca Poch. Puzzled, Melchor wonders why his friend is getting off there when she should stay on for two more stops, until Port de Pollença, where he rented her an apartment a few days ago; then he realises that there is barely an hour and a half left until the meeting with Carrasco in Pollença and understands that the sergeant has decided it doesn't make sense to go as far as the port only to have to come straight back to town almost immediately.

Following the directions on his mobile, Melchor forgets about Paca Poch and walks into the old quarter of Pollença, an intricate medieval labyrinth of narrow cobbled streets, passes the Convent of Sant Domingo, crosses the main square and takes a right on calle Major, walks between tourist shops, stately brownstone mansions, with green blinds and wrought iron balconies, and, before reaching the plaza de Sant Jordi, turns left on calle Sant Sebastià and rings a bell. Salom answers, having arrived in Pollença that morning.

"All good?" Melchor asks.

"All perfect," Salom replies. "The rest of them won't be long."

The apartment is a tiny two-bedroom affair, with a bathroom, dining room and kitchen, furnished with sober pragmatism; there is natural light everywhere, except for the bathroom and kitchen, but the dining room is illuminated by a large window overlooking the calle Sant Sebastià. The others start to arrive before the expected time. Paca Poch is the first; Vàzquez, second. A little while later Carrasco appears, in a suit and tie, carefully shaved and with his hair closely cropped. The former guardia civil says hello to Melchor and allows him to introduce him to his friends; then he asks if he's got all the equipment and weapons that he's requested and, when Melchor assures him he has, sits down at the dining table and pulls out a notebook and several maps from the leather satchel he's carrying. Observing him, Melchor is no longer thinking of an ancient warrior or a samurai, like the first time he saw him; now the image that comes into his head is that of a top executive, or a hired assassin.

The sixth person to enter the apartment unsettles them all a little, except for Carrasco, who introduces her as a former sub-ordinate now affiliated with a security company (he does not specify the name of the company, or where it might be based). Her name is Catalina and she is a tiny, very slim, dark-haired and compact woman, with a childish face and a nervous gaze that in the blink of an eye scans the room and everyone in it; she can't be much older than Paca Poch, but she's barely half her size. Carrasco, who calls her Caty, invites her to sit beside him and the two start to talk. Until, a few minutes after seven, Inspector Blai barges into the apartment. His first words don't seem addressed to anyone in particular:

"I haven't seen so many anarchist flags since my father used to take me to CNT rallies."

"It's not an anarchist flag," Carrasco explains, shaking his hand after Melchor introduces them. "It's the flag of Pollença."

Blai's second comment is a rebuke and only for Paca Poch:

"You could have dressed a bit more discreetly, Paca."

"You have to draw attention to avoid drawing attention, boss," the sergeant replies.

After Blai's arrival, Melchor sits down opposite Carrasco and tells him:

"We can start whenever you want."

Carrasco looks at him uncomprehendingly. Blai and Salom take seats across from him, one on either side of Melchor; Paca Poch sits on his left and Vàzquez on Caty's right. Carrasco observes them one by one before turning back to Melchor:

"And the rest of them?"

"We're all here," he answers.

"I told you we need to be ten," Carrasco reminds him. "I'm only counting seven."

"I couldn't get anybody else," Melchor admits. "We'll have to make do with who we've got."

Carrasco observes him with a furrowed brow. He has knotted his tie conscientiously and is wearing a very clean shirt and impeccably pressed suit, as if he has dressed for a ceremony. Suddenly, he almost smiles, his brow smooths and, for a moment, his stony boxer's or miner's expression slackens a little.

"It seems I didn't explain myself clearly," he says to Melchor and no-one else. "If I told you we needed ten people, it's because that's how many we need. One or two more would not go amiss, but any fewer and it would be too risky."

"If it's too risky, we'll leave it," Blai interrupts.

"I'm not leaving anything," Paca Poch hastens to say.

"You be quiet, Paca," the inspector says.

"I'm with her." Vàzquez points to the sergeant. "I haven't come this far to back out now."

"Melchor, what did we agree the other day?" Blai asks.

Melchor does not respond. Sitting on his right, Salom also remains silent, as does Caty.

"Too risky," Carrasco repeats. "Mattson's house is a fortress. Ten people is the minimum we need. There's no other way to be sure it'll work. I told you."

"You also told me there was only one opportunity to do it," Melchor reminds him; he brings in his companions with a barely perceptible movement of his head and adds: "Well, then this is the opportunity. We have everything: the right material, the right day, the right people. Fewer than you wanted, OK, but we have them." He turns a little bit to his left. "You said it yourself the other day, Blai: what ten people can do so can seven." Turning back to Carrasco: "And I'm sure we can find a way to do it. Just us. I can assure you of one thing: each one of these people is worth two."

"Bullshit," says Paca Poch. "I'm worth three."

Vàzquez laughs. But he's the only one.

"This is the opportunity," Melchor repeats. "Do you really think you're going to get another?"

Carrasco does not take his eyes off him, as if mulling over his reply.

"He already told you, Melchor," Blai insists. "It's too dangerous. The joke's over. We're here because you told us this guy has spent I don't know how many years preparing this and that he knew how to do it, if we do it the way he says, it'll all work. Great . . . But now it turns out that this same guy says no, that it's impossible, that it's too dangerous and we should leave it. So do what he says and that'll be that, just as we were going to do what he said before. It makes sense . . . We also agreed, that if we reached the conclusion that it's all madness, we would leave it and be all square. Well, it's not us who've reached that conclusion. It's him."

"I haven't said it would be impossible," Carrasco corrects him. "Or that it was madness. I only said it was too dangerous."

"As things stand, it amounts to the same thing," Blai says. "Enough of this insanity, Melchor. You also told us you're no madman or kamikaze. Well, prove it. Press formal charges against Mattson and let's all go home. That's what needs to be done . . . Let the justice system deal with him."

"The justice system is not going to deal with Mattson," Carrasco corrects him again. "Go home if you want, but forget about that."

This last comment unleashes an argument between Blai, Vàzquez and Paca Poch; Salom and Caty follow it without getting involved, while Melchor wonders if Blai joined the operation at the last minute not to help execute it but to sabotage it (he even wonders if that was precisely what Rosa asked of him). Opposite him, Carrasco listens to the argument looking weary, or maybe as if, in spite of having his eyes open, he were asleep and dreaming; but then he seems to lose all interest, unfolds the map he had set down on the table a little while before and starts examining it with an absent expression. Until a comment from Blai seems to tear him out of his abstraction, or his despondency.

"Besides, I don't trust this guy." The inspector gestures towards Carrasco. "And I don't understand why you trust him . . . Let's see, how many times have you talked to him, Melchor? How do you know he's not tricking us? How can we be sure he's not a lunatic?" Blai and Carrasco look at each other face to face. "Don't take it the wrong way," the inspector says. "I don't have anything against you personally. But I'm sure that, if you were in my place, you'd think the same thing. You understand, right?"

A solid silence follows this last question; only the one who was questioned is brave enough to break it.

"Perfectly," he says, locking eyes with the inspector. "And you're right: If I were you I would think the same thing." He shrugs, starts to fold up the map and adds: "Anyway, some other time."

"The captain is not a lunatic," Caty chimes in at that moment. "And he's not deceiving you."

It's the first time the woman has intervened in the argument. She has spoken in a sharp, imperative voice, and now everyone, curious and puzzled, looks at her; all except Carrasco, who, as if he hadn't heard, finishes folding up the map and puts it in his bag.

"I've known Captain Carrasco for years," Caty explains; her upper lip trembles slightly. "I've worked under his command. And I know there is nobody more trustworthy than him."

"Congratulations," says Blai. "We, however, do not know that. And that's why we're going home."

"You're making a mistake," the woman insists.

"Caty, please," Carrasco murmurs, with a gesture of fatigue. "This is over."

At that moment the woman notices that Carrasco is putting his things away in his leather satchel, and her gaze begins to leap urgently from Melchor to Blai and from Blai to Melchor.

"Do you remember the Spanish diplomats who took refuge in the Brazilian embassy in Guinea?" she asks.

"Come on, be quiet, Caty," Carrasco murmurs again.

"No, you be quiet, captain, sir," Caty replies. "Do any of you remember, yes or no?"

Melchor remembers. In fact, he's sure everyone there remembers; the reason is that, although the episode happened eleven years ago, for several months it was on the front pages of all the papers and the first item on the television news. It happened just after the Islamist revolution that overthrew Santiago Nsue Mangue in Equatorial Guinea, when the insurgents accused the Spanish government of having conspired to keep the dictator and his wife in power and an angry mob stormed the embassy, lynched several diplomats and held the rest hostage for four months. Six officials, however, managed to escape the invasion and sought refuge in the Brazilian embassy, where they remained for several weeks while the new Guinean authorities demanded they be handed over, accusing them of very serious crimes. Until finally they were extracted from the country and returned safe and sound to Spain."

"The Brazilians took credit for the escape," Caty says after reminding them of the events. "But it was the captain who organised and executed the operation."

"Don't pay any attention," says Carrasco, who has been listening to the woman with his head down and a sad smile on his face. "Caty is a good girl, but she's always been very imaginative."

"What I've told you is the truth," Caty squirms. "Believe me. The captain entered Guinea alone, got into the embassy and brought those people out. The Spanish government said they had nothing to do with the matter and that it had been the Brazilians, because they didn't want to poison relations with Guinea even more, and especially because there were still hostages in the embassy."

"How do you know it was Carrasco?" Paca Poch asks.

"Because I was working under his command at the SIU and helped him from Madrid," Caty responds; her upper lip has stopped trembling. "I told you this because it's an event everyone remembers, but I could tell you quite a few more things . . . Don't be fooled. You're police officers, ask any of my comrades. The captain was a legend in the Guardia Civil."

"Were you also thrown out of the corps?" Vàzquez asks.

"No," Caty answers. "I left. When they accused the captain of all that narco shit, tried him and sent him to prison, I left. Me and two others who worked with him. The three of us decided that, if there was no place in the Guardia Civil for this man, then it was no place for us either." She pauses, and lets her gaze wander around her audience, until coming to rest on Melchor.

"That's all I want to say: if the captain says he can do something, it's because he can do it."

When Caty concludes her defence, Melchor feels she has managed to sow doubt among those who were doubting, including Carrasco himself, who is still sitting in his chair facing him, with his leather satchel on his lap. Blai is again the first to react.

"The problem is that he said himself that it can't be done," he argues, pointing at Carrasco again.

"He didn't say that," Vàzquez returns to the charge. "He just said it's dangerous, not that it can't be done. And Melchor's right. There won't be another opportunity."

"Now or never," Paca Poch backs him up.

"Well then, never," Blai says.

The three of them get embroiled in the argument again. It's only been a couple of seconds, but, feeling that Vàzquez and Paca Poch are ganging up on him, Blai looks for an ally.

"What do you think, Salom?" he encourages him. "Am I right or not?"

The former corporal is the only one of those present who hasn't declared a position yet, and perhaps for that reason all six of them look at him with interest, especially Carrasco and Caty, who seem not to have noticed his presence until then. Far from feeling uncomfortable in the spotlight, Salom takes his time answering. First, he takes off his glasses and then, while he cleans the lenses with a folded handkerchief, he seems to meditate, his lips a pale red sticking out of his greying beard, his short-sighted eyes lost above Paca Poch's head.

"Yes and no, Blai," he answers, putting his glasses back on and addressing the inspector. "I think that, now that we're here, the least we can do is listen to what this man has to say." He points to Carrasco. "Let him tell us his plan . . . Then, if we

306

think it can work, we carry on. And, if not, we go home. Isn't that actually what we agreed from the start?"

The question is for Melchor, who first nods and then turns towards Blai, who lets a couple of seconds go by, and in the end, with a gesture of resignation or boredom, agrees to Salom's proposal. Then Melchor's gaze slides over all the rest of them, until it stops on Carrasco.

"OK?" he asks.

Still with his satchel on his lap, Carrasco looks at Melchor for a moment; then he sighs deeply and stares at the table, as if looking for something on its surface on which the declining light from the window seems to shimmer. Before anyone can say anything, Carrasco looks up. With a severe expression he enquires:

"Which of you supports Barça?"

The question confounds all of them, and they look at each other uncomprehendingly. Carrasco repeats what he has just said.

"Is this a joke?" Blai asks.

"I'm serious," Carrasco replies. "Tomorrow is the final. Are any of you Barça supporters, yes or no?"

Visibly impatient to move on from that dead end, Paca Poch is the first to raise her hand; Vàzquez imitates her; then, less convinced than intrigued, Blai and Salom raise their hands. Paca Poch urges Melchor:

"Raise your hand, you bastard."

Melchor raises his hand. Then Carrasco leans over to Caty and whispers some words in her ear which Melchor does not manage to decipher but which manage to provoke the woman to produce the first smile of the evening.

"OK then," Carrasco again, opening his leather satchel. "Might as well be hung for a sheep as for a lamb."

4

"Mattson's house is here, in Punta Conill," Carrasco begins, placing the tip of his index finger on a point on the map he has just spread over the table, above which hangs a lamp, just now switched on. He is still sitting in his chair, completely focused on the map, as are Melchor, Blai and Caty; as for Salom, Paca Poch and Vàzquez, they have sat up a little, with their arms or elbows leaning on the table, to get a better view and follow the explanations. "This is the Formentor peninsula, about a twenty-minute drive from here. A very exclusive zone. Mattson's neighbours are some of the richest people in the world."

Carrasco explains that Mattson's mansion is quite isolated. So much so that, by land, it can only be reached by a road that goes from the Hotel Formentor, a luxurious establishment more than a century old, where a multitude of celebrities have stayed. A kilometre or so separates the hotel from the tycoon's property, he assures them, a distance with barely six or seven homes, all very luxurious, all empty at this moment; beyond it there is only one more house, abandoned and going to ruin.

"Mattson's is spectacular," Carrasco continues. "I don't

know how much it's worth right now." He turns to Caty. "Seventy-five million euros? A hundred?"

She half-closes her eyes and purses her lips.

"More or less." Then, speaking to the rest of them, she explains: "During the construction they had legal problems, they were accused of violating environmental laws. In fact, it went to trial."

"As expected, Mattson got away with it," Carrasco takes over. "The judge took his side and the house stayed the way it was. But at least there was a trial, and considering it was Mattson that was an achievement in itself. Obviously, the environmental crime is a verifiable fact."

Looking back at the map, Carrasco describes the mansion's surroundings, with the sea on one side and a steep, rugged mountain known as Na Blanca on the other, a rocky outcrop covered in rough bushes and pine trees, and he insists, apart from the sea, there is only one way to enter and leave the property, a road that ends a little further on.

"This, for us, is an advantage," Carrasco assures them. "But it can also be a problem."

"Sure," Vàzquez deduces. "If things get complicated, we could get trapped over there."

"Exactly," Carrasco says.

"And then?" Melchor asks.

"Then we'd have to escape down Na Blanca," Carrasco answers. "Not easy, and even less so in the dark and at night, but doable. I know that mountain like the back of my hand. Besides, in the worst case we could stay up there, hide all night and escape in the morning . . . Although that would not be ideal, of course. Ideally, we'll do it all in a few minutes. Get inside the house and out again without anyone noticing and then escape by the same route we came. So, we should avoid complications. And that's why we have to start by taking maximum precautions."

Carrasco picks up his satchel, begins to take out phones and distribute them among those present.

"More mobiles?" Paca Poch asks.

"I bought them from some gypsies in Son Banya," Carrasco says, handing Caty hers. "We'll only use them tomorrow night. Then we'll get rid of them. You've each got everybody else's number written on a piece of paper stuck on the back."

"We're sliding too easily into the future conditional," Blai points out, receiving his phone and turning it over. "I'll just remind you all that nothing's been decided yet."

"I suppose I don't have to tell you these are burners," Carrasco carries on with his explanation, ignoring Blai's comment. "And that you should leave your own phones switched off in the apartments. So we'll be undetectable."

"We left our own mobiles at home," Salom says. "The ones we've brought are different."

"Doesn't matter," Carrasco says. "These will be even more secure."

Once he's finished handing out the material, Carrasco moves on to firming up the way in which, the following night, they will carry out the approach to Mattson's mansion.

"The match starts at nine-thirty, if it doesn't go to extra time, it'll be over by eleven-thirty. For us, those two hours are a gift from the gods. Barça–Madrid in the final of the Champions League, who could believe it: facing such an event, planet earth will stop spinning, the streets will empty, people will hold their breath, a stellar silence will descend. Anyway . . . That will only be from nine onwards, but we'll get started a little earlier."

After asking a few timely questions, Carrasco establishes the following: at nine-fifteen, Blai, driving the Audi Q7 loaded with the weapons and equipment, will pick up Melchor and Salom at the Pollença bus stop, and then the three of them will collect him, at the entrance to the port, on a roundabout where there's a metallic sculpture of a seaplane. Meanwhile, behind the wheel of the car hired at the Palma airport, Vàzquez will collect Paca at the main door of the apartment building where she's staying, which is also in Port de Pollença, next to a restaurant called La Vall. The two cars will meet at the exit from the port and, keeping a safe distance between them, drive to Formentor.

"What about her?" Blai asks at this point, gesturing towards Caty.

Carrasco says to forget about her for the moment and then, grazing the map with his index finger, he sketches out a road that, as he describes in detail, passes next to the military aerodrome on one side, zigzags its way up the mountain, with the sea on its right and a rocky slope with pine trees and fan palms on its left, until it reaches the peak of the promontory, begins to descend towards Formentor beach and heads for the hotel.

"You're in luck," Caty comments. "Now you can drive that route without problems. It used to be impossible to get to the hotel unless you were staying there or had a house nearby. It was a public road, but there was a security guard blocking the way."

"That's the rich for you," Carrasco growls. "They've always done whatever the fuck they want."

He then explains that the party would have to cross the car park of the Hotel Formentor, take the road to Mattson's mansion and stop a hundred metres away, before a curve where a high voltage transformer stands, with Na Blanca mountain on the left and the sea to the right.

"That's where we start to rock and roll," Carrasco says. "First off, at that moment we get out of the cars, put on the equipment and distribute the weapons. Then, the first car will go up to the house while the second stays at the curve, to provide perimeter security to the operation."

"What?" Vàzquez hastens to ask.

"Worst case scenario," Carrasco replies, stretching his neck until he locates the former sergeant on Caty's right. "Suppose things don't go well and, while we're inside the hacienda, Mattson's people alert the police. In that case, before we knew it we'd have Benavides and his people on their way up there and we'd have to stop them. How?" He points again to the curve on the map. Chopping down a couple of trees and felling them across the road here, so they don't catch us in the act and we have time to escape down the mountain." Now Carrasco looks for Melchor. "You did say you got the chainsaws I asked for, right?"

"Three of them," Melchor says. "Husqvarnas."

"We'll have a spare," Carrasco says. "Only two of us will be able to stay there, on the road, chopping down trees while the rest of us go to the house. It would have been much safer with three, but . . . The two who stay will have to cut down the trees very quickly, leave them on one side of the road and then start praying that we don't call from inside the house, because that would mean that someone had discovered us and raised the alarm. If that happens, if someone sees us, the ones inside will advise the ones outside – the ones who have chopped down the trees – and they'll have to drag the tree trunks across the road and run full tilt to the house, so we can all flee down the mountain."

"And if those inside don't advise those outside?" Paca Poch asks.

"That would mean everything has gone as planned," Carrasco says. So those outside would just have to wait for the rest of us at the curve, so we could all leave that rathole together."

312

"Also at full tilt," Blai surmises.

"Yeah," Carrasco confirms. "Tomorrow we have to do everything at full tilt. Really well and at full speed."

"Not have to," Blai insists on spelling out. "Would have to. We still haven't decided anything."

"I have a question." Salom looks at Carrasco, who meets his gaze. "You know the area, but we don't. If we have to get inside this house, wouldn't it be good if tomorrow morning we took a glimpse at it from outside, to get an idea? . . . At the house and the surrounding area."

"Not a bad idea," Carrasco says. "Well, actually it's a really good one, as long as you proceed very carefully. I especially think it would be helpful for the two drivers."

"I could be one," Salom offers.

"OK," Carrasco says. "That would mean you and not Blai would bring the first car from Pollença, the lead car. Those of us who will infiltrate the house would go with you . . . Me and two others. If you go there tomorrow morning, check out the entrance. It's a big gate, an armoured sliding door, with two surveillance cameras and a small service entrance on one side. Beside that little door you'll see an intercom and another surveillance camera. We'll get into the property through there and you should make use of the time it will take us to enter to turn the car around on the level area in front of the house, so we're ready to go back the way we came. And you should do it in absolute silence and in the dark, well, with the headlights off, because tomorrow the moon will be almost full . . . That is also an advantage and a disadvantage. But, for you, at that moment, it'll be an advantage."

Carrasco asks who's going to take charge of chopping down the trees.

"You're all police officers," he adds. "Or you used to be. So you don't need me to tell you that the ideal would be for each of us to have one single job. One and only one. But, with so few people, one of the two lumberjacks is going to have to double up and drive."

As he has already given to understand, Carrasco excludes himself from tree felling and includes himself in the group that will enter Mattson's house, among other reasons, he claims, because he has it memorised, even though he's never been inside.

"I'm going in too," Melchor hastens to say.

"So am I," Paca Poch says.

"I don't mind what I do," Vàzquez admits. "I've never in my fucking life cut a tree down, but I don't think it can be that hard."

"Not with a chainsaw, no," Carrasco says. "Have you ever used one?"

"Sure," Vàzquez says. "Dead easy. The problem is: what about the noise?"

"Husqvarnas are very quiet," Carrasco says. "Besides, you'll be far away from the house. Nobody will hear."

"Done, then," Vàzquez says. "And I can drive the car too."

"That leaves you and me on the road," Blai says, pointing to Vàzquez. "It would leave, I mean."

"Great," Carrasco approves. "Tomorrow morning, when you go up there, have a good look at that curve . . . You'll rec-ognise it by the high voltage transformer hut. A few metres before it we'll stop and put on the gear, get the weapons and equipment. You –" he looks at Blai – "don't need to get back into the car: grab a chainsaw and start chopping. And you –" turning to Vàzquez – "take the wheel of the second car, fol-low us to the curve and turn around there, drive back to where you've left your comrade and you get chopping too. Between

314

one site and the other there's thirty or forty metres, no more. And there are lots of trees beside the road. Calculate that you have to chop down two in less than ten minutes; if it could be five, even better. And don't forget the fundamental thing: you should only block the road with the trunks in case of maximum necessity. And only if we tell you to."

"We being you, Melchor and Paca?" Vàzquez asks.

"If we're the ones going in, yes," Carrasco answers. "And we will only ask you to cut off the road if we realise we can't get out the way we came in. If we don't send you a message or call you, wait with the cut trees in the ditch, but don't do anything, don't put them across the road. Whatever happens . . . It's important that this is clear."

Vàzquez and Blai nod. Then the latter asks a question:

"How many people guard that house?"

By way of reply, Carrasco takes a black cardboard file out of his satchel, and from the file a plan that he unfolds on top of the map. It is a plan of the house, neat and detailed, drawn in ink with some parts highlighted in three different colours: blue, yellow and green.

"I was just getting to that," he says "This is Mattson's house. A fortress, as I told you. The whole year round, whether Mattson's there or not."

Melchor and Paca Poch ask at the same time if the tycoon will be at his mansion the next day.

"No," Carrasco answers. "He's not in Pollença. And that's another advantage for us. When Mattson arrives, the protection multiplies. But, if he's not there, the house is still fortified, especially this part, which is what interests us." Carrasco gestures to a blue rectangle separated from the rest of the dwelling by a sort of isthmus. "In that house they call it the recreation zone. In reality, it's the place where Mattson and his guests

315

get up to their debauchery." Then, sliding his fingertip over that zone of the plan, he enumerates: This is the gymnasium, here's the heated swimming pool, in this other place they have a sauna, and massage room and things like that, these are all bedrooms . . ."

"And this other?" Paca Poch points to a square and a hexagon, situated a certain distance apart from one another and circled in red. "What's in here?"

Carrasco moves his index finger across the plan to the edge of the square.

"That's the epicentre of the house," he says. "From that room the whole security system is controlled. There are always two armed people inside. All the time . . . The rest of the property is guarded by two other people, also armed, who make rounds night and day, but those two don't leave that room."

"Is there anyone else in the house?" Melchor asks.

"There's a man and a woman there permanently," Carrasco answers. "A married couple of Chilean immigrants who worked for Mattson in Sweden until he brought them here. People he trusts completely. They look after the house, keep everything running smoothly, hire extra staff when Mattson comes . . . Anyway." Leaning over the floorplan a bit, Carrasco pauses, as if he'd lost the thread of his explanation or as if he'd discovered an error or a fissure in his plan; but he soon straightens up, leans back in his chair and goes on: "The security system is very sophisticated. Caty knows it well, because the company she works for installed it." He turns towards his former subordinate. "Caty?"

"More than sophisticated, the system is perfect." Now it's Caty, leaning on the left armrest of her chair, who bends over the floorplan. "At least in theory."

She immediately takes over from Carrasco and begins to

316

set out with professional rigour the defence mechanisms that protect the mansion and the strategic points in which they are situated: she states that there is a conventional alarm fitted on every window in the house, she points out on the plan the twelve surveillance cameras and the ten steel security doors, describes the operation of the anti-aggression alarms, the reinforcement system against possible intruders, that of evacuation and fire-proofing, as well as the motion detectors.

"As soon as any of these alarms is triggered," Caty continues, indicating the square in the red circle on the floorplan, "the people who are in this room know it. So, as the captain says, from there the security of the whole house is overseen, all the alarms depend on this room . . . To put it a better way, they depend on a programme called Odín and that's what controls them all."

"I've heard of that," Paca Poch interrupts. "It was created three or four years ago. They say it protects the Congress of Deputies and Moncloa."

"They don't just say." Caty nods. "It's true."

"And why would Mattson want such a powerful security system?" Carrasco asks rhetorically.

"I've already told them," Melchor says, gesturing around at all his friends.

Ignoring him, Carrasco returns his concentration to the floorplan.

"Just to protect this room," he answers himself, now placing the tip of his index finger on the hexagon circled in red. "This is where our man stores his treasure chest, this is the objective of our operation, in here is what we have to take out." He pauses, scans the faces of those present, who wait in silence for him to continue. "Unfortunately, we can't take everything that's in there, I mean we can't take, for example, the trophies the

317

guy keeps of his victims, personal objects, parts of their bodies, things like that . . . Mattson, I suppose Melchor also will have told you, is a sexual predator and, as you know, people like that sometimes keep those kinds of things. It would be great to photograph them, but there probably won't be time, I had planned on two people entering that room, but now we'll only be able to have one, so we'll have to make do. Besides, it's something else we're really after."

According to Carrasco, the room houses a computer where over the years thousands of photographs, documents and videos that bear witness to Mattson's sexual misdeeds and those of his guests have been stored; of course, most of them are unaware this material exists, they only find out when the tycoon decides to blackmail them, if he ever does. In any case, the computer in question has a hard drive with twenty terabytes of memory, enough not to need to connect to the cloud and, therefore, is invulnerable to incursions by hackers.

"That's the treasure chamber," Carrasco states. "The whole house is iron-clad in order to protect the computer's hard drive." He looks up from the floorplan again, but this time only at Melchor, Blai and Salom, sitting across the table from him. "There is more than enough material there to destroy Mattson. If we get it, we'll unmask him and he'll be finished."

"Getting the disk out of the computer tower is easy," Caty says. "It's an old-style tower, for security, but you just need a screwdriver to get into the housing."

"Sure, that's a piece of cake," Paca Poch agrees. "The tricky thing must be getting into the room."

"Even harder than you think," Carrasco says. "Because to get in you don't only have to bypass the house security system. You also have to get through an iris-recognition system that only recognises Mattson's eye."

This last piece of news engenders a stunned silence. Paca Poch and Vàzquez stare at Melchor as if they can't quite believe what they've just heard, or as if what they've just heard changes everything. On the other side of the table, Caty's restless eyes seem to observe the reactions of those present. The first to speak is Blai.

"Let's see if I've got this straight," he says in a tone halfway between patient and sarcastic, like someone who's just reached the end of a dead-end street. "You're proposing that we attack a fortress full of thugs armed to the teeth, a fortress that, to make things worse, is protected by the world's most sophisticated security system . . . Or one of the most sophisticated. But, hang on, that's not all. Because it turns out, supposing we were able to get in, we'd have to enter a room in which, physically, you can only enter if you are Rafael Mattson, or, if you have Rafael Mattson's eyes . . . Is that what you're saying? Have I missed something? And, if I haven't missed anything, do you want to tell me how the fuck we do that, if we don't happen to be the great Houdini, but in reverse?"

In theory, Blai is posing the question to all of them, but in practice it is aimed only at Carrasco. However, it is Caty who answers.

"You don't need to be Houdini," she says. "You just need to trick the system, make it think it has committed an error . . . And prove that, as I said before, it's only perfect on paper."

5

"**D**eep down, the most sophisticated cybernetic system is as simple as the simplest," Caty says out loud. Around her, the group now seems held prisoner in a circle of gold woven by the light from the lamp that hangs over the table; it's the only light on in the kitchen: through the window, a bloodless dusk barely enters. "This, for example." The woman picks up the telephone Carrasco has just given her and shows it to the rest of them. "It's happened to all of us: every once in a while, we don't know why, our mobile crashes and we have to restart it. Sometimes it crashes because there's been an error in the system, or not exactly. Sometimes it crashes as a security measure of the system itself. Or for whatever other reason . . . Sometimes it even crashes for no reason, just because." She sets the phone back down on the table, in front of her. "Well, the most sophisticated systems do the same thing. The only difference is that Odín is so sophisticated that it doesn't need to be restarted, it restarts itself without anyone telling it to . . . Seven minutes, it takes. Seven minutes exactly: not a second more or less. During this time, all the security of Mattson's house would be blocked, suspended. That means the surveillance cameras, the alarms, the iris-recognition system: none of them will be functioning.

Nothing. For seven minutes, the whole property will be out in the open, with no protection. Defenceless. A person could stroll in and walk from one side to the other as easy as you like . . . For the system, it's a blind spot, its Achilles heel."

"And, for us, a providential way in," Carrasco says.

Caty nods, picks up the phone again, but immediately puts it down again, as if it burned her hand.

"When those seven minutes are up everything goes back to normal," she continues, her gaze leaping from Melchor to Blai and from Blai to Salom, who are sitting across from her. "The system will reactivate itself and carry on working, as if nothing had happened. But Odín is Odín and, if that stoppage was not the result of a simple error of the system itself, if it wasn't spontaneous, if someone provoked it, it'll know that something strange happened. That is, after that seven-minute parenthesis the system realises that it wasn't its own error, that someone had forced it to restart, that it has been deceived and, in effect, has been the victim of a cyberattack." Now she looks at Vàzquez and Paca Poch, on their side of the table. "Therefore, it acts accordingly and, to protect itself, locks down the house, closes the doors and windows and launches jets of smoke to blind the intruders and prevent them from escaping . . . From that moment on, it'd be impossible to get out of the treasure chamber. Out of there and the whole house, which closes tightly, hermetically sealed." She pauses and adds: "In other words, in theory, the system shutdown would give you seven minutes to get inside the house, reach the treasure chamber, grab the hard drive and get out again."

"And in practice?" Melchor asks.

"Just three," Carrasco interjects. "Ideally we would do it in three minutes."

"And is that possible?" Melchor asks again.

321

"No," Carrasco admits. Why would I try to deceive you. It's almost impossible. But it would be ideal."

"For a very simple reason," Caty says, so in tune with her former superior officer it's as if the two of them had rehearsed the exposition beforehand, or as if this weren't the first time they'd done it. "Because, three minutes from the moment the system has begun its automatic reboot, a warning goes off in the control room. And that's where the problems would also start for you . . . They're not insoluble problems, of course, because the warning is nothing too exceptional, nothing that doesn't happen fairly frequently, the guards must be quite accustomed to dealing with it. Actually, the warning is no more than a signal that, for whatever reason, which might be a perfectly natural one, the system is resetting itself, or that there's been some fault that the system can correct on its own, or is even already correcting . . . I'm sure those who are in that room have seen an alert like this more than once. As I say, these things happen now and then, those who know the system and work with it do not tend to get alarmed. But, despite that, in normal circumstances the logical thing to do would be, at that moment, three minutes after the stoppage, for the guards to take the trouble to leave the room to see what's going on, or to advise someone else to."

"That's, under normal circumstances," Carrasco picks up the thread, to modify its course. "But remember that Barça–Madrid, in a Champions League final, is the least normal circumstance in the world, at least the least normal in the history of football."

"I see where you're going," Blai says. "But what if the guards are less interested in football than Melchor?"

"I'll pretend I didn't hear such nonsense," Carrasco says, without looking at the inspector. "Tomorrow night, people who don't give a flying fuck about football will be glued to the telly, and that's not even those who have to be locked up in a bunker, as in this case . . . By the way, did you not watch the semi-final against Juve, Melchor?" To Blai's bewilderment, Melchor says yes while Paca Poch winks. "Anyway," Carrasco continues, "let's just hope the match is at a boiling point at that moment and the guards decide it's not worth the bother of leaving the television . . . In short, let us have faith in the blessed alienating power of football."

"I do have faith in it," Caty declares. "But that power won't fix everything. Because, supposing things work out the way we want and the guards don't leave the room, that would only give those of you who are inside an extra two minutes. After that another alarm goes off, and then there'll be no doubt that something's happening. And, final of the Champions League or not, one of the two guards will leave that room to see what's going on. For sure."

"That means," Melchor deduces, "that we would have under seven minutes to get into the house, steal the computer's hard drive and clear out. Have I got that right?"

"Precisely," says Caty.

"Although ideally we should do it all in under five minutes," Melchor goes on. "In that case, when the guards want to react we would already be out of the house. If we take more than five minutes, we could have problems."

"Exactly," Carrasco approves. "First of all, as Caty said, after five minutes one of the guards would try to leave the room to see what's going on, and naturally we'd have to prevent that any way we could. And when I say any way I mean any way. That's why we'd need to leave two people there, guarding the door to that room, while the one in the treasure chamber is getting the hard drive out of the computer and leaving with it . . . My plan consisted of two people going in there, one to take photos and the other to get the hard drive. But now only one can go in. So, we'll have to confine ourselves to the drive."

"If you want, I'll go in," Paca Poch suggests, exhibiting her pianist's fingers and wiggling them rapidly. "I can get a drive out of a computer in thirty seconds."

"If it could be twenty, even better," Carrasco says. In any case, Melchor and I will try to make it as easy for you as possible. Or the least difficult."

"Could we do all that in five minutes?" Melchor asks.

"That's the 64,000-dollar question," Carrasco says.

"I think it's impossible," Caty says. "Or almost. There's just not enough time."

"We at least have to try," Carrasco argues. "If it can't be done in five, then let it be seven." Looking back and forth from Paca Poch and Melchor, he continues: "As I was telling you before, I have never been inside that house, but I know it like the back of my hand, so, when we go in, you would just have to follow me. I had planned to leave a person at the door, to cover our withdrawal if there are any problems, which there could be. But that won't be possible either . . ." Now he turns to Salom. "There is one important thing: we won't stop the car in front of the entrance because the security cameras would pick it up. We'd have to leave it a little bit before that, just after the curve where the transformer is." He turns again to Melchor and Paca. "We can cover the ground between the car and the control room, after opening the service door, at a run in less than two minutes. I would leave you, Melchor, at a bend in the hallway, with the door of the room in sight, and then go with Paca as far as the entrance to the treasure chamber, leave her there and come back to where you are."

"And how do I open the door to the chamber?" Paca Poch asks.

"That's no problem," Carrasco replies. "With the iris-recognition mechanism deactivated by the reboot, the door opens like a normal everyday door. So you go in, get the hard drive out of the computer, come back to where we are and the three of us get the hell out of there . . . That we can do in seven minutes. Maybe even five. But, in seven, for sure. It all depends on us. Do you agree or not, Caty?" She nods. Melchor notices that her upper lip has started quivering slightly again. "Oh yeah, it would be important that before we go into the house we activate the frequency inhibitor, to prevent those inside from alerting Benavides and his guys. I assume you've brought one."

"It's in the false bottom of Blai's car, with everything else," Melchor says. "Apparently, it's a really good one. But we were warned that it's not completely reliable."

"No inhibitor is completely reliable," Caty says. "And less so against the anti-inhibitors they have in Mattson's house."

"Entirely sure, no," Carrasco accepts. "But it would at least protect us for a short time. Which is all we need."

"That's true," Caty says.

"Everything you've said seems all well and good," Vàzquez says then. "But there's one thing I don't understand."

"What's that?" Carrasco asks.

"How do we trick the system?" Vàzquez says. "I mean, how would we provoke the stoppage that would let us get into the house?"

"You don't have to worry about that," Caty says; Melchor notices that she has dominated her lip quiver and replaced it with a slight smile. "I'll take care of that. And don't bother asking me how I'll do it because I'm not going to tell you . . . That's under a gag order. I'll just say that, however things work out, if anyone tries to trace the attack they'll believe it was launched from Lahore, in Pakistan. They can go and look for me there if they want."

That said, Caty consults Carrasco wordlessly while she opens her arms and shows her palms in a gesture Melchor translates as implying: "For my part, that's all."

"Well then," Carrasco concludes. "That's more or less the plan."

"Seems perfectly feasible to me," Paca Poch hastens to declare.

"Me too," Vàzquez seconds her.

Melchor grips Blai's forearm, as if trying to contain him, and, turning to his right, asks:

"Salom?"

The former corporal looks up from the floorplan of Mattson's house and shrugs.

"For my part, no objections."

All eyes then merge on Blai.

"You've heard," Melchor says, letting go of his arm. "We're going to do it with or without you. You decide."

The inspector also has his eyes fixed on the floorplan; deliberation is hardening his mouth and making his chin pulse. In the lamp light, his shaved head shines like a recently varnished leather dome.

"What are you asking me for?" He turns to look at Melchor. "You've decided for me, no?"

"Olé, boss, well done," Paca Poch says.

"You and I will talk at the station," Blai mutters, standing up and requesting a break by banging the fingertips of his right hand against the palm of his left. "I'm going to the bathroom."

Paca Poch, Salom and Vàzquez also stand up to stretch their legs. Opposite Melchor, Caty whispers in Carrasco's ear; his face reveals not the slightest emotion. When everyone's sitting around the table again, Carrasco takes the lead.

"There is an important matter." He looks at Melchor. "You and I have already talked about this, I don't know if you told the rest of them . . . I mean what we're going to do with the stuff we get out of Mattson's house."

"I've thought about that," Melchor says.

Then, he sums up the conversations he's had with Rosa Adell: he tells them what she has told him about Héctor Abad, Gonzalo Córdoba and Caracol Televisión.

"That seems like an excellent idea to me," Carrasco admits when Melchor finishes speaking. "We'll keep the originals though, and just give those people a copy. More than anything in case it doesn't work and we have to look for another solution, of course . . . But in principle this seems unbeatable, especially if the Colombians broadcast the images quickly. This is important. No, not important: vital. We can't allow Mattson time to react. We need to maintain the element of surprise. That's why speed is of the essence . . . Any more questions?"

They all look at each other, but nobody says anything.

"Very good." Carrasco spreads out the map of the Formentor peninsula over the top of the floorplan of Mattson's house. "Let's go over the plan again."

During the next hour and a half they review the spaces, the times, the meeting places, and most of all the exact mission each of them needs to carry out and the way it must be done. When they finish there is a very short round of questions and answers. Once this is finished, Caty is the first to say goodnight to the group. Carrasco does so soon after. Melchor looks at his watch: it's a little after eleven. He goes to the bathroom, urinates, washes his face and splashes water on his neck, looks in the mirror and runs his wet fingers through his hair. When he comes out, his friends are still in the dining room, as if they were waiting for him. The atmosphere is not uneasy, but nor is it euphoric.

"OK, I'm off," Blai announces, picking up his jacket. "I'm starving. And don't look like that, fuck, everything's going to be fine." He turns to Vàzquez: "I'll wait for you in the car."

The inspector hasn't finished putting on his jacket when Salom, sprawled out on the sofa, his gaze lost in the rectangular night of the window, murmurs:

"I'd pay to know what it was he whispered to the girl." Perhaps surprised to find he'd said it out loud, he turns his bearded, bespectacled face towards them and clarifies: "Carrasco, I mean . . . what he said to the girl before he agreed to tell us his plan. After asking us what team we support."

Hours earlier, Melchor had wondered the same thing, but he keeps from confessing that now. There is silence.

"I read his lips," Paca Poch eventually reveals.

They all turn towards her.

"And?" Salom asks.

The sergeant's mouth curves into a sardonic smile.

"You don't want to know," she says.

Now it's the sergeant who, one after the other, looks at them all; as she does so her smile vanishes.

"It was just a joke," she says.

Nobody says anything. Paca Poch clicks her tongue and gives in.

"What he said was: 'Just my luck. I'm going to get killed with a bunch of Barça supporters.'"

The next day, when Melchor wakes up, Salom is in the bathroom, taking a shower. In the kitchen he finds bread, ground coffee and cheese and, while he's having breakfast, the ex-corporal reappears.

"I'm going to go and see the house with Blai and Vàzquez," he announces.

"What about Paca?"

"She wants to sleep in."

"Be careful."

"Don't worry. I'll be back at midday."

Melchor spends the rest of the morning reading Turgenev's *A Sportsman's Sketches* in the apartment. The one he likes best is the last one. It's called "The Forest and the Steppe" and it is simply a collection of impressions of a hunter's life. Melchor has never in his life gone out hunting in the countryside, but the story, and especially its innocent ending ("Farewell, dear reader! I wish you unbroken prosperity"), makes him feel melancholy.

Salom comes back just before half past one with a bag of provisions and, while he fries a couple of hamburgers, a couple of tomatoes and a couple of green peppers in a pan, the ex-corporal describes the road to Formentor, the hotel of the same name, the Na Blanca mountain, Punta Conill and Mattson's house or what he was able to see of Mattson's house. Melchor knows it all, has seen it all; now he realises, however, that it's as if he doesn't know it, as if he's never been there.

"Carrasco's right," the ex-corporal concludes. "That is a rathole. But we'll manage."

They eat at the table, the same one where the previous night Carrasco spread out his maps, and they haven't even finished when Melchor asks Salom if he's thanked him yet. The ex-corporal's answer does not consist of asking him what for; it consists of a smile.

"What's so funny?" Melchor asks.

"Nothing." With his fork Salom spears a piece of hamburger, another of tomato and one of pepper, improvising a sort of brochette. "I was thinking that the last time I did a favour like this for a friend I ended up in jail."

After a second of confusion, Melchor realises Salom is referring to the Adell case, and a wave of heat floods his face.

"This is nothing like that," he objects.

Peering at Melchor with the pieces of meat and vegetables suspended two centimetres from his mouth, Salom asks while still smiling:

"Are you sure?"

After eating, the ex-corporal falls asleep on the sofa, his glasses folded on the floor beside him, and Melchor, who doesn't want to connect to the internet so he won't leave any trace of his stay in Pollença, makes a pot of coffee and rereads the stories in Turgenev's *Sketches* that he liked best: apart from "The Forest and the Steppe" – "Birouk", "Yermolay and the Miller's Wife" and "The Singers". In front of him, Salom snores softly with his hands crossed over his belly, while his thorax rises and falls with his rhythmic breathing; the air entering and leaving his nostrils stirs the hair of his moustache like a breeze. Melchor looks up from his book every now and then and observes the man who was his most faithful companion and best friend for years, without thinking anything or only thinking that, until the hour of truth arrives, when all masks fall, a person never knows who he is.

When he wakes from his siesta, Salom makes another pot of coffee and, while they both drink a cup, Melchor asks if he has seen Albert Ferrer, Rosa's ex-husband who was also found guilty in the Adell case. Salom says no and tells him the only thing, he says, that he knows about his friend: that he got out of prison a couple of years ago and since then has been living in Barcelona or somewhere on the outskirts of Barcelona. They spend the rest of the afternoon talking as if they wanted to catch up on fourteen years of not seeing or speaking to each other. When Melchor asks Salom if his two daughters know where he is, Salom replies:

"I told them I'm in Mallorca, with some friends. They didn't believe it, of course. I bet they think I'm having an affair or something like that . . . In any case, they were happy. It's the first time I've gone away since I left prison."

At a quarter past eight they begin preparations, and shortly before nine they leave the apartment separately and retrace the route Melchor took last night: they walk to the centre of town along calle Major, cross the main square and, passing the Sant Domingo convent, reach the bus stop. Night is falling. Five minutes later Blai drives up in the black Audi Q7, Salom takes his place at the wheel and, practically without exchanging a word, the three of them head off in the direction of Port de Pollença, where they pick up Carrasco beside the metal seaplane sculpture at the second roundabout.

"Everything in order?" he asks.

"Everything in order," Melchor answers.

On the way out of the port the Porsche Cayenne that Vàzquez picked up the previous day at the Palma airport is waiting for them, let's them pass and follows at a discreet distance. It is night now, and they soon begin to climb along a road that snakes up the mountainside passing a mass of shadow on their right where they can barely make out the shapes of rocks, pine trees and fan palms. They meet no vehicles coming the opposite way. Inside the car the only sound is the silky purring of the engine and the whisper of the bodywork slicing through the air, and Melchor contemplates through the window to his right, Port de Pollença stippled with the trembling lights of the boats anchored in the bay. Once they reach the pass they begin the descent, still zig-zagging, still with the sea silvered by the moon on their left and the mass of darkness on the right, and, when they get down to sea level, the headlights illuminate two signs. Pointing to the one that says Formentor, Carrasco murmurs:

"Straight ahead."

Salom, who knows the way because that morning he has driven it with Blai and Vàzquez, obeys, passes the Formentor beach on the right (Melchor catches a glimpse of it through a curtain of pines), drives up a road that stretches between walls of vegetation and comes out in front of the Hotel Formentor, passes its illuminated facade, takes the dirt road that leads to Mattson's mansion and drives up until the headlights hit the high-voltage transformer hut a few metres ahead.

"There's the curve," Carrasco announces.

Salom stops the car and, while the rest get out, opens the boot, puts the car in reverse and turns on the indicator. Behind them Vàzquez pulls up in the Porsche Cayenne, with Paca Poch in the passenger seat. In absolute silence, with only the sound of waves breaking against the cliff a few metres away from them in the background, they all put on their equipment – the balaclavas, bulletproof vests, the clips – and each grab a pair of zip-tie handcuffs and a torch and attach the sites to the barrel of a Heckler & Koch UPM submachine gun, load the ammunition into the magazine, snap the cartridge into the gun and the strap over their neck. Then Blai, armed with a chainsaw, starts cutting down a tree at the side of the road and Vàzquez gets back behind the wheel of the Porsche Cayenne and Melchor and the rest get back into the Audi Q7 driven by Salom. He accelerates a little and begins to drive very slowly, almost in slow motion; they go around the curve to the right hearing the stony ground flattened by the tyres and leave behind the high voltage transformer hut. Behind them, a few metres away, Vàzquez is executing a three-point turn in the Porsche Cayenne.

"Stop here," Carrasco orders, and, after giving Vàzquez a few seconds to complete his manoeuvre and get back to Blai, he sends a message from his mobile phone and switches on the frequency inhibitor. Speaking to Melchor and Paca Poch, sitting behind him, he explains: "When I give the word, we set off for the entrance. It's right up there." Then he adds for Salom, pointing to the driveway in front of the house: "As soon as we leave, turn the car around and wait for us there."

Carrasco is speaking in a calm, level voice, or that's how it seems to Melchor, who knows that he has just notified Caty and is waiting for her to authorise the assault, sending the signal that the house security system has been suspended and they can storm it. The signal soon arrives.

"OK," says Carrasco, opening the door of the Audi Q7. "Here we go."

6

Melchor gets out of the car behind Paca Poch and Carrasco, and in a few strides reaches the small door, which the latter opens in a fraction of a second while, behind them, Salom turns the Audi Q7 around in front of the main entrance to the house. Preceded by Carrasco and followed by the sergeant, Melchor runs down a concrete ramp barely lit by a string of lights set into the edges, on the other side of which he can make out a vast lawn descending towards the sea. He runs in a crouch as far as the first wall of the mansion – enormous, white, smooth and rectangular, with huge dark windows in the upper part – he presses against it and, sheltering in the dense shadow it casts, follows it until, sixty or seventy metres along, he climbs an exterior stairway and, always behind Carrasco, goes through a door and down a corridor lit by the latter's torch. They soon reach a corner from which they glimpse, at the end of another corridor on the left, a little red light above the lintel of a closed door. Using only gestures Carrasco orders Melchor not to move from that spot and disappears with Paca Poch down the other end of the corridor. Sheltering at the corner, without turning on his torch, with his heart racing and the submachine gun pointing at the door down the hall while hearing in the distance the voice of a football pundit commentating on the Champions League final, Melchor counts to twenty-seven, at which point Carrasco reappears like a silent shadow next to him. By then Melchor's eyes have begun to adjust to the semi-darkness, so he manages to exchange a glance with Carrasco, who nods without a word as if assuring him that everything is going as planned and positions himself in front, panting in the woollen balaclava.

The seconds that follow seem to last for ever. Melchor examines the quiet of the corridor, but only hears the distant voice of the TV commentator mixed with his own breathing and, for some moments, with Carrasco's; he also feels a drop of sweat trickle down his neck like a shiver. At a certain moment, the light at the end of the hall turns from red to green with no warning, someone half-opens the door from inside and a burst of gunfire from Carrasco's submachine gun tears the silence to shreds. The door closes again, some confused voices can be heard on the other side of it and the silence reigns once more, only now it's a silence from which even the weak hum of the televised match has disappeared, a silence so deafening and so tense that it seems on the brink of exploding again. However, nobody tries to come out of that door again, and with their submachine guns at waist level Melchor and Carrasco aim at it without exchanging words or looks, while the corridor remains submerged in a fog broken only by the bright red glow at the end, as if nothing had happened. After an uncertain period of time, or a time Melchor feels incapable of specifying, but that can't have been more than ten or fifteen seconds, Paca Poch reappears. She is running, waving an object Melchor does not have enough time to make out in the shadows because Carrasco snatches it out of her hand, and the three of them rush away, back up the corridor they came down minutes earlier, open the door to the outside, run down the stairs as fast as they can and run through the garden seeking the cover of darkness, until, when they are starting up the exit ramp, they are dazzled by a very bright beam of white light almost at the very instant the first shot rings out. The second and third come almost immediately after it; by then they are very close to the main gate. Paca Poch charges through the service door and Carrasco is right behind her, when Melchor is about to follow them, he is brought down by a burning sensation in his knee. With the submachine gun on his back, he struggles to the little door dragging his useless leg, and just at that moment, as if that nightmarish pain had slowed down reality, he sees a man get out of the car in slow motion or as if, instead of running, he were swimming in amniotic fluid, and in spite of the balaclava he recognises Salom, sees him advancing ducking a hail of bullets, sees him make a tiny abnormal movement and then feels him grab hold of his arm and tug him through the service door and drag him across the stony ground until Paca Poch pulls him by the armpits up into the car.

What happens in the following minutes is confusing, but, each time Melchor recalls it in the future, he will clearly remember four things or four lumps of things. The first is that, while Salom starts up the Audi Q7 skidding over the driveway and, in the back seat, Paca Poch tries to find out where he's been shot and takes off his balaclava, submachine gun, clip and bulletproof vest, Carrasco shouts over the phone to Blai, or maybe Vàzquez, not to block the road with the tree trunks, that everything came off and to make their getaway, that they will follow. The second thing he'll remember is that at a certain point Salom lifts his right hand off the steering wheel asking where the hell all this blood was coming from, and suddenly his hand disappears into his side and re-emerges drenched in blood, and then the ex-corporal swears out loud: "Fucking hell, I've been hit too." The third thing he'll remember happens next, and it's that Paca Poch begins to beg Salom to let her replace him behind the wheel, and Salom, in spite of now only driving with his left hand because he's using his right to try to stop the haemorrhage, refuses to pull over assuring her he's fine, all of which happens at the same time as Carrasco calls Vàzquez, or maybe Blai, and demands that they pull over and let them pass, to then hang up and call another person and tell them he has to ask a big favour, that he has two wounded men in the car, who urgently need a doctor and to send one to Can Sucrer as soon as possible. And the fourth and last thing he'll remember – the one he'll remember above everything else each time he brings to mind those frenetic minutes during which they raced from Mattson's house to Can Sucrer, with the tyres squealing on every curve and the car swerving and lurching next to the cliffs of Formentor and a silence illuminated by the full moon and spattered with cursing and moaning, with Paca Poch's hand squeezing his and exhorting him and Salom to hang in there – is that a cold and sticky sweat bathed his skin and his leg hurt as though someone was cutting it off with a handsaw.

Salom collapses over the steering wheel as soon as he stops the Audi Q7 at the entrance to Can Sucrer and, almost immediately, Vàzquez and Blai burst into the car, pick up the ex-corporal and carry him inside the house as fast as they can. Meanwhile, Paca Poch gets Melchor out of the car as well, carries him in her arms, walks into the house and sits him down in an armchair, right in front of the television and under a ceramic sign that says: CALLE DEL TEMPLE. The sergeant props Melchor's leg up on a wicker chair, disappears and reappears with a pair of scissors, cuts his jeans up to his thigh exposing his wounded knee: an indecipherable mash of blood and splintered bones; then she leaves again and reappears with a couple of cushions she places under his knee. The pain is still brutal and, when Paca Poch offers him a glass of water, Melchor asks how Salom is.

"I don't know," she says, pointing to a bedroom door, which is ajar. "The fucking bullet got him just below the vest. That's what he gets for being fat . . . Anyway, the bastard saved your life."

Melchor asks Paca Poch if she managed to get the hard drive out of Mattson's computer.

"That's the third time you've asked me." The sergeant reassures him. "Carrasco's got it."

While Melchor struggles to endure the torment of his leg, trembling and clenching his teeth, Paca Poch stays by his side gripping his hand, drying his sweat and trying to distract him. In front of him, wrapped in a sort of mist that seems to segregate his pain, human shapes come and go, but Melchor could not say if they were coming in or out of the house, the kitchen or the bedroom where they'd taken Salom. Sometimes it seems as if there are more people around than there should be; other times, that he's been left alone, that everyone has disappeared. At some point he hears a vehicle parking at the door of the property. Paca Poch leaves his side and immediately comes back with a man in his fifties, with grey hair and glasses, carrying a small case in his hand who, when he comes into the room and notices the blood-soaked knee, rushes to him to attend to it. Melchor gestures to the bedroom.

"Go and see my comrade," he urges. "He was shot in the gut."

The doctor obeys without hesitation, and a little while later Blai replaces Paca Poch, who vanishes behind Salom's bedroom door. The inspector sits down beside him.

"Don't worry, *españolazo*." He dries his damp forehead with a handkerchief and tries to smile. "You're not going to die." He adds, pointing at the knee without looking at it, "But that must fucking hurt."

"What about Salom?"

Blai is slow to reply. Despite being very close to him, the mist seems to pull him away.

"I don't know," the inspector admits. "But it doesn't look good, he's bleeding a lot. We'll wait and see what the doctor says . . . Is it true what Paca told us?"

Melchor exchanges a grimace of pain for an inquisitive one. The other clarifies:

"That he went in to get you out and that's when he was shot."

Drawing strength from weakness, Melchor specifies:

"They shot him while he was getting me out." And then: "If not for him, I'd still be there."

At that moment Carrasco appears, looks at his knee while Melchor asks him more or less the same question he's just asked Blai; Carrasco gives him more or less the same answer. Melchor then asks about the hard drive from Mattson's computer.

"Don't worry," he says. "I'm going through it."

Before Melchor can ask another question, Carrasco disappears again, but he reappears almost straight away, this time with a big cup in his hand.

"Drink this," he says, holding it up to his lips. "It'll make you feel better."

Melchor takes a sip: it's cognac. Then he takes another and chokes and starts coughing. Carrasco meanwhile goes off again, leaving him with Blai. Although he drinks the rest of the cognac in the cup, the alcohol does not alleviate the pain, which is much more intense than the anguish he feels over Salom's fate, but does not cancel it out. For several minutes he lets Blai speak, though he doesn't understand what he's saying, or not entirely. He can barely tear his eyes away from his knee: he is startled by how little blood is flowing from the wound, but fascinated by that increasingly dry scarlet and white melange of ooze, burnt skin and bone shards. Every once in a while, the inspector stands up and, without avoiding the blood darkening the floor, goes back and forth to the bedroom door and Melchor's armchair and from Melchor's armchair to the bedroom door. At a certain moment the pain grows so intense that it seems to freeze time, and almost immediately the bedroom door opens and frames the silhouette of Vàzquez. The former sergeant is pale, suddenly aged, with his sleeves rolled up and his eyes wide open. Melchor stares at him as if he were an apparition, suddenly believes he understands and for a second the pain vanishes, transformed into an abysmal vertigo.

"It's alright," Vàzquez then announces. "He's not going to die."

Blai observes the ex-sergeant from the middle of the room, immobilised by the news.

"Are you sure?" he asks.

Vàzquez nods yes while a euphoric smile gradually illuminates his eyes and, with a sort of relief, Melchor feels the pain that has been torturing him for more than an hour return. The relief lasts barely a second, after which the torture resumes. Blai and Vàsquez are hugging a few steps away from him. When the two men separate, Melchor notes that Blai's eyes are shining, as he pulls out a bottle of cognac from somewhere, pours himself a shot in Melchor's cup and knocks it back. Vàzquez blocks his path when he heads for the bedroom.

"Wait till the doctor finishes," he says. "Paca's with him."

A few minutes later, the doctor bursts into the room again, and, avoiding Blai and Vàzquez, who rush to interrogate him about Salom, sits beside Melchor and begins to examine him. Melchor also asks him about the ex-corporal.

"The Virgin appeared to your friend," the doctor answers, trying to find the entry and exit wounds of the bullet in Melchor's knee. "He should really be dead. If that bullet had strayed three millimetres, your friend would not have made it to this house. As simple as that."

Melchor takes less than a second to change the subject:

"And what have I got?"

The doctor tries to straighten Melchor's leg and he stifles a groan of pain.

"What you've got is a wrecked knee," the doctor diagnoses. "The bullet came in from the back, destroyed your kneecap and everything around it: the tibial plateau, the femoral condyle . . . All shattered. I don't know where the fuck you guys went, but this was a massacre."

"Give me something, doctor," he urges. "It hurts like hell."

"That's what I was going to do," the doctor says, digging through his bag. "What I don't know is how you haven't fainted yet."

While he continues pondering the implausible fate of Salom, who seems to have had a bullet pierce his abdomen without grazing a single vital organ ("If it had touched his spleen, your comrade would have lasted fifteen minutes; if it had hit a major artery, less than five"), the doctor pushes a sleeve of Melchor's shirt up and ties a rubber strip around his arm, pulling one end with one hand and holding the other end in his teeth; at the same time, with his free hand he loads a dose of morphine into a syringe, locates a vein in the arm and, without cleaning it with the usual alcohol and cotton swab, sticks the needle into the vein and injects the shot of opiate. He hasn't yet completed the operation when Melchor asks what he's going to do with him.

"I'm going to clean you up, disinfect you and, if someone finds me a couple of boards around here, I'm going to put a splint on your knee," the doctor answers. He has blue eyes, and two days' stubble darkens his cheeks. "Then we have to see how to get you somewhere to fix that mess."

Blai and Vàzquez rush out to the patio, the doctor gets down to work, and three or four minutes later Melchor notices, with an incalculable feeling of joy, that the torment is beginning to ease, that the mist is beginning to clear, that he's not sweating as much as before and that little by little he feels better, and the doctor is already finishing applying a dressing to his knee, with a bandage and surgical tape, when he sees Salom come out of the bedroom, leaning on Paca Poch's shoulder, his right hand on the left flank of his abdomen and his shirt and trousers soaked in blood; his beard is dirty and his thick glasses a bit steamed up. Blai and Vàzquez, who have just come back into the room, stare at him, and the ex-corporal takes a few shaky steps towards Melchor.

"How are you?" he asks.

Vàzquez answers for him.

"He's got his colour back," he says, pointing at him with a wooden board; Blai also has one in his hand. "You should have seen him five minutes ago. He was as pale as a corpse."

Melchor's response consists of moving his head towards the doctor, who is still leaning over his knee.

"As you can see," he says. Then asks Salom the same thing: "How about you? . . . The doctor here says the Virgin appeared to you."

Blai and Vàzquez leave the boards within the doctor's reach.

"It's not that I say so," the doctor mutters. "It's what happened."

Salom nods with an awkward smile and at that moment

Carrasco bursts into the room from the kitchen, brandishing the case of the hard drive; his face seems transfigured by joy. When he sees the doctor, however, his expression changes, and he conceals the hard drive behind his back. Then he approaches the physician, introduces himself as a friend of Biel March and asks him how Salom and Melchor are.

"This man is going to need his knee reconstructed." The doctor looks up for a second from his task to look at Carrasco and asks for a washbowl with water and soap. "As for the other, he's fine, out of danger . . . I stuck scissors into the entry wound, and where the bullet came out, and I didn't find anything. But it'll have to be checked to make sure nothing is still inside, any sherds of material or anything like that. If there is, it could cause an infection and complicate things, so it would be best if someone operated on him and cleaned the internal trajectory of the wound . . . In short, they need to get to a hospital."

"Can they wait till tomorrow?" Carrasco asks.

"Impossible," the doctor answers. "It has to be right away . . . Tonight. Right now." When he finishes bandaging the boards to the inside and outside of Melchor's leg (including the joint), he continues talking while he washes the Betadine stains off his hands in the tin basin full of foaming water they've brought him. "We need an anaesthetist and an operating theatre. And a traumatologist: I can look after the abdomen injury, I used to be a military medic; but not the knee. We can't go to a public hospital, it's obvious these are bullet wounds and whoever attends to your friends would be obliged to report them. If not, they're at risk of losing their licence."

"Where then?" Blai asks.

The doctor dries his hands on the kitchen towel that Paca Poch has passed to him, and meanwhile looks at each of them in turn, distrustfully.

"I'm only doing this for my friend Biel," he finally says to Carrasco. "If it weren't for him, I wouldn't do it."

While they interrogate Carrasco in silence without daring to ask him directly who Biel March is, the doctor finishes drying his hands and picks up his phone. The conversation that follows is extremely brief.

"Paco, it's Lluís," the doctor says, looking around at the walls of the room. "I have an emergency . . . Yeah, I know the match isn't over, but it doesn't matter. I'll meet you in a quarter of an hour in the operating theatre. Call a trustworthy anaesthetist. And no questions." He hangs up, picks up his bag and nods towards the door: "Let's go. We're heading for a hospital in Alcúdia."

They agree that only the two wounded men and the doctor will go, plus Carrasco and Blai; they also decide that, in order not to call attention to themselves, they'll just take two vehicles, and that Vàzquez and Paca Poch will return in the other one to Port de Pollença, where they'll await news. The doctor divides up the injured men: Salom will travel with him, in his car; Melchor will travel with Blai in the back seat of the Audi Q7, which Carrasco will drive. As soon as they leave Can Sucrer and file down the Can Bosch road following the doctor, Carrasco holds up the hard drive from Mattson's computer in the semi-darkness.

"I've been taking a look through this," he announces. And after a pause: "There's enough stuff here to destroy that son of a bitch ten times over. It's not everything he's filmed, but . . ."

"How do you know it's not all of it?" Blai asks.

"Because it says so on the drive itself," Carrasco answers. "Only the material Mattson accumulated in the first years of the house is saved on this one. Maybe I was misinformed and in the treasure chamber there's not just one computer, but two. Could be, we'll have to ask Paca, perhaps she had time to check . . . In any case, it doesn't matter: we've got more than enough here."

During the twenty minutes it takes them to get to the hospital, Carrasco speaks of the photographs and videos he's been examining, as if he himself is surprised to have found exactly what they'd gone there to find. While he listens, Melchor doesn't know whether to celebrate or regret that what they've just taken from Mattson's mansion cannot contain images of Cosette. Carrasco also explains to Melchor that he'll entrust Mattson's drive to him to make a copy to give to Rosa Adell, who in turn should get it to her Colombian friends so Caracol Televisión can broadcast it as soon as possible.

"We can't leave time for Mattson to react," Carrasco insists. "We need to act very quickly to catch him off guard and take advantage of his confusion . . . It's important the Colombians know that."

They don't meet a single soul on the road to Alcúdia, but, when they get to town, they hear car horns and the streets begin to fill up with cars decked out with blue and red striped flags waving everywhere: Barça has won the Champions League.

"We can't have everything in this life," Carrasco murmurs.

In the Port d'Alcúdia hospital they are met by a tall, angular guy in his thirties and an older heavy-set, red-headed woman, who turn out to be the traumatologist and the anaesthetist. Salom goes into theatre first; the doctor from Can Sucrer goes with him, after first advising Melchor that the operation they have to carry out on the ex-corporal is more urgent than his, but less complex and laborious. Melchor waits in an adjacent room with Blai and Carrasco, lying on a stretcher with his injured leg elevated, and, in spite of the doctor's warning, he is still surprised to see Salom wheeled out of the operating theatre after barely forty-five minutes, asleep on his way to a recovery room.

"He's perfectly fine," the Can Sucrer doctor answers when they ask after Salom. "He'll wake up in an hour and a half, with a bit of pain, not much. Then he can go home . . . just like that. In two weeks the wound will have scarred over. The only thing you have to watch out for is making sure there's no infection in the next seventy-two hours. I already told you that your comrade's case was a miracle." He points to Melchor. "Your knee, however, is more complicated."

After examining the wound, the traumatologist confirms the doctor's diagnosis, explains to Melchor that he's going to have to reconstruct the damaged joint, that the operation is going to be long and that, as with Salom, they're going to have to put him completely under. With that, they proceed to do so. The anaesthetist finds a vein in his left arm, sticks a needle into it, connects an intravenous catheter, tapes it down, injects the serum. After a few seconds, the anaesthetic begins to take effect and Melchor loses consciousness. He recovers five and a half hours later, without pain, but dazed and with discomfort in his throat, as if they'd put a stick down it. Smiling, the anaesthetist explains that this is exactly what happened: they intubated him while he slept, they introduced an endotracheal tube into his mouth so he could breathe. The traumatologist and doctor soon appear next to his bed, and the first explains that everything went as well as it could have, why he has a brace on his leg and how he anticipates the process of rehabilitation should go. When Melchor asks if he'll ever walk the way he used to again, the traumatologist answers:

"I doubt it." And he adds: "Although you never know with these things . . . What you can't do today is get on a plane,

346

because the incision would open. It would be better if your friend didn't either. I already told him."

Once the traumatologist has left, the anaesthetist gives him five ampoules of morphine, five syringes and five needles.

"When the pain comes back, give yourself a shot of this," she recommends. "Or better, don't let it come back: give yourself a shot every four hours."

Melchor leaves the clinic sitting in a wheelchair pushed by Blai, with his leg immobilised in a rigid plastic brace. Outside dawn is breaking. Melchor says goodbye to the Can Sucrer doctor at the door of the hospital, and Blai helps him into the back seat of the car, where Salom waits.

"How are you?" the ex-corporal asks, once Melchor has managed to get comfortable.

The Audi Q7 is driving down the empty streets of Alcúdia, very close to the sea.

"Isn't this the second time you've asked me that tonight?" Melchor answers. Then he says: "OK . . . A bit dozy, but OK. How about you?"

"Isn't this the second time you've asked me that tonight?"

The two men look at each other for a moment; the next moment they burst out laughing, first just a little and soon uncontrollably, which makes the stitches they've just received tauten, and both of them double up with pain. Blai, who is listening to Carrasco from the passenger seat, turns around for a moment while the former guardia civil looks at them in the rear-view mirror.

"What's going on back there?" he asks, and, beginning to be infected by their laughter, adds: "What a pair of lamebrains."

Epilogue

On 26 May 2035, the nightly newscast of Caracol Televisión opens with a worldwide exclusive: the television station's investigative team has a series of documents showing the American tycoon and philanthropist Rafael Mattson taking part in sexual activities with underage girls. According to the news anchors – María Teresa Orozco and Kevin Martínez, perhaps the two most influential journalists in Colombia at the time – the images that were taken in a pleasure mansion Mattson owns in the municipality of Pollença, Spain, are very numerous and feature not only the famous Swedish-born multimillionaire, but also a considerable line-up of international personalities from the worlds of finance, politics, television, cinema, sports and journalism, who Mattson invited to his sexual amusements and, probably, filmed without their consent. The two anchors point out that, although the images might offend their audience's sensibility, due to their journalistic value the channel feels obliged, both morally and professionally, to broadcast exclusively a small selection of the contents. Next, three brief fragments appear on the screen. They're in black and white, of uneven quality, but good enough to identify without room for doubt who is in them, although Mattson's presumed victims' faces have been blurred to make them unrecognisable. In the first fragment, Mattson appears completely naked and surrounded by several teenage girls; the tycoon kisses them, caresses them and is caressed and kissed by them while they dance, drink, smoke and snort a white powder which is probably cocaine. In the second fragment, Mattson forces himself on a young girl with the help of a woman and a man. In the third, another underage girl gives a massage to Mattson, who lies on a trolley bed, until the film is cut off when the girl begins to masturbate him. While the images are being shown, the two journalists take turns describing or commenting on them, as if they weren't explicit enough in themselves, and at the end announce in a solemn tone that the station is offering to provide a copy of the documents in its possession to the relevant Spanish authorities, so they can take appropriate legal action.

The news is a viral bomb. Social media networks are immediately saturated and all the television and radio stations, digital editions of newspapers and news media the world over reuse the images or parts of the images broadcast by the Colombian news programme with Caracol TV's permission.

"Carrasco says this was predictable," Melchor tells Rosa, just back from Bogotá, where she handed Gonzalo Córdoba a copy of the drive extracted from Mattson's mansion two days ago. "But I didn't expect so much."

"Me neither," Rosa confesses. "Although, the fact is the images are dreadful."

Melchor nods and assures her that, before the Colombian news programme broadcast them, he hadn't seen them. Rosa is surprised.

"What was I going to look at them for?" Melchor asks, surprised by her surprise. "Cosette can't be in them . . . I thought whoever needs to see them can see them, so I made the copy and that's all. By the way, your Colombian friend has really come through: he couldn't have got the news out faster."

"I insisted on the speed. That's what you asked for, isn't it?"

"It's what Carrasco asked of me."

"Now are you going to tell me the truth about what happened in Pollença?" Rosa points to the rigid brace protecting Melchor's leg. "It's fine to tell people it was a motorbike accident, but I've earned the truth, don't you think?"

Melchor tells her she hasn't just earned the truth but heaven as well, and proceeds to tell her what happened in Pollença. That night, after making love as best they can, Rosa suggests Melchor invite Salom over for dinner.

"Invite Blai and Glòria as well," she adds. "And Paca Poch. That'll make things easier."

"Are you sure you want to see Salom?" he asks.

"Completely sure," Rosa replies.

"I always thought Salom did what he did for money," Melchor says. "To pay for his daughters' studies . . . I was wrong. I'm not saying the money counted for nothing, but he was also trying to help out a friend, just as he helped me. It took me fifteen years to understand it, but that's what he did. Well, fifteen years and a bullet in the knee."

"I don't know what Salom did," Rosa admits. "But, whatever it was, he saved you. One makes up for the other."

The scandal provoked by the images broadcast by Caracol TV catches Rafael Mattson in Stockholm, the city that houses the headquarters of Loving Children, the NGO dedicated to fighting childhood illnesses and malnutrition in the Third World of which the tycoon is founder and president. His reaction is surprising, or at least it is for those who study the case in the future. Mattson has the worst things he could have against him from the legal point of view: images in which he appears committing various extremely serious crimes and in which, as the Caracol TV journalists emphasise over and over again the first time they were shown, Mattson is perfectly recognisable. Despite that – and despite the media uproar that immediately surrounds him and the universal indignation he is the object of – the tycoon does not seek to shelter himself from justice, or even take the slightest precaution in case he must eventually evade it; quite the contrary: instead of seeking refuge in a safe place or leaving for the United States, where he is a citizen and might remain better protected from legal consequences, he remains in the city of his birth. The most plausible explanation of this temerity, or at least the most generalised, is hubris. At first, Mattson miscalculates the tremendous global impact those dreadful images have, and does not understand that neither his crushing financial power nor his aura of a benefactor of humanity could protect him from them; and much less in Sweden: it's true that, in that country, Mattson represents for many a sort of national hero, but it is no less true that Swedish legislation is implacable when it comes to sex crimes. Furthermore, Mattson would have considered it beneath his dignity to hide from justice in some African or Middle Eastern satrapy: he would have been very welcome there, but his elevated concept of himself would not have tolerated the humiliation of running away. It's even possible that those around him might have advised him badly or, most likely, that he felt himself to be so invulnerable that he hadn't even sought advice.

What is sure is that the first public reaction from Mattson's representatives is no less clumsy than his. Two days after the scandal broke, one of the tycoon's right-hand men is interviewed on the US television channel CNN about a megaproject of investment in renewable energy that one of Mattson's companies has just approved. The interview will be remembered for years, but only for its finale. At that moment, the interviewer asks Mattson's representative about the video footage that has gone round the world, and the interviewee, by the name of Paul Hammer, smiles with a mixture of pity and haughtiness and claims that those images are false and have been manipulated and disseminated by enemies of Mr Mattson, who are also, he assures the viewer, enemies of the democracy and solidarity that Mr Mattson promotes on five continents; finally, Hammer appeals to the interviewer's journalistic ethics. "We've known since the Gospels that truth creates free women and men," he states, "which means that lies only create slaves." "You journalists have a great responsibility,' he concludes. "You must choose what kind of world you want to build: a world of free men and women or a world of slaves. Mr Mattson made his choice years ago." In light of this, and other similar declarations, everything indicates that, at least at this stage of the case, Mattson, and Mattson's circle are convinced the scandal will blow over in a few days and vanish like smoke in the air; it's possible that might also be the dominant hypothesis in the newsrooms of some important media organisations, as well as the majority of Western governments and chancelleries.

This is another miscalculation, as the subsequent course of events demonstrates. Given the magnitude of social alarm created, the Spanish legal reaction is unusually rapid. The day after the Colombian news programme's broadcast, the attorney general presses the public prosecutor of Inca, through the prosecutor's office in Palma de Mallorca, to press charges against Mattson, filing a criminal complaint for alleged sexual abuse. The Inca prosecutor, who is the relevant authority for the case, obeys his superiors and, before twenty-four hours have passed, presents in investigative court number 2 a complaint which requests a series of investigative procedures, including getting a statement from Mattson, who is under investigation, to respond to an alleged sexual offence, and the identification of his alleged victims.

That is when another error is committed in the long chain of errors that explains the scale the case will eventually take on. At this point it is the judge who receives the complaint who commits the error; who, instead of activating the appropriate investigation, almost immediately dismisses it. The decision, judicially incomprehensible, explosive for the media, is quickly revealed by a *Diario de Mallorca* reporter; as a result, the dimensions of the scandal expand, indignation explodes and overflows. What is now at stake, however, is not just Mattson's prestige, but also the credibility of the Spanish justice system, which is hung out to dry in articles and editorials all over the world. So, dragged by that invincible tide, the Inca prosecutor, again pressured by the attorney general (and perhaps by the Spanish government), presents a devastating appeal against the case's dismissal before the provincial high court in Palma. A tribunal formed by three magistrates assigned to that court is given ten days to resolve it; but, after evaluating the reasonable evidence of criminality that supports the prosecutor's complaint, they wrap it up in three. Their resolution, passed by two votes to one, consists of two parts: in the first they order the Inca judge to reactivate the case against Mattson ipso facto and urge him to carry out the appropriate investigations; in the second they consider the judge's resolution so manifestly absurd that, in the same decree, they oblige the Inca prosecutor to issue a warrant for prevarication against him. The latter complaint almost coincides with another, issued against the same judge by the International Association of Victims of Abuse (IAVA), constituted as a class action suit. As a result of all that, the judge from investigative court number 2 in Inca is removed from his post awaiting trial, and his place is filled by his natural substitute, the presiding judge of court number 3, who immediately commences the investigative procedures the accused judge tried to frustrate. The substitute is called Ricardo Lozano and he is the magistrate who brings the case and will see it through.

"Some get the glory, others do the work," Paca Poch complains. "Those Colombian journalists are going to get the Pulitzer, and that judge has won the lottery. But we're not even going to get a thank you."

"You've chosen the wrong job, Paca," Blai laughs. "If you want applause, you should have gone on the stage."

"And if they knew we were the ones who went into Mattson's house, we'd be in the nick," Salom points out. "And I've had enough of that."

"The worst isn't that we'd be in the nick," Melchor says. "The worst is that the trial would be quashed. Mattson's lawyers would rightly say that the evidence against him was acquired in an illegal manner, violating I don't know how many of the defendant's fundamental rights. Result: the case would be declared void and Mattson would get off scot-free."

"That's what the lawyers have started to argue, isn't it?" Rosa asks.

"Sure," Blai says. "As soon as the judge demanded Mattson present himself for interrogation. But now it's much more difficult to demonstrate the videos were acquired illegally. In fact, the Colombians have already said so many times that a stranger left the drive in their newsroom . . . Let Mattson's lawyers prove it didn't happen like that. It won't be easy."

"There is one thing that strikes me as strange," Rosa admits.

"Just one?" Paca Poch asks.

"It seems strange to me that the next day nobody heard

anything about what happened at Mattson's house," Rosa says. "Especially, after the commotion you made."

"Strange why?" Paca Poch replies. "Most likely nobody found out what happened. Apart from the ones in the house, of course. Remember it was Barça–Madrid."

"And those at the house?" Rosa insists.

"They would have no interest in reporting it," Salom says. "The opposite, really, they'd want to hide it."

"Who knows what they thought," Blai wonders, without contradicting Salom. "Maybe, that we were simple thieves and that, after we took the videos, we would want to negotiate with them, to see what we could get out of them. In any case, they needed time."

"Do you remember what Carrasco said?" Salom replies to his own question: "'We have to act quickly. We can't give Mattson time to react. We have to take him by surprise.' He was right."

"That they needed time is clear," Melchor says, picking up Blai's line of reasoning. "But, after the break-in, the first person they would have thought of is Carrasco. That's for sure."

"Any news of him?" Paca Poch asks.

"We've only spoken once on the phone," Melchor says. "He was euphoric."

"Do you know where he went?" Blai asks.

"He didn't tell me," Melchor says. "And I didn't ask either. But I'm sure he's left Mallorca, at least Pollença. For his own good."

"And Vàzquez?" Paca Poch answers. "Do we know how Vàzquez is doing? Shouldn't you invite him to come down for a weekend? Poor guy, lost up there in La Seu d'Urgell . . ."

"I was wondering when you'd get around to asking about Vàzquez," Blai mutters. "How many times do I have to tell you he's happily married?"

"Don't worry, boss," Paca Poch says. "I'm not jealous . . . Besides, it's not even true that I shagged your friend in Pollença, as you believe."

"I'm pleased to hear it."

"Not that I didn't want to, truth be told."

"Why don't you fuck off for a while."

Melchor is mistaken: after the assault on Mattson's house, Carrasco has not left Mallorca. He finds this out three days later, when he opens the digital edition of the *Diario de Mallorca* as he does every morning, looking for fresh information on the Mattson case, and finds the news of a shoot-out that happened the previous night on the outskirts of Pollença. "Settling of accounts between drug traffickers," says the headline. The unsigned piece could have escaped his notice, but, when he skims the lead-in, he recognises a name: Can Sucrer. The information the reporter offers is scant: the skirmish took place in the early hours, lasted no more than ten or fifteen minutes, after which they picked up five corpses in Can Sucrer and the Guardia Civil considers that the massacre was a particularly bloody episode of the war between mafioso clans in the struggle to control the drugs trade that has been tearing the archipelago apart for years.

"Bullshit," says Biel March, whose phone number Melchor has managed to find after searching for Caty's in vain. "It was Mattson's people. They went after Carrasco, wanting to demonstrate that he'd been the one who'd stolen the videos from the house. For sure."

"Could be." Still in a state of shock after finding out that one of the five bodies at Can Sucrer is Carrasco's, Melchor comprehends immediately that Biel March's explanation is correct. "If Carrasco had stolen the images, the evidence against Mattson would be ruled out. And, if there's no evidence, there's no case."

"Exactly," Biel March says. "They weren't going to kill him. They were going to search the house. They were going to pump him for information. They wanted to interrogate him and make him confess. But Carrasco didn't let them."

It's nighttime, and Melchor feels that, on the other end of the line, Carrasco's friend and the owner of Can Sucrer is possessed by an icy rage. He had found his phone number on the internet, under text that identifies him as an artist who lives and works in Pollença and next to a photograph in which he is posing – tall and dishevelled, with a straw hat and a grey, ungroomed beard – in front of one of his installations: a large natural myrtle hedge in the shape of a cube. Melchor has not asked how he knows who broke into Mattson's mansion: he is aware that Carrasco called Biel March as soon as they left the property, and that it was Biel March who managed to get a doctor to go to Can Sucrer in the middle of the night to look after him and Salom.

"What I don't understand is why he didn't leave," Melchor says. "He knew this could happen."

"Of course he knew," Biel March says. "I told him a thousand times: 'Get out of here,' I said. 'You've got what you wanted now. Leave. If you don't go, they're going to come for you.' And do you know what he answered? 'This is my house, Biel,' he said. 'I'm not leaving. They should go.'"

"Don't cry," Melchor begs him.

"'Let them come for me,'" Biel March continues. "'I'm waiting for them here.' He told me that too . . . Fucking hell."

"Don't cry," Melchor repeats.

"Do you know what I think?" Biel March asks. "What I believe is that Carrasco wanted this story to end with him, he didn't want anybody to connect it to you lot. First, because he thought it was a story between him and Mattson. And second, because of what you said: because, if anyone was able to connect you to the break-in, Mattson might get off. So he cut his losses. Destroyed his archive and sacrificed himself."

"I don't entirely understand," says Melchor, having understood perfectly.

"What I mean is that Carrasco's death wasn't murder," Biel March says. "It was suicide. Carrasco took four of Mattson's hitmen down with him, but that's what it was . . . Anyway, don't you worry, this is not going to end here."

"What are you thinking of doing?" Melchor asks.

"Report what happened," Biel March answers. "Tell who killed Carrasco, denounce the Pollença Guardia Civil agents and the Inca judges who've been on Mattson's payroll and who we've all known were on Mattson's payroll, bring to light all the shit we've been accumulating for so long . . . That's what I'm going to do. Now or never."

Melchor tries to calm Biel March, asks him to be careful, tries to divert conversation to another subject, but does not succeed. The two men carry on talking about Carrasco long into the night.

"Did he ever tell you he was a Communist?" Biel March asks, calmer now. "Well, he was. A card-carrying Communist . . . Incredible, isn't it? He must have been the only Communist in the Guardia Civil. He didn't have enough money to buy a pair of shoes, but he kept paying his party dues, and that's when nobody even knew there still was a Communist Party in Spain . . . I used to laugh at him. I said: 'Damián, you must be the last Communist left in this country.' And do you know what he answered? 'Don't bust my balls, Biel,' he'd say. 'My grandfather was a Communist, my father was a Communist and I will die a Communist.'"

At some point in the conversation, Melchor remembers

the password Carrasco gave him in the letter to confirm by WhatsApp that he accepted his project to break into Mattson's house, and asks Biel March if he knows what it means.

"Yours is the earth?" Biel March asks.

"Yes," Melchor says. "Earth with a capital 'E'."

"I don't know," Biel March admits, after a moment of silence. "It rings a bell, but I don't know where from."

By the time he says goodbye to Carrasco's friend, his initial rage has turned into a sort of tranquil despair, but he has not abandoned his intention to launch a campaign against the corruption Mattson had established on the island.

"At least Carrasco won't have died for nothing," he says. And then: "Come back over here whenever you want. You know any friend of my friend is also a friend of mine. And don't be fooled: no matter what happens, this is still a wonderful place."

The first order from Ricardo Lozano, presiding judge of Inca's investigative court number 3 and examining magistrate for the Mattson case, surprises locals and foreigners, but most of all surprises Mattson's lawyers: it consists of issuing a search and seizure warrant for the tycoon's mansion in Formentor. A double objective drives the procedure: on the one hand, to find evidence and preserve proof of the crimes Mattson is accused of, before anyone can destroy them; on the other hand, to verify that the images broadcast by Caracol TV – a copy of which has been submitted to the judge on its own volition by the Colombian network – were indeed filmed in that house, as the journalists maintain.

An integrated squad of Guardia Civil and Policía Nacional officers carry out the operation by surprise, in the presence of

Judge Lozano himself and an attorney from the Justice Department, and that same day images of what Carrasco called the treasure chamber are leaked to the press; barely a few hours later they are making their way around the world. The effect they produce in worldwide public opinion is devastating to Mattson's battered prestige – in a display window of reinforced glass can be seen dozens of sexual trophies accumulated by the tycoon, some conserved in formaldehyde – and the investigating judge immediately issues a European Arrest Warrant (EAW) against Mattson, who only at this moment realises that his armour-plating is about to be pierced and forgets his pride and elevated concept of himself and tries to get to safety by fleeing from Sweden. He does not succeed: the Scandinavian police arrest him at the Arlanda airport, when he is about to board his private jet to fly to Brasilia, and, in light of the high flight risk the detainee represents, a tribunal assembled at the Stockholm Palace of Justice agrees to an extradition hearing and orders his detention in the Österåker prison as a precautionary measure. Four days later, when nobody had yet recovered from the impression of seeing Rafael Mattson handcuffed and escorted by police, with the bewildered air of a man who doesn't know what's happening or can't quite believe it, the same Swedish court, after considering that the evidence against the philanthropist is overwhelming and evaluating the enormous social alarm created by the case, orders Mattson extradited and transported to Spain for trial without delay. To add to the tycoon's complications, one of the women identified as his victims by Judge Lozano, thanks to the videos kept in the Formentor mansion, files a complaint against him on the very day he lands at the Mallorca airport, and over the next two days so do another four, two in Palma and another two in Barcelona.

"Serves him right," Blai says. "And prepare yourselves, I'll bet whatever you like, within a month, that judge won't be able to keep up with all the complaints."

"The victims are going to lose their fear," Rosa predicts.

"Not even God could save that son of a bitch," Paca Poch says.

"I'm going to have to see it to believe it," Salom tries to dampen the euphoria. "Anyway, it's possible: the judge might not believe one complaint, but he can't not believe ten."

The one person who doesn't say anything is Melchor, who knows the others are asking themselves in silence a question they don't dare ask out loud. The question is whether Cosette will join the complainants and testify against Mattson.

Melchor hopes with his whole heart that she won't, and he is sure that, at least for the moment, his daughter is not considering it. Cosette left the Mercadal Clinic two weeks after their assault on Mattson's mansion, when the scandal had already blown up, but she didn't even comment on it, not at least to Melchor, nor to Rosa. She didn't do so over the following weeks either. "Don't think that your daughter is cured," Doctor Mercadal told him the last time Melchor was in his clinic, the day he went to pick up Cosette. "Here, in these weeks, we have stopped the blow, Cosette has emerged from her depression, has become aware of what happened to her, is no longer a victim of self-destructive impulses and has recovered her self-esteem to a certain extent, enough to discharge her, so she can go out and live an apparently normal life." "Apparently?" Melchor asked. "She seems well, but she's not well," answered Dr Ibarz, who had joined the departure meeting. "She can't live a normal life, but she can pretend to live a normal life. So normal that nobody around her will notice anything, probably not even you. But that doesn't mean the trauma is not still inside her and that she's cured . . . To put it another way, it's good for Cosette to try to normalise her life as far as possible, which she is anxious to do. But it's not good for us to forget that she is still suffering, that the process is still going on inside." "Now Cosette knows she has a wound," continued Dr Mercadal, rubbing his forearm as if it were sore, "she knows what she has, knows how and who gave it to her, and we have even helped her bandage it, so no-one can see it . . . But that doesn't mean the wound is healed. Come to that, if it doesn't heal, it will fester." Next, Dr Mercadal gave him the name of a psychologist who specialised in traumas treatment who has an office in Tortosa, and recommended taking Cosette there. "He will help her to get entirely well," Dr Mercadal said. "He'll help her take that bandage off each week and cure that wound so it can scar over." "It's what we told you on that first day about the process of integration," Dr Ibarz reminded him. "It might not be easy . . . Cosette will almost certainly not want to know anything about what happened to her again. For a start, because she believes it's over. And, especially, because it's too painful for her to want to relive it . . . But, if she wants to be completely cured, she has to do it. She has to return to her body, make peace with it, reconcile herself with it, that is, with herself. If not, her body will make her pay and her life will be filled with distress." Melchor asked how long it would take Cosette to get entirely better, when she would get back to being herself again, how long the healing process would take. Both doctors shrugged at the same time. "We don't know," Dr Ibarz said. "It takes as long as it takes." "It depends on the person," Dr Mercadal backed her up. "Normally, in a case like this, it takes many years: after all, we are talking about serious, very intense abuse. But I told you the other day that your daughter is special, stronger than you think she is . . . Do you remember Nietzsche's line?" "What doesn't kill you makes you stronger," Melchor quoted. "Exactly," Dr Mercadal said. "Well, however long it takes Cosette to get well, this will make her stronger. Much stronger. You can be sure of that. Simply put, rest assured she'll get better, and everything else will collapse under its own weight . . . Your daughter is a fantastic girl, if I had a daughter like her I'd be proud."

Cosette returned to Terra Alta bursting with energy and agreed without protest to go each week to see the psychologist recommended by Dr Mercadal, whose name is Lluís Arbeloa and his office is in the centre of Tortosa. By that time classes had finished at Terra Alta High School and Cosette had missed the last semester before the selection exam, the test she had to take if she wanted to go to university next year. She was undaunted by the setback: she asked for the notes from the previous trimester, and now, at the end of June, after having spent two weeks shut up at home barely going outside, she has just sat the final exams. That's the reason Melchor is sure Cosette is not considering denouncing Mattson: she is exhausted after the effort of the exams and too concerned about her results to think of anything but passing them.

Predictably, she doesn't pass, or not all of them, so she cannot apply to sit the ordinary selection exam and spends the rest of the summer studying to apply for the extraordinary exam, in September. Melchor cannot understand that determination to pass the entrance exam when his daughter hasn't even decided what she wants to study at university, but he's pleased to see her happily cramming several hours a day, sharing the housework with him and going out with her friends, so he doesn't pry, doesn't interfere, doesn't question. At the beginning of August, Cosette tells him she's going out with a boy, the cousin of a friend from La Pobla de Massaluca, who spends his summers in the village.

"He's from Barcelona," Cosette informs him. "His name's Albert."

Melchor looks at his daughter; she asks him:

"Don't you have anything to say?"

"What do you want me to say?" Melchor says. "I think that's fantastic."

"Well say that you think it's fantastic."

"I think that's fantastic."

They laugh. That year is the first time they don't spend their summer holiday with Carmen and Pepe in Llano de Segura, Murcia. Melchor calls his mother's old friend to give her the news; he puts forward one lie and one truth: the truth is that Cosette has to study for the selection exam and doesn't want any distractions; the lie is that he had a motorbike accident on holiday in Mallorca and damaged his knee and he was still in rehabilitation. Even this last bit was false: even though three weeks after returning from Pollença he was able to do without the brace that was protecting his knee and begin the process of rehabilitation, the reality is that a few days earlier he had given it up, because the traumatologist and the physiotherapist assured him they couldn't do any more than they'd already done, that he would never walk normally again and would have to get used to living with his limp.

In the middle of August, Melchor and Cosette move into Rosa's house and put their flat on calle Costumà up for rent. One night, shortly after they finished moving, Melchor gets a call from Biel March. He is pleased, because he thinks Carrasco's friend is calling to comment on the good news about the Mattson case. He is mistaken.

"Do you remember that thing you asked me about?" Biel March says.

"What?"

"The password Carrasco gave you. 'Yours is the Earth.'"

"Oh, yeah."

"Well, I know where it comes from."

"Where?"

"From a poem by Rudyard Kipling. I don't know how I could have forgotten. It's called 'If' and seems to be super famous. Do you know it?"

"I know Kipling, but I don't know the poem. And I didn't know Carrasco liked poetry."

"He didn't. But he liked that poem. Once he told me, after he read it, he decided never to read another poem, because it was impossible that anyone had ever written anything better than that. Read it, see what you think. 'Yours is the Earth' is in the penultimate line."

As soon as he hangs up the phone, Melchor looks on the internet for Kipling's poem. It goes like this:

If you can keep your head when all about you
    Are losing theirs and blaming it on you,
If you can trust yourself when all men doubt you,
    But make allowance for their doubting too;
If you can wait and not be tired by waiting,
    Or being lied about, don't deal in lies,
Or being hated, don't give way to hating,
    And yet don't look too good, nor talk too wise:

If you can dream – and not make dreams your master;
    If you can think – and not make thoughts your aim;
If you can meet with Triumph and Disaster
    And treat those two impostors just the same;
If you can bear to hear the truth you've spoken
    Twisted by knaves to make a trap for fools,

Or watch the things you gave your life to, broken,
   And stoop and build 'em up with worn-out tools:

If you can make one heap of all your winnings
   And risk it on one turn of pitch-and-toss,
And lose, and start again at your beginnings
   And never breathe a word about your loss;
If you can force your heart and nerve and sinew
   To serve your turn long after they are gone,
And so hold on when there is nothing in you
   Except the Will which says to them: 'Hold on!'

If you can talk with crowds and keep your virtue,
   Or walk with Kings – nor lose the common touch,
If neither foes nor loving friends can hurt you,
   If all men count with you, but none too much;
If you can fill the unforgiving minute
   With sixty seconds' worth of distance run,
Yours is the Earth and everything that's in it,
   And – which is more – you'll be a Man, my son!

Melchor reads the poem twice; when he reads it a third time he thinks it's the first poem he's ever understood in his life; when he reads it a fourth time he thinks it's not him who understands the poem but the poem that understands him; when he reads it a fifth time he thinks he has just come to understand Carrasco; when he reads it for the sixth time he remembers the grey court official with the walking stick who, when he was looking for Cosette, attended him at the Inca courthouse, and then put him on the trail of Carrasco (or that's what Melchor thinks): he doesn't even know the man's name, but he wonders if he's aware that it was his small act of anonymous courage that started the case against Mattson; when he reads it for a seventh time he realises he almost knows it by heart. After memorising it completely he sends it by email to his daughter.

The next day, while they're having breakfast on the balcony, Cosette asks Melchor why he had sent her that poem.

"Have you read it?" Melchor asks.

"Yes," Cosette says.

Melchor tells her the story of Carrasco.

At the beginning of September, Cosette sits the selection exam and passes with a mark of 83 per cent. To celebrate, father and daughter eat at a restaurant in Horta de Sant Joan called Can Miralles. During the meal they talk about Vivales, the old lawyer who for years was like a father to Melchor and a grandfather to Cosette; they also remember Puig and Campà, Vivales' two best friends, who they have hardly seen since the lawyer's death, and Melchor declares his intention, which he will not fulfil, of calling them to find out how they are and invite them to Terra Alta. When they order coffees, Cosette announces:

"I have two pieces of news for you."

"Shoot."

"I'm not going out with Albert anymore."

Melchor looks at his daughter without blinking.

"I think that's fantastic," he says.

"That's the same thing you said when I told you I was going out with him."

"It's just that lately everything seems fantastic to me."

They laugh.

"What's the second bit of news?"

Cosette waits to answer while the waitress serves the coffees and then leaves again.

"I am going to lodge a complaint against Mattson."

Maybe because deep down he expected it, the first piece of news does not take Melchor by surprise; the second one does. Melchor asks Cosette if she knows what it means to denounce Mattson.

"No," she admits. "But I can imagine."

"You can't imagine," Melchor corrects her. "You'll have to give a statement to a judge. You'll have to go to the trial. You don't know what that's like."

"No," Cosette admits. "But I'll find out."

For a good long while, Melchor tries to dissuade his daughter with a complete set of arguments he finds within reach, especially with the argument that, the way the investigation of the Mattson case is developing, right now the tycoon has no possible escape, and therefore will most probably be sentenced to many years in prison, even if she doesn't testify at his trial.

"I'm glad," Cosette says. "But it doesn't matter. I want to testify against Mattson. I want to tell what he did to me. And I want to say it to his face. To him and the rest of them."

Melchor does not manage to convince her; the only thing he manages is to get her to agree to speak to Blai the next day so that he can explain, with a wealth of intimidating details and worst-case scenarios (although he doesn't tell Cosette this), the consequences of the decision she wants to make.

The next afternoon, just as Melchor is leaving the library, Blai phones.

"She takes after her father," he claims, after talking to Cosette for an hour. "Stubborn as a mule . . . We're waiting for you at the station to take her statement."

That very evening they submit her statement to the Gandesa judge, who accepts it on behalf of his counterpart in Inca.

By then, the middle of September, the Mattson case has

acquired a different aspect. Twenty-six women have now come
forward with complaints against the tycoon, accusing him of
different sex crimes, and the number of accused in the case –
among them two US senators, a sheikh of the small emirate
of Sharjah and an ex-prime minister of Sweden – has reached
nineteen, all of them men identified by their victims in videos
or photographs taken in the Formentor mansion. Some of those
personalities have fled or disappeared and, although Judge
Lozano issues search and detain orders for them, it doesn't
seem likely that they'll be extradited in the near future from
the countries where they've sought refuge, which means the
magistrate will be obliged to file a separate case to try them
when he might have them at his disposal, as well as the rest of
the suspects who appear in the images and have not yet been
identified. Everything also points to the preliminary investigations into that mega-case lasting a minimum of two years,
that the prosecutor could end up seeking centuries of prison
time for Mattson and the court could end up sentencing him
to forty-five years, the maximum allowed by the Spanish penal
code. And there is no shortage of jurists who predict that the
Mattson case could take much longer, and that it could take up
to two decades, which Spanish law establishes as the statute of
limitations for the crimes, for all those responsible for the outrages committed in the Formentor mansion to be put on trial.
As for public opinion – which in a slightly arbitrary manner
had baptised the place as the Fortress of Evil – the generalised feeling is that the Mattson case represents a parting of the
waters in the combat against impunity for abusers of women,
and many analysts compare it to the Weinstein case, almost
twenty years earlier, which brought to light the sexual outrages
of the all-powerful mogul of the North American film industry,
catalysed Western women against their eternal subjugation to

men and unleashed the MeToo movement, which sought to put an end to that secular scourge and later gradually deflated.

The hero of this new feminist insurrection is Judge Lozano, the investigating magistrate in the Mattson case, who in just a few months goes from being a complete unknown to become a global star whose likeness appears on T-shirts, stickers and graffiti halfway around the world, and whose name becomes an emblem of ethical integrity as well as a feminist ideal of the new masculinity. Perhaps this explains in part why an article by the *Diario de Mallorca*'s star reporter, Matías Vallés, called "The Star Judge" barely has any repercussion outside the local area. The text forms part of a series that Vallés has been writing for two months on the web of corruption that Mattson wove for years in Mallorca; the series has been published in parallel with the arrests made over the same time period by the magistrate of Palma who, almost from the start of the Mattson case, has been investigating the Inca judge removed from his court for perversion of justice after he ordered the hasty and unjustifiable dismissal of the case, an investigation that has produced, so far, the arrest of two magistrates of the Inca court and one attached to the Superior Court of Justice in Palma, as well as a Judicial Police captain in Inca and a sergeant, a sergeant major and several Guardia Civil agents from the Pollença post, all of whom, according to the judge, were allegedly on the tycoon's payroll and blocked or manipulated or watered down the complaints lodged against him. Vallés' article maintains or insinuates with diabolical ingenuity, quoting anonymous inside sources from the Inca courthouse, that, in fact, Lozano formed part of Mattson's web, and that all his actions are overreactions and respond to an aim of hiding his links to the tycoon dictated by the judge's sharp media nose, having intuited from the beginning that the images broadcast by Caracol TV were going to unleash a tidal wave that would sweep away anyone who tried to resist the evidence.

"Didn't I tell you some do the work and others get the glory?" Paca Poch says when Melchor sums up the article for them. "There you have it."

"And didn't I tell you, if you want applause, you should run away and join the circus?" Blai says.

"You said go on the stage, boss," Paca Poch corrects him.

"Don't bust my balls, Paca," Blai says. "Theatre, circus, what difference does it make?"

"Come on, didn't you have a good time in Pollença," Vàzquez says to the sergeant. "How bored you must be in Terra Alta."

"Come and live here and I'll give you some boredom, macho," Paca Poch says.

"Paca, for fuck's sake, his wife is right here beside him," Blai reprimands her.

"Who knows," Salom wonders. "Maybe the journalist is not mistaken." He gestures vaguely towards Melchor. "When this guy first arrived here, he spoke less than a mute, but he never missed an opportunity to say that the worst bad guys are the ones who seem good."

"Well, at least in the case of Mattson he was right," says Vàzquez.

"Whether or not what the journalist says is true, nothing's going to happen to Lozano," wagers Melchor, who knows that behind the magistrate's investigations that are uncovering Mattson's corrupt conspiracy there is a statement from Biel March, who is also a friend or informant of Matías Vallés. "As soon as that article was published, social media came out in force to defend him: they accused the journalist of sexism, of defending Mattson, of being a country bumpkin incapable of appreciating Lozano's greatness, of being jealous of his fame and I don't know how many other things. The people love Lozano."

"Shhhh." Vàzquez waves his arm. "Here comes Vero."

"What is it that you don't want us to hear?" asks Verónica, bursting onto the terrace arm in arm with Glòria, Blai's wife. "Gang of thugs. You lot are a gang of thugs."

It's Saturday afternoon and, for the last almost twenty-four hours, Rosa's house has been bustling with festivities that have obliged her to hire two waiters to assist Ana Elena. Friday afternoon Vàzquez and Verónica arrived from La Seu d'Urgell and, from Barcelona, Rosa and Lídia, Rosa's two eldest daughters, with their husbands and children. Salom, Paca Poch, Blai and his wife showed up at dinner time, which went on for several hours and finished up with dancing in the garden that went on almost till dawn. Now the party seems to be winding down, especially since Rosa's daughters and their families left for Barcelona and Verónica advised Vàzquez she's not planning to spend another night in Terra Alta. But the group of police officers and ex-police officers does not seem very willing to disperse and carries on chatting on the first-floor balcony. At some point Cosette reappears there, accompanied by Rosa – with whom she's been talking for a while in the library – and tells her father she's going out because her friend Elisa Climent is coming to pick her up.

"I'll see you out," says Melchor, standing up.

Cosette says goodbye to everyone and then father and daughter walk downstairs to the front hall, Melchor limping down the stairs behind Cosette, out of the building and towards the entrance to the property, through the open gate, which gives them a glimpse of a vast expanse of countryside and, beyond, the irregular profile of the mountains standing out against the setting sun, bristling with wind turbines. A long way before reaching the gate, Cosette stops.

"I've been thinking," she says.

Melchor turns to look at her.

"I know what I want to do this year," Cosette says.

Just at this moment a car brakes in front of the gate, the passenger window lowers and Elisa Climent sticks her head and shoulders out; smiling and waving one arm, Cosette's friend shouts something, which Melchor doesn't manage to catch. Cosette responds with a smile and a raised index finger, while he notices that a boy is driving the car and another travels in the back seat.

"You don't have to do anything," he says. "There's no rush. If I were you I'd take a year off, and meanwhile think about what it is I want to do."

Melchor tries to argue for his suggestion, but Cosette interrupts.

"I'm not in a rush," she assures him. "But I've already thought it over. I just told Rosa."

Melchor reads in Cosette's eyes that she has already made a decision, and that it's irrevocable. The sound of the car horn destroys the rural quiet, and Elisa Climent emerges again out of the passenger window, making an elaborate gesture, with which she seems to be hurrying her friend and apologising at the same time. Cosette turns back to her father and announces, very seriously:

"I'm going to be a police officer."

Author's Note

I could not have written this novel without counting on much disinterested help. To start with, I should mention several members of the Guardia Civil assigned to the command headquarters in Palma or the post in Port de Pollença: Sergeant Antonia Alanzol, Sergeant-Major Víctor Manuel Rubio Martos and Corporal Francisco Molina Cárdenas; Juan Manuel Torres is no longer a guardia civil, but he used to be and, like the previous three, put his time and considerable knowledge at my disposition. The conversations I had with Pedro Herranz, Chief Inspector of Missing Persons in the Spanish National Police, and with Miquel Barnera, psychologist and family therapist specialising in gender violence, were also of great help. Raquel Gispert opened wide the doors of Mallorca to me, Mateu Suau those of the Hostal Borràs and Biel March those of his house (and much more); the latter also was generous enough to read and improve the manuscript. As was Marco Antonio Jiménez Bernal, Mossos d'Esquadra sergeant, who educated me on an infinite number of police matters, and Carles Monguilod and Juan Francisco Campo, who have spent years trying to keep me from making legal and medical errors. Antoni Cortés continues to be Terra Alta's best possible ambassador.

I am grateful to them all.

JAVIER CERCAS is a novelist and columnist for *El País*. He is the author of *Soldiers of Salamis* (which sold more than a million copies worldwide and won the *Independent* Foreign Fiction Prize among many others) and its companion volume *Lord of All the Dead* (which won the Prix André Malraux). His other books include *The Anatomy of a Moment*, *Outlaws* (which was shortlisted for the Dublin Literary Award in 2016 and was made into a film directed by Daniel Monzón) and *The Impostor* (winner of the 2016 European Book Prize). In 2015 he was the Weidenfeld Professor of Comparative Literature at St Anne's College, Oxford, and his lectures there are collected in *The Blind Spot*. His books have been translated into more than thirty languages. He lives in Barcelona.

ANNE MCLEAN has translated Latin American and Spanish novels, stories, memoirs and other writings by many authors including Héctor Abad, Julio Cortázar, Gabriel García Márquez, Enrique Vila-Matas and Juan Gabriel Vásquez. She has twice won the *Independent* Foreign Fiction Prize, with Javier Cercas for *Soldiers of Salamis* and with Evelio Rosero for *The Armies*. In 2004, and again in 2016, she won the Premio Valle Inclán for her translations of *Soldiers of Salamis* and *Outlaws* by Javier Cercas. In 2012, Spain awarded her a Cruz de Oficial of the Order of Civil Merit. She lives in Toronto.